MW01470820

Tell It Not In Gath

by
C. Vernon Hines

authorHOUSE™

1663 LIBERTY DRIVE, SUITE 200
BLOOMINGTON, INDIANA 47403
(800) 839-8640
WWW.AUTHORHOUSE.COM

First published by AuthorHouse 07/08/05

ISBN: 1-4208-7117-X (e)
ISBN: 1-4208-4454-7 (sc)
ISBN: 1-4208-4455-5 (dj)

Library of Congress Control Number: 2005905039

Printed in the United States of America
Bloomington, Indiana

This book is printed on acid-free paper.

Dedication

To My Wife
Laurabel
"Miss Luck"

Foreword

This book was written by our father, C. Vernon Hines, a prominent Nashville attorney, in the early 1950s. Upon his sudden death in 1958, the manuscript remained in storage until the recent death of his wife, our mother.

Because of his steadfast belief that all blacks could become equal citizens in this country if it were not for the barriers of segregation, discrimination, subjugation, and humiliation imposed by the ruling white society, he wrote this book in an attempt to expose those injustices. By today's standards, the book is not politically correct and for this, no apology is given. The text reflects the conditions of the era in which the story is told.

In hindsight, the reader may see that many of the injustices described no longer exist. Some have been removed through legal means and others through education. However, many injustices remain that can only be eradicated by acceptance from within each of us that everyone deserves the right to equality in a free society.

Louis C. Hines
Hendersonville, Tennessee

Robin H. Hines
Tullahoma, Tennessee

C. Ruth Hines Dickson
Lookout Mountain, Tennessee

The beauty of Israel is slain upon thy high places:
 how are the mighty fallen!

Tell it not in Gath, publish it not in the streets of Askelon;
 lest the daughters of the Philistines rejoice,
 lest the daughters of the uncircumcised triumph.

II Samuel, 1:19-20
The Holy Bible
King James Version

Chapter 1

It was a bitterly cold day with a raw, penetrating wind in the January of his fifth year when Sam came to the Alley. His mother had put all his heavy clothing on him and had wrapped him in a quilt, but still he suffered from the cold. A niche had been left in the family's household goods at the rear of the truck so that he and his brother, John Henry, could be protected from the wind as much as possible. Although it was a good place to ride, it would have been better if they had been allowed to sit up front so that they could see the sights as they came to them instead of after they had been passed. Because it would have been too cold facing the wind, their mother insisted that they ride in the rear of the truck. Not that they passed anything worth seeing; but Sam did not want to miss a thing; not a house, nor a barn, nor even a billboard. It was all new and exciting. This was the first time that he had ever been more than a few miles from the place where he had been born.

He never complained of the cold even though sometimes he had to pull the tattered quilt over his head and risk missing something interesting to see while he snuggled up to John Henry to dispel some of the cold. Occasionally, when they stopped at the top of a long hill to put more water in the leaky radiator, his mother would leave the cab of the truck and would come to the rear to check on the well-being of her sons. Sam would not admit that he was cold. He knew that if he complained of the cold, his mother would probably insist on taking him to the cab with her where he would be unable to see as much. The glass on the right side of the cab had been long gone and covered by a sheet of corrugated board. The windshield in front of where he would sit was so cracked that it was almost impossible to see through.

Sam couldn't make up his mind which he liked better, going uphill or going downhill. In going uphill, the truck labored and strained, and sometimes it seemed as if it wouldn't make it to the top; but it gave Sam the opportunity to see all the sights. At the slower pace, he could more closely observe the smaller details; the livestock with heads down to reduce the effects of the cold wind, the frozen ponds, the frost covered fields, and even once, a farmer tending his winter chores. Only a few sheep that he saw seemed to be content in the winter landscape. Going downhill, the truck seemed to go almost as fast as it was originally designed to go, but the increased speed caused eddies of cold air to swirl into the brothers' niche and brought tears to their eager eyes. Sometimes, Sam was forced to pull the blanket up over his head in a survival mode.

The family was moving to Rock City. The truck belonged to Mr. "Boss" Beecham for whom William, the husband and father, had worked intermittently for years for twenty dollars a month, "dry time." The truck was being driven by Tom Cowan who worked full time for Mr. Beecham. Because William had always been a steady worker and was always available on a moments notice, "Boss" was to let William have the use of the truck and Tom's time to move the family to their new destination.

The move had been debated and argued for a long time by William and Maria. The two boys were the reason for the move. John Henry, the elder, was approaching the age when he would be thinking of leaving Brierville, just as most of the other boys usually do. The only thing that a Negro could do in the country was to hire out as a farm hand to a white farmer and there were a lot more Negroes needing work than farmers needing to hire. John Henry had finished the fourth grade. That meant that John Henry had graduated since four grades were all that were taught at the Brierville grade school under the assumption that that was all the education necessary for a country Negro. William and Maria knew that it was not always best for a country Negro to go to the city. Often times, those who did were brought home to be buried in Old Bethel Cemetery; victims of industrial accidents, or fights, or traffic. Others wound up in the county workhouse or the state penitentiary. It was hard for an ignorant and ill-prepared country Negro to survive and succeed in the harsh reality of the fast pace of city life.

Sam would begin school next year. Sam and Maria had heard that the schools for their kind were better in the city and more grades were taught. They could if they wanted to do so, go all the way through high school just like the white children could do in the country. Sam already knew his letters and could spell quite a few words. William and Maria were proud of his accomplishments and hoped that with an early start, he could amount to something. Maybe a preacher or a teacher was not out of the question. Like most illiterate people, they had a profound respect for book learning and they wanted their boys to get all the book learning they could. This would be possible only in the good schools of the city.

The matter of making a living in the city was something they had seriously considered. All William knew and had ever done was farm chores. In the city he would only be able to do common labor and that work would not be easy to find. He told himself over and over that when he did find a good job that he would be the best worker that he could possibly be and that the white boss would never want to let him go. He knew that in the city, he had to work for his family to eat. In the country, he did not always have work but the family always had food that the family grew on the small plot of garden that was always available to sharecroppers and farm laborers. In the fall, everybody had a hog or two to kill. There was corn to be ground into meal or made into hominy. Turnips and turnip greens grew throughout most of the winter. Can goods from the summer crop abundance would stretch throughout the lean winter months. In the city, everything they ate would have to be bought, but going hungry was a chance they would have to take if they expected the boys to have any schooling. In a pinch, a person could go a mighty long way on very little.

The thing that caused the most concern in moving to the city was the rent. William had gone to the city the previous week with a white neighbor who had carried a load of cattle to the stock yards and he had rented a house. He had to pay as much rent for just a week as he had to pay for a whole month in the country. In Brierville, the small two room house with a "dog-trot" to the kitchen was one of a dozen scattered haphazardly over a rocky hillside. The rent was only three dollars a month. If he didn't always have the money on time, Aunt Sarah Smith, who had inherited the house from her father, would wait until he was able to pay. No one had ever been known to have been put out of a house in Brierville.

Aunt Sarah's father had been given the house by his former owner, Colonel Reed Smith, after the Yankees had set the slaves free. The Yankees might free the Negroes, but they couldn't kill the sense of responsibility the masters had for their former slaves. Aunt Sarah had buried three husbands and she had homestead rights in houses owned by each of them. At her death, there would be four sets of heirs to inherit her property. She lived at the foot of the hill near the state highway in the house that was owned by her last husband who had been killed in a sawmill accident over in Big Bottom. This was the best place in Brierville for it had an acre of ground, which unlike the others, did not dry out in the summer from being so close to rock. An automobile might have difficulty in going through Brierville because of the rocks, but none had ever been stuck in the mud there. There wasn't enough dirt to make enough mud for an automobile to become stuck no matter how much it might rain.

Maria grew sick at heart every time she thought of having to leave her neighbors. These were people whom she knew would lend a helping hand in times of sickness or distress. Old Bethel cemetery was where her mother, her father, and three of her children were buried. No longer would she be able to linger among the tombstones after church re-living again the happy moments spent with those buried there. She would lose the feeling of nearness to her in this world, for she knew that once she left, her chances of ever returning would be remote.

John Henry was anxious to leave Brierville as soon as possible and the sooner the better. He knew there would be too many chances in the city for a smart Negro like himself to make money and have a good time for him not to like it there. He listened to his parents' plans for his future without comment, but he had no intentions of wasting his time going to school. There were too many other things to do.

Sam looked eagerly to moving. It was the most important and exciting thing that had ever happened in his young life. He didn't have any regrets about leaving. There was nobody there he liked to play with since Eula Shires had died of flu the past summer. He hated to leave Shag, but since the dog had caught the mange and the mixture of lard and sulfur had not cured it, he could no longer play with him. Charley Jones had promised to take good care of Shag. Charley had also promised William, outside of Sam's hearing, that he would take the dog up in the woods and shoot it as soon as the Martins were gone.

The family had gotten up long before daybreak. Breakfast was eaten and most of the things were ready to load when Tom drove up shortly after the sun rose. Tom brought a pork shoulder, a slab of bacon, a gallon of sorghum molasses and a sack of meal as farewell gifts from his employers. Mrs. Beechem had also fixed a sack of sandwiches for them to eat on the way. After giving away all the things they could not carry and telling all the neighbors a final good-bye, it was nine o'clock before they bounced down the rocky road from Brierville and turned onto the state highway to their new destination and new life. Maria had made a great fuss of fixing the quilt about her shoulders and she kept her head down to hide her tears. William stared stonily ahead, but John Henry merrily waved "good-bye" to the neighbors as long as he could see them before he too settled down under the quilts.

They reached the house in Mills Alley late that afternoon. Sam was so cramped with cold that he could hardly move, but he soon recovered from his stiffness in the excitement of unloading and looking over the new house. It was larger than the one they had in the country. It had two large rooms opening onto a porch with another small room at the end.

Sam was appalled at the number of houses about them. As far as he could see, there were houses; many of them so close together that a person could not walk between them. He wondered if he would ever be able to know all of his neighbors like he had in Brierville.

A number of children gathered about the truck to watch the unloading and Sam felt important at being the object of their interest. To properly impress them with his importance, he kept busy carrying into the house such lighter items as he could handle. He kept getting in the way so much that finally William, in exasperation, ordered him to take a seat on a box in the far corner of the room. He again became conscious of the cold. When he complained to his mother, she threw a quilt over him and ordered William to stop what he was doing and put up the stove. Some kindling had been brought with them and John Henry was given a dime and a grass sack to go get some coal. When the fire got going, it made Sam drowsy. Since the beds had not been brought in yet, Sam quickly fell asleep on the floor.

When the furniture was finally unloaded, Maria made a pot of coffee. She woke Sam, and Tom joined the family in eating the rest of the sandwiches. As Tom prepared to leave, he was given admonitions by William and Maria to remember them to this person and to that person, and particular messages for certain ones as if they had been away from Brierville for months instead of hours.

When the sound of the truck died away down the alley, a sense of loneliness swept over Sam and tears filled his eyes. Life in Brierville had always been interesting. Everything and everybody there had been familiar to him. Here, everything and everybody were strange. Everybody in Brierville had been friendly to him. The children he had seen here looked sullen and had been unfriendly toward him. He decided that he did not like Mills Alley and the city. He would rather be back in Brierville.

Thus, Samuel Martin came to Mills Alley. It was to mold him and shape him; and as long as he lived, he would never get away from what it contributed to his life.

5

Chapter 2

It was about the middle of the afternoon when there came a knock on the door. When Maria opened the door, she saw a short, very black woman who was almost as broad as she was long and was standing with her feet far apart.

"Howdy," said the woman and her face broke into a wide smile. "I'se Sarah Brown–yore nex door naybor," and she jerked a pudgy thumb over her massive shoulders. "I thought I'd be rite nayborly and come ober and see effen dey's ennything I kin do fur you."

"Dat's rite nice uv you to do," replied Maria. "Won't you come in, iffen you kin fine yore way in; eberthing being tore up and out of place with jes' movin' in."

"I knows jes' how hit is," replied Sarah. "Movin' is one of de hardest jobs dey is. You move two, t'ree times and eberthing yo' got is done busted to pieces. I won't stay but jes' a minnit. I t'ought maybe dey is some help I kin give yo'all."

"I don't know yet. Maybe yo' kin later on. Hyar, take dis cheer."

"Yo'all frum de country, ain't yo?" asked Sarah, taking the proffered chair. "Now you jes' go on wid yore work. I'll jes' sit a minnit."

"Yea, we'se moved hyar frum Brierville. Dat's down in Adams County."

"How come yo' moved to town?"

"We think maybe we kin do better hyar. Den we wanted de boys to go to school. The colored schools in Adams County ain't so good. We'se heerd de schools fur colored people are pretty good here."

"I reckon dey's all rite, but I don't see dat goin' to school is goin' to help de colored folks much. Jobs ain't so plentiful an' 'bout all I kin see dat an eddication does for a colored person is jes' to make 'em dat much mo' mis'able. If you had enough to eat, maybe yo'all would have been better off to have stayed in de country. Yo' kin get might hungry in town."

6

"We know dat works kinda scarce but hit war'nt so plentiful in da country either. I reckon William will find sumpin' to do. He don' mine workin'. He's a mighty good hand. He's gone to de grocery to git some coal oil. He'll be back in a minnit."

"Oh, I reckon yo'll will git by some how. Everybody else does. I'll tell yo', dis depression is sumpin' kinda awful."

"Hit sho' is frum what I'se heard of it," replied Maria, who only had the vaguest idea of what the other was talking about. 'Good times' and 'bad times' she knew, but there had never been a great deal of difference between them.

"De white folks, dey's all de time talkin' 'bout de depression; what caused hit and how to git rid of hit, but what caused hit is so simple dat I don' see why de white folks don' see hit and do sumpin' 'bout hit."

"How's dat?"

"Dey caused hit when dey started makin' de money smaller. Hit jes' stands to reason dat when de dollar is smaller hit ain't worth so much. De depression set in rite after dey started makin' dat small dollar bill. All dey got to do is jes' to take up all de little dollar bills and start makin' dem big dollar bills again. Den when yo' got money, yo's jes' naturally got more of hit."

"I reckon yo' is rite," replied Maria.

"Well, I reckon I'll be runnin' along," declared Sarah, struggling to her feet. "Seein' as yo'all are new to de city, iffen ennything come up what you don' ritely understan', you jes' let me know and I'll see yo straight. Yo'all have to be mighty kerful. Dey's a lot of sharp niggers as well as white folks about dat will try to beat yo' outa yore back teef. But I know 'em. Yo' jes' ast me," said Sarah as she waddled her way out of the house.

Monday morning, John Henry was ordered to go to school.

"There's no use in me starting into school right off," he argued. "I ain't been to school since it closed in Brierville in November. I never could catch up. I'd better look around a few days. Maybe I can get me a good job."

7

"Job nothin'" sniffed Maria. "Yo' ain't big enough to do no kind uv work. 'Sides, iffen yo' stay out o' school at all, you never will go back."

"But I'll be too far behind the other boys my age," argued John Henry.

"Dat don't make no difference, yo's goin' to school if dey starts yo' in de first reader. Dat's one uv de reasons we come to town; for you and Sammy to go to school."

Sullenly, John Henry went to school and registered. He was placed in the fourth grade. William had started out early that morning looking for work. Maria and Sam stayed at home all day by themselves except for the few moments that John Henry was there after school.

William came home late that afternoon, tired, hungry, cold, and with no job. He was not discouraged, however.

"Dey ain't a lot goin' on," he explained. "'Sides, de cold has made work kinda slack. I'll get me a job of work in a day or so. A man jes' can't walk in and get a job enny time he wants."

It was two weeks before William got a job. It paid two dollars and a half a day, and lasted only a month. He helped clean up the debris from a large warehouse fire. In March, he got a job as a laborer at a rock quarry. This job paid twenty dollars a week. This was not sufficient to feed, clothe, and house a family of four; and by the time William got a steady job, most of the cash that the family had when it came to town was gone. They had eaten many a supper of only sorghum molasses and cornbread. Some extra money must be made somehow. Maria decided to help out by taking in washing.

Her plan for getting work was simple but direct. From Fanny Moore, who lived diagonally across the Alley from her and with whom she left Sam, she learned the general direction of the city where the better class of white people lived. With a dime securely tied in the corner of her handkerchief for bus fare in case she got lost, she started out. Her plan was to keep walking until she came to a section of the city where, judging by the appearance of the houses, there lived people who could afford to have their washing done. When she reached such a section, she started from house to house.

She always went to the back door. It had never occurred to her to go to the front door. In the first place, being a Negro, she was supposed to go to the back door. In the second place, the woman of the house was far more likely to be in the kitchen this time of day.

When her knock was answered by a white woman, she would take one step back from the door and simply state, "Misses, I'se jest lately come to town from de county and I'se lookin' fur some work to do. I'se jes' wonderin' if you needed a wash woman?"

If her knock was answered by a Negro woman, she knew her mission was doomed to failure for people who kept full time maids either had the maid do the work or they patronized a laundry.

By the middle of the afternoon, or "evening" as she would call it, she would turn her footsteps homeward. She knew that the white women would be busy getting supper and would not want to be disturbed by her. The constant repetition of negative replies to her query was disheartening, but she had no idea of giving up. She knew that sooner or later she would come to a house where a wash woman was needed, and if she got the job once; she would not have to worry after that. The work would be so well done that not only would the customer continue, but would help her get other customers. On the third day, she called on a woman who had her come the next day to clean house.

Maria put in a hard day at work. She had never seen a house where there was so much to clean and scrub. At five o'clock when the woman for whom she was working announced they were through, Maria was so tired she thought she would drop in her tracks.

"Come into the bedroom and I will settle with you," her employer said to her.

The white woman went to a closet and took out several hats which she spread on the bed. She picked up each in turn and carefully examined them. She finally handed one of them to Maria asking her, "What do you think of this one?"

Maria eyed the hat wondering what it was all about. She judged it to be the worst of the lot.

9

"I reckon hit's all rat," replied Maria, handing the hat back to the white woman.

The woman handed the hat back, but Maria made no move to take it.

"Don't you want it?" she was asked.

"You mean you are jes' goin' to give hit to me" asked Maria.

"Oh, no. I thought I would give it to you in settlement for the day's work."

"Oh, no; I doesn't need a hat," replied Maria, hastily.

"That hat you are wearing is not fit to be seen on the street," argued the white woman.

"I can't help dat," returned Maria. "It's good enuff for me. I ain't nothin' but an old nigger woman noways and I don't want a hat. I jes' wants my money."

"It seems to me that you are being very obstinate in this matter."

"I don't know nothin' 'bout dat, ma'm. All I knows is I'se done de work de bes' I knows, and I wants my pay. I don't want no hat." replied Maria.

"I am very sorry, but I cannot pay you today. My husband didn't leave me any money this morning. You will have to come back on Saturday."

"Yess'm," replied Maria. She was afraid to say anything else for fear she would not be able to conceal her anger.

She was so tired she spent a precious nickel for bus fare home. She was hurt that she had not been able to collect her pay which she needed so badly, but every time she thought of how the white woman had tried to give her the worn out hat for her services, she became so angry that tears came to her eyes. By the time she got home, though, she had managed to control her feelings; and simply announced to the family that the white woman would be unable to pay her until Saturday.

When she presented herself at her employer's home on Saturday, the woman laughed lightly and said, "You know, I forgot all about having to pay you today and my husband left me only a dollar; and I've got to buy some groceries with that."

"I'se sorry 'bout dat," replied Maria, "but I put a good day's work for you and I earned a dollar. I'se had to come back after it and now you wants me to come back again for it. Hit looks like I got to do a lot to get that dollar."

"If that's the way you feel about it, I will give you your money," snapped the woman as she turned on her heel and went to the back of the house. She returned in a moment and handed Maria a dollar bill. "I don't think I'll be needing you any more," the woman shouted at Maria.

"Yess'm, I'se satisfied o' dat," replied Maria, meekly.

"What do you mean?" demanded the woman.

Maria did not reply. She was already going down the steps. Years later, she told Sam of her first day's work in Rock City and she was able to laugh about it. Sam did not laugh when she told him.

The next week, Maria fared a little better. She got two washings. One of them was at the home of a Mrs. Mason and she did the work on the place. Mrs. Mason liked her work so well that she engaged Maria regularly. The two washings netted her one dollar and seventy-five cents.

Chapter 3

The Martin family had not been in town long when one evening after they were in bed, there was a heavy knocking on the door.

"Who dat?" called out William.

"It's the law; open up," came the answer.

William got up and was groping on the mantel-shelf, trying to find a match to light the lamp; when the knocking was repeated, only more vigorously.

"Come on, open the door!" roared the person on the outside.

William gave up the search for the match and threw a piece of kindling on the dim bed of ashes in the stove in hopes that it would catch on fire and shed some light. He hurried to the door. When he unlocked it, a uniformed policeman flung it back and stalked in. With his flashlight, the policeman made a quick survey of the room.

"Boss, I wuz jes' tryin' to git de lamp lit," explained William.

"When the law says open the door, Nigger, it means open the door. Who all's in this house?"

"Jes' me, my wife, and two boys."

"Is that your wife there?" asked the officer, bringing the beam of light to rest on Maria's frightened face.

"Yassah," replied William.

"Where are the two boys?" demanded the officer.

"In de next room," replied William, pointing to his right.

The officer strode into the room, flashed his light about, looked in the closet and glanced under the bed. He came back into the room and remarked as he did so:

"Hell, they are nothing but children. I'm looking for a man."

Flashing his light on William, he asked, "Nigger, how long you been in town?"

"We's been hyar 'bout two weeks." replied William.

"And where are you from?"

"From Brierville in Adams County."

"Humph, you'd better have stayed there. A country nigger like you'll starve to death in town. All right, go on back to bed," he told William and abruptly left the house. William heard the officer tell someone on the outside "there's nobody here but a country nigger, his wife, and a couple of boys."

Sam had been awakened by the pounding on the door, and he was frightened. When the officer came into the room and flashed the light on the bed, he pretended that he was asleep. After the officer was gone, he was too scared to go back to sleep. He nudged John Henry.

"Are you asleep?" he asked.

"How come you think I would be sleeping wid de police beatin' on de dor and stomping all over de house wid a flashlight?"

"Did you make out like you was asleep when he come in here?"

"Yea, did you?"

"Uh-huh."

"I didn't think you had that much sense. It's a wonder you didn't set up a squawk."

"I was too scared," replied Sam. "I wonder what he wanted?"

"I don't know. He said he was looking for a man."

"I bet he was looking for a burglar, don't you, John Henry?" exclaimed Sam, excited by the thought.

13

"I don't know. Maybe."

"What if he was in the house, hid under the bed or something?"

"Den that policeman must be blind 'cause he flashed his light under the bed. 'Sides, what would a burglar want in here? We ain't got nothin' Shut up and go to sleep."

Sam decided, before he dropped off to sleep, that if things like that happened in the city, he was going to like it even better than he had thought. Nothing so exciting had ever happened in Brierville.

Chapter 4

One cold, rainy afternoon about a month after the Martins had moved to Rock City, Maria was ironing and Sam was playing with some cardboard boxes which were his "town." The weather had been so bad that Sam had not been able to leave the house enough to meet any of the other children in the Alley. He was growing tired of playing by himself. There was a knock on the door. When Maria opened it, she saw a black, skinny girl of about twelve years old. She had an old coat draped over her head and under her arm she clutched a coverless magazine.

Without any ceremony, the girl walked into the room. "I'se come to play with your little boy," she announced to Maria and immediately turned toward Sam.

Sam jumped up with a squeal of delight. "I know who you are," he cried. "You're the girl who lives in the house across the road. I've seen you over there. What's your name?"

"My name's Malvoy Tanksley. What's yourn?"

"Sammy Martin. I'm making a town out of all these old boxes. Come on; you can help."

"It's real nice of yore mammy to let you come over and play wid Sammy," commented Maria.

"I ain't got no mammy," returned Malvoy. "She done been dead seven years now."

"Who's dat woman I sees ober to yo' house?"

"Dat's my step-mammy. I calls her Mammy Susan."

"Anyhow, it's mighty nice of her lettin' you come over hyar."

"She didn't let me come. I jes' come of my on accord."

"Didn't you ask her to let you come or nothin'?"

15

"Naw. I don't asks her nothin'. I jes' ups and does it. De baby's been crying, and little Susie's not feelin' so good so I jes' wants to play wid somebody." She had flung her coat aside and as she settled down on the floor, she opened the magazine disclosing a pair of scissors. "Let's cut out paper dolls," she invited Sam.

"All right," replied Sam, gleefully.

Maria picked up the damp coat and hung it over the back of a chair to dry. She had one or two more questions she felt compelled to ask.

"What's yo' pappy's name?"

"His name's Frank Tanksley, Mam."

"Don't yo' ask yo' pappy iffen yo' wants to do anything?"

"Naw, I don't ask him neither. Besides, he ain't home much. He's got work to do. He mostly never says anything about what I does, 'cause if he do, he's gonna have an argument and he ain't much to argue," replied Malvoy, busy with her scissors.

The children were engrossed in the paper dolls for the next two hours until Maria reminded Malvoy it was time for her to go home. Her first impression of the child was not favorable. She didn't like "biggerty" children, but as the afternoon wore on, she modified her opinion some. Malvoy and Sam got along well together in spite of the difference in their ages. Later, when Maria came to know the family better, she decided Malvoy had been spoiled by the years when she did not have a mother and Susan Tanksley did not have the strength of character to control her.

Thereafter, Sam spent many hours playing with Malvoy and Little Susie. Little Susie was so young that she could not take an active part in their games, and for the most part, was merely a round-eyed spectator at whatever Malvoy and Sam were doing. She was tractable and easy to keep quiet, so it was easy to fit her into their games. She was hardly more than a living doll. Since the baby was at the crawling age, if she interfered with their games, Malvoy put her in a wooden box.

Maria learned that since Malvoy did not obey her step-mother, Susan Tanksley had wisely given up asking the child to do anything,

16

but so long as Malvoy looked after the children, she felt she was amply compensated in preparing the food, washing and ironing for her.

Once Maria was hanging up some clothes to dry in the house. Sam was looking at a book.

"Sammy, get me that bucket of clothespins offen de porch," Maria ordered.

Sam did not make a move.

"Did yo' hear me, Sammy?" Maria demanded sharply.

"I don' want to," whined Sam.

Maria dropped the sheet she was ironing and turning around, gave him a slap that set his ears to ringing. Sam let out a yell, more from surprise than pain.

"When I tells yo' to do somethin', I don' want no back talk from you," admonished Maria. "Now you march right out on dat porch and get me dem clothespins like I ast yo'."

Sam hastened to obey her orders. He returned to the room carrying the bucket in one hand and holding the side of his face with the other. He was sobbing.

Maria took the bucket from him and set it down.

"Now let me tell you somethin', Young Man," she said, holding him under the chin so he had to look up to her. "Jes' because you been playin' wid dat Malvoy Tanksley, don' go to gittin' it in yore haid dat you can do like her. You's been raised a country nigger and yo' gonna go on bein' raised a country nigger. Me and yore pappy was raised dat away and dey folks before dem. When I tells yo' to do somethin', I means you to do it and widout any sass or squirming. Dat Malvoy ain't got no mammy to tell her what to do, but, Young Man, don' you forget dat you's got a mammy and she 'spects you to mind her."

Chapter 5

Maria had been a faithful member of Old Bethel Church near Brierville, and one of the first things she did when she got to Rock City was to locate a church. She joined Mt. Zion Missionary Baptist Church and was soon recognized as one of the most faithful members of the congregation. Every time the doors opened for services, Maria was there. The church had three regular services a week, two on Sunday and one on Wednesday evening. This, in Maria's opinion, was the greatest advantage the city had over the country, for in Brierville, services were held only once every other week.

Maria's religious beliefs were simple. One was eternally punished in an afterlife in a hell of raging fire and brimstone, whatever that was, for the sins committed in this world; but the virtuous life was rewarded with eternal bliss in the New Jerusalem which would have streets of pure gold and be watered by the River of Eternal Life. There would be a sort of perpetual Sunday in which no thoughts of a coming Monday would ever interlude. The question of sin was set down and clearly defined in the Bible, but if any doubt arose covering any set of particular circumstances, the decision of the Reverend Isaac Hutton, pastor of her church, was final. Sin could be of two kinds, one of commission, which was to be most guarded against. The other was the sin of omission, which at the best, was a little vague; but which wouldn't bother one if one didn't pay much attention to it.

The Bible presented to her no problems of theology. Everything was there in black and white, and one had only to read it with an open heart and an understanding mind. Divine commands were clear and required little or no interpreting. One either did or didn't according to the requirements of the circumstances.

For the most part, the Bible, to Maria, was a series of personalities. This was why she liked the Old Testament best, for it contained the most interesting people. There were Adam and Eve who committed the Original Sin; Cain and Abel, the principals in the first blood-shedding; Abraham and Sarah; Esau and Jacob with his dreams; Joseph and his wicked brothers; Moses and the children of Israel in the Wilderness; Saul and David and Solomon; Samuel, for whom she had named her second son, and many others. Against this, the New Testament, with the exception of Jesus, had

18

only a few who were colorful. There were only Paul, Peter, Silas, and Barnabas who interested her.

All of the characters in the Bible were real and close to her, far more real than many of the people whom she personally knew. She would not have been a bit surprised if she had gone around a corner some day and run right into any one of them.

Maria's religion was a complete emotional outlet for her and she poured her soul into her religious devotions. It gave her a philosophy that enabled her to live her hard lot without complaint. She had so much faith in the rewards of her religion that if she had thought about it at all, she would have considered the hard work and poverty of her life as merely the preparation for a Greater and More Abundant Life beyond the Grave.

Often at night while William was dozing in his chair and the boys were studying their school lessons, she would get out her worn Bible and laboriously spell out some passage. Her education had been meager and it is doubtful if she gained much from her reading except to call to mind some of the things she had learned in church.

The Reverend Isaac Hutton was a man of massive proportions. He wore a Prince Albert coat of black broadcloth and fascinated Sam by the ponderous manner in which he carefully parted the tails of this coat when he sat down. The fact that his wing collar was sometimes not changed for days in no way lowered his standing among his flock.

His voice was a deep bass and he used it most effectively when preaching. At times he would be speaking in a low, soothing tone when, suddenly, he would blare out and storm at the congregation so that it was as if a mighty blast of wind had struck the building. Those who were dozing would wake with a start and sometimes cry out; those that were awake would sit up straighter in their pews. His listeners could then begin to have an understanding of the meaning of "The Wrath of God."

When he prayed, he did so in a loud and fervent voice, and at great length. There was nothing uncertain in his manner and he prayed directly to the Throne of Grace. His listeners were made to feel that they were practically standing in the presence of the Lord. Sam could not always understand what the prayers were about, and they would have been boresome had he not discovered a source of entertainment in them. He knew sooner or later some member of the congregation was going to express approval of the prayer, after which, the expressions would become general. He rated the prayer on the length of time it took some devout worshiper to become audible. Usually, Deacon Chadwell gave the first response, but if someone else came in first, Sam felt the deacon's privileges were being assailed and resented such usurpation; though the deacon never gave any indication of any similar feeling. Rather, the deacon seemed to encourage such initiative, and if the deacon was not first with his "Amen", he could always be counted on for the second and given in a hearty manner in a way to encourage the others to keep up the good work. It was almost as if he had said, "That is the spirit, but get a little more enthusiasm in it."

Brother Hutton would wrestle on with his prayer, calling the Lord's attention to all the details of the lives of the members of his flock which needed Heavenly attention, mentioning names where reward was to be given for good works or faith, but charitably omitting them in cases of sin where Divine Grace was sought to bring repentance to the sinner. Blessings were invoked in general and then worked down to personal references beginning with the pastor of the flock and on through the board of deacons, the Sunday school superintendent, to the humblest worker in the church. No particularity was stressed in the invocation of the blessings and Sam often wondered just what it took to make a blessing. He had heard of people being blessed with happy dispositions and ability to pray or sing or do other things, and he wondered if this was what was meant; but finally decided against this conclusion in favor of one in which the blessing in some way was like baptism. As the preacher would warm up to his prayer, the interjections would become more frequent and varied. From the first "Amen" there developed "Blessed de Lawd," "Glory in de Lamb," "Hallelujah," and "Save us, Jesus," until the entire congregation would be in a ferment of religious ecstasy. Just when it seemed that more violent action was in order, the preacher would bring his prayer to a close with a flourish; and amid a chorus of "Amens," the members would settle themselves back in their seats thoroughly cleansed, refreshed, and definitely lined up on the side of God.

While the Reverend Isaac Hutton was spiritual leader of the church, Deacon Chadwell was unquestionably the lay leader. His rank as lay leader and chairman of the board was not due so much to his religious fervor nearly as much as the amount of money he was able to bring to the coffers of the church. He was a porter in a large industrial plant. There was not an employee in that place but with whom this wielder of the broom and dustpan came in contact. At work, Deacon Chadwell was one of those Negroes "who knew his place." This meant that he was uniformly cheerful, was never given to moods, was always clothed in an air of humility, and was ever ready to do the slightest wish of every employee of the plant. He addressed everyone as "Mister," even the youngest helper and office boy. He was ever ready to lend a sympathetic ear to the woes and complaints of all, offering consolation and encouragement.

These might or might not be the natural qualities of the man. Certainly, he did not display them at the meetings of the board, yet where he worked, they paid good dividends. If the broom and dustpan were the implements of his work and no picture of him would be complete without them; not far behind in that same picture of him would be a small cardboard box. This box had a slot in the top for the reception of coins, and pasted on the side, there was a legend, "The Lord Loves a Cheerful Giver." Hardly a week passed but this box was passed for one reason or another, and when a coin was dropped into it, the donor was overwhelmed with profuse thanks and an invocation of the Blessings of the Almighty.

Whenever the church gave an ice cream festival or a chicken supper, it was always Deacon Chadwell who brought in the most money for tickets sold. Practically all the tickets sold by him were clear profit as, of course, the white people to whom he sold the tickets never used them. Even when a chicken supper was given which cost thirty cents, the tickets were printed in ten-cent units so that it took three of them to get a meal. One ticket was for the chicken and dressing, one was for the bread and vegetables, and the third was for coffee and pie. This strange division of prices was done in order to sell tickets to the white people. Scarcely any white person who knew the Negro offering the ticket would refuse him a dime for it, but very few would give thirty cents. Therefore, the tickets were offered at a price that would bring in the greatest cash returns.

Deacon Chadwell was careful not to let any of the white people ever see him with more than one ticket. He would sidle up to his prospective customer, and in a low voice, offer the ticket for sale, explaining the good cause for which it was being sold. The white man knew he was being victimized, but it was only a dime. Since the offering was being done by Uncle Dan for a good cause and the attitude of the whites toward the blacks who worked for them being what it was, the deacon rarely failed to make a sale. Every man in the plant who bought a ticket knew that he was a victim of a gentle racket worked by the old Negro, but so long as the Negro kept the victimization a secret from the others, the victim was willing to be mulcted, hence the secrecy. Should the deacon offer the tickets for sale openly, he would not be able to sell a single one. Invariably, the would-be buyer would return the ticket back to the deacon.

Chapter 6

The changing seasons were best noted in Mills Alley by the change in temperature. If spring came with a rush in other places, it came only with a few faltering steps in the Alley. The crab grass sprouted and grew in the few places not worn bare by the passing of feet, the chick-weed grew rank and insolent around the water hydrants, and the misshapen heaven-wood trees put forth their offensively odored leaves. The only flower that grew and blossomed anywhere in the Alley was the volunteer sunflowers which grew between one side of the Martin house and the sagging board fence that marked the property line separating the yard of the house next door; an un-numbered generation of the flowers which sprouted from the seeds fallen to the ground after the sparrows had fought over them in the fall of the previous year.

Hot weather meant more stenches, some of which came from more or less communal privies that harbored swarms of flies. The discomfort of cold and drafty houses, inadequately heated in the winter, changed to the discomfort of airless, sun-baked houses of summer. Spring and fall were merely fleeting interludes of relief from the extremes of the winter and summer.

The older houses on the Alley were originally either stables or servants' houses when the wealthy people lived in the houses facing on Felts Street to the south and Johnson Street to the north. As the families of the original builders died out or moved away, the properties were bought by people who made a business of renting, and Jerry-built houses were erected on the spaces between the stables and the servants' houses. The newer structures had been so stinted with paint and up-keep, that one would be hard put to determine which were the older. A closer look revealed that the solidly built houses were those which were built for a pride of possession and not a desire for profit. The profusion of sway-backed roof combs, sagging porches, broken steps, uneven chimney tops, and missing window panes that were stuffed in winter with rags or covered by pieces of corrugated board, all combined to give the entire area the appearance of being on the verge of total collapse from sheer weariness. The board fences gave their own answer as to why they didn't fall. Part of each leaned one way and the other part leaned the other way so that the two parts mutually supported each other. Property lines with no fences were probably the result of all the fences leaning the same way.

23

Felts Street was a through street from the business section of the city to some of the less fashionable suburbs. Its section near which the Martins lived was a shopping area. The stores had been built, for the most part, on to the front of the original houses and extended to the sidewalk. They, too, must have been built at some remote time, for they seemed to be as ancient as the houses which they fronted.

Most of one side of the street in this particular block was occupied by a furniture storage warehouse and a factory of some sort which had long since been abandoned and was heavily placarded by signs printed in bright red to the effect that the building had been condemned by the city. On the corner at Eighth Street was a grocery where more food could be bought for the money than probably any other store in the city if one was willing to be satisfied with chine bones, "chit'lings," hog heads, grits, sauerkraut in bulk, slightly sprouted potatoes, and wilted vegetables. Quantity was the prime consideration of shoppers on Felts Street. In the same block was a shoe repair shop operated by a wizened Jew from the Ukraine, who, in spite of almost twenty years in this country, still had difficulty in making himself understood in English. His wife and such older children who happened to be home from school assisted in translating with the customers. In this same store could be bought shoes that were called "factory outlet" by the large sign over the door but were usually factory rejects. The family lived in the rear of the store.

In the block were two eating places where beer was sold. The foods ran to stews, hamburgers, and pig ear sandwiches. Both did flourishing business on Saturday night when the juke boxes blared incessantly and the interiors were heavy with tobacco smoke and the fumes from burnt grease. One of these places was run by a Syrian and the other by a Negro. The patronage of each was about equal. Mid-way in the block was the "Family Emporium" but commonly known as the "Jew Store" where serviceable work clothes and finery of doubtful value could be bought. One place, by the signs on its windows, selling new and second-hand furniture, made liberal uses of the terms. The amount of new furniture was practically negligible and the second-hand furniture could more properly be termed third, fourth, or even fifth. Liberal terms of purchase could be arranged, which meant that the down payment would usually cover the cost price and anything the seller got after that would be all profit.

At the corner of Ninth Street was the Elite Drugs. This business was operated by "Doc" Meade and the title was not deserved. Meade had an old barber chair just back of the shelves on which he kept his medicines in the prescription room, and there he treated those who sought his help and came within the scope of his abilities. "Doc" Meade made no pretensions of being a physician and to his credit; if a patient were running a fever, he would usually advise the ailing one to consult a real doctor. He unhesitatingly undertook to remove objects from eyes, splinters from various parts of the body, cleansed and bound up minor cuts and gashes. He made no charge for these services other than the necessary salves, ointments, and bandages used, although he may charge a little higher price for these items.

Doc had long since learned there were several types of the so-called patent medicines that he could prepare and sell under his own label more profitably than he could if he bought them from the jobbers. His two leading sellers were a cough syrup prepared from tasteless kerosene and honey as a base and a product that he frankly labeled "crap shooter," which obviously told its purpose. So far as was known, no stomach-ache had ever developed into a ruptured appendix by the use of this preparation. Some of its users said that if you took one bottle of it, you had to buy another bottle to clean out the privy.

Meade was tall and thin with his head topped with a shock of snowy white hair that tended to inspire confidence in his customers. He wore steel rimmed glasses which he kept pushed upon his forehead and only lowered them to read the labels on his products or a prescription. He insisted that he did a cash business, yet he never refused to fill a prescription when his customer was unable to pay for it. He made a pretense of writing down the charge, and even had a book for that purpose; but when the charge was once written, he never consulted it again. His prescription department never showed a profit, but year in and year out, he managed to show a fair profit in the business.

Mills Alley was a backwash in the flow of progress in the city. In spite of the fact that electric lines were on the adjoining streets, there was not an electric line in the Alley. With possibly two or three exceptions, there was no one in the Alley who could afford to pay for the service nor did they have the money to put up the deposit required by the electric company. All of the lighting was done by kerosene lamps and sometimes the accidental breaking of a lamp or its glass chimney had the aspects of an economic tragedy.

Not only was there not a bathtub in the Alley, there was not even a faucet inside a house. All the water was obtained by hydrants placed in the yards and sometimes one hydrant had to serve several families depending on the number of families living on that particular lot. Water was the only thing free in the Alley. The landlords had long since learned that it was more practical to pay the water bills themselves since most of the tenants never had the money to make the necessary deposit for service with the water department. Without water, of course, the prospective tenant could not occupy the premises. To keep water from being wasted, all the hydrants were supplied with spring faucets that required the consumer to hold his hand on it as long as he was drawing water.

The sanitary laws of the city prohibited outside privies. When this law was passed, the owners complied with it by installing frost proof commodes in the existing outhouses. Sometimes, one such facility would have to serve several families and the early morning rush to them was the cause of frequent and heated arguments. On more than one occasion, blows were struck and blood was shed. They were hot in the summer and cold in the winter, but not through lack of ventilation; none was in such condition to afford complete privacy to the occupant. While answering the call to nature, one could observe, through cracks between the planks or through the sagging door, everything that was going on in the neighborhood. In the event it was raining, it was a matter of sheer luck that the commodes happened to be under a part of the roof where there were no leaks. When one became clogged, it was sometimes a matter of days before the complaints lodged with the owner would bring results. Meanwhile, its enforced disuse threw a bigger load of use on the other toilets. It was only when one of the structures collapsed entirely that any sort of repairs were made on them.

The houses were heated by coal, either in grates that were installed when the houses were originally built for servants' quarters, or by stoves. Coal was usually bought by the bushel from the itinerant peddlers of coal and kindling in the winter and ice in the summer. Several of these peddlers passed through the Alley each day calling out their wares. What coal was bought in ton lots was usually bought by the tenants' employer who took out so much a week from wages to pay for it. The weekly take-out had to be gauged rather closely to be sure that the coal had been paid for before it had been used and the employee would be in need of another lot. Coal bought by the bushel usually brought from three to four times what it could be bought from the yard in ton lots. While the peddler made a good profit, he had to hustle to sell as much as a ton a day.

All the houses in the Alley were rented on a weekly basis and the rental usually amounted to one-fourth of the tenant's weekly earnings. The weekly rental period was based on sound economic reasons. No tenant had enough money at any time to live through the week if he had to pay a full month's rental.

Sunday morning was the rent paying time. It was the logical time for it. The tenant was more likely to be at home then than on Saturday night, for then he would be out buying his groceries and shopping for what other necessities he could afford to buy that particular week. Most of the tenants resisted the strong temptation to spend the rent money on Saturday night for he knew he had to have a roof over his head. The landlord might excuse him for missing one week, but on the next Sunday morning, if he did not have two week's rent ready, his name would be turned over to a deputy sheriff or a constable that very day. These officers usually had detainer warrants signed in blank by a magistrate, and all the officer had to do was to fill in the name and he would be there to serve it Monday morning by the time the delinquent got out of bed. Experience had taught them that no excuses were accepted by the magistrates, so as a consequence, no one ever appeared in court to contest the warrants. When a warrant was served, there was but one thing to do and that was to start looking for another place to live for in ten days, the time allowed by law, the officers would come back and set all the possessions out into the Alley.

As a result of these practices, the collecting of rent on this and similar property was easy and the ownership of them was highly profitable. The returns on the investments were high and the maintenance costs were practically negligible. About the only thing the landlords felt they were under obligations for were to keep the tenants' feet off the ground and the rain off their heads; that is, except for the privies. Anything beyond this minimal effort that the landlord did for his tenant would have been considered as pampering.

The Alley began to come to life at about five in the morning. In the winter, the windows lighted up, one by one, illuminated with the yellow glow of kerosene lamps. Soon the smell of boiling coffee and frying side meat began to overpower the stale odors of night. In a little while, doors began to open and slam closed again, to disgorge the bread-winners on their way to work; men and women in about equal proportions. The men went to work on trucks, as labor gangs on construction projects, in mills and factories for none of them were skilled workers. The women went to laundries, to chicken dressing plants, and to the homes of the white people where they worked as domestics.

There was a lull for a time and then came the children on their way to school. With their passing, the Alley was left to the children too young to go to school, the women who looked after them, the aged, and the jobless of which there was always a few.

Scarcely a day passed but one or more young white men came into the Alley carrying loose-leaf books calling at some of the houses. These generally fell into one of two classifications. They were either agents for industrial insurance companies working their debits or collectors for installment firms. Of the two, the insurance men were just a bit more welcome in the Alley and received more cooperation from the inhabitants.

As a rule, a Negro will carry some life insurance. He has a horror of dying without the means of being decently buried, yet experiences great difficulty in keeping the premiums paid.

An insurance company solicitor will go up to a door, knock, and step back a pace. His debit book would rest along the inside of his left arm with a finger inserted at the sheet for the policyholder. From somewhere within the depths of the house, a voice would call out.

"Who dat?"

"Collect on your insurance, Maggie."

"Is dat de Metropolicy man?"

"Yeah."

"Yo'll have to come back Wednesday; I ain't got no money for you t'day."

"I can't come back Wednesday; your policy will have lapsed by then."

"Well, yo' will jus' have to collapse it den, cause I ain't go no money t'day."

"You better make arrangements to pay me. Suppose I collapse this policy and you die. What are you going to do then?"

"I dunno. De county will jus' have to bury me, I guess."

"All right, I will tell Mr. Metropolicy, but he ain't going to like it," and he starts off.

The door opens. A Negro woman sticks her head out.

"How much does I owe Mr. Metropolicy?"

The finger flicks the book open. A pencil is run down a column of figures. "Let me see. You didn't pay me last week. Six bits altogether."

"I can't pay yo' no six bits, Man. Dat's jus' too much money. How much yo' gotta really have?"

"Six bits is what I got to collect."

"I ain't got but a quarter. I was saving that to buy my old man some meat for supper. I can give yo' dat and maybe the grocer man will credit me for da meat."

"All right, give me that, but have the money for me next week 'cause if you die and this policy ain't paid for, you won't get money to be buried."

She goes back into the house and returns. She gives the man a quarter and a premium receipt book. He pockets the quarter, receipts the payment in the book, and returns it to her and marks the payment in his own book. He starts for the next house. So far so good. A quarter was all he expected to get anyway for that was all the woman really owed. Had she surprised him by paying the seventy-five cents, and he would have been surprised, the surplus would have been credited on the book against the time when she really would not have been able to pay.

The collector for the installment firm does not fare so well. Only after a lengthy argument and threats to repossess the goods is there a payment forthcoming. The payment included muttering to the effect that the price was too high in the first place, the goods weren't any account anyway, and the wish that people would quit bothering folks when they had work to do.

During the week, life in the Alley was intense. Everybody concentrated on the job of making a living. The Alley folks worked long hours. They had to leave early in the morning and got home late in the evening, too tired to do much except eat and go to bed to rest for another day. Even the older children in school had to contribute towards making a living, if possible. Some of the boys, such as John Henry, caddied at the golf courses if the weather permitted. Others had regular customers among the white people for whom they fired furnaces, cleaned out basements, washed windows, and in the summer months did yard work. Some of the girls did housework for people who could not afford a full-time servant; others looked after babies while mothers visited or caught up on their much needed rest. Only the very small children in the Alley led care-free lives.

On Saturday and Sunday the Alley relaxed. From the time men who worked at places which closed at noon on Saturdays began to come home, the thoroughfare began to take on a different atmosphere. Neighbors would yell good-natured greetings to each other and there was much laughter for no apparent reason. Suppers as a rule were eaten very early or very late, depending upon the amount of food in the house as to whether or not the important weekly visit to the grocery would be before or after the meal. The man and wife always went to the store together; she to do the pricing and he to do the buying.

The grocers on Felts Street did half of their week's business between noon and eleven at night on Saturday. A charge account at a Felts Street grocery was practically unheard of. The class of people who patronized them was not given credit. Their incomes were too low and their employment too uncertain to entitle them to such consideration.

Should the average Negro in that locality be given credit at a grocery, it is doubtful if he would know how to use it. He would try to buy out the entire store the first week. Groceries were not bought so much on the basis of present needs, but on the basis of how many groceries can be bought with the immediate buying power. Therefore, the amount of cash on hand determined the amount of food bought. There were two fundamental needs that must be cared for on Saturday. One was the house rent that would be due in the morning and the second was the food for the coming week. It was planned to buy all of the weekly food needs on Saturday. There might be one or two items that would have to be bought during the week and probably some money could be found for them; but for the most part, if enough food for the coming week was not in the house on Saturday night, rations would have to be spread mighty thin before the next Saturday.

One could readily judge the amount of a family's income by the type of groceries bought. If the purchases ran principally to salt butts, meal beans, and molasses, the past week's earnings were low. If chine bones and stew meat were added to the list, the finances were in better condition. The heavy wage earners bought round steak, chuck roasts, and green vegetables. Invariably, if it were in any way possible to do so, fresh fish was bought to provide the Sunday morning breakfast.

Saturday night was the time for social festivities, but rarely were they arranged in advance. The gatherings were spontaneous and usually occurred around a bottle of whiskey or a pair of dice. Fan-tan was the usual card game. The men played the leading part in these events. About the only game in which the women indulged was a card game known as "rise and fly." Bridge had not yet penetrated the Alley.

These Saturday night social activities might sometimes end in brawls with one or more of the participants in the hospital, but grudges were not harbored. Likely as not, the assailant and his victim, if the latter were out of the hospital by then, would be as friendly as ever the next Saturday night. Most of these disturbances were not investigated by the police. The officers only came out when, as occasionally happened, death resulted. Convictions were rare. Self-defense pleas were easily sustained. The dead were past helping. The living, who needed and could use help, could nearly always get enough witnesses to clear him.

31

The Alley came to life at a later hour on Sunday mornings and the tempo was slower. The first to appear were usually the children, either to play or on their way to Sunday school. These were followed by the men, who, if the weather was pleasant, would take seats on the porches and from time to time, engage in conversation with other idlers; some of whom were as much as a half a block away.

Later, the women would appear on the scene, some to join in the conversations and others on the way to church. As the church-goers would pass along the Alley, there would be a profusion of courteous greetings and flattering compliments on both sides. All the world would be at peace and cheerfulness and goodwill would pervade the Alley. Gradually, as the day progressed, there would be further drinking and gambling with probable resulting brawls; but none of this was evident during the placid Sunday forenoon.

Chapter 7

One of the city's dumps was only two blocks from the Martin home in Mills Alley, but sometimes its presence came even closer. When the wind blew from the northeast and acrid smoke from its ever smoldering fires wafted through the Alley, eyes were made to smart and fits of coughing erupted. The area of the dump was low and flooded just as soon as the nearby river left its banks. Streets had been built over it on fills. The land was owned by a man close to the city administration, who, by giving to the political campaign funds, had been rewarded for his generosity by the sanitation department dumping the city's refuse on his land. He was slowly converting worthless sinkholes to potentially valuable industrials plats. The dumping had been going on for years so that only a small portion of the area remained to be filled.

The owner of the property kept the top leveled off as it was filled and a part of this level area was used by the Negro boys in the neighborhood as a playground. On part of this area and grouped together were five or six shacks where lived some of the human derelicts who eked out an existence by picking over the refuse. These shacks were made principally of tin, odd pieces of boards, and corrugated boxing all of which came from the dump and were furnished from the same source. Once a day, an itinerant scrap buyer came to the dump to buy the accumulations of the dump pickers.

The dump pickers crawled up and down the face of the dump, sometimes knee deep in the loose trash. They raked through the more recent dumpings of the city trucks and salvaged anything that might possibly have some market value. They carefully avoided the smoldering fires which burned continually and sometimes broke into flames. When this happened, the city fire department was required to extinguish the blazes. These occasions were always of interest and crowds from the neighborhood gathered to watch the firemen lug the unwieldy hoses down the loose face of the dump to the flames.

Several times, people of good intent, having their attention called to the plight of the dump pickers, suggested the unfortunates would be better off if placed in the county poorhouse where they would be adequately housed, clothed, and fed. However, the mayor, a strong proponent of the free enterprise system which "built America," always opposed such suggestions, declaring that the dump pickers, instead of wanting to become charges of the public, were willing and able to care for themselves through their own initiative and efforts. The truth of the matter was that the dump pickers voted in every election. They didn't always know for whom they were voting, but they voted just the way the ward heeler, who hauled them to the polls and gave them a dollar and a sip of "Jack" for their trouble, told them to vote.

The leader and patriarch of the dump pickers was a man of uncertain advanced age known only as Uncle Mike; that is, except on election day. Comparatively speaking, he was a man of affluence. He owned a wagon, an animal to pull it, though ever so slowly, and a house. While it was true, the wagon had been salvaged from the dump, part by part; and as a consequence, no two wheels were the same size. The draft animal was a decrepit donkey which had been salvaged from the city pound for fifty cents. The one room house had been built mostly from grain doors and stood at the back of the stock yards on the banks of the river. A lean-to shed provided shelter for the donkey.

The site of the house had its distinctive advantages. The river provided drinking water for the donkey as well as the needs of Uncle Mike. The river bank provided some sort of pasturage for the animal except during the most severe weeks of winter and the stock yards were another source of feed. Uncle Mike didn't exactly steal the feed, but nobody ever objected to him gleaning enough left in the troughs by the animals which had already been sent to the packing houses. By an unwritten consent, Uncle Mike assigned the areas on the dump where each of the dump pickers was to work and his word was the final law in all matters of encroachment on territory and the ownership of salvaged articles in cases of dispute over ownership.

The day was hot and sultry when Sam, clad only in a shirt and a pair of well patched pants, wandered onto the dump. Behind him he was towing two cigar boxes, one tied behind the other. He was shuffling his feet and from his mouth there came a puffing sound. He was not a little Negro boy but a speeding train hurtling through space.

The section crew on this particular railroad had been lax for suddenly the train stopped and the locomotive gave out an agonizing screech. But it was not the whistle of a train but was the cry of a small boy in pain. He had slid his foot over a piece of glass that was partially buried in the ground and he had received a painful cut.

The boy was near Uncle Mike's donkey, standing in peaceful repose, blinking its eyes in solemn meditation, oblivious to the onrushing train. At the cry, it looked around in idle curiosity, but seeing only a Negro boy, a familiar sight, it resumed its meditations. Uncle Mike, whose head and shoulders were just above the level of the dump, also looked up, but allowed no further concern at the cry to interrupt his work.

The boy stood on one foot, and raising the other, he turned it up so he could see the bottom. When he saw it was bleeding, he began to cry in earnest. Not knowing what to do, he stood thus for some seconds until tears had blinded his vision. He then decided that under the circumstances home was the best place for him. He picked up the boxes, and walking on the heel of the injured foot, started to hobble away.

He had taken scarcely a half a dozen steps when he was attracted by a cry at the bottom of the dump. Through his tears, he saw Uncle Mike straighten, and start down the dump with the speed that was amazing for one so old. From the bottom of the dump, there came a blend of mixed shouts and cries. The boy halted.

He saw some of the dump pickers struggling up the fill bearing a limp burden between them; the body of an old Negro woman, apparently lifeless. When they reached the top and laid her on the ground, she roused a bit and began to moan. About her was a medley of voices, some inquiring what had happened, and others trying to give the answers. Someone suggested they get her to the hospital.

"Put her in Uncle Mike's wagon," suggested someone. As if glad to be doing something, they tried to lift the woman, but they were so clumsy, they got in each other's way.

Sam forgot his cut foot; he even forgot to cry. He gazed with curiosity and pity at the woman, whom he recognized as Aunt Jennie, who lived in one of the huts on the dump. She had always been thin and scrawny, but lying there so flat on the ground, she looked thinner than ever. Her partially opened mouth revealed several jagged teeth, and the skin was drawn so tightly across her cheeks that Sam was reminded of the picture of a skull he had once seen, only this one was black instead of white.

The efforts to place the woman in the wagon started out tenderly, but was done so awkwardly, that two or three times she was almost dropped. She was finally practically heaved into the wagon. Another old woman, in not better shape physically than Aunt Jennie, climbed into the wagon, and, sitting on the flat on the floor, held a folded paper over the stricken woman in a kindly meant, but feeble-hearted attempt to shield her from the burning rays of the sun. Uncle Mike climbed into the wagon, and picked up the pieced out ropes which served as lines.

He had been clucking to the donkey for some time, and the donkey had just about made up its mind that Uncle Mike meant it. It was showing signs of developing movement when a patrol car drove up. A policeman jumped out and came bustling up. He had been attracted by the commotion on the dump and he made up his mind that he was going to make an arrest if there was the slightest excuse.

"Hey, what is going on here?" he demanded.

The throng drew back from the wagon as if yielding to the superior right of the officer to take charge. Someone explained to him that a woman had fainted. He went to the wagon and peered in as if to satisfy himself that he was being told the truth.

"Damn, she looks about played out," he cried.

Aunt Jennie moaned feebly.

"Hey, Aunty, what's the matter?" he inquired heartily, unmindful of the fact that the woman was practically unconscious, but probably under the impression that his vigorous manner and the authority of his uniform had the power to revive her; at least enough to answer his questions.

Aunt Jennie's only reply was a feeble moan.

With a vague feeling that somehow his failure to receive an answer was something of a rebuff, he had to get a definite answer from someone to restore his prestige. He asked Uncle Mike, "What are you going to do with her?"

"We's fixin' to take her to de horspittle," replied Uncle Mike.

"What! In that thing? My God, she would have died of old age before you could have gotten her halfway there."

"Yassah," acquiesced Uncle Mike in a manner that indicated he had no doubt of the truth of the statement.

In the meanwhile, the clucking having ceased, the donkey had relapsed into his state of somnolence.

"Hey, Pete," he called to his partner who had never left the patrol car. "It looks like a hospital case. You'd better call for an ambulance."

The officer in the car picked up the radio-phone to place the call.

During the wait for the ambulance, someone brought some water in a fruit jar and the woman in the wagon bathed Aunt Jennie's head with a dirty rage she had pulled out of one of her pockets. The policeman idly listened to the recitals of what had taken place. Aunt Jennie was picking over the dump, when suddenly, she fell forward on her face. Some thought it was the heat; others suggested heart trouble, but the officer, viewing the scrawny body, decided for himself it was most likely starvation.

The siren of the ambulance was heard, and several people ran out into the street, waving their hands, to direct the driver to his destination. The ambulance drew up to the wagon with a flourish, and two white coated interns jumped out, and merely gave the policeman a perfunctory nod when he pointed out to them their patient. When the woman was put into the ambulance, and as the interns were getting into the machine, the policeman strolled over to them.

"What do you think is wrong with her, Doc?" he queried.

"Oh, I don't know. A sun stroke probably. There's been several of them in the past few days. Let 'er go, Bill" The last remark was addressed to the driver. With a low wail of its siren, the ambulance gingerly picked its way across the dump.

The dump pickers stood in a group for a few minutes and discussed what had just taken place. They talked in hushed tones, as if Death was already in their midst.

"I seed her kinda jerk her head up and den fell fo'ward on her face. I knowd sumpin' wuz wrong den," said one of the scarecrows.

"I seed her 'bout dat time. She wuz rat near one of dem places what wuz burnin' and I wuz afeerd she'd fall in de fire," observed another.

"She didn't look so good to me," said one of the women.

"Dat's rat," said another cronie, shaking her head dolefully. "I'se afeered dat's de last we seen of her."

"Youse rat about dat. Even if she don' die, some o' dem perky social workers 'll git hold of her and she'll wind up in de pore house."

"She shorely will dat," said one of the women. "Hit jes' seems lak dem folks jes' naturally likes to send folks to de pore house."

"Maybe she'll be better off at de pore house," said one of the men. "She warn't doin' no good here. She musta been ailin' fur some time. She ain't been doin' no good lately."

"Ain't nobody better off at de pore house," spoke up one of the women. "Iffen you dies out dere and you ain't go no folks, dey turns yore body off to dem medical students to cut up. I ain't thinkin' about goin' to no pore house and I'se goin' to keep up de payments on my burial policy even iffen I has to go hungry to do hit."

"Dat's shore de God's troof. Dat's one thing I always had de money fur. Dey ain't goin' to cut my body up."

"Well, hit won't do dem students much good to git her body," said one of the men, pointing vaguely over his shoulder with his thumb in the direction the ambulance had taken. "A couple of swipes wid de knife and dey'd have all de meat offen her bones."

"Dat's de God's troof for certain."

The group broke up and went back to the tasks of gleaning on the dump.

No one had paid any attention to Sam, and when the group broke up, he became conscious of the pain in his foot. He started home, walking on the side of the foot that was cut. In spite of the pain, he did not cry. He was thinking of Aunt Jennie.

When she was lying on the ground, she seemed so small and thin. Really not much larger than a baby. He had no doubt but what she was going to die. Those people back there had said as much, and they were grown people, and grown people usually knew about those things. He wondered if she died at the City Hospital, if they would turn her body over to the medical students to cut on. That must be just about the most awful thing that could happen to a person. How would the good Lord get a person's body back together on Judgment Day if it had been cut up and scattered by the students. Maybe the Lord would give a person like that a new body. He'd sure hate to be a medical student and have to cut up bodies. He wondered if medical students went to hell on account of cutting up people like that. He resolved that when he was grown, he would see that people didn't have to be poor and have to pick around on the dumps to make a living; especially colored people.

Chapter 8

"You, Sammy Martin, where you been?" his mother yelled at him when he entered the yard. She was emptying a wash tub into the drain at the hydrant. She gave the last of the water a swish to stir the dregs.

"I'se been playin'," returned the boy.

"I called you and I called you. I wanted you to go to de store and git me a box of blueing," she said as she ran some fresh water into the tub and rinsed it. She hung the tub on a nail on the side of the house.

"What's happened to yore foot?" she queried sharply, noticing his limp.

"I cut it on a piece of glass, Ma. I couldn't help it. I was playing train, and it was sticking up out of de ground."

"Huh, come here and let me look at it."

She set the boy in a chair on the porch. When she turned up his foot to see the cut, she grunted. She got some clean rags and tore them into strips as she drew a basin of cold water. The foot had become slightly fevered and the water was soothing to it. Sam watched his mother's capable hands as they ministered to him. He noted the deep wrinkles, the result of having been in water for a long time, and wondered if the wrinkles would ever come out.

When the foot was properly cleansed, Maria applied a thick strip of fat bacon to the cut and tied it in place with a strip of cloth. "Dat's to draw out de poisons," she remarked. She wrapped other cloths about the foot and tied them in place. The last act in her treatment was to hold up the child's foot and saturate the cloths with turpentine. The boy winced and cried out with the pain when the turpentine ran into the open wound.

"Tain't no use in you takin' on dat way," she admonished. "Hit's supposed to hurt. Dat's what the turpentine's for, to take out de soreness. Now you set right dere and don't you dare put yore foot on de ground because I don't want to put 'nother rag on yore foot fo' you goes to bed. Dat's a fine thing for you to be doing, and yo' startin' to school next month.

You can sho' go barefooted, 'cause I don't spose yore pappy can buy you enny shoes no how."

Sam tried to think about school, but his mind kept wandering back to the old woman on the dump. Tomorrow, he would go down to Aunt Jennie's house and see if anybody there knew how she was getting along.

His reverie was interrupted by the arrival of his father. William showed the day's ravages of heat and toil. His face was tired and worn, his shoulders drooped, and his shirt showed irregular rings where the sweat had dried.

"Hi, Sonny, where's yo' mommy?" was his greeting.

His wife answered the question herself. "I'se right whar I belongs. I'm here gittin' yo' supper. Whar you think I is?"

The man grinned. "Now, ole woman, yo' needen be gettin' on yo' high hoss. I jus' wanted to know whar yo' is. What's the matter wid yo' foot?" he asked Sam as he noticed the makeshift bandage.

"I cut it on a piece of glass," replied Sam.

"Yes'n, I 'spect you cut it at some place what yo' didn't belong, didn't yo'?"

"No, Sir; I was just playing on the dump an' old Aunt Jennie fell down and died and the police came and got her in an ambulance and took her away."

"Maria, what's this boy talkin' about?"

"I don't know. Pay him no mind. He jus' likes to talk."

"But they did. I saw it when I cut my foot."

William filled a wash basin at the hydrant and placed it on the edge of the porch. He took off his shirt and gave his face and neck a vigorous scrubbing. He emptied the pan by flinging the water down the drain. Replacing the pan on the shelf, he sat on the edge of the porch to await the summons to supper. His wife would rinse out the shirt and hang it up so it would dry by morning. He was a picture of weariness itself. His knees were crossed, and his tired body rested on his arms which were loosely crossed over his legs with his head hung forward between his hunched shoulders.

He might be tired, but William Martin was at peace with the world. He had just finished a hard day at the quarry, but on Saturday, he would collect the pay for what he had done. This money would enable him to pay rent and buy food to carry his family through another week. He had all a man needed. A job, a place to lay his weary body at night, and a woman to lie with him. He did not have all he wanted to eat all the time, but his lack made him appreciate what he did get. He had two boys, and, while one of them, John Henry, was somewhat harum-scarum and was inclined to be "too uppity" for his own good; he was a good boy who did not give him any trouble. His younger son, Sam, seemed more thoughtful and had a leaning towards book learning. Already, the boy knew his ABC's, and could spell out the headlines in the newspapers. His own education had been one of the meagerest, consisting of only a few weeks in a country school and like the illiterate, he had the greatest respect for book learning. He had high hopes for Sam.

For his labor, William received two dollars a day. The hours were from seven in the morning until noon and from twelve-thirty until five except on Saturday when work stopped at four o'clock but the men were not docked that last hour.

Out of this twelve dollars, William had to pay house rent of three dollars a week, pay for food, clothing, light, fuel, medical care and insurance on himself, his wife, and his two sons, and his daily bus fare to and from work. His wage was not adequate to the burden placed upon it; but with what Maria brought in from her washing, they were getting by.

Maria had six families for which she was doing the washing. The most she got from any family was one dollar since all of her families were small and the fee was based on the size of the bundle. They made more money than they did in Brierville, but they did not live any better. It took a sight of money to live in town where you had to pay for everything.

When Maria's washing dropped off, the family felt the pinch because there was never enough money to carry them over the lean days. The washing dropped off for various reasons. Maybe the white people would decide to do their own washing for a week, or skip a week's washing to help catch up on some of their own expenses, or maybe she would lose a customer permanently because of some fault had been found in her work, or some other Negro woman had cut the price for washing.

Maria had only one customer she could absolutely depend upon. This was Mrs. DeWitt Mason. Mrs. Mason would not allow the clothes to be taken from her home, so Maria did the washing there. Every Tuesday morning, she was at the Mason home before the family had breakfast. Maria had a twofold reason for this. Mrs. Mason wanted Maria to get through as quickly as possible, and never paid her less, no matter how early she finished. The other, Maria got her breakfast there as well as her lunch. Since the family consisted of only Mr. and Mrs. Mason and one daughter, Florence; Maria was able to do both the washing and the ironing in one day. For the day's work, she was paid seventy-five cents and her bus fare. Additionally, she was frequently given some of Mr. Mason's worn-out clothes, and occasionally, one of Mrs. Mason's old dresses but always, a package of food to take home. This seventy-five cents did not represent a net profit, for she had to give one of her neighbors fifteen cents to look after Sam. Sometimes she was so tired at the end of the day that she afforded herself the luxury of a ride home on the bus although the distance home was only about four miles--a walk she did not mind when she was feeling good.

Tuesday at the Mason's was the highlight of Maria's week. She counted Mrs. Mason her benefactor, and when she mentioned the family, while talking to some of her neighbors or friends at church, she always referred to them as her "white folks."

During this summer, John Henry was caddying at the country club. Although he rarely said anything about what he made and he never gave his father or mother any of his earnings; he did buy himself a pair of pants and occasionally, brought in something to eat. That something was usually something that particularly appealed to him such as a pound of catfish, a watermelon, or some fruit.

43

Maria called her son and husband in to a supper of boiled cabbage and fat bacon, stewed tomatoes, grits with bacon grease, and corn bread. Just as they were sitting down at the table, John Henry breezed in.

"Had a good day today. I caddied for Judge Lasater and Mr. Jones what owns the furniture store downtown and one of them gimme two bits and t'other gimme twenty cents." He didn't add that he had won thirteen cents matching pennies, but had lost ten cents of it betting with another caddy on a golf match.

While he was talking, he pulled three ears of fresh corn from inside his shirt.

"Heah. I got yo' some roastin' ears."

"Boy, whar did yo' get dem roastin' ears? Yo' didn't steal 'em did yo'?"

"Naw, sir. They fell off a farmer's truck what was goin' to the market and I picked 'em up. It wasn't no use in hollering at him 'cause his truck was makin' so much noise he couldn't have heard me." John Henry could have added that he had ridden the tail gate of the truck from near the country club to within two blocks of home. The corn had really fallen off the truck with an assist from John Henry when the truck had stopped at a traffic light where he had gotten off.

John Henry gossiped of the doings at the country club, and to hear him tell it, all the white men lined up to take their turn at getting him for a caddy. He who failed to get John Henry felt that his day of golfing was wasted.

John Henry was relating an incident that had occurred that day in which he had advised the man for whom he was caddying on how to play a certain hole.

His father interrupted him to observe, "John Henry, yo' mine how yo' go about tellin' white folks what to do. Remember yo' is a nigger and yo' got to keep yo' place."

"Naw, Sir. I does. I knows what white men I can tell things like 'at and what I can't. Now yo' take old Mr. Jacobs. Yo' can't tell him nothin'. He keeps on doin' like he always does and raises Cain cause he don' do no better."

"What does a nigger do to keep his place?" asked Sam.

"Hush," said his mother. "John Henry is talkin' and it ain't polite to inter'upt folks."

"That means to 'member yo' is a nigger, and bein' like one around white folks," explained his father.

"But if yo' are one, how can yo' help remembering it?" persisted Sam.

"Yo' will know later on as yo' gits older. If a nigger wants to get along, he has got to keep his place 'round white folks. If he does that, the white folks will like him. If he don't, he will just get in trouble," advised William.

Disregarding the interruption, John Henry went on with his story which was meaningless to everyone but himself.

When the meal was finished, William sat on the porch and watched the passing to and fro of life in the Alley until the fading light drove him into the house and to bed. While his mother cleared away the supper dishes, Sam heeded her warning and sat in his chair and successfully resisted the lure of the sounds of other children playing farther down the Alley until it was time for him to go to bed.

John Henry grabbed his hat, and with a "Yes'm" to his mother's caution not to stay out late, ran out, and did not return until long after the remainder of the family were in bed.

Maria enjoyed telling about the families for whom she did washing. Sometimes there wasn't much to tell about families where she brought the washing to her own home to "do," because her contacts were necessarily fleeting; but on the nights when she had "done" the laundry at the home of her employer, she was full on conversation. In addition to what she saw

45

and heard, the cook always had something to say about the family. The only member of the Martin family who paid much attention to her idle and harmless gossip was Sam, and he never tired of hearing about the white people and particularly the children. He asked endless questions about them, many of them over and over, and although he knew what the answers would be, he never grew tired of hearing them.

He knew the likes and dislikes of each child in the families where Maria worked, which child ate its food without grumbling and which child was fussy about its eating; which child went to school and which didn't; what kind of toys each one had; which ones had been naughty, and which ones had been good. He came to know so much about the children, that he felt that he knew each one personally.

Chapter 9

One night, Maria announced that he could go with her the next day to deliver a washing she had finished and then go with her to the Masons' where she was to make arrangements to do the laundry the next day. Sam had never dreamed such a thing could happen to him. Not only would he be getting a long trip away from home, but also he would be able to see some of the children he had heard so much about. It was difficult for him to go to sleep that night.

The next morning when they started out, Maria had a large wicker basket containing the laundry balanced on the top of her head. Sam rolled a metal hoop which had formerly been the wheel of a coaster wagon he had found on the dump, and out of which he had knocked all the spokes. He propelled it by a stiff wire which he had twisted into a U shape at the end.

On the way, Maria warned him that when she delivered the washing, he was to remain at the gate in the alley; and at the Mason's house, he was to remain in the yard and to bother no one. He was not to speak unless spoken to first, and then he was to reply politely while not forgetting to say sir or ma'm if the person speaking to him was a man or a woman. She told him that his behavior would depend on whether or not he would ever be able to go with her again. He promised to obey all her instructions.

It was almost two miles to where they were going, but it never occurred to Maria that she could ride a bus although her customer would give her the bus fare. This was a custom of the city. No matter what a Negro's compensation was, there was always the bus fare added extra. There might be considerable give and take at arriving at the day's pay, but when this amount was agreed upon, the Negro could always be depended upon to add "and bus fare," and the white woman had to pay this additional charge. Undoubtedly, the white woman always took this condition into consideration in her bargaining; and probably, the Negro always felt that she was getting something extra. This was particularly true if the distance was such that it could be walked on pretty days. The distance was also a factor, and cases have been known where the Negro lived so close to her prospective work that she could easily walk it. If the employer objected to paying the fare, then the Negro would refuse the employment. Certainly on this day, Maria never even gave a thought to riding the bus. She had all the forenoon to deliver the washing and stop by Mrs. Mason's

This was the first time Sam had been more than two blocks away from home since moving from the country. After several blocks, they left the Negro section and came to a region where white people lived. The houses were old and not so well kept, but they were far better than those in the Alley. Several times they passed yards where groups of children were playing, and Sam kept looking at them as long as they were in sight. Once he was so interested in a group that his mother had to warn him of a cross street.

At one place, his interest attracted a white boy about his own age. This boy stopped what he was doing and sang out:

"Nigger, nigger, black as tar,
Tried to get to heaven on a 'lectric car.
Trolley broke and nigger fell,
And nigger went straight to _____."

As he started singing this doggerel, the other children stopped their playing and listened to him. When he got to the unspoken last word, all of them broke into uproarious laughter.

Sam dropped his head, not in shame at what the child had said, for he had not understood the meaning of the words, but in shyness at being noticed.

His mother, misinterpreting his attitude, cried out, "poor white trash," but kept her head rigidly facing forward.

The appearance of the city gradually improved until eventually they came to a section where the houses were far apart and behind large expanses of well kept lawns. Sam decided that everybody who lived in these houses must be awfully rich. They went down a cross street and up an alley a few doors. True to his promise, Sam remained at the gate. His mother was in the house only a few minutes, but to Sam's disappointment, he did not see any of the members of the family.

From there to the Masons' was not far. Sam accompanied his mother to a tree almost at the kitchen door where she told him to remain until she came out. The grass felt good to his feet. It had been so long since his bare feet had walked on grass that he had forgotten what it was like and he had never walked on grass as thick and smooth as this. He sank down on the lawn and rubbed it with one of his hands. He looked about him at the shrubbery and flowers. The air smelled fresh and sweet. This was far different from Mills Alley with its bare clay ground, its dust, and its odors of laundry soap, fried grease, and sewer gas. For the first time, he noticed a group of children in the far corner of the yard, partially concealed from him by the shrubbery. He tried to see what they were doing. They were playing some sort of a game; a girl was facing the others who were sitting in a row on the grass.

The girl who was standing was facing Sam. He knew she was the most beautiful thing he had ever seen. The fair skin and the mass of yellow ringlets reminded him of the pictures of angels he had seen on the walls at Sunday school. He quickly moved a few feet so he could see them better. The movement attracted the attention of the girl, and she called him to the attention of the others. They turned to look at him and he became very interested in a small cut on one of his hands which he had not noticed before.

"Hey, aren't you Aunt Maria's little boy?" the girl called out to him.

Sam did not reply or even raise his head. She was too far away to reply politely. You couldn't very well be polite and yell at people at the same time. He glanced at her through his lowered brows. One of the boys scrambled to his feet and started towards him followed by the girl.

"Are you Aunt Maria's boy?" the boy asked.

Sam nodded.

"What's your name?"

"Sam," he scarcely uttered the word.

"My name is Robert and her name is Florence. She lives here and your mother does the laundry here. I know Aunt Maria. Do you want to play with us?"

"I can't. Mammy tole me to stay here."

49

"Aw, I know Aunt Maria," countered the girl. "She likes me, and she won't mind you going just over here. We are playing school and I am the teacher. You can play with us if you want to."

Robert took him by the shirt sleeve and not daring to refuse, Sam allowed himself to be led over to the other children.

"This is Sam, Aunt Maria's little boy, and he is going to play school with us," announced Robert.

"He can't play with us. Whoever heard of a nigger in school with white boys and girls," objected a girl.

"Why, Agnes, they do up North. We can play like this is a northern school. I've got a cousin in Cincinnati and she says there are colored girls in her class," argued Florence.

"He can just be the janitor," offered one of the boys.

"Besides, he hasn't any books," continued the objector.

"I'll lend him one of mine," offered Robert. He turned to Sam. "You go to school, don't you?"

Sam shook his head. "But I start next week," he proudly proclaimed, "but I know how to play school," he added.

"You sit here then. You will have to be at the foot of the class because you've just started," Robert directed.

The game had hardly started when Maria came out of the house accompanied by Mrs. Mason who was giving some last minute instructions about tomorrow's work. Maria called to Sam and he went to her.

"Is that your boy, Maria?" asked Mrs. Mason.

"Yes'm, he's my young 'un."

"What is your name?" asked the white woman.

"Sam," he responded.

"Were you playing with the children?"

"Yes'm."

"Maria, you can bring him back with you sometimes if it is not convenient to leave him at home. He seems like a nice boy and I think the children would enjoy playing with him."

Sam and his mother had walked several blocks in silence. He was thinking deeply. Finally, he spoke.

"Mama, why is it wrong to be a nigger?"

"Not nigger; Negro," with the accent on the last syllable. "It ain't wrong, honey," and her tone was softer. "The good Lord made us what we is and what He does is all right. I suppose they just has to be black folks as same as white. Why? Did somebody say somp'n 'bout yo' bein' a nigger?"

"No. I was just thinking," and thereafter, they walked in silence again.

It was the following summer before Sam had a chance to go back to the Mason home, but Maria told him that Florence nearly always asked about him. This pleased him very much. At Christmas, Florence sent him, by way of Maria, a small toy automobile. He was so proud of it that he would not allow any of the other children in the Alley to play with it. He kept it under his pillow and only played with it when he was alone.

When Sam went back to the Mason home with his mother the following summer, he was greeted by Florence and Robert with shouts of joy. Many times that summer and the two following ones, he went to the Mason home and played with the white children while his mother was doing the laundry.

He was always given a lunch of sandwiches and milk and he, Florence, and Robert ate them on the wide and cool side porch. Other white children joined in the games, and if there was any ever any objection to the presence of the Negro boy, neither Maria nor Sam ever heard of it.

When the children tired of playing, they would stretch out in the shade of the tree near the kitchen steps and talk. Often they talked of what they were going to do when they grew up. Usually, the ambitions changed from week to week, but no one ever told Sam he could never attain any of his ambitions because of being a Negro.

The summer Sam was ten years old, Florence and Robert went to camps, and Sam never went to the Mason home again.

Those summers spent with the white children remained pleasant memories all of his life.

Chapter 10

The waning of summer and the approach of the first day of school was reflected in the games played by the children in the Alley, for naturally, they played school. He enjoyed the game but wished the others did not fuss so much about who was going to be the teacher. He never offered to be teacher for he had never been to school, but all the children who had been to school wanted the part. That could have been worked out all right and was done when Malvoy was not present by each taking turns at being teacher. When Malvoy was present, she wanted to be teacher all the time.

Malvoy didn't like the game because she didn't like school. The only reason she played at all was that the other children would play no other game. Since they would play no other, then she would take the part that was most desirable. Malvoy was not dumb, but she stayed out of school so much because of the need for her at home and her liking for playing hooky that it took her two years to put in the required time for a passing grade. Her attitude toward school was reflected in the way she played the part. She was a stern disciplinarian, giving her pupils orders to do this and do that so that she seemed more like a drill sergeant with a bunch of boot camp recruits than a school teacher. She didn't like to give lessons and ask questions for she realized that most of her pupils knew more than she did. Until the children got tired of Malvoy and started drifting away, the game was fun; but when there was only Sam and Malvoy, he didn't like it much.

Several times a day, Sam would count off on the coal company calendar which hung behind the stove the number of days before school started. They passed so slowly that it looked as if he would never get to school. The first day of school was even slower in coming than Christmas or Easter. When the great day finally arrived, he could hardly realize it. Even though he wasn't to report to school until eleven o'clock, he insisted on his mother getting him ready as soon as William had left for work. Maria told him that there was plenty of time, that if she got him ready too early, he would get his clothes dirty. Finally, after repeated promises to sit quietly on the porch until time to leave for school, Maria got him ready.

She heated water and gave him a bath. This seemed odd, for he had had a bath only two days before. She scrubbed him until he glistened and then had him put on a clean shirt and his Sunday pants. He was to go barefooted and would continue to do so for a month or six weeks before it would be cold enough to need shoes. He didn't have any now, but Maria had promised to buy him a pair before cold weather. The lack of shoes didn't bother him and was nothing unusual. All the other boys and girls were barefooted, too.

Faithfully heeding his mother's warning to keep his clothes clean, Sam took his seat in a chair on the porch. He sat perfectly still with a pencil clutched tightly in one hand almost fearing to move lest he mar his pristine cleanliness and prevent his going to school. That would have been a real tragedy for him. He lost himself in imagination as to what school would be like. He saw himself answering all the questions so quickly that all the teachers were astonished and talked about him among themselves.

He thought of the time a month ago when he sat in that same chair and could not get out of it. Then his foot had been cut. He tried to turn his foot up so he could see where the cut was, but he didn't succeed. He took his foot in his hands and held it up so he could see the bottom. The cut was almost well. On dropping his foot, he notice that he had gotten dust on his hands. Without thinking, he rubbed them on his pants legs. One of them left a black streak. He rubbed it vigorously with the back of his hand, and while he did not make it entirely disappear, he got rid of enough of it so that his mother probably wouldn't notice it.

After a wait which seemed as though the morning was going to stretch on endlessly into eternity, Maria announced it was time for him to leave. She left her wash tubs to give him a final inspection and dismiss him with a grunt. She didn't have to tell him how to act. She knew she had "raised" him right.

When he entered the school, he found himself in an immense room filled with desks. No one noticed him and fearful lest he get in someone's way, he sidled over to one of the desks and took a seat. There were not many pupils in the room since the older students had been there, received their books, and left. Three teachers were busy taking names and addresses of the pupils and one of them was working her way down the row in which Sam was sitting.

When she reached the boy in front of him, Sam had an impulse to slip out and run home. While he was debating this question with himself, the teacher came to his desk. His heart began to pound and the palms of his hands became moist. He felt as if he were trapped.

"What is your name?" inquired the teacher.

Sam gulped and managed to whisper, "Sam Martin."

"What's that? I did not hear you."

"Sam Martin," he blurted and felt better.

"Where do you live?"

"In the rear of Felts Street."

"What number?"

"1109 rear of Felts Street."

This was the customary way of giving an address. No Negro ever lived in the rear of a street address; it was always at the rear of the street.

"Is that in Mills Alley?"

"Yes'm."

"Have you ever been to school before?"

"No'me," which was not the name of a city in Alaska but a polite negative.

"Have you been vaccinated?"

"Yes'm," and Sam produced the certificate that had been given to him by the public health nurse.

The teacher passed on to the next boy and Sam was sorry she had no more questions to ask him. The experience had been delightful.

In a few minutes, the teachers began to call the pupils to the platform, one by one, and giving each a new tablet, a reader, and a pencil; dismissed them by way of the front door. Hugging the tablet and book clasped against his chest with one hand and the pencils grasped in the other, Sam ran all the way to the mouth of the Alley. There on more familiar ground, he slowed down to look at his book. In spite of the fact that it was dog-eared and covered with pencil marks, ink spots, and just plain grime; he was immensely proud of it, for it was the first book he ever had.

As he walked up the Alley, he turned its pages, looked at the pictures, and wondered if the words he saw would ever have any meaning for him. The remainder of the day, he sat on the porch thumbing through the reader, and once he turned each of the pages in the tablet in the hope he might find something of interest there.

That night, he proudly asked his father to sharpen his pencil for him. He opened his tablet to the first page as if he were going to do some work. He wanted, ever so much, to write something on the clean white page and he would have made some sort of a mark, but he was fearful the teacher would see it the next day and expel him from school.

"Mind you learn all that yo' can," cautioned William as he handed the pencil back to Sam. "I never had no chance to more'n learn my letters and sign my name an' figger a little," he continued. "Anyways, I reckon that was jes' about all de schoolin' dey figgered a country nigger needed. All he needed was a strong back an' a weak mind. My paw, he could read rat good. He wuz one ob de slaves of ole Dr. Bauman. He owned all dem ribber bott'm lands below Mt. Nebo. He says dat mos' ob de slave owners didn't want their niggers to read and rite, but his marster was different. He wanted his slaves to do pretty good. Hit may be that he had so many that he had to hire out a lot of 'em. He got a lot ob slaves frum his daddy and both of his wives had a lot. Maybe he figgered a nigger what could read and rite was worth more when he wanted to hire out his time. Ennyways, my paw said sure as ebery Fall came, ole Doc Bauman would line up all de young nigger boys on de place on de big side porch and give each of dem a Blue Back speller and tell dem what de lesson would be fur de next day. De nex' day, when he had 'em all lined up on de porch for de lesson, he would ax one of dem how to spell a word."

"'I don' know how, Doc Bauman,' de boy'd say.

"'How come you don't know?'

"'I los' my book.'

"'How did you lose it?'

"'I don' ratly knows.'

"'Did you look for it?'

"'Yassuh, I looked ebery whar but I couldn' fid hit.'

"'How about you,' he'd ask de nex' one.

"He said he lost his book, too.

"In a few days, jes' about eberybody in de class would say de lost dey book, and he would give up de class in disgust. Come nex' spring when dey would plow de fields fer corn plantin', dey would turn up Blue Back spellers all ober de place."

From the very beginning, Sam liked school. He learned to read quickly and early on he developed a love for reading which in the years to come, was to cause him to read nearly every book he could lay his hands on. To him, his teachers were infallible. They were beings imbued with all the world's learning. The fact that a teacher said it was all the proof he needed that a statement was true. He talked so much about his teachers that John Henry, who had no such respect for them, took to avoiding him. So absorbed was Sam in school for the next several years, he was never afterwards able to place it in its proper relationship with the life he lived. School was a place where the cares and worries of the world did not intrude. The family might be behind in the house rent and there would not be enough food on the table to satisfy the hunger of all, yet, all these and other concerns were forgotten when he entered the schoolhouse. School was a different world. It was a place of beauty, of love, of ambition, and a place where rewards were earned and success achieved.

Chapter 11

It was a summer night. Sam and his two boon companions, Lige and Tom, had been idling about the streets. They were on their way back to their own neighborhood, when they were accosted by a huge black Negro. They could tell at first glance that he was under the influence of liquor and was in high spirits.

"Whar yo' boys gwine?" he inquired.

"Home," they responded almost in unison.

He took them by the shoulders and arranged them in a row in front of a store that was closed for the night.

"I bet yo' all ain't heard no singing tonight, an' I'se gwine to sing to yo'" and with that, he stepped to the edge of the sidewalk and throwing back his head; he began to sing in a rich, full voice.

When he finished the song, he cut a shuffle, shifted his position, and sang another song.

A crowd soon gathered about him.

When he had finished his third song, he remarked he "had to wet my whistle," and pulling out a bottle of white corn whiskey; he placed it to his lips, threw his head back, and drained it. When he had finished the next song, his legs began to give way. A well-intentioned member of his audience took him by the arm and started to lead him away, saying, "come on, Big Boy, let's go; the men will be along in a minute and take yo' home."

"Don' wanna go, wanna sing," protested the singer, trying to twist from the grasp. He lost his balance and would have fallen, had not his new-found friend held him up.

The singer protested that he wanted to sing just one more song and then he would go. His friend, evidently thinking that would be the path of least resistance, agreed to just one more.

The big Negro had hardly begun his song when he was interrupted by two policemen pushing their way through the crowd, demanding to know what was going on.

"Jes' doin' a lit'l singin', Boss," exclaimed the Negro with an unsuccessful attempt to appear sober.

"Drunk, eh," commented the larger of the two policemen. "I've got a place for you." Taking the Negro by the belt, he turned to his partner and said, "Call the wagon; I'll bring him on down to the corner."

"Don't arrest me, Boss; I ain't drunk. Hones', I ain't. I'se jes' feelin' good."

"Not drunk? Hell, you are drunker than a fiddler's bitch. Come on," and he jerked on the Negro's belt.

The sudden jerk and the condition he was in, caused the Negro to lose his balance. He saved himself from falling by clasping the arm of the policeman.

"Take your arms off me, you black son-of-a-bitch," and before anyone realized what had happened, he hit the Negro on the side of the head with his night-stick.

The Negro pushed the policeman in an involuntary attempt to protect himself, and the officer hit him again. The Negro threw up his hand and grabbed the stick and pleaded:

"Don' hit me again, Cap'n I ain't done nothin'."

In a frenzy of rage, the policeman wrenched the night-stick from the Negro and hit him again and again. The Negro kept throwing his hands up to ward off the blows.

"Boss, please don' kill me," pleaded the Negro.

"Keep your hands down," screamed the officer in a further frenzy of rage.

Exercising masterly self-control, the Negro held his arms rigidly against his sides and closed his eyes for what he knew was coming. The policeman drew back his arm and brought the club down over the helpless man's head with a resounding blow that laid open the scalp. Blood spurted and with a sigh, the Negro slumped to the sidewalk and rolled impotently into the gutter.

A murmur of anger ran through the crowd. With a mighty roar, the officer commanded everybody to move on. The other officer, returning from the call box, added his commands to those of his partner and made a threatening forward motion. The crowd began to disintegrate.

Sam stood paralyzed in his tracks and felt as if he was going to be sick at his stomach. He had heard of Negroes being beaten up by officers, but he had never dreamed of such brutality as he had just witnessed. He had winced at every blow struck. He couldn't avert his gaze from the bloody head. So far as he could see, the Negro had done nothing to deserve such a beating. He couldn't realize this inert, bleeding hulk of humanity was the happy, singing Negro of a few moments ago.

"What happened?" queried the second officer, glancing at the Negro who gave a slight moan like a puppy whimpering.

"The black son-of-a-bitch wanted to fight and I had to hit him once or twice."

"Why didn't you kill the black bastard?"

"Oh, I didn't want to hurt him seriously," replied the officer magnanimously.

"Git up, Nigger," commanded the policeman, shoving the man with the toe of his shoe.

There was no response from the man in the gutter.

"I expect the bastard has tapped out," suggested the first officer. "He was all inked up and raising hell when I got here. Leave him alone and we'll let the wagon men 'tend to him." Then noticing that the boys were still present, he bellowed, "What the hell you boys gaping at? Didn't I tell you to move on?"

The boys quietly slipped away.

Sam was sitting on the curb thinking. He was thinking about being a Negro. Until recently, the fact that he was a Negro never had any particular meaning for him. A Negro was a Negro and a white person was a white person. That was all there was to it. Things just happened that way. Like a house was a house and a street was a street. They had always been that and there was no reason that they should be otherwise. He had known ever since he was old enough to know anything that he was a Negro but that was nothing unusual. He was a boy, but he never thought about being a boy. Sooner or later, he would grow up and then he would no longer be a boy.

He thought of the first time he had played with the children at the Mason house. This was the first time anybody had objected to him on account of his color. It was true that he had never played with white children before, but that was because few lived in his neighborhood. You did not play with them because they were dirty and filthy like the Hooberrys whose mother and father got drunk and fought and were nearly always in jail. Or they were strange people with different ways of eating or doing things like the Jews or Syrians. They were just people that you didn't play with simply because you had playmates in the neighborhood that you would rather play with and who just happened to be Negroes.

Sam had known that he was a Negro but it had no particular meaning for him. He had studied about Negroes in school. They lived in Africa where it was hot and there were jungles where they lived. There was a picture of one in his geography book with his hair tied up in a knot and he was holding a shield and about to throw a spear. But these were strange people who lived across the ocean. He had been told that his ancestors came from Africa, but he couldn't connect himself with the picture of the savage in the book. He wondered if the white boy whose ancestors came from Germany or England thought of himself as being a German or an Englishman or just simply what he was--an American. To Sam, that was all being anything at all had ever meant; simply--he was an American.

Then the incident of the happy drunken man who was so badly beaten by the policeman had frightened him. He had thought of it often since it had happened. The man was not harming anyone. It was true he was drunk and Sam thought that it was sinful to get drunk. He had learned that in church and his mother and father had also told him that. They didn't get drunk but he had seen many people drunk, both black and white. Sometimes, he had been just a little in awe of the white people he had seen drunk because they seemed so different, but the Negroes had always been funny. Certainly that poor man was not harming anyone and was happy, but then that policemen had beaten him so severely and for apparently no reason. Sam had tried to think what the man had done in any effort to justify the policeman's action, but for his life, he could not think of a thing. He had seen drunken men arrested by the police before. In fact, there was hardly a Saturday night but what one or more drunks were arrested down on Felts Street but this was usually because they got down on the street and had to be moved. He had seen Mr. Myers arrest drunken people and he always laughed and joked with them. He would tell them that they had gotten their nose full of red ink and it was boiling over, but he didn't beat anybody unless they tried to get mean and disturb other people. But this man wasn't disturbing anybody. Certainly, he was not mean and had not tried to hurt anybody. Sam knew that the policeman was not telling the truth when he told the other policeman that the drunken man had tried to whip him. The beating the man had received was brutal and without reason. He couldn't understand why the policeman should have cursed him so. Sam had heard people curse before, even when angry, and good-natured cursing was a part of life in the Alley; but he had never heard anyone curse with such hatred. When the policeman had referred to the man's color, he had spoken in such a way that made Sam feel that being black was not only a crime, but also a sin.

There was nothing strange about a person being black. A person was what his parents were. White folks had white children and black folks had black children. That was the way things were. It would be strange if it were otherwise. It was true that there were more white people then there were black and most of the white people lived in better houses than the Negroes, but there were some of the white people Sam knew of that lived in worse houses than the Negroes did. The real rich people were white and all the bosses, the people who had charge of things, were white; but that was because the white people had once owned the black people. But when the blacks were set free, they didn't have anything to go on but to go to work for the white people and they would expect to go on working for the white people because they owned most of everything. All this had been explained to him by his father and it looked reasonable to him.

A white man passed down the street and Sam looked at him closely observing his color. While this was a white man, Sam saw that he was not white but pink, and he realized that most white people were pink.

He remembered some white people he had seen who were dark in color, in fact as dark as some Negroes he knew, and concluded that after all, very few white people are really white. Sam looked at his own skin. It was black. There was no mistaking that fact. Never, under any circumstances, would anybody ever mistake him for anything except what he was, unless a miracle occurred. He was so black that his skin was shiny. He tried to realize what it was to be black. He thought about it but he could not feel different from what he had always felt. Looking intently at the back of his wrist didn't help any. He was still a Negro boy.

He looked up and saw old Uncle Andy Epperson slowly shuffling his way along dragging a grass sack behind him on his way down to the feed store to buy some corn for the horse that he had not been able to drive for weeks and would probably never drive again. Uncle Andy was old and he had heard a neighbor tell his mother that he wouldn't be here long. He hadn't paid much attention to it then, but he knew now that Uncle Andy was to die soon. Sam looked at him closely. Uncle Andy was black; just as black as Sam. All but his hair and that was snow white. There is a man thought Sam, who was born a Negro, lived a Negro all his life, and would soon die a Negro. Had he felt any difference in being a Negro? After all, was there any difference in being a Negro? Different from what? Different from being a white man? That was silly, for if you had never been a white man, how could you know that there was any difference. And, after all, what was the difference between being a white man and a Negro? Since there didn't seem to be a logical answer to that problem, he got to his feet, shied a rock he had idly picked up, and threw it at a campaign poster tacked to a telephone pole across the street. The rock hit squarely in the face of the candidate pictured on it and left a gaping hole. He quickly ducked into the alley for he realized that the picture was of a white man. He or his friends could make trouble for a little Negro boy caught throwing rocks at it.

Chapter 12

One day, Sam, Tom, and Lige were shooting marbles in the yard at Sam's house when Uncle Andy Epperson drove his horse and wagon through the Alley, ringing a bell, and crying out his chant of "Any rags and bones and bottles today? I buy old junk and give good pay."

Sam paused as he was about to shoot and looked at the old man. He wondered what had happened to him. Last year, everybody said the old man was about to die and now he seemed to be as strong as ever. Suddenly, a thought struck him.

"Say, I know how we can make some money."

"How?"

"By gathering up junk and selling it to Uncle Andy."

"Where are you going to get this junk?" asked Lige. "They won't let boys pick over the dump. Nobody but old men and women."

"Most anywhere else. In alleys and folks' back yards where they have thrown stuff away. I bet we can make a thousand dollars."

Both boys agreed that the idea was good. In a few minutes, each boy had a burlap bag slung across his shoulder and they were off on a search for junk. For no reason that any could give, they walked several blocks before making any attempt to find anything. Then they started down the alleys with a fine tooth comb. No piece of bone or iron was too insignificant to be overlooked. In the course of an hour, each had accumulated a load and they started back.

"Gosh, this stuff gets heavy," cried Tom, swinging his sack from his shoulder to rest a minute.

"I'll say it does. It didn't seem so heavy while we were gathering it," observed Lige.

"We need a wagon for this business," put in Sam.

"A wagon would come in mighty handy," admitted Tom.

"Let's keep a look out tomorrow for some old wheels and some axles. We ought to be able to find some from an old coaster wagon somewhere and we can get us a board and make a wagon," said Sam.

The boys carried their loads to Sam's house and there they separated the metal from the bones. When this was done, they carried their wares down to Uncle Andy's shack in the next block, and received seventeen cents for their afternoon's labor. Each took a nickel, and it was agreed that Sam should hold the odd two cents until they had made some more money. Elated over the success of their first day's work, they decided to start out right after school the next day.

As the boys moved further away from home and into the section of the city occupied by white people, they were more successful in finding junk. They were amazed at the amount of stuff white people threw away and particularly in the way of whiskey bottles. The state was "dry" and bootlegging was a flourishing industry. They soon learned they could get two and three cents for all the whiskey bottles they could find. Usually, when they found one bottle, they found many more.

In several days' search, they found enough parts to old coaster wagons to make themselves a wagon of their own. The construction of their wagon was simple. They nailed several planks together by means of cross pieces so they had a bed about eighteen inches wide and three feet long. Across one end of this they nailed an old axle with staples and the wheels were held on by nails bent in the original cotter-key holes. The front axle, in the absence of a fifth wheel, was a board. A hole bored through the wagon bed and in the center of this enabled them to drop a bolt through both so the wagon could be turned. With this fairly adequate outfit, the boys were able to bring back larger loads of junk.

In a short while, they learned a few principles of the business they were in. One of them was to never ask a white person for any junk lying in a yard. All white people were uniformly suspicious of Negro boys and it was easier for them to say no than to say yes. Another was to never take anything out of a yard that was not lying in a trash pile. Most of the yards that had rear fences nearly always had gates that were either down or stood open. Because the trash piles were usually close to the gates for the convenience of the trash collectors, the boys did not have to go far into the yards. Only on rare occasions were they ever noticed and ordered out. If anybody was in sight at a house, the yard was not entered. Even if the trash pile was on the edge of the alley, and someone was in sight, it was passed up. They learned that white people sometimes acted funny and there was no sense in taking a chance in getting into trouble.

Once Sam found an electric motor of good size and when he brought it out of the trash pile to the wagon, the three boys gloated over the find. Although they had never found anything like it before, they felt sure that Uncle Andy would pay a good price for it. Then, as though all were struck by the same idea at the same time, they returned feverishly to their prospecting as if discarded electric motors came in bunches and they would be sure to find more.

Sam came out of a gate into the alley when a rock flew past his head and hit the fence beside him. He glanced down the alley and saw three white boys throwing at him. Just as he yelled for Lige and Tom, one of the rocks hit him on the shoulder. He grabbed the rope of the wagon and started to run just as Tom and Lige came running into the alley. Sizing up the situation at once and gathering up some rocks of their own, they started returning the fire and holding off the attack until Sam could get away with the wagon. They slowly retreated down the alley dodging the barrage of stones as best they could, but occasionally, receiving a direct hit which, in the excitement of the moment, did not hurt much. When the Negro boys reached the cross street, a rock thrown by one of the white boys sailed over its intended objective and crashed into a window of an automobile that was passing by the entrance of the alley. There was the sound of falling glass and the screech of tires sliding on asphalt followed by a verbal blast from an irate motorist as he jumped from the car.

The white boys fled back up the alley while Tom and Lige disappeared around the corner, but Sam stood his ground.

"Who threw that rock?" demanded the motorist.

"I don't know. Some white boys ran us out of de alley, an' one of dem threw it."

"Who were they?"

"I don' know; I never seed dem befor'."

"Don't lie to me; you know who they were."

"Honest, Mister; I never saw them before. We were just up in de alley lookin' for junk, when dey started throwing at us."

"What have you got in that sack?"

"Just some stuff we found," and Sam opened the mouth of the sack to show its contents.

"Somebody is going to pay for that glass," the man stated grimly as he peered into the sack. "What the hell are you going to do with all that trash?" he added.

"Sell it. That is how we make money."

"You stay here. I am going up that alley and you had better be here when I get back. If you don't, it won't be good for you."

"No, Sir," replied Sam.

While this answer might have been a little ambiguous, coming from a Negro, the white man knew that what the Negro meant was, "I will be here when you get back, because I know it won't be good for me if I am not."

The man started up the alley looking into all the yards and finally darted out of sight of Sam. Just at this moment, a police squad car drove up and two policemen stepped out.

"Boy, what is going on here?" Sam was asked.

"Some white boys were throwing rocks and one of them hit that car over there. The white man who owns the car has gone up the alley looking for them," replied Sam.

"What did you have to do with it?"

"I didn't have nothing to with it."

"You know damn well you had something to do with it. Were they throwing at you?"

"Yes, Sir. At me and two more boys."

"I thought so. Where are the two boys who were with you?"

"I don't know; they ran off. I couldn't run with the wagon."

"What have you got in that sack?"

"Just junk."

"Junk, eh. I bet you rats have been stealing. Here, let me see it," and picking up the sack by one corner, the officer spilled the contents onto the sidewalk.

"No, Sir, Boss; we ain't stole nothing'. We just picked this stuff up."

"Well, what the hell is the difference? What is this?" and he picked up the electric motor.

"I found that in a trash pile," replied Sam.

"What trash pile?"

"At that big house up there," returned Sam, pointing.

"Like hell you did. Who would throw away a motor like this? I am going to arrest you."

"No, Sir, Mister; please don't arrest me. I ain't stole nothin'." and Sam began to cry.

At this juncture, the white man came out of the alley. At the sight of the policeman, he stopped.

"Hello. Why are you fellows here?" the man asked.

"Somebody turned in a call that there was a wreck here."

"There wasn't a wreck, but if I had been a little slower, probably there would have been. That rock just missed my head; and if I find the little bastard who threw it, I'll make a wreck out of him."

"This nappy here throw it?" asked one of the officers.

"No, he didn't. I saw him and the other two. They were throwing in the other direction."

"What difference does it make which direction they were throwing? If they were not throwing at the white boys, the white boys would not have been throwing at them; so, what the hell."

"That's what I say; what the hell? I bet the white boys started it. Whoever heard of a bunch of Negroes coming into a white section and starting a fight? It's those little white boogers I want. I think I have two of them located. Would you know any of them if you saw them again?" This last statement he addressed to Sam.

"Yes, Sir. I believe I would," nodded Sam, whose sobbing had died into a sniffle. He was conscious of a hurting in the shoulder where the rock had hit him.

"Come on with me and you officers, too," and he led them up the alley and into a yard where two boys were sitting on the rear steps of a house.

"That is two of them," Sam said.

"Which one of you boys threw the rock that broke this man's car window?" one of the officers asked.

"We don't know anything about any rock throwing," answered one of the boys.

"We have been down the street and just got here," added the other.

"Are you sure these are the boys?" one of the officers asked Sam.

"Yes, Sir. I am sure of them. It was both of them throwing rocks."

The rear door of the house was opened by a woman who asked the meaning of the gathering. One of the officers outlined what had taken place.

"Henry," she asked one of the boys, "what do you know about this?"

"I don't know anything about it. We just got here when that white man came up."

"Henry, look me in the eye. Have you been throwing rocks at those colored boys? Tell me the truth."

Henry began to squirm.

"Henry, tell me the truth. Have you been throwing rocks?"

"Yes'm," he weakly replied.

"Did you break the glass in this gentleman's car?"

"I don't know whether I did or not. I heard the glass break just as I threw, but I don't think I broke it. I think one of the other boys must have done it."

"That is enough. I might excuse you for rock fighting, but I can't excuse you for lying. You march yourself inside this house," and turning to the motorist, she said, "I am sorry this happened. Will you have the glass replaced and send me the bill?" With that, she gave the man her name.

When the group reached the alley, one of the policeman asked the motorist, "What are you going to do with this boy?"

"Do with him? I am not going to do anything with him. He hasn't done anything to me so why should I want anything done with him?"

"If the little son-of-a-bitch had stayed where he belonged, none of this would have happened."

"I am not going to argue this with you. If I had not been driving by, my glass would not have been broken. There is no use in 'iffin' about it. You can turn him loose as far as I'm concerned."

"I will be damned if that is so. I am going to arrest him for larceny."

70

"Suit yourself about that. It doesn't look to me as if he had done anything wrong. I understand he was trying to make a little money collecting junk; but that is your business, not mine. If I were you, I believe I would try to find out if any of the stuff was stolen before you make an arrest."

"Say, we don't need you to tell us how to make our cases."

"I am certain of that," said the motorist as he started off in his car.

"Hey, that sounds like a crack to me," returned the policeman.

"Figure it out for yourself when you go off duty tonight, if you are not too tired," yelled the motorist as he drove away.

"I have a good notion to run that guy in."

"You had better figure out first what you are going to run him in for. You already have one case that you don't know what to charge with," returned the other policeman.

"You stay here with the nappy. I am going up there and investigate this matter," and picking up the motor, he started up the alley. In a few minutes, he came back still carrying the motor. He nodded significantly.

"Just as I thought. Stolen. Load him up and let's take him to the station."

Sam started crying again.

"What am I going to do with my wagon and junk?"

"We will take the junk to the station with us for evidence. Leave the wagon here, nobody would want it. Put it up next to that fence. You can send somebody for it. Where you are going, you won't need no damn wagon. They will give you a wheelbarrow."

When Sam was escorted into the police station, the desk sergeant asked: "What have you got there, Hoyt?"

"Just a little thief; charge him with petty larceny."

71

The officer booked Sam and then released him telling him to report to the juvenile court the next morning.

When Sam got home, he found Tom and Lige had already returned with the wagon. They had hidden in the next block until the officers had left with him.

The next morning, Sam reported to juvenile court with his mother. When his case was called, he went up before the judge.

"What is this case about?" asked the judge.

"Call the prosecutor," called the officer who had arrested Sam.

The clerk called out a name and a man stood up. He approached the bar.

"I arrested this boy with a motor he stole from this man yesterday," said the officer as he pointed to the man whose name had been called. "He is the prosecutor."

"There must be some mistake here," the man spoke up. "I am not prosecuting anybody."

"This is your motor, isn't it?" belligerently demanded the officer.

"It was, but it burned out so I threw it away. My wife said that yesterday afternoon an officer came to the house with this motor and asked if was hers. After she told him that it was mine, the officer told her to tell me to be here in court this morning. I didn't want anybody arrested and this boy can have the motor if he wants it. I understand he got it out of the trash pile. When I threw it away, I didn't care who got it; but I resent being called into court and away from my business like this."

"It would have been different if something was of value had been stolen," spoke up the officer as if trying to justify his action.

"That is true," returned the man. "It would have been entirely different; I would never have seen my property again and you would not have arrested anybody."

The judge rapped on his desk with the gavel. "Here, that is enough of that."

The officer spoke up. "Judge, this boy and two others have been going around getting stuff out of people's back yards and selling it. He told me so himself."

"Do you have any complaint about his stealing?"

"No, but you know he is bound to be stealing some of the stuff he is getting."

The judge turned to Sam. "In the future, you don't take anything out of anybody's yard unless you ask them for it. Case dismissed. Call the next case."

Sam couldn't understand what had taken place. If he had been sent to the reform school, he would not have been the least bit surprised. He was certain the policeman would get the white man to say that the motor had been stolen. Besides, it would have been easier for the man to say that than to get up there and make the policeman look foolish. What could a little colored boy mean to him? White people sure were funny. They would pick on a Negro themselves but would not let anyone else do it. He decided he would never understand white people, but taking them as a whole, he did not like them. They made it hard on Negroes, even when the Negroes tried to do right.

Chapter 13

That part of Johnson Street that paralleled Mills Alley was forbidden ground to Negro boys. Negro men, women, and girls could use the street, but not a boy unaccompanied by an adult. Grocery delivery boys, newspaper route carriers, or others who had business there were tolerated because they were carrying out orders, but a Negro boy who tried to use the street for his own convenience would find himself the center of a barrage of rocks hurled by the white boys who lived in the two blocks. They were the ones who enforced the unwritten ban.

Occasionally, the Negro boys, resentful of the rule, would band together and try to repeal it by open violation; but they were never successful. If they were in sufficient force to drive the white boys from the street, the latter could always take refuge between the houses and behind fences and from those safe advantages, harass the Negroes who were forced to stay in the open. The Negroes might have the field of battle, but they could not follow up their victory. They dared not throw in the direction of a house occupied by white people. To do so would be inviting arrest, for the white people could not permit such an attack on their prestige to go unnoticed. The Negroes would eventually have to withdraw with nothing gained. The next Negro boy who tried to pass along the street would be rocked.

This enmity between the boys of the two races existed only in the neighborhood. Away from there, they were good friends. They played baseball and swam in the river together. Even, at times, they had helped each other in rock fights with boys from other sections of town.

The white boys were not so restricted as the Negroes. They could pass through the Alley, but they were not allowed to stop. To linger was an invitation to a battle. If a white boy should be injured in a fight in the Alley, the Negroes would be relatively safe from prosecution because of the unwritten law, "that a white person had no business where Negroes live except on business."

Sam was coming down Johnson Street one day with a sack of junk over his shoulder. He had been on the street for several blocks and had forgotten to turn off and go through the Alley so he walked through the restricted zone. He was lost in thought, but was brought back to reality by a rock hitting the sidewalk in front of him. As he looked up, another rock sailed past his head. He quickly got his bearings. He was in the middle of the block. To turn and run back to the next cross street with the load he had was impossible and he did not want to abandon his load of junk. He thought to run down between two of the houses. As he started to run, he saw some of the boys, as if divining his intentions, start toward the alley to head him off. He decided then that when he reached the alley, he would go in the direction opposite to that he had been going and get over onto Felts Street. This was a congested street and rock throwing was not permitted there. But this line of retreat was not to be permitted him. The boys had evidently planned this ambush well as others were coming up the alley from this direction. He was being closed in on from three sides. There was but one course--take out over the fences until he could find an opening between the stores that faced Felts Street. He broke into a yard that had an old barn on the Alley. When he disappeared from view, the white boys gave shouts of victory because they thought they had him trapped and let loose a barrage of rocks against the barn. Sam was looking for a place to hide his sack in the hopes it would not be found and later he would come back after it, when he heard someone say, "Psst. Come in here."

He looked around and saw a Jew boy of about his own age standing in a door of the barn. Sam had seen the boy before and knew his father ran a store on Felts Street. The family lived in rooms over the store. This barn must be on the lot at the rear of the store. He darted into the barn and the boy quickly closed the door and hooked it from the inside.

"Come on. We will hide up here," the white boy called out as he began climbing up a ladder to the loft. Sam followed and had no sooner reached the loft when his pursuers came together in the alley.

"This is where the bastard went," one of them said.

"Hell, yes; I particularly noticed he went in by this old barn," said another.

"He is not in this yard," said a third, walking past the barn and glancing around.

"He didn't run through old man Moskovitz's store or go over any of the dividing fences because I climbed up on a telephone pole to see," said one who had just come up, thus explaining why he had lagged behind.

75

"I'll bet he's hidden out in this old barn."

"You know he is. Where else could he have gone?"

"Let's search it then."

"Here is a door and its locked from the inside. I'll bet the son-of-a-bitch went in there and locked it."

"I don't know about that. Here is another door on this side and its locked from the outside. Whoever uses this barn locks that door and goes out this one."

"He is not in there. These cracks are wide enough so that you can see all over the place."

"Yeah, but how about the loft? The bastard could be hiding up there."

"Suppose he is. He's gonna stay up there until we leave. Meanwhile, he's just hiding up there laughing at us."

"We could just bust open this door and go up in the loft."

"Yeah, and get in trouble for breaking into a building. Not for me. Hell, we chased him off Johnson Street. That's all we wanted to do in the first place. Come on, let's go; he won't be back."

Sam and his savior lay side by side on the floor of the loft.

"What were they going to do with you?" asked the Jew when the white boys were out of ear-shot.

"They already did it. They rocked me."

"Yes, but suppose they would have caught you. What would they have done?"

"I don't rightly know. I have never heard of a Negro boy being caught."

"Why don't they allow you on Johnson Street?"

"I don't know unless it's because they don't like the idea of colored people gradually taking over the houses of white people. Colored people are already in the second block below this one on Johnson Street and I suppose it's only a matter of time until they will move farther on up. They just don't like to live so close to colored people."

"Where do you live?"

"I live in this alley, down in the next block."

"What's your name?"

"Sam Martin. What's yours?"

"Max Moskovitz. I live here. My father runs the store and we live upstairs over it. Why do Gentiles hate colored people and Jews?"

"What are Gentiles?"

"Gentiles are,--Gentiles are,--" and Max looked at Sam in amazement. "Why Gentiles are people who are not Jews, but come to think of it, I don't know whether that includes colored people or not. It must not because the Gentiles don't like Jews and Negroes."

"I know why they don't like Jews. It's because they killed Jesus."

"I've heard my father say that although I don't understand why they should hold it against us. That happened almost two thousand years ago in Palestine. Jesus was a Jew."

"Naw," cried Sam.

"He was, too. What did you think he was?"

"I don't know. I'd never thought about it but I didn't know he was a Jew."

"Well, he was."

"The Jews don't believe in him and my mama says all Jews are going to hell when they die because they don't."

"Our rabbi says we won't."

"That's funny. I wonder who's right about it," mused Sam.

"I don't know; but I don't think it's right for us to be mistreated now for something that happened such a long time ago."

"How are you mistreated? You are white."

"That doesn't make any difference. We are mistreated in lots of ways. The Gentile boys sometimes throw rocks at me on the way home from school. I always run when I see them."

"That's the only thing to do. There's no sense in standing up and let them knock your brains out," advised Sam.

"That's the reason why I asked you what they would do if they caught you. I have wondered what they would do to me if they ever caught me."

"Nothing, I suppose. At least they wouldn't kill you. Leastways, I've never heard of anybody being killed."

"Besides throwing rocks at me, they are always making dirty remarks at school and saying all sorts of nasty things about us. Even the grown people are nasty. Sometimes a Gentile will say mean things to my father and mother in the store."

"But you are white. You can go anywhere you want to go."

"Not everywhere but at least we can go to more places than colored people can go. Some restaurants don't want us. Some hotels and apartments won't allow Jews."

"I didn't know that. I didn't know there was any difference in white people. What do you do about it?"

"Nothing. There is nothing to do. The only thing to do is to 'Tell it not in Gath'."

"What's that?"

"I don't exactly know. It's from some place in the Bible. That's what my father always tells me when the Gentile boys have rocked me home, or I've have been in a fight with one of them on the school yard. I think it means not to let them know that they have hurt you. Just keep quiet and put up with it the best you can, and in time, everything will be all right."

"Maybe that's true. Reckon that same thing would be true for colored people. 'Tell it not in Gath'. Most of the time when people do something to you, it's just because they want to see you suffer. If they didn't know they were hurting you, maybe they would quit."

"I don't know whether it will work or not. If it does, it's a long time doing it for the Jews. It's been going on for centuries. The only satisfaction you can get out of it is just in not letting them know they are hurting you. The only thing to do is to remember, 'Tell it not in Gath', and dig in deeper in whatever you are doing so you can do it better than anybody else."

"What do you mean by that?"

"Here in America, everybody has a chance to make something out of himself. He can be a doctor or lawyer or teacher or businessman; just anything he wants. In Europe, a Jew couldn't do that."

"Can a colored person be anything he wants to be?"

"Why not? He has the opportunity. I don't care what it is, if he just makes himself just a little better than the next one, he will be recognized and accepted. That is why I am going to be the best surgeon in this city."

"It's easier for a Jew. After all, he's white."

"I don't see why that makes any difference. Even a Negro can be successful. They tell me that there's a Negro dentist in this city who doesn't have any but white patients."

"I've never heard of him."

"That's true. And if a dentist can be that good, why not any other profession?"

79

"You can do it because you have the money to go to school and learn all that."

"I've got money? Where is it?"

"You are a Jew, ain't you? All Jews have got money."

"I don't know any rich Jews, although there are some here. And my father doesn't have any money."

"He's got that store."

"He owes a lot of money and he just barely makes enough to take care of us. There are five of us children. That's why we've got to help out as much as we can. We pitch in and sweep out the store and wash windows, and sometimes on Saturdays, my sister and I help out in the store."

"Then how are you going to get all this schooling?"

"I'll get it. You watch and see."

"Do you suppose a colored boy could do the same?"

"I don't see why not. You can go through high school and right here in town, only a few blocks away, is Semmes University. It's for colored people."

"I never had thought about going to college before, but I suppose I could," mused Sam. "You know, I'm glad I met you for more reasons than one. I think I'll figure on going to college and making something out of myself; something more than just an ordinary colored person."

"You can do it," enthusiastically declared Max.

Thereafter, the two boys had frequent contacts with each other. If Sam were passing through the Alley and Max was doing some work in the yard, Sam would stop and they would engage in conversation. Sitting on the back steps of the store or swinging their legs from the open hay door in the loft of the barn, they had long talks about questions that usually interested adolescent boys, but mostly they talked about what they were going to do when they grew up. Sam decided that he, too, would become a doctor.

In his talks with Max, Sam came to realize more and more that there was considerable prejudice in the world. He had always been taught that he was a Negro, and there was a certain place in the world for him and he couldn't expect things to be any different. As a Negro, he would always "stay in his place", and if he undertook to get out of it, he would get into trouble. He began to readjust some ideas and put them into their proper places. The mere fact that he was a Negro did not necessarily mean that he could not have ambition. From what Max said, in many respects, a Negro was not much worse off than a Jew. It meant that he might have to work harder and overcome more; but it could be done.

Most of the Negroes he knew seemed to be satisfied in just being what they were. They were content in working and eating and having a good time on Saturday night and sleeping all day Sunday, or some like his mother and father had to use all their time in just trying to stay alive.

He wondered why the white people should be so "down" on Negroes. The Negroes had not done anything to them like the Jews had killed Jesus. The only thing they could say about the Negro was that he was once a slave owned by the white man, and now he was free; but it was the white people who had freed him. The more he knew of white people, that is, white people who were not Jews, the more puzzled he became. They didn't like Negroes, didn't want to have anything to do with them; yet, there were people like Mrs. Mason and the white man whose automobile glass was broken, who were kind to him. He had heard older Negroes say that a Negro was always a whole lot better off if he had some white man who would take an interest in him. If he got into any kind of trouble, you could always depend on the white man to look out for you. They were certainly hard to figure out.

The more he thought of the matter, the more important the white race loomed in his existence. He began to see that not only would he have to overcome the handicaps of the lack of money to get sufficient schooling, but he would also have to overcome the opposition of the white race towards all the people of his own race. His fight for success would have to be fought not only for himself, but for his own race, for he saw that his greatest handicap was that of color. Then he began to wonder why the white people hated the Negro as they did. He didn't hate white people. In fact, he never paid much attention to them. He didn't come in contact with them much, and, after all, he didn't know a great deal about them. Certainly he had nothing against them and he couldn't see why the white people should have anything against him. Their attitude towards the people of his race was unfair.

There slowly began to develop in him a dislike of the white race, and this, coupled with a dogged determination to make something of himself, gave him a sensation altogether new. He couldn't tell just how it affected him. He couldn't say it made him happy, but it did give him a greater interest in life.

He wanted to talk to someone of his own race about this new feeling he had. He knew his mother would not be interested, and she would be afraid he was getting ideas over his head. He had never talked with his father much, and he knew the older man would not be able to offer anything on the subject. One night after supper, John Henry did not immediately leave, but sat down on the edge of the porch.

"John Henry, what are you going to do when you grow up?" Sam asked his brother sitting down beside him.

"What do you mean, what am I going to do?"

"I mean, what kind of work are you going to do? What are you going to be?"

"I don't know. Most anything that comes to hand. I am gettin' damn tired of caddyin'. Besides, I'm gettin' too big for that. I am almost a man. Mr. Biggers offered me a job delivering packages for his drug store, but, hell, that's a boy's job. Besides, it don't pay but three dollars a week, and I make more'n that at the country club. I would like to be a caddy master or a truck driver."

"Is that all the ambition you got? Just a truck driver."

"What the hell's wrong with that?"

"Oh, nothing, if that's all you want. I want to be something more than that. You know what? I'd like to be a doctor."

"What the devil you talkin' about, Nigger. You bein' a doctor. Hell, you have to go to college to be a doctor and then what you got? Doctors ain't so much. Not a nigger doctor, noways. You been readin' too damn many of them books from school. You had better cut it out 'fore you get in trouble."

"I don't see why a Negro can't amount to as much as a white man."

"I do, and I'll tell you why. 'Cause 'fore the nigger amounts to so much, some white man has done pushed all his teeth down his throat. That's why. You'd better forget about them things and be thinkin' about gettin' you a job o' regular work."

"Oh, I don't know," returned Sam, becoming angry, "I'm not doing so bad. I make a little money selling junk besides going to school."

"Yeah, and yo' are agoin' to get in trouble about that junk business, too. You almost got in trouble once."

"I know, but I hadn't done anything wrong. The police just wanted to arrest somebody 'cause that white man made 'em mad."

Sam didn't try to discuss the subject of his ambition with any of his family after that. He did want to talk with someone of his own race. He had thought of talking to some of his teachers, but decided against it. They probably would not understand, and most of them acted as if they were about to lose their jobs. Then he happened to remember that Mattie Carr had gone to college. Mattie and her husband, Jeff, lived in the Alley. Most of the people did not have much to do with them because they had a reputation for bootlegging. Not that Mills Alley people had any objections to bootlegging, but they were afraid that some day Mattie and Jeff would be caught by the law, and they might be involved. The Carrs were friendly enough with their neighbors, and in spite of the fact that they were apparently making money, did not try to give themselves airs. Jeff was also a cabinetmaker and worked at a furniture factory.

Sam strolled past Mattie's house and found her sitting on the porch.

"Howdy, Miss Mattie; how are you today?" Sam asked her.

83

"Fine, Sam, and how are you?" returned the woman.

"I'm all right," replied Sam. "Miss Mattie, I would like to ask you a question."

Mattie hesitated a moment before replying, but noting the serious look on Sam's face, she said: "Why certainly, Sam. What is it? Sit down there on the edge of the porch."

"You have been to college, haven't you?"

"Yes. I had two years at the Negro State Normal."

"What do you think about Negroes trying to make something out of themselves?"

"I think it is a pretty good idea. Why do you ask?"

"I don't know. I've just been thinking. I want to be something, but everybody keeps reminding me that I am a Negro and it seems like the white people don't want the Negroes to do anything."

"It's not as bad as that. After all, the white people have established some pretty good schools for Negroes."

"Yes, I suppose that is so."

"The big trouble is that so few Negroes have the money to go to school, and it takes money, in spite of the fact that the schools are free. I wanted to be a school teacher, but I could go to college only two years. It takes four years to get a degree to teach."

"I suppose a fellow could work and make enough money to get through school."

"Yes, and that is what most Negroes do. You can do it if you want to hard enough."

"What gets me, though, is that most Negroes don't seem to want to better themselves. I mean all they think about is just getting a job and going to work."

84

"That is probably because that is the easiest thing to do," replied Mattie. "Ambition is an uncomfortable companion to have. I am afraid that the trouble with you is the same as that of most ambitious colored people. They can't just be ambitious for themselves. They want to be ambitious for the whole race. That is too big a job for anybody regardless of his color."

"I don't understand what you mean."

"When a Negro starts out to do something, he begins to think about being a Negro and when he does that; he realizes that his race has still a long way to go. Then he wants to take the whole race along with him so that before long, he realizes that he can't do it. Then he gives up in despair."

"Why shouldn't he feel that way?"

"Why should he? Do you think the average white person ever gives a thought about his race except in the most general way? He goes ahead and does what he wants and lets his race take care of itself. I am glad to see you are ambitious. I know you have a good mind. If I were you, I would go ahead and do what I wanted to do, and forget the race."

"But how can I when I am being reminded of it all the time?" cried Sam.

"I don't know," softly returned Mattie. "If I did, I would do it myself."

Chapter 14

"What is that stuff I see you and those other two boys hauling in sacks?" Max asked Sam one day.

"Junk. Me and Tom and Lige are in the junk business."

"Is it hard to find?"

"Naw. You can find plenty of it most everywhere. Most people will give it to you to get rid of it."

"Where do you sell it?"

"To old man Epperson, who runs a junk wagon. You know him. You have seen him driving an old horse and ringing a bell. An old fellow who looks like him is about to die. He is not, though. He's looked that way for years."

"What does he pay you?"

Sam gave him the current prices.

"What would it be worth to you to get more money for your junk?"

"I don't know. How are you going to get more money?"

"That's up to me. What I want to know is what is it worth to me to get you more money for your stuff?"

"What do you want?" asked Sam, assuming the caution natural to his race in dealing with white people.

"I'll tell you what. You and Tom and Lige meet me in my back yard after school tomorrow, and I'll show you how all of you can make more money, and I can make some too."

"How are you going to do that?"

"There's no use in me telling you now. Meet me tomorrow and I'll tell you then. If you don't think it's fair when I tell you, you don't have to do it."

The three Negroes met the Jewish boy the next afternoon.

"I'll tell you what I've got on my mind," began Max. "You guys have been going around collecting junk and carrying it in that little wagon. How much more could you get if you had a bigger wagon to haul it in?"

"We could get a whole lot more if we had something bigger to haul it in," replied Sam.

"All right. I've got a push cart and you can haul ten times as much in it as that wagon can carry," and Max dragged a push cart from beneath the porch steps.

"Good gosh," exclaimed Lige. "I'll bet we can get twenty times more junk with that."

"Don't be silly," scolded Tom. "I don't care how much junk you can haul in that. You got to get it and bring it back, don't you?"

"Yeah," responded Lige.

"Well, how much junk you get depends on how far you have to go to get it."

"You boys have been selling your stuff to old man Epperson," explained Max. "Now what does he do with it? I'll tell you. He takes it down to the junk house and sells it for more money."

"That's right," agreed Lige.

"With this push cart, we can take it down there and get what he is getting for it, can't we?"

"Yes, if they will give us what they pay him," argued Sam.

"Why can't they give us the same prices? All they want is the junk. They don't care who they buy it from, do they?"

"I don't know what the man what runs the junk house wants," declared Tom.

"Here is my proposition. I'll furnish the cart. You get the junk and bring it back here and we'll sort it. You get more money if you do that. Then we take it down to the junk house and sell it. For furnishing the cart and helping you sort it, you give me one-half of all over what you are getting now for the junk."

"Huh, you'll get it all then," objected Tom.

"If you get just twice as much junk with this cart than you are now getting, you will make more money, won't you? Then if I get a better price for it than you, you'll still be ahead that much, won't you, because you are not getting it now."

"That's right, Tom," agreed Sam. "Let's try it anyway. We can't lose because if he doesn't get more money, we are not out anything and we'll be getting the use of the cart free."

"It won't make any difference how late you get back. We will sort it tonight and take it down and sell it in the morning before school," Max called to them as they started out.

With their improved facilities of transportation, the boys went into entirely new territory that afternoon in their quest for junk and came back heavily laden. By the time the boys had separated it into its various kinds, it was dark. They agreed to meet early the next morning and take their stock to the scrap material buyer.

Max did the talking when they sold the junk and much to the surprise of all three Negroes, they were offered prices greatly in excess of what they had been getting. After Max took his part of the excess price and the Negroes divided the remainder, each of them had more for his part than he had ever made before for one day's work.

Later, on the way to school, Tom said, "See there. That's why Jews always got money. He got almost as much money as any one of us did and he didn't do any work at all. Why didn't we think of that? We could have gotten us a bigger wagon somewhere and that man would have given us as much as he gave Max."

"Maybe so," responded Sam. "But you'll have to admit, it took a white boy to show us how to do it."

"We could have done the same thing."

"Yes, but why didn't we? I'll tell you why. It's because we think like niggers. That's why."

Chapter 15

Sam got a job delivering the afternoon newspaper. His route included the Alley along Felts Street and on out to Twelfth Street. The corner of Felts and Twelfth Streets was the center of the city for its Negro population. Here were two movie houses; several eating places that ranged all the way from Nick's Ten Cent Lunch to the Royal Palm named for the two giant palms in tubs just inside the front doors; beauty shops with French names that featured hair straightening processes; several clothing stores that carried fairly good and stylish merchandise; a Negro owned drugstore that was as good as any in the city; and the city's only Negro owned bank. Most of the businesses were legitimate enterprises but a few of them were merely fronts for activities beyond the pale of the law. In closely guarded rooms at the rear and upstairs; bootlegging, gambling, and prostitution flourished.

The police made spasmodic efforts to clean up these evils and at other times they preyed upon them to raise campaign funds. The occasional raids only succeeded in curtailing the activities for a few days. It was difficult to make a case since usually the evidence would be destroyed by the time the officers had effected an entrance. The police department's usual policy was to leave things alone so long as they did not become too open or too rough, then the police would exact a penalty in the form of campaign assessments. The operators gave willingly to these exactions and merely considered them a form of taxation.

On Saturday evening, the whole area took on a festive air. This was the best place in the city to have a good time, and every Negro who had a quarter to spend felt he was getting extra value if he spent it at Twelfth and Felts. Those who had the money in their pockets and were looking for a good time could be accommodated there. Good-time houses were available to fit all purses. It made no difference that a person might wake up in the police station, the city hospital, or in the Alley and his money all gone; a good time had been had the night before.

The sidewalks began to become crowded late in the afternoon and by dark, it was almost impossible to walk past the corner. Nobody cared, though, it was Saturday, and everybody was out for a good time. Even those Negroes who were intent only on buying food for the coming week enjoyed the excitement of the street. They might not have money for anything other than beans and grits, at least the gala atmosphere did not cost anything. A drink could be bought for as small a sum as ten cents, and while its quality might be such that the drinker would have to be rushed to the hospital to be cleaned out with a stomach pump, its kick was such that it was really worth far more than he paid for it. A nickel would enable one to get into a crap game and a woman could be had for "two bits."

Sometimes the gaiety of the area would be extinguished with the suddenness of an explosion and tragedy would stalk the streets. If a person had a grievance against another and wanted to have it out with him, he was almost certain of running into that person on Felts Street sometime on Saturday night. Or under the influence of liquor, a man might receive a fancied insult from a friend, something at which he would ordinarily laugh. There would be shouts and curses, a scuffle, the flash of steel, and in a moment, a Negro would be lying dead or dying and another Negro would be the object of a search by the police. In spite of the hundreds of people who might be on the street and witness the affray, by the time the police would arrive, not one person could be found who could tell anything about what had happened. A conviction for a murder on Felts Street was rare. Even if the murderer was caught and witnesses found who had seen the fight, a plea of self-defense could usually be sustained. Probably such a plea would have been just as good if the murdered Negro had done the killing instead of being the one killed.

One of the places where Sam delivered papers was the Rosebud Café. It had a counter with the customary stools along one side with a row of tables along the other side. In the back of the counter was a wide shelf stacked with fried pies, doughnuts, pyramids of fruit, and breakfast cereals in individual packages. At one end of the counter was a shiny coffee urn. The proprietor of the place was a tall, slender Negro who always wore a greasy cap with the bill pulled far down over his eyes. A glance at the eyes under the cap bill would leave no doubt as to where the man got his nickname of "Frogeyes."

The Rosebud Café did not seem to be very popular for Sam rarely saw many customers. He wondered about this since the place was neat and attractive. In the course of time, he came to recognize some half dozen men who seemed to make it their headquarters. At least two or three of them were always in the place. What struck Sam as being so strange was that these men had nicknames that were just as ridiculous as the owner's.

91

He learned to know "Dry Bread," "High Pockets," "Hot Corn," and "Hog Meat" by sight. He learned these men were all professional gamblers and used the Rosebud Café as their hangout while their henchmen were out organizing games for them among the unsuspecting Negroes.

Frogeyes never had anything to say to Sam beyond a grunt. Sam grew to like the man and felt that Frogeyes liked him. Probably, this idea was based on the fact that every time he collected for the paper, Frogeyes always wrapped up a fried pie and gave it to him.

Sam had a subscriber on the second floor of one of these buildings who was not in one day when he made his regular collection round. When he delivered the paper that afternoon, he heard people talking in the room. Instead of dropping the paper on the floor by the door as usual, he knocked on the door thinking that he could collect the weekly payment while he was there. From within, came a significant silence followed by "Who's dar?"

"Paperboy. Collect for the paper," sang out Sam.

The door was cracked open by the subscriber who ran his hand in a pocket to get out the money. Sam glanced into the room and saw a number of men on the floor on their knees around an army blanket spread on the floor.

One of the men glanced up and saw Sam. Sam had seen the man in the Rosebud Café several times and had heard someone call him Jupiter. Whether this was his real name or a nickname, Sam did not know. He suspected that it was the latter since it seemed that everyone around the Rosebud went by a nickname.

"Looka dere. Dere is de paperboy," Jupiter called out gleefully. Sam could see that the man was very drunk. He recognized Dry Bread and High Pockets in the group. He did not know any of the other men.

"Come on, Nigger. What if it's de paperboy? It's yore shot," declared Dry Bread.

"I wanna see de paperboy," asserted Jupiter, arising to his feet. "Come on in, Boy," he yelled as he motioned at Sam with a grandiloquent sweep of an arm.

"Dat boy don't wanna come in here. He's gotta deliver his papers. Come ona shoot. You got de dice."

"I don' care. He's gonna gib me luck."

"Let dat boy alone. He ain't studyin' you."

"I ain't gonna shoot until he comes in here and gives me some luck. You niggers been gittin' my money and I'm gonna get it back 'cause 'at paper boy is gonna be lucky for me."

"Listen, Fool, you is gonna get us all raided," High Pockets spoke up.

"Come on in and close the door until that fool shoots," said Sam's customer to him. "Then you can go on about yo' business."

Sam came inside the door and closed it.

"Go ahead and shoot, Jupiter; everything's all right now," one of the Negroes ordered.

With one hand, Jupiter took off Sam's cap and with the other, he rubbed the dice on Sam's hair. Then he dropped down on his knees, and after rattling the dice in his hand, he threw them across the blanket.

"Wham," he cried. "Dat's my point and I gets de money," and he picked up two dollar bills from the blanket.

"What you mean, 'at's yo' point? That's a six and eight's yore point," cried High Pockets.

"Listen, Nigger, when I says I made my point, I'se made my point."

"I'll be damned if dat's so. When yore points an eight, you're gonna make an eight; and yo' ain't gonna make it on a six. Not on dis nigger, you ain't. Now youse lay dem two frogs down on de blanket, and yo' shoots for an eight."

"Listen, Nigger, who in hell yo' tellin' what to do?"

93

"You, you son-of-a-bitch, that's who I'm tellin'."

Sam did not know what happened next. He had a recollection of a mass of humanity surging from the floor. Someone snapped the light switch throwing the place into pitch darkness. There were sounds of shuffling feet, a heavy grunt, and a jar that shook the room. The door was flung open and men began to stream from the room. Sam joined the procession, grabbed the paper sack he had left in the hall, and ran down the stairs. There was no sign of any of the men who had been in the room. They had disappeared as if by magic.

He continued on his route and made his deliveries; but when he came back up the street, a crowd had gathered at the foot of the stairs.

"What's happened?" he asked, fearing the answer he might hear.

"A bunch of niggers was shooting dice in there and it ended in a ruckus. One of them killed another," one of the bystanders volunteered.

"How did he kill him?"

"Cut his throat. He had done bled to death by the time the law got here."

"Who was it?"

"I don't know 'ceptin' I heard somebody say it was a big black feller what is called Jupiter. I don't know him."

"I'se seen him about but I don't rightly know who he is."

"Who killed him?"

"Nigger, how come you think I know who killed him? I don't know nothin' about it. Let the law find out. That's they job."

Sam slipped quietly away. He asked himself what he should do. Should he go to the police and tell them what he knew? After all, what did he know? Just that there were a bunch of men in the room shooting dice and an argument started. Just who did the killing, he didn't know. Maybe if the police knew who was in the room they could find out. At the same time, they would ask him a lot of questions. He didn't like the idea of being asked a lot of questions by a policeman. Maybe he didn't know enough, after all, to tell the police. In the end, he decided he would keep his mouth shut. Let the police find out what they could in their own way. They could find out who had rented the room; and from him, they could learn who all were in the room.

Several days passed and Sam did not hear of any arrests. In fact, he didn't hear anything at all about the murder. The only change was that High Pockets was absent from the Rosebud Café. Since High Pockets was not one of his customers and it was not any of his business anyway, he did not ask about him.

About two weeks after the killing, Sam came into the café to deliver the paper and High Pockets was standing at the rear end of the counter talking to two other men. Their glances met, but neither gave any sign that either had ever seen the other before. Sam laid the paper on the counter and left. High Pockets went on talking to the other men.

At Christmas, when Sam went to the Rosebud Café to offer the carrier's annual calendar for sale, Frogeyes gave him two dollars for one, remarking as he did so, "This is mostly because you got sense enough to mind your own business."

There was never an arrest for the murder of Jupiter. Sam later learned that as a rule, the policemen, if the identity of the assailant was not quickly learned in Negro murder cases, spent very little time in the investigations, assuming with a callous indifference that a few dead Negroes, more or less, didn't make much difference anyway.

Chapter 16

There were two deputy sheriffs in Rock City who were generally referred to by their combined names of Fenton and Scruggs. This was the result of the practice of endorsing the surnames only of the arresting officers on the outside of warrants and indictments. These men had been partners for years and so linked had their names become around the courthouse that any reference to either was by their joint monikers. For all practical purposes, they did not even possess given names.

They had been deputies for years and no sheriff had seen fit to refuse them commissions. This was probably due to two factors. One was that the sheriff received certain fees out of every prisoner lodged in the jail, and in the course of a year, Fenton and Scruggs would bring in a lot of prisoners. The other was that they worked out of Squire Boles' office and Squire Boles was a power in county politics. Since he received a dollar for each person convicted in his court, it was money in his pocket to keep two such active officers as Fenton and Scruggs working out of his court. No matter how much the public might condemn the abuse of the fee system as practiced by Fenton and Scruggs, the money produced by the arrests they made insured their continued appointments.

The two men were decided contrasts. Fenton was of an enormous size, slow and deliberate in his movements, and he spoke in a foghorn voice. Scruggs was small and scrawny, quick and alert, and was never still so that gave one the impression of a sparrow. He spoke in a high piping voice that enhanced that impression. Fenton patronized the best tailors in town and, in spite of his bulk, was always neat in appearance. Scruggs might have been wearing his partner's cast-off clothing, except for the quality. The cuffs of his coat came almost to his knuckles and he was constantly pulling up his trousers to keep from walking on the cuffs. He wore a faded derby hat, both winter and summer.

The two men lived next door to each other, and owned and operated their automobile jointly. They had several Negroes regularly employed as spotters and to attract dice games. These Negroes would go out on Saturdays, Sundays, and holidays; and if they could not find a dice game or "party" which they could tip off the officers, they would start one. In the subsequent raid, these Negroes always "managed" to escape. The officers got two dollars for each arrest they made. It didn't take but two or three of these raids to turn a profitable weekend.

Fenton existed in a wholly or partially inebriated state. He drank constantly but most of the time he was not drunk enough to prevent him from carrying out his work. Every few weeks he would speed up his drinking until he got past going. Then Scruggs would carry him to a second-rate hotel and take care of him until he toned down on his drinking enough to return to circulation.

The larger man was the directing genius of the partnership, and while Scruggs might suggest and counsel, it was never his to command. He didn't mind, though. He had never made any money until he had teamed up with Fenton as a deputy. What money he made, he saved against the inevitable time when something would happen to destroy their business.

One day, Fenton was sitting in Squire Boles' second floor office staring moodily out of the window when Scruggs bustled into the room. He leaned over Fenton and whispered, "Say, I know where we can make us some jack. Just got a tip on it."

"Spill it," ordered Fenton without diverting his gaze.

"There is a nigger couple by the name of Carr in Mills Alley who are bootlegging. We can knock them off."

"Hell, it ain't worth it. Won't you never learn not to make state cases? If we catch them we'll only get four dollars and maybe have to spend several days in criminal court making the case. You want to make misdemeanors where they can plead guilty and pay off the magistrate's court. You get your money quick and you are through with it."

"Damn, I know all that. This is different. They been at this bootlegging a good while. The police tried to catch them several times but couldn't, and finally laid off them. They been doing a good business and ought to have some stash. If we can catch them, they'll pay off regularly."

For the first time, Fenton showed some interest.

They decided they would make a raid that night.

They drove through the Alley that afternoon to get a lay of the land. That night, when they got to the Carr house, Fenton went to the front door, as was their custom, and Scruggs rushed to the back door to prevent anyone from escaping or trying to destroy evidence.

"Who is it?" called out Mattie in response to Fenton's knock.

"Officers of the law. Open up!"

When Mattie opened the door, Fenton tried to open the screen door, but it was locked.

"What can I do for you?" asked Mattie.

"We are going to search you for liquor. Unlatch this screen."

"Do you have a search warrant?" inquired Mattie blandly.

"Don't have to have one. We got a complaint," shouted Fenton in a voice that usually brought results.

"I'll let you in," replied Mattie, slipping up the latch on the screen door, "but I want you to understand that I am not giving you permission to search this house, and I have asked for a search warrant."

"By God, you're a smart bitch, ain't you?" demanded Fenton as he flung open the door and stalked into the house. "Who in the hell has been telling you the law?"

"Never mind who told me. I happen to know the law." replied Mattie, sure of her position.

"Not where Fenton and Scruggs are concerned. We make our own laws," replied the officer with a grunt which meant to be a laugh. He went through the house and unlocked the back door to let Scruggs in.

"Did you find any whiskey? How many did we catch in here?" excitedly asked Scruggs looking about as if he expected to find bottles of whiskey hidden in Easter egg fashion.

"Shut up and get busy," ordered Fenton.

In a few minutes the officers had ransacked every drawer and closet, stomped on all the planks in the floor to test for loose ones, and measured with their eyes all the walls for hiding places; but they did not find any whiskey. Not even an empty bottle.

"Where do you keep it?" Fenton demanded of Mattie who watched their search with amused tolerance.

"Keep what?" she asked innocently.

"Hell, you know what I'm talking about. Whiskey, of course."

"I don't have any whiskey here. Why did you think I'd have any?"

"Skip it. Where's your old man? Gone after some liquor?"

"No, Sir, he's gone down to the drug store after some medication."

"What's the matter with him?"

"Headache."

"Must have been drinking some of his own head splitter."

"I still don't know what you are talking about."

"Are you Carr's wife or his woman?"

"Your questions are insulting. I refuse to answer."

"Damn your stuck up hide. I've got a great mind to crown you once," put in Scruggs, drawing his black-jack.

"Here, none of that," said Fenton, holding up a warning hand.

Mattie contemptuously turned her back on Scruggs.

"Is that your old man's picture there?" asked Fenton, nodding to a picture on a table.

"Yes."

"What does an old buck nigger like him want with a good-looking wench like you?" asked Fenton, looking her up and down as if he was seeing her for the first time.

Mattie did not reply.

"Come on, let's go," put in Scruggs, not liking the tone of Fenton's voice and the way he looked at the woman. "Hell, they've either just sold out or they've got it stashed out somewhere."

"Might as well. Listen, girl, we're coming back and I may be looking for something the next time besides whiskey?"

"I don't know what you'll be looking for, but you won't find anything here that you'll have a right to," replied Mattie.

"You know, that's a damn good looking wench," said Fenton to Scruggs as he crawled into their automobile.

"Yes, but after all, she is a nappy," replied Scruggs, stepping on the starter of the car.

"Did you notice how clean she was? And there wasn't any niggerery smell about the place, either," observed Fenton more to himself than to Scruggs.

Two days later, the officer paid another visit to the Carr house. Again, their search for illicit liquor was fruitless. While he was searching the kitchen, Fenton raised the lid of a pot that was bubbling on the stove.

"That smells good," he said, sniffing. "What is it, turnip greens?"

Mattie nodded assent.

"How about a mess of them?" he asked.

"They're not quite done," replied Mattie.

"That's okay. I can wait," and taking off his coat, he hung it on a door knob and sat down at the table.

"Hey, what are you doing," demanded Scruggs as he was coming into the kitchen from the outside. He had been looking under the house.

"I'm going to eat me a mess of good turnip greens and hot corn bread. You want some?"

Scruggs stared at him for a minute before asking, "Have you completely lost your mind?"

"Well, I'll be damned," yelled Fenton, pounding on the table with his fist. "Can't a man eat a little turnip greens without somebody wanting to know if he's crazy? By damn, I like turnip greens and I'm going to get some, and I don't care who doesn't like it!"

"All right. I'll wait for you in the car," returned Scruggs and he left the house.

Half an hour later on the way back to the office, Scruggs remarked, "I thought we went there after liquor, but you wind up eating turnip greens."

"What's wrong with that?"

"Just the idea of eating in a nigger's house."

"You're crazier than hell. What the hell is the difference in eating in their house when it's clean like hers or having one of 'em come to your own house to do the cooking?"

"I don't know. There ain't nothing else there you're after, is there?" and Scruggs gave his partner a side-long glance.

"No way. Why?" but Scruggs didn't catch the grin on his face.

"Just that if your are, I've got a hunch that says lay off. It might be bad business."

Chapter 17

Sam was sitting with his back to the window eating his lunch one day after school, when Selene Jones and Liza Boone met in the Alley just outside his window.

"I see'd dat white man's car settin' on de street jes 'round de corner as I come by," observed Selene.

"Yep, I see'd him come down de Alley and slip in dat house a li'l while ago."

"Dat white man might be smart but I don' think he is. He's jes' askin' fer trubble and some day he's gwine to get it."

Sam quit chewing so he would not miss anything that was said.

"You mean Jeff might come home sometime and find him there and cause some trouble?"

"I don' know how hit'll come 'bout but hit's jes bound to cause some trouble. What bizness has a white man got visitin' a colored woman so much? That ain't right and you knows hit, even if she didn't have no husband. Dat's whut I means. Whites and blacks ain't go no bizness doin' dat a way, if whut's goin' on is whut I thinks hit is."

"I blames her for lettin' him come 'round so much. She don' have to let him, even if he is white."

"Jes' plain commonality, I calls hit."

"So far as dat goes, he's a whole lot commoner dan she is. After all, she is a nigger and folks don' look for much out of a nigger but he's a white man and a officer of de law at dat."

Sam couldn't swallow another bite. He spit the food out of his mouth and laid it on his plate. He felt sick at his stomach. He'd seen the car parked around the corner a lot and once when he delivered the paper, he had seen the man there thinking that he was the insurance collection man. Not Mattie Carr. Mattie who'd gone to college and had told him he could be what he wanted to be and talked to him about going to college and making something of himself. People like Mattie didn't do that sort of a thing. If it was Malvoy, it would be no more than you could expect, but not Mattie. Those two old women were just gossiping. They should attend to their own business and let other people's alone. Yet, that weak feeling in his stomach persisted.

Sam always looked forward to collecting at Mattie Carr's. He had had several talks with her since that time she had advised him not to try to be too ambitious for the whole race. The Mattie who had always encouraged him in his ambitions. She usually had a word or two with him when he went there. Sometimes she would talk to him about the books he had read and would suggest others for him to read. Often she would give him some fruit or candy, and on hot days in the summer, she would give him a glass of lemonade. Had he been a little older, and Mattie wasn't already married, Sam was sure he could fall in love with her.

He did admire and respect her, for to him, she represented something that all Negroes could be without too much effort. She was always neat and clean, and while her clothes were not expensive, in fact, most of the time she wore simple house dresses, she wore them with an air of being well dressed. Her house was kept ever so clean, and to Sam, it was elegantly furnished.

Sam had heard that Jeff and Mattie bootlegged, but he hadn't paid much attention to it. They kept none of the liquor in their house, and did not sell it to any of their neighbors. They sold mostly to white people to whom they delivered the liquor. There was never any coming or going around their place as it was with some other places he knew of where bootleg whiskey was sold. At least, they didn't drink the stuff themselves, and otherwise, tried to live decent lives.

Fenton had arrested and unjustly accused too many people with minor offenses for the sole purpose of collecting the fees for his relations with Mattie Carr to remain long a secret from his wife. She took no immediate action after reading the anonymous letter, but discreetly kept silent for more that a week. Then one morning at breakfast, she guardedly asked him a few questions about his activities. His evasive answers caused her to decide that the matter needed looking into.

After her husband left the house, she got ready, and went downtown to the office of Paul Allen, a well known divorce lawyer. She told Allen of the letter and her suspicions, and gave the lawyer the money to hire a private investigator to look into the matter. Allen could have told her that her suspicions were justified because he had been about the magistrate's court enough to have heard the gossip. It was just a matter of procedure to get the evidence to be used in court. After Mrs. Fenton left, he sent for Ken Rundle to get the evidence, and then called in his secretary and starting dictating the divorce petition. He rubbed his hands in anticipation of the fee he would get out of this case. He knew Fenton made a lot of money and had taken good care of it. There should be a large property settlement that would justify a good fee. He would ask for an injunction tying up Fenton's property and bank account.

After arriving at the office, Fenton developed an uneasy feeling. He didn't like the tone of the questions his wife had asked him. Not that it mattered a damn, but there was no use in starting up a stink. He wondered if she had heard anything. He got a bottle of whiskey out of his desk drawer and slipped back to the toilet and took a drink. It was good stuff and he felt better. On coming back into the office, he told Scruggs he was going down to the corner drug store for a few minutes. Scruggs watched him from the window to make certain that he did go into the store.

When an hour had passed and Fenton had not returned, Scruggs went to the drug store. In response to his queries, he learned that Fenton had come into the store, bought a cigar, and then had gone on through the store into the Alley. Scruggs rushed around the corner to where they usually parked the car and found it was still there. Mystified, he returned to the magistrate's office to await his partner's appearance.

Later in the morning, one of the loafers who hung around the courthouse came in, and getting Scruggs off in a corner, talked to him a few minutes in an undertone. Scruggs gave the man half a dollar for the information he received.

He got the automobile, drove out Felts Street to Twelfth Street, and circled the Alley. He found a car parked on Eleventh Street near Johnson which he recognized as Rundle's. He parked his car in behind it and got out. When he turned into the Alley, he saw Rundle near the Carr house and Rundle saw him at about the same time. Rundle turned and started walking in the other direction, looking at the houses on both sides of the street as if he were looking for a particular one. Scruggs walked through the Alley and around the block; but when he returned to where he had parked his car, Rundle's was gone.

He went to the Carr house and Mattie answered his knock.

"Tell Fenton I want to see him," he ordered.

"Mr. Fenton is not here, Mr. Scruggs," replied Mattie, feigning surprise.

"Damn it, Woman, don't lie to me. This is serious. I've got to see him."

Mattie started to close the door, but Scruggs threw himself against it and flung it open. Ignoring Mattie, who was hurled back against the wall, he strode into the adjoining room. Fenton was lying on the bed, partially clothed. At a glance, Scruggs could see that he had been drinking heavily. Scruggs marveled that a man could get so drunk in such a short period of time, but he had always marveled at the drinking prowess of his partner.

"What the hell do you want?" demanded Fenton.

"Come on and get away from here. There is going to be hell to pay."

"I'm not goin' anywhere."

"Your wife has seen Paul Allen and he has got Rundle to get the goods on you."

"Why, that dirty bitch. She doesn't know when she's well off."

"It's not going to do you any good to stay here. That bastard may go off and come back with a warrant and catch you here."

"I am not worried about Rundle or Allen, either. I've got enough on both of those bastards to make 'em lay off. Besides, if you stay here, it won't amount to anything if they do come."

"I am not going to stay. I am going and you are going to come with me."

"No, by God. I am staying and you are staying with me. If we leave, we leave together, feet first," giggled Fenton, rolling over and starting to reach for his pistol that was lying on a table at the head of the bed.

"Don't reach for that gun, Fenton; I don't want to have to hurt you."

"Then you are going to stay?"

"No, I'm leaving, and be damned to you. I tried to help you out, and you wouldn't let me."

"You are not going to leave me now," and Fenton placed his hand on the pistol.

"By damn, I told you about picking up that gun. If you pick it up, I am going to kill you if it's the last thing I do."

"Then, damn you, you dirty bastard, start shooting," screamed Fenton as he grasped the pistol.

Instantly, the room rang out with a fusillade of shots and almost as quickly, Mills Alley filled with Negroes all wildly excited and yelling to one another trying to find out what had happened.

By the time the police squad car careened into the Alley, the knowledge was general that the shooting had taken place in the Carr house, and it must be serious since no one had come out. Not one of the assemblage had the courage to venture into the house to find out what had taken place. The house was pointed out to the officers who piled out of the car and rushed into it with drawn pistols.

The police found Scruggs lying in the door of the back room and Fenton on the floor by the side of the bed. Both were dead. The Negro woman was cowering behind a cabinet in the kitchen, too frightened to move or speak. She collapsed when one of the officers spoke to her.

The Negroes in the Alley crowded about the door. Several ventured up on the porch and one was so bold as to walk up to the front door, but he did not linger. He returned to the edge of the porch shaking his head which could have meant he did not see anything, or what he had seen was too horrible to relate.

One of the officers came to the front door and called out, "Who knows anything about this?"

Each person looked at the officer and then looked at one of the neighbors as if expecting him to speak up, but no one said a word. There was a restless movement through the crowd and one or two at the outer edge turned and started to walk slowly away.

"Come on. Speak up. Some of you are bound to know something about this," commanded the policeman.

Complete silence met his question. Several more started to leave.

"Wait a minute. Don't anybody leave. What were those two white men doing in this house?" This last question was addressed to Uncle Andy Epperson.

"I don't know, Boss," Uncle Andy answered. "Don't know what business the white folks had there."

"Who lives here?"

"Jeff Carr. His wife's supposed to be in there."

"She's in there, but she's too scared to talk. Where is this Jeff Carr?"

There was no answer, and Uncle Andy had turned and started pushing his way through the crowd.

"Where is this fellow Carr? Hey, you," the policeman yelled at Uncle Andy.

"I don't know, Boss. Where he belongs, I 'spect is at work. He works at a furniture factory on the east side. Jes' whar 'bouts, I don't know 'xactly." Uncle Andy had turned half way around with one foot outstretched as if to take a step after the officers were through with him.

"Had these two white men been coming here much?"

No answer. The officer repeated the question and looked directly at the old Negro. Uncle Andy turned his face slightly and caught the eyes of the officer on him.

"Who? Me?" he asked, as if surprised at being asked such a question.

"Yes, damn it. You."

"Boss, I don't know nothing about them white genmen comin' to dat house. What dey do is dey business and this ole nigger ain't puttin' his nose in nobody else's business. Yo'll hafta ask somebody else about it 'cause I don' know. I lives down at de udder end of de alley." Uncle Andy turned and made his way through the crowd, muttering to himself. The remainder of the Negroes either began to leave or had such blank looks on their faces, the officers, wise in the ways of the race, knew it would be useless to ask any more questions. The only way he could get any more information from them would be to question them singly and in private. This they did do later, after the bodies had been sent to the morgue and Mattie had been sent to the police station. There, they were able to piece together the whole sordid story.

Lacking any other charge, Mattie was booked at the police station for disorderly conduct. Jeff put up a fifty dollar cash bond for her that was forfeited the next day. That night, a moving van hauled away the Carr furniture, but neither Mattie or Jeff put in an appearance. It was six months before the owner could induce a tenant to occupy the house, and then only after he had painted it throughout and gave a month's free rent.

Even after listening to many of the discussions of the tragedy and the circumstances leading up to it, Sam could not believe that Mattie had been guilty of any wrongdoing. To him, she had represented an upward step for the race. She was intelligent, well educated, and with a quiet manner that he imagined was like those of the best white people, but at the same time, was without any indication of snobbishness. He had respected her and appreciated her friendship.

Accepting all the things they said about her as true, he could not blame her for what had taken place. She had not been just a Negro "whore" of a white man. The white man must have forced himself on her, and being a Negro, she could not complain without getting him, and possibly herself, in trouble. Why couldn't the white man have gotten himself a woman of his own race? Why did he have to lower both races by taking up with Mattie? Were the Negroes in the United States to be forced to keep their women unattractive, like the Ubangies of Africa, so other men would not want them? Didn't the white people ever do anything to better the feeling between the races instead of doing things to make it worse?

Mattie owed him twenty-five cents for papers. He made no effort to find out where she had moved to. Even if he saw her again, he would not ask her for the money. After all, he owed her something.

Chapter 18

Early one morning, a collector for an installment clothing store was in the Alley looking for one of his firm's customers who had been so thoughtless as to move without leaving a forwarding address. He was staring at the Tanksley house and had just made up his mind that this was the place for which he was looking, and had started toward the door, when he was startled by a loud noise from within. There was a sudden scuffling of feet, the second door on the porch flew open, and Malvoy ran out, slamming the door behind her. The door was almost immediately opened and Frank Tanksley ran out with a razor strap in his hand.

"Come back in the house, Gal," called Frank to his daughter.

"And let you whop me with that strap? You're crazier'n hell. If you wants to whop me, come on outside and take yo' chances like any udder nigger," and Malvoy gathered up a handful of rocks.

"Now, Gal; yo' put dem rocks down and come in dis house. Eber since yo' been workin', yo' been gittin' too big for yo' britches. Yo' needs takin' down a buttonhole."

"Supposen yo' make me come in de house."

"I don' wanna have to come out dere and git yo'."

"Yo' don' wanna and yo' ain't gonna. I'm tellin' yo', don' come outen dat dor."

Frank took a step towards his daughter. Malvoy threw the rock she was holding in her hand and it hit the side of the house near where Frank had been standing. The rock hit just as he had jumped inside the house and slammed the door.

"Come on out you ole buzzard," sang out Malvoy, as she hurled another rock against the door. Getting no response from her invitation, she threw several more rocks against the house.

The commotion had attracted the attention of Fanny Moore, who lived next door. Being of a peacemaking spirit, she raised a window and sang out, "Malvoy, ain't you 'shamed of yo'self, throwin' rocks against yo' pappy's house like dat?"

"What yo' gonna make of it, you ole snuff-dippin' slut? Don' yo' go stickin' yo' nose in my bizeness," returned Malvoy, and she heaved a rock that just missed Fanny's head but went through the window and knocked a bucket of grease off the back of the stove. Fanny withdrew her head and slammed down the window with one swift motion. Her peacemaking efforts came to a quick end.

When Malvoy turned back to the point of the original attack, she saw her father slipping between the two houses on Johnson Street. He had taken advantage of Malvoy's distraction to sneak out of the other side of the house.

"What do you know about that?" demanded Malvoy, dropping her rocks and placing her hands on her hips, "that kinky-headed bastard said he wuz gonna whop me and he runs off jes' 'cause he's gonna get a little fightin'."

Susie came to the door and called to her step-daughter, "Come on in de house and finish yo' bre'kfust, Malvoy. I don' know how come yo' has to fret yo' pappy lak yo' does."

"And I don' know how come he has to fret me, neither," returned Malvoy, accepting the invitation to go back in.

The collector who had been a dumbfounded witness to the scene, decided these were not the people for whom he had been looking. When he turned away, he noticed Maria Martin leaning out of her front room window, which opened almost on the Alley. She had been a spectator of all that had taken place.

"What kind of business is that?" asked the man.

"Jes' Malvoy Tanksley havin' annuder of her tantrums," replied the Negro woman.

"Something ought to be done with her. I never saw anything like that."

"Malvoy's all right," returned Maria. "She's jes' young and full of life. I've knowed her eber since she's a li'l gal. She don' mean no harm."

"Humph. You are more charitable towards that kind of goings on than I am," replied the collector, resuming his search for the errant customer.

A few minutes later, Malvoy passed down the Alley on her way to work at the Apex Laundry. The Howards; Christy Lavergne and Jenks were just coming out of their house.

"Say, Skinny Gal," called out Jenks, "What kinda ruckus was that goin' on up at yore house a while ago?"

"None o' yo' damned business," replied Malvoy without looking around and striding on down the Alley.

"What do yo' mean speakin' to that common laundry rat?" demanded Christy Lavergne, giving her husband a push that threw him off his stride.

Malvoy overheard the remark and without even looking around or slowing up called out, "Listen, you stuck-up bitch, I heard what yo' said, and iffen I wasn't in a hurry to get to work, I'd come back dere and mop up dis Alley wid yo' and iffen yo' ses ennything else, I'll take de time."

If Malvoy had one virtue, it was expressed in the remarks she made to Christy Lavergne. She did work and she got to work on time. Her foreman had long since learned that if Malvoy was not at work on time, it was because she was either in jail or the police station. He had worked out a routine to handle this situation with a minimum of trouble. After calling and finding out in which place Malvoy was held, he would have her released and later in the day, he would send the cash bond to be posted for her. In fact, this had happened so often that on several occasion, the police had turned Malvoy out in time to go to work with instructions to have her boss send the money up sometime during the day.

The laundry took the perpetual bailing out of Malvoy as part of the price to be paid for a good worker. She fed a flat work ironer, and kept the other three people who worked with her in a steady trot all day. A dollar a week was taken out of pay to apply against the money put up for her fines. Sometimes, if the account grew to a good size, the laundry would double the take-out until the debt was somewhere near the liquidation point. There were few weeks in which Malvoy did not have to make a payment on her escapades.

Malvoy had only gotten to the fourth grade by the time she was sixteen and when the Compulsory Education Law could no longer keep her in school, she got the job at the laundry. She had not missed a day's work since.

It was only on rare occasions that Frank tried to exercise any control over her and these usually met with failure for him. Malvoy was a law unto herself. She went her own way, enjoyed life as she saw fit, and had no fear of the consequences.

She was a natural-born rowdy. She liked to drink, she liked to eat, and she like to love; but above all, she liked to fight. Keeping up Malvoy's succession of lovers would broaden one's acquaintance, to say the least. She had no lack of men friends. Something about her must have appealed to their sporting instincts--to see how long they could last, for she certainly had nothing to offer in the way of looks. She was lean, spindly, and always looked as if she had found her clothes in a trash pile. She never wore stockings on her legs, but winter and summer, her head was covered with a cap made from one. Usually, one good fight with her was enough to cool the passions of the most ardent swain. The rupture in the relationship was usually mutual for Malvoy had no use for a lover who wouldn't fight.

Frank knew Malvoy was not a good influence on his younger children, but he could not bring himself to drive her away. The younger siblings worshiped her and Malvoy was good to them. She regularly brought them candy, cakes, and toys from the five and dime. Malvoy and Susie had never had any major differences. Malvoy had started off by simply ignoring Susie and had kept it up. Susie had accepted the situation without feeling or rancor. She took care of Malvoy the best she could as the child was growing up and she was never heard to utter a complaint against her step-daughter. Malvoy contributed greatly to the family's welfare in the abundance of food she brought home. It was true that she brought it to satisfy her own appetite, but she freely shared what she had with the others. In this way, she was some help to Frank and he was willing to tolerate her disruptive behavior.

The Howards had not been in the Alley long and nobody liked them. Everybody thought they were stuck-up. They occupied a second-story room overlooking the Alley down near the lower end of the block. Jenks drove a delivery truck for a wholesale grocery and made good money for someone in the Alley. Christy Lavergne was a maid for one of the wealthiest families in town, and due to her position, was the recipient of what to Mills Alley was "mighty stylish" clothes. The Howards kept to themselves and in the Alley where everybody was friendly with everybody else, temporary differences excepted, this did not go well. People wondered why the Howards ever moved into the Alley and once, when Christy Lavergne was asked, she replied that it was because of the cheap rent since both she and her husband worked they didn't need much of a place to live. In this way, they could save their money to buy a home. This explanation did not increase their popularity.

Malvoy and Christy Lavergne disliked each other on sight. Malvoy did not like Christy's good looking clothes and the "prissy" way she wore them. When she learned the newcomer's name, she didn't like that either, especially when she learned that the bearer was proud of it and insisted on it being used in its entirety when she was addressed. Christy Lavergne didn't like Malvoy's sloppy appearance and her dislike increased when she learned of Malvoy's way with men. Christy Lavergne knew her husband and knew he was weak as far as women were concerned. Although he was mortally afraid of her, a close watch had to be kept on him to keep him from straying.

There was some justification of Christy Lavergne's dislike of Malvoy. When Malvoy first saw Jenks, she made a mental reservation that she would get around to him some day; but after she knew him better, she decided that it would be a waste of time. Jenks didn't seem like a drinking man and evidently wouldn't fight or he wouldn't live with Christy Lavergne. To interest her, a man had to love, to drink, and to fight. So, as far as she was concerned, Jenks was a total waste.

All that day while at work, she thought of the remark she had overheard Christy Lavergne make about her and the more she thought about it, the madder she got. She finally made up her mind to give the woman a good whipping the next time she saw her.

That night as Malvoy came through the Alley, she glanced up at the room occupied by the Howards in the hope of seeing Christy Lavergne.

Jenks was sitting on the second-story porch reading the evening newspaper. He had changed into his good clothes. Malvoy smiled. This was going to be better than whipping Christy Lavergne.

"Hello, Handsome," she called to him.

Jenks lowered his paper.

"Hello, Baby," he responded.

"What's the news?" asked Malvoy.

"All 'bout a skinny black gal what lives in Mills Alley and makes all the men folks step around."

"How come there's anything like that in the paper?"

"A newspaper is supposed to publish the news and that's the mostest news in Mills Alley."

"Is that in the paper?"

"Yeah, you want to see it?"

"Uh-huh."

"Come on up and take a look."

"How about that stuck-up woman of yourn?"

"There's a party where she's working and she won't be home 'til late. Besides, you ain't scared of her, now are you?"

"Hell, no! I wuz jes' wonderin' how come yo're so brave."

When Malvoy mounted to the second-story porch, Jenks opened the screen door for her.

"Come on in here. The flies ain't so bad," he said.

"Yeah, but the light ain't so good either, neither," replied Malvoy as she stepped into the room.

"Listen, Hon, we don't need no light," returned Jenks as he slipped an arm around her, "You shore got what it takes, ain't you, Skinny Gal?" he continued as Malvoy responded to his advances.

Malvoy did not return home to supper. Later, she and Jenks went down to the Blue Moon Café to eat some sandwiches and drink some home brew.

The next time Malvoy saw Jenks, his wife was with him. He acted as if he had never seen Malvoy before. This so angered Malvoy that she started to tell Christy Lavergne right there what had taken place between her and Jenks, and if necessary, whip both of them. On second thought, she decided not to say anything. There was the possibility that something would develop that would be even more fun.

A few nights later, Malvoy was passing the Howard house when Jenks asked her to come upstairs a minute.

"How come you acted like you didn't know me t'other day?" asked Malvoy when she entered the room.

"Honey, you don't understand," explained Jenks, taking her in his arms.

"I understand you think you are too damn good to speak to me when you are with that bitch of yours," retorted Malvoy, stiffening.

"That ain't it at all. There just ain't no use in startin' something' when it ain't necessary. If I'd said anything, she would have gotten suspicious and I couldn't have gotten to see you anymore."

"I don't believe you, but it sounds all right," returned Malvoy, relaxing.

Several times after that, Jenks gave Malvoy the high sign that Christy Lavergne was not at home, and she went to his room with him. Malvoy didn't enjoy the assignations. Jenks was so much of an ox and so afraid of his wife, that her contempt for him grew. She tried to provoke him into a fight, but Jenks refused to become angry. A good fight with him would be fun and maybe Malvoy could also have a good fight with Christy Lavergne.

On the other hand, Jenks fell desperately in love with Malvoy and offered to leave Christy Lavergne if she would marry him.

"Big Boy, you are too damned scared of that woman of your'n to leave her," laughed Malvoy.

"I ain't afraid of her either. I'll admit I take a lot 'cause I'm a man what wants to keep the peace, but if you'll say the word, I'll leave her and get it all over with at once."

"If you'll go out wid me and get good and drunk then come back and beat up dat heifer, I'll do it."

"Honey, how come you wants me to cause such a ruckus?"

"Damn it, 'cause I likes ruckuses, dat's why."

The seduction of the husband of the proud Christy Lavergne was too good to keep, so it was inevitable that she was told about what was taking place. Christy Lavergne loved her husband, and she did not want to lose him. She decided she would handle the matter in such a way so he would never think of even looking at another woman again. Instead of going home and accusing him of his transgressions, she would arrange to catch him in the act.

The next morning when she started to work, she told Jenks she would be late getting home that night because there would be a baby shower for an expectant co-worker. That evening as Malvoy came through the alley, Jenks signaled to her. She started to ignore him and go on home. She was too tired to be bored by him, but then thinking that a good fight would lift her spirits, and she might provoke him into one, she changed her mind and went upstairs.

"Listen, Big Boy; how come you wants to be loving all the time?" asked Malvoy while resisting his advances.

"I just naturally wants to love you."

"Don't that bitch you're married to do any loving?"

"Listen, you ought not to talk that way, Honey. Besides, I am talking about you and me; not me and her."

"I don' want to talk about that stuck-up bitch. I don't give a damn what you want to talk about."

"Now, Honey Baby, let's don' do any talking at all. Let's do some lovin'."

Christy Lavergne had slipped up the stairs and was listening at the door. The word had been passed around that something was about to happen, and a crowd gathered at the foot of the stairs. Christy Lavergne had heard all she could stand. She threw open the door and strode majestically into the room.

"So this is the kind of husband you are?" she demanded of Jenks who was trying to get as far from her as he could without showing too much sign of motion. He was just edging along the bed toward the window realizing that was the only way open, even if dangerous, line of retreat. "And as for you, you common whore," she screamed at Malvoy, "get out of my house."

Malvoy exulted. No longer was she tired and listless.

"Suppose you puts me out." she replied, her arms akimbo.

Christy Lavergne let out a roar and made a dive for her. Malvoy met her half way. While Malvoy was outweighed twenty pounds, she made up in speed and wiriness what she lacked in weight. The two women went together and rolled over in the floor. Round and round they went, knocking over tables and chairs, and generally making a wreck of the room while Jenks sat on the bed, too dazed to move.

Christy Lavergne's intention was to get Malvoy out of the house, and whether or not it was the results of her efforts, the two women rolled out onto the porch, over to the stairs, down which they plunged one over the other, gouging, scratching, and pulling hair. The crowd, which had edged up the stairs, made way for them. The two hit the bottom with a crash. Malvoy jumped up but Christy Lavergne lay there with her head resting on the lower step screeching at the top of her voice.

"Come on and get up, you Hyena," dared Malvoy, and grabbed her by the foot as if to drag her off the porch.

"Save me, save me," yelled Christy Lavergne. "Help, help. She's killing me."

Frank Tanksley broke through the crowd and grabbed Malvoy by the arm.

"Come on, Gal. Get out of here. The cops will be here in a minute."

"I'm not going anywheres. That black heifer said she was going to throw me out, and I want her to do it," cried Malvoy, trying to shake off his grasp.

"Dey ain't no use'n you stayin' here and gettin' arrested. You done whipped her all over her own house. Come on wid me." Malvoy took his advice and allowed herself to be led away.

The police did come, but Christy Lavergne had gone upstairs. The people downstairs were laughing and re-enacting the fight. Someone told the police that it was just a couple of women having a little spat over a man, that they had been separated and both had gone their ways. The officers accepted the explanation and returned to their rounds.

There wasn't anymore fighting in Mills Alley that night, but it was some time before quiet reigned. When Christy Lavergne got back upstairs, she started in on Jenks with her tongue and when she had rested sufficiently, she sailed into him with her fists and feet. It wasn't a fight. The action was all Christy Lavergne's. Jenks just lay in the floor and let her maul him. Later, when an armed truce had been declared between them, Jenks suggested they move out of the neighborhood.

"No, Sir, we are not going to move," emphatically declared Christy Lavergne. "You are going to stay right here and face the music. You oughta thought of this when you tied up with that laundry rat. It ain't goin' to be said that I ever let any woman run me out of the neighborhood 'cause I was afraid she would get my man. We's goin' to stay right here, whether you like it or not, until I gets ready to leave. And I don't think you will look at any other woman either."

Christy Lavergne was a good prophet. From then on, Jenks never so much as looked up from his evening paper when Malvoy passed through the Alley.

Chapter 19

One night, Malvoy did not come back at the usual time, but no attention was paid to this. At around eleven o'clock, when everybody was asleep, she came home accompanied by a man. She stumbled into the house and was preparing to go to bed with the man when her father awoke and came into the room where they were. Two of the children were asleep in another bed in the room.

Frank lit the lamp.

"What's going on in here?" he demanded.

"I'se just goin' to bed," explained Malvoy, drunkenly.

"Who's that man?"

"That's Slats, my boyfriend."

"What's he doin' here?"

"He's goin' to bed with me."

"Not in my house. I'se a respectable man, and I ain't goin' to have no strange men sleepin' wid women in my house," roared Frank.

"Yo' ain't got no say 'bout what I does. Slats ain't got no place to stay, and he's sleepin' here."

"I'll have none of yore whorin' around here. It's bad enough the way you do enny ways without you bringing it home."

"Go on, ole man. Go back to bed whar you belongs. I ain't goin' to have no trouble wid you tonight," and with that, Malvoy undressed by the simple expedient of kicking off her shoes and slipping her dress over her shoulders and stepping out of it. "Come on, Slats, get in bed," she said to the man, who had been standing in the middle of the floor, apparently oblivious of what was going on.

"No, you are not either. You get out of this house, you bastard," yelled Tanksley and started for the man.

"Don't you do that," screamed Malvoy, raising up in bed.

Frank grabbed Slats with the evident intention of shoving him out of the house. Slats suddenly galvanized into life and reaching behind him on a table, picked up a vinegar bottle and brought it down on Frank's head. Frank sank to the floor with a sigh.

"Why, you son-of-a-bitch," screamed Malvoy. "Dat's my pappy. What cause you got hittin' him like dat," and she jumped on Slats with all the force of her feet, teeth, and fingernails. It didn't take Slats long to realize he was in danger of great bodily harm. From trying to overcome Malvoy, he quickly changed his tactics into efforts to make a strategic retreat, but Malvoy clung to him like a leach kicking, biting, gouging, and clawing.

The house was in an uproar. Susie had come to the door of the room and taking in the scene at a glance and thinking that Frank was dead, started screaming. The two children in the room were jumping up and down on their bed while the child in the other room was crying at the top of her lungs. Malvoy and Slats fought all over the room, wholly unmindful of the unconscious Frank who was occasionally trampled on. Susie, with much dodging and twisting, was able to get the two children into the other room. The combatants fell against the table overturning it and throwing the lamp to the floor. Fortunately, the flame went out before the lamp broke so that it did not start a fire.

The commotion aroused the neighborhood and a crowd gathered about the house wondering what was taking place. It was suggested that someone go in and find out what was happening. It was agreed that this was a good idea, but the difficulty lay in getting anyone to be that person. Several suggested the police should be called, and while it was agreed that this, too, was a good idea, no one wanted to take any chances on missing some of the excitement by leaving long enough to locate a patrolman or call the police station.

Suddenly, the door of the house flew open and out came Slats with all the speed fear and pain could give him with Malvoy right behind him, naked as the day she was born. The crowd opened a passageway for them and the last seen of the chase was when they passed under the street light at the corner. Slats was widening the gap between himself and his pursuer. The crowd yelled encouragement to Malvoy.

When some of the neighbors entered the house, they found that Susie had lighted another lamp and was sitting on the floor holding Frank's head in her lap and bathing it with a damp cloth. He had recovered consciousness. The three children were in the other room crying hysterically.

While the neighbors were trying to find out what had happened, Susie was trying to explain as best she could and, at the same time, was trying to quiet the children. Some of the women were trying to straighten up the room when Malvoy returned.

Frank tried to rise.

"Get out of here, you slut," screamed Frank. "Ain't you caused enough trouble for one night?"

"I am gonna get out. I wouldn't stay in this damn house 'nother minute. I jes' came back to get my shoes and dress."

She dropped her dress over her head and stepped into her shoes.

"Here comes the cops," someone near the door yelled.

Malvoy climbed through the window and dropped to the ground. She was not see again in Mills Alley for weeks, although it was reported that she was at work at the laundry the next morning at the usual time.

The officers shouldered their way through the crowd and into the room.

"What's going on here?" one of them demanded.

Frank managed to get to his feet.

"Nothin', Cap'n. I just had a row with my daughter and she's run off."

"Anybody hurt?"

"Naw, Sir, Cap'n. I got a little hickey on my head, but it don' amount to much."

"You want her arrested?"

"Naw, Sir. She's my daughter and I'll take care of her."

"See that you do and if I hear of any more disturbance here, I'll run the whole kit and kiboodle in. All right, you people, clear out. The show's over for tonight. Ain't no niggers killed yet. I'll be damned if I can understand it," this last to the other officer. "These nappies will try their damndest to kill each other, yet, when the law comes in, they just been havin' a little friendly argument."

In a short while, peace again reigned in Mills Alley.

Chapter 20

Susie had come from the country. In the town near where she had lived, there was a canning factory and during the season, there was a big demand for labor. Susie had always tried to go back to her old home each summer to visit a sister who still lived there so she could work in the factory. Thus, her vacation was both pleasurable and profitable. After she had paid her board, she usually had a few dollars to bring back to town with her. This money came in handy to buy shoes and winter underclothing for the children.

She made her annual pilgrimage a few weeks after Malvoy had left home, taking her three children with her. While she was there, a young Negro man who was employed to drive a truck up North to deliver produce, came home sick. After lying in bed several days, a doctor was called in and he diagnosed the illness as typhoid fever. No particular attention was paid to the illness since the patient did not seem to be seriously sick. He was up and around by the time Susie and the children left to go home.

Susie had been home only a few days when she became ill. Remembering the young man who had been sick, she sent the oldest child down to the grocery on Felts Street to call the city health office. When the public health nurse arrived, Susie talked to her for a few minutes. She left to return with a doctor. The doctor pronounced the illness as typhoid fever, and the house was placarded. The children were given inoculations.

Susie's condition grew worse, and Frank became ill a week later.

Frank and Susie were carried to the general hospital the next day. Carrying them away seemed an impersonal thing. The doctor from the health department decided that their conditions were such that they could only be properly treated in a hospital so he sent a nurse to call an ambulance. No mention was made of the children, and nobody gave them a thought until the parents were being carried out of the house. The children, who had been in the background all this time, started crying and calling for their mother.

"What are we going to do with the children?" the nurse asked the doctor.

"I don't know. Probably some of the neighbors will care for them. If they don't, you check up on them again this afternoon and notify the juvenile authorities. Keep track of them because we will have to continue their shots. They will probably come down with the fever in a few days."

"I don't want you to carry my mammy away," screamed Little Susie.

"I want my mammy," cried Tommy, the youngest.

Mary Lynn sobbed quietly in her arm against a post of the porch.

"I'll take care of the chillen," offered Maria, who had come over to help prepare the patients for the hospital. "Come on, Honeys," she said, sweeping Little Susie and Tommy into her arms.

As they started to raise the cot into the ambulance, Susie protested feebly.

"I wants to tell my chillen good-bye," she said. "I may never see them again."

The attendants waited long enough for the children to kiss her, and Frank gently squeezed the arm of each of them.

"You be good chillens 'til I get back," admonished Susie. To Maria, she gave the name and address of her sister in the country and requested her to send the children there if she and Frank didn't return from the hospital.

The two patients were lifted into the ambulance and it started off amid the wails of the children.

Someone locked up the house and gave Maria the key.

"Come on, Babies, you all are going over to Aunt Maria's house to visit for a few days," said Maria to the children, taking Tommy by the hand. The two girls walked close to the woman as if given strength by her immediate presence.

"How come you goin' to take them chillen to yo' house?" asked Rachel Drake. "You ain't got no call to be feedin' 'em yore grub. They ain't no kin of yourn."

"No, and how come that no 'count Malvoy ain't takin' 'em. After all, they's her half brother and sisters. She makes good money down at de laundry. Ennyways, how come she ain't around? She ain't been here since Susie's been sick. Layin' up wid some man somewhars, I 'spect," argued Fanny Moore.

"Never you mind about Malvoy. I 'spect she don' know about de trouble de family's having. She ain't such a bad gal. She just likes to have a good time," replied Maria.

Maria took the children to her house. She gave them an old magazine she had picked up somewhere and a pair of scissors. They were soon busy cutting out paper dolls.

When her husband and sons came home, she briefly explained the situation to them, William merely grunted, but his grin at the children showed how he felt. Sam said that there was nothing else she could do. It made no difference to John Henry.

Maria was cooking supper when she glanced out of the window and saw Malvoy coming up the Alley with her arms loaded with bundles. Maria stuck her head out of the window and called to her.

"Malvoy, the chillen's over hyar."

At the sound of their sister's name, the children jumped up, ran to the window, and greeted her with shouts.

"Dey done tooken mammy and pappy to the horspittle," exclaimed Mary Lynn.

"What has happened to de folks, Miz Martin?" asked Malvoy.

"Yo' mammy and pappy is been took mighty bad wid de typhoid fever," explained Maria, "and de health doctors sent 'em to de city horspittle. I'se keepin' de chillen fo' yo'. I knowd yo' would turn up as soon as yo' heard 'bout it."

127

"I just heard dis evenin' dat dey was sick and I stopped by de grocery to get some grub."

"Ain't no use in you goin' down dere and cookin' supper. Yo' come on in hyar and eat wid us. I'se got plenty already cooked."

"Thank yo', Miz Martin, but I reckon not. I'se got food here and I'll take de chillen on down to de house and cook it for dem. I'se de onliest one dey got to look after dem while de ole folks is in de horspittle."

"We wants to eat here," argued Tommy.

"Dat's right. De chillen, dey wants to eat hyar and we's done fixed it for dem. Yo' come on and eat wid us. Yo' house is all in a muss and yo'll be half de night gettin' it straight."

Malvoy stayed and ate supper with her brother and sisters at the Martin's. Maria explained to her all that had taken place.

"Is dey took bad?" asked Malvoy.

"Frank, he didn't seem so bad but Susie's right sick. Dat typhoid fever; I'se scared of it. I had a brother dat had it when I wuz a little girl and he didn't get well. I remember it same as wuz yesterday. We wuz livin' down at Cottage Grove den. My pappy, he was a farmin' for old man Denny dat year. Dey buried Lafe in de Elm Hill graveyard dere."

"I wonders would dey let me see 'em iffen I went out to de horspittle?" asked Malvoy.

"I don' know but it seems like dey would. After all, he is yo' pappy, and she is yo' step-mammy."

"They will let you see them if you get there at the visiting hours. I think it is between seven and eight," said Sam.

"I wants to go see dem den. Iffen I had been hyar I wouldn't let 'em take 'em to no ole horspittle. I'se afraid of dem places. If dey carry niggers out dere dat can't pay, dey don' do nothin' for dem. Dey jus' lets 'em lay dere and die so's dey can take 'em out to de medical school and let dem students cut dem up. A nigger jus' as same as dead when dey's carried out dere."

At this, Mary Lynn started to cry.

"De nurse, she say dat dat's de onliest way dey can get well is by bein' took to de horspittle," argued Little Susie, her chin quivering.

"Of course they will get well. That's what the hospital is for," consoled Sam. "Malvoy, you ought to be ashamed talking that way. You know they don't let people die if they can help it. What would a hospital be for if they did that?"

"Jes' de same, iffen I gets sick, I don' wanna go to no city horspittle. You just let me die right whar I is if I am gonna die."

After the supper of turnip greens and hog jowl, Malvoy offered to help Maria with the dishes, but the latter insisted that the girl go to the hospital to see her parents. "'Sides, I wants to know myself how dey is," she added.

The nurse had come to check up on the children and she explained to Malvoy how to clean up the house and care for the bedding so that the disease would not be spread. She also told Malvoy to have the children at the health office at the proper time so they could get their remaining typhoid serum injections. Malvoy didn't pay any attention to this order since she didn't understand what it meant.

After Malvoy had left for the hospital, Maria went to the Tanksley home and started cleaning it. Sam had missed her at home so he went looking for her and found her there.

"Ma, how come you have to come over here and start doing that?"

"This house is in such a turrible mess, I jes' hates to think of dat girl comin' back to it from de horspittle."

"Have you ever been given the typhoid fever shots?" he asked.

"No, Chile. I ain't got no time for dem fancy medical doings."

"You come on and leave this house alone. You are liable to mess around in there and get typhoid fever yourself."

"I ain't goin' to get no typhoid fever. I done been aroun' hit too much and know too much about hit for me to be gettin' hit. I'se got my turpentine."

"What's turpentine got to do with it?"

"Hit's got everything. Don't you know dat turpentine is a shore pertekshun against typhoid fever and enny other kind of fever? You jes' keeps a bottle wid you and ever onct in a while you touches de bottle to yore tongue so's you gets jes' a drop. You keep doin' dat and won't no typhoid fever ever bother you."

"Turpentine is no good to prevent fever. If it was, the doctor would be using it."

"Yes, it is, too. Ever' time I hears dey's any fever about, I gets out de turpentine bottle. Why, Chile, I bet I'se give you gallons of hit. Hit's good for a lot of things. Dat turpentine's so strong dat it jes' naturally kills all germs. Dey didn't give hit to yo' Uncle Lafe and he died. Dat's Uncle Lafe what died 'fore yo' was borned. I wuz jes' a little chile den myself. Den I knowd a woman what had typhoid fever onct and dey give her up to die. She tole 'em all dat she wasn't goin' to die; dat she had too much yet to do. She had a passal of younguns to be raised. She says to de doctor, 'Is you done all you knows to do for me?' De doctor, he say 'Yes.' And he wuz a white doctor, too. Dat wuz way out in de country where dey didn't have no colored doctors. Den she say, 'All right, den I'll try my remedy.' 'Ole man,' she says to her husband, 'you go and get me a quart of peach brandy and a peck of red onions. And I don't mean for yo' to get no white ones. And a bottle of turpentine.' Her husband asks de doctor what about it. De doctor says hit don' make no difference 'cause she gonna die ennyways. 'All right,' she says, 'you cut dem onions up in a bucket,' and he did. 'Now pour dat brandy over 'em,' she says and he did. 'Now, pour in dat turpentine and stir it all up together good and set it by de bed,' and he did. 'Now give me de dipper,' she says and dey give her de dipper. Then she reached in dat bucket and got her a dipper full of dat mixture and drunk hit. Then she kept on drinking hit 'til she got so drunk she couldn't drink no more and den she went to sleep. When she woke up, she started drinking dis 'til she drink hit all up and when she got sober, she was a well woman. She lived to be way past eighty and raised all dem younguns and a lot of granchillen besides. 'Cose de brandy jes' kep' her drunk so she could sleep; it wuz dem onions and dat turpentine dat cured her. Dey jus'

130

went in her guts and killed off all dem germs. Don' you worry about me, I ain't goin' to have no fever. And dem chillen ain't neither 'cause I been givin' 'em some turpentine, too. Dey can shoot dat stuff in dey arms all dey wants to but give me my turpentine eber time."

"All right," laughed Sam, "but I wish you wouldn't do it, anyway."

When Malvoy returned, she said she had seen both her father and step-mother and both of them were pretty sick. Susie didn't know her, but her father was glad to see her. She promised him that she would look after the children until he and Susie got out of the hospital.

She got the groceries that she had left with Maria and took the children home.

The next morning, she stopped by Maria's and told her that she would appreciate it if Maria would "sorter" keep an eye on the children since she had to go to work to get money to feed them and to pay the house rent.

That day, the hospital authorities sent word to Malvoy at the laundry to come to the hospital right away. When she got there, she was told that Susie was dying. Malvoy stayed at the hospital until time to go home and fix supper for the children. Susie died late that night.

When Malvoy arrived at the hospital the next morning, she was told that her father had taken a sudden turn for the worse and was in a critical condition. She called the undertaker to take charge of Susie's body and went upstairs to see her father. He was unconscious. She remained with him all that day, and when she went home that night, she did not tell the children that their mother was dead. She had already instructed the undertaker not to make any announcement of her stepmother's funeral for at least another day. Frank died the next morning shortly after Malvoy arrived at the hospital. Malvoy called the undertaker and arrangements were made for a double funeral. Both Susie and Frank had small industrial insurance policies, and the undertaker agreed to give them a good funeral since he was going to be paid for two funerals and it would take no more time than one.

The funeral of Frank and Susie was the biggest ever seen in Mills Alley. A funeral was an event under any circumstances, but a double funeral was something out of the ordinary.

The undertaker and the preacher let themselves go. The services lasted for almost two hours. When they were finally over, everybody was as limp as a dishrag but spiritually exalted. Frank and Susie had both been good people, and dying so close together as they did, and leaving three small children, gave the preacher everything he needed for his oration. He did not overlook one point by which he could arouse emotion. The weeping and sobbing shook the church and Little Susie was hysterical. Everyone agreed it was a beautiful funeral. In spite of the fact that it was almost three miles to Mount Nebo cemetery, fully a hundred mourners followed the two hearses on foot. The procession slowly wended its way through the streets of the city, singing hymns and mourning in unison, something that only the American Negro can do.

After the funerals, some of the close neighbors gathered in the Tanksley home.

"What are you going to do now?" Malvoy was asked.

"I ain't a goin' to do nothin'. In de mornin', I'se goin' to git up and go down to de laundry like I'se been doin' for years."

"I means about de chillens."

"I ain't goin' to do nothin' 'bout dem. We'se goin' to go on livin' hyar jes' like we always did. So longs I kin work and pay de rent and buy food. After dat, I don' know what we does, but I ain't worryin' none about dat so longs I can work."

"Who's gonna look after de younguns?"

"Little Susie's gettin' big enuff so she can look after de odder two. 'Sides, when school starts, dey will all be in school most of de day. Tommy, he's big enuff to go now."

"But will the law let you do it?"

"Will de law let me? What has de law got to do wid me takin' care of my own flesh and blood? Ain't dey mine and ain't I'se all dey got to look arfter dem? Dey mammy was always good to me, jes' lak I wuz her own chile, and warn't dey pappy my pappy? I'se gonna look arfter dem, and de law ain't gonna have no say 'bout it. 'Sides, why should dey keer so longs as it's me doin' it? It won't be costin' dem nothin'."

Malvoy had not reckoned without her old enemy. Christy Lavergne saw a chance to get even for the humiliation she had suffered at the hands of Malvoy. On her Thursday off, she went to the juvenile court. She explained to the judge the situation at the Tanksley house. She gave him a history of Malvoy's love affairs and of the brawls she had been in and an idea of the number of times she had been arrested. A check of the records at the police station verified these. She further explained that while Malvoy was at work, the children were allowed to roam the streets at will getting into all sorts of mischief and subjected to all sorts of bad influences; that they were not being given the proper care and attention they should have. Christy Lavergne heard the judge order the clerk to issue a warrant to have the children taken into custody and placed in a detention home until a hearing could be held to determine their final disposition. Christy Lavergne left the court with a smirk on her face and satisfaction in her heart.

That evening when Malvoy entered the house, instead of the children rushing to meet her, she was met with an ominous silence. A hurried search of the house gave no indication as to what had become of them. With fear in her heart, she went to Maria Martin's in the hope that the old woman could tell her what had happened to them. Maria met her at the door.

"Malvoy, if you is lookin' for de chillens, de jubilee officers done got 'em."

"What do you mean, de jubilee officers got 'em?"

"Dat's what dey said dey wuz. A white man an' a colored woman. Dey said sumpin' about you not bein' a fitten woman to have de chillens, and dey wuz goin' to put dem in de 'tention home, whatever dat is. Some kin' of orphants home I 'spect."

"Now what kind of business is dat?" raged Malvoy. "And I wonder who could've did it. You reckon it was 'at no 'count Christy Lavergne? I wouldn't put nothin' past that hussy. Dat's all right. I'll see my boss in de mornin'. He'll tell me what to do. Ain't nobody goin' to have 'em. I'll show that heifer a thing or two."

The next morning, Malvoy went to see her boss and explained what had happened. He called his lawyer, and in a few minutes, the lawyer called back. He said the case was set for two o'clock the next afternoon and explained that Malvoy would have to show why she should be permitted to have charge of her half sisters and brother. Malvoy's boss told her just what she would have to do to prove her case and gave her that afternoon and all the next day off. He offered to furnish her with a lawyer, but Malvoy replied that she didn't need no lawyer; all she wanted was a chance to talk to that judge.

The next day, it looked as if all Mills Alley had moved to the juvenile court. Practically all the women, a great many of the children, and some of the men who were able to leave their work were there. Susie, Mary Lynn, and Tommy were in court and when Malvoy came in, they ran to her with yells of joy and threw themselves upon her. Since the judge was not present and the court was not in session, no harm was done by the disturbance. They were seated on the first row of benches by the court officers. Sam came in with Maria who would be a witness for Malvoy.

In a few minutes, the judge entered. Court was formally opened, and the clerk called the case against Malvoy Tanksley.

The judge picked up a sheaf of papers and while thumbing through them said: "Malvoy, complaint has been made to the court that you are not a fit person to have the care and custody of your two half sisters and brother. An officer from this court has investigated those complaints and she has found that practically all of these charges are true. Some are even worse than charged. I find from reading these reports and talking with the officer that you have a very bad record. For years, you have been a heavy drinker and your morals as far as men are concerned are very bad. In fact, they were so bad that you left home because your father objected to you taking a man to bed with you in your home and in the same room in which two of these children here were sleeping. That you remained away from home until after your father and his wife became ill and were taken to the hospital where they died. The police blotter shows you have a long record of arrests, mostly for fighting and engaging in drunken brawls. It is true that you have never had to serve time for any of these offenses because none of them were ever serious enough to justify a jail sentence.

134

You either paid fines or forfeited cash bond in all of these cases. There is no instance of you ever having been declared guilty of any charge.

"The only thing we can find in your favor is your steady employment. Your employer gives you a good name and says you are one of his best workers. That is fine and I must commend you for it. The other good thing I find in your favor is your return home and your desire to care for your orphaned brother and sisters. That is a most laudable act, but, Malvoy, in case you didn't know it, the state has a most definite interest in these children. Some day they are going to grow into adults and what kind of adults they become is a matter of deep concern to the state. It does not want them to become criminals, nor persons of bad morals and ill reputation. It wants to make citizens of them, and to do that, it must see that they are properly reared. That is the purpose of this hearing today; to determine if you are a fit person to continue to have the control of these children. It may become necessary for me to take these children from you and place them in a state school. In fact, it looks as if that is what I am going to do, but I will do it only for the best interests of the children. Believe me, I have no personal feelings in this case one way or the other.

"I see you are not represented by counsel. You will have nothing to lose by that lack. The court will look after your interests for you. Now, we have a number of witnesses here today. I have not talked with any of them, but I have read the statements of some, I have talked to our investigator, and I know what they will say. If you want to, we will call them to the stand and ask them to give statements. You will have the right to question them about any statement they might make in connection with this case."

"Now, Judge, yore Honor," began Malvoy.

"Wait just a minute and then you can talk. I just want to tell you that this court holds its hearings without any particular set of rules. Our only desire is to reach the truth and try to decide cases so that the greatest good will result. Sometimes, what we do seems hard, but in the long run, it usually turns out to the best. Now, we are ready to proceed. Whom do you want called as the first witness?" This last statement was directed to the Negro woman attached to the court who had made the investigation.

"Jedge, yore Honor," spoke up Malvoy, "it ain't no usen'n callin' any witnesses to tell what kind of a girl I been. If you is satisfied they's done told you all dey knows about me, and dat's what you said a little while ago, I reckon dat's enuff. Iffen dey's been tellin' some lies on me, you will find it out.

"Jedge, I admits I been a bad girl. My daddy, he was a good man and my step-mammy was a good woman. Dey wanted me to do right but I jes' nacherally wouldn't do it. I likes to fight, Jedge. They just ain't nothin' 'at'll do yo' so much good as a good fight." The judge smiled a bit at this. "Then I likes liquor and I likes to run around with men and have a good time. I knowd those things warn't right, Jedge, but somehow I jes' had to do 'em. Now them chillen, I loves 'em. I nussed ever one of dem. But dey pappy and mammy done gone and dey ain't nobody to hab dem but me. Jedge, dey's my 'sponsibility. I'se willin' to work hard for dem to keep dem in clothes and food and send dem to school.

"Jedge, yore Honor," and Malvoy walked a little closer to the bench, "I promise you dat if you won't take dem chillens away from me, I won't drink no more and I won't run around and I won't have nothin' to do wid enny men. I'll be a good mammy to dem chillens. Please, Jedge, yore Honor, let me hab dem chillens. Dey's all I got. Jes' gib me a chanct wid dem and I'll promise I'll do right. If I don', den you can take dem, and I won' say a word."

"Malvoy," said the judge, "what you have said greatly impresses me. I have never heard a more moving appeal. I have no doubt as to your sincerity, but I do as to your ability to do as you say. It is not reasonable that you can reform over night."

"Yes, I kin, Jedge, yore Honor," put in Malvoy. "Jes' try me onct."

The judge shuffled some papers on his desk, looked at one of them for a few moments, and raising his head, he asked, "Is Maria Martin in the courtroom?"

"Yassah, here I is," replied Maria, scrambling to her feet and raising her hand.

"Maria, it seems from the report of the investigator that you have been living near the Tanksley family for some time and know them pretty well. It further seems that you have a good reputation and are highly thought of by people who know you."

136

"Thank ye, Jedge," interposed Maria.

"What do you think of Malvoy?" asked the judge.

"Well, Jedge, I'll tell you. Hit's like this," explained Maria. "I'se knowd Malvoy since she was a little girl and I knowd her pappy and her step-mammy. Dey wuz good people but dey couldn't never do enny thing wid Malvoy 'cause dey jes' didn't know how to handle her. Now dat Malvoy has done a whole lot of bad things and a whole lot of 'em is what I thinks is badder than most folks thinks, 'cause I wuz raised a country nigger, Jedge, and country folks don' put up wid a lot of things city folks thinks is right. But dat's nedder here nor dere. Malvoy jes' ain't been handled right. She's de kind, Jedge, dat needs 'sponsibility. I 'spects you is a pretty good jedge but I 'spects befor' you got to be jedge you warn't as settled as you is now wid all dese sort o' things to look atter. Malvoy, she needs 'sponsibility and takin' keer of dem chillen is it. I know dey's a lot of folks as what wouldn't agree wid me on dat but dey don' know dat gal like I does."

The judge nodded his head. "I think I understand what you mean," he said.

"Malvoy," he continued, addressing the girl. "I believe Aunt Maria knows what she is talking about, and I really believe she is sincere in what she has said."

"'Deed I is, Jedge," interjected Maria.

"I'll tell you what I am going to do. I am going to allow you to have these children. I know it will be far better for these children to have a home of their own with someone to love and care for them than to put them in some institution, although there is nothing wrong with the state schools."

Malvoy started to say something, but the judge held up his hand and continued.

"If I return these children to you, I will expect you to live up to every promise you have made. I will have our investigator keep a close check on you, and if you are not properly caring for them, or if you bring evil influences about them by your associates or conduct, I will take them away from you immediately. Is that clear?"

"Yes, Sir, Jedge, yore Honor. I understands."

"Now, there is one condition. I am going to ask Aunt Maria to sort of keep an eye on you for me, and if she gives you any advice, I want you to take it. Is that understood?"

"Yassah, Jedge, I'll do what ever she tells me."

"Will you undertake this task, Maria?"

"Yassah, Jedge, an' if she don' do what I tells her, I'll come tell you."

"That's right. I am not going to dismiss this case for the time being. I am going to hold it open, subject to the entering of an order at any time. Take those children with you, and I hope I will not have to see you or them again."

It was a laughing, happy throng that trooped out of the courtroom and back to Mills Alley. That is, all but one. Christy Lavergne remained in the courtroom until all the others had left. Jenks' desire to move out of the Alley was fulfilled.

Chapter 21

The courthouse barbershop was on the west side of the square near where Felts Street took off to the west through the Negro section and Third Street took off to the north leading to the stockyards and the industrial section near the river. In the early days of the city, the square was the location of the retail stores, but the better ones had moved to the southwest and were now congregated on Spring Street two blocks away. The north and east sides of the square had been taken over by the wholesalers and what retail stores that were left on the south and west sides of the square catered mostly to the farmers and the laborers who were looking for bargains.

The courthouse barbershop was the only business on the square that was owned and operated by Negroes, but its customers were exclusively white people and it was financed by white capital. When the Civil War broke out, George Lavender, who had just been elected the circuit judge, joined the Confederate army and took his valet, Silas Burke, with him as his servant. Both Judge Lavender and Silas went through four years of the war without either being wounded, but both experienced many sieges of illness so that sometimes the master nursed the servant and sometimes, the servant nursed the master. When the war ended and that state re-admitted into the Union, Lavender resumed his position on the bench, but, as he could not afford the luxury of a valet out of his small salary as a judge, out of his meager savings, he rented the space, bought the equipment, and set Silas up as a barber and became his first customer.

Thirty years later, when Silas' hands had become so crippled with rheumatism that he could no longer hold a razor, Judge Lavender said that nobody but Silas had put a razor to his face, and he would be damned if anybody else ever would. So, at a time when most men were getting rid of their beards, Judge Lavender grew one for the first time in his life. Since he could not very well allow his hair to grow unshorn, he grudgingly allowed the son of Silas, who had grown up in the shop, to cut it, but every time he got a haircut, he fussed and fumed, claiming that young Burke did not know the first principles of cutting hair; that his life was in imminent danger; that he would never take such a fool-hardy risk again, and that his hair would probably be ruined.

The younger Burke was a deacon in the church attended by the Martins and Sam never heard him called anything but Deacon. So far

139

as he ever knew, Deacon Burke had no other given name. Deacon gave Sam the job of shine boy in the barbershop the summer Sam finished elementary school. Sam had to get to the shop at seven in the morning, make a fire in the water heater, clean up the two bathrooms; sweep out and clean up the barbershop which meant emptying and washing out the six cuspidors in the shop. He had to help customers off and on with their coats and hats, brush them off after the barbers had rendered their services, and shine the shoes for such customers who wanted this service. Sam received no wages, but he was allowed to keep all the receipts from the shoeshine stand, out of which he had to buy his own polish and cloths and he was allowed to keep what tips were given to him. He had to see that soap and clean towels were always in the bathrooms.

He did not like the job and would not have taken it except this looked like his only chance to go to high school. Deacon had always made a point of giving the job to a high school student, and while the student was at school, the barbers assisted the customers and no shoes were shined. He despised the subservient position the job placed him in. He was nothing more than a servant, waiting on men, many of whom he knew he was better than they were. It would not have been so bad had he not had to work on the shoes of the customers, many of whom were customers just having delivered cattle to the stockyards, and whose shoes were caked with mud and manure. And what made it worse, this particular group rarely gave tips, apparently feeling that the ten cents charged for the shine was greatly in excess of its worth. Sam's contacts with the white race so far had not given him a very high opinion of it, and his work in the barbershop did not improve it any.

His feelings must have been reflected in the shop, for one afternoon, Tom Brown, the youngest barber in the shop, and as such, had the rear chair and the one closest to the shoeshine stand, called Sam over to him. Brown had only been in the shop for fifteen years and was still looked upon by the other barbers as a newcomer.

Brown said, "I notice that you are not getting the tips you ought to be gettin'."

"Is that right? I thought I was doin' pretty good."

"You oughta be gettin' a whole lot more."

"What am I supposed to do to get more? I do everything I am supposed to do."

"It ain't what you do, it's how you do it. You don' make over people enough."

"What do you mean?" asked Sam.

"Everybody likes attention," answered the older man, "and especially in a barbershop. The more attention they get, the better they like it, and they will pay for it. You'll notice there are several kinds of people who come in here. There are lawyers and the county and city officials. They'll always give a tip irregardless, but it won't be much, except sometimes maybe one of the lawyers will have just won a big lawsuit and he's feelin' good and will give you a right good tip. Now the farmers, dey ain't goin' to give you no tip at all. Dey are payin' for what dey are gettin' and don't see no sense in payin' for somethin' dey ain't gettin' and since dey're usually wearin' their farm clothes, dey know it don't do no good brushing dem off. Now dere's the class who are folks that naturally like to loaf around the courthouse. They are either tryin' to get some kind of job or dey just like to be around the politicians for the feelin' of importance it gives 'em. It's with this bunch you are losin' out. They'll do everything they can to keep from givin' you a tip, but dey won't be belittled. When dey come in, rush up to 'em and take dey hat and help dem off with der coats. When dey gets ready to leave, brush off dey hat, help dem on with dey coat and give 'em a good brushing. Sometimes dey'll stand around talkin', makin' out like dey don't know you are around but just keep on brushin' even if it wears out dey coat. Sooner or later, dey'll have to notice you and give you a tip."

"That doesn't seem just right to me," observed Sam.

"Sure, it's all right. It's part of the business. You just do like I says and see if de tips don't get better."

Sam followed the advice and the number of tips did increase. He was so gratified over his increased income that he became adept at charming a tip out of the most reluctant of the customers, but at the same time, he felt some contempt of the white men who could be flattered into parting from even such small sums as they gave.

Chapter 22

During Sam's second year in high school, the freshman class gave a musical program at assembly. He came to the meeting prepared to be bored. He knew what to expect. There would be one or two popular numbers and then there would be a quartet singing spirituals. My God, why did Negroes always have to sing spirituals? Couldn't they sing anything except something that characterized them as Negroes? Wouldn't they ever learn?

The program had been built about the girl who played the piano, but he had never seen anyone who was so good with that instrument. She seemed absolutely sure of herself; and with her mastery of the piano, number succeeded number in a smooth flow. There was a lot of the music he did not understand, but so far as he could tell, all of it was good. And there was not even one spiritual. It was plain to see that the success of the program was due to this girl.

She seemed too much of a child to be in high school. Her figure was small and slender, but gave the impression of health and vitality. Her infectious smile gave assurance to the others on the program. He decided that he would like to know her better had she not been so much of a child.

The next day when he took a seat in the cafeteria, he found himself sitting next to the girl who had played the piano. She did not seem so childish today and somehow, this embarrassed him.

"Hello," he greeted her. "I enjoyed the program yesterday. You were the whole show."

"I am sure you are saying that to be nice, but I appreciate it just the same," returned the girl with a smile.

Sam felt uncomfortable. He had never met anyone so self-possessed.

"No, I really mean it," protested Sam. "I had made up my mind not to like the program. I didn't think freshman could get up anything that would be so entertaining but you changed my mind for me."

"My, my. You worldly sophomores are so blasé. We should feel flattered that we were able to interest you."

"I didn't mean it that way at all," stammered Sam. "I suppose it does sound awfully conceited. I am sorry."

The girl laughed merrily. "I believe you do feel badly about it," she said. "I won't say anything else. After all, you are being nice."

"You know, I like you," blurted out Sam.

"This is so sudden, Mister," returned the girl, drawing back in mock surprise. "Or maybe that is your usual approach?" she added thoughtfully.

"No, it is not. I don't think I have ever told anyone that before. In fact, I am sure of it."

"Then I am honored," said the girl with a light bow.

"You seem to have a ready answer for everything," observed Sam.

"Oh, then I am supposed to sit dumb while listening to your words of praise?"

"No. I don't mean that at all. Why is it that you give a different meaning to everything I say?"

"I didn't know I did that. I am only taking what you are saying at face value."

"Let's change the subject before I say too much. What is your name?"

"Rosemary Jones. It starts out very romantic, but it ends so ordinary."

"I like it."

"Thanks again. Are you usually this nice, or are you on your good behavior today?"

"I can't say, but I am glad you think I am nice. Would I be saying something else out of the way if I told you that I like the way you talk? You use good grammar and you pronounce your words so distinctly and without any put on."

"There seems to be no end to your niceness it seems. The explanation is simple. I am one of six children and my father is a school teacher. About all he can give us is the benefit of his education, which is a good one. He always insisted on our using good English, but to use it naturally. He says so many educated Negroes make the mistake of becoming a slave to the language instead of its master."

"Your father must be a remarkable man."

"At least I think so."

"I would like to meet him. Of course, I would like to be coming to see you when I do. Do you have dates?"

"A few," replied Rosemary in mock seriousness. "My father will allow you to come see me once, and if you are half as nice to him as you have been to me, he may allow you to come again. That is, if you want to come more than once."

"May I come next Sunday afternoon? I work after school and on Saturdays, and I can't go out much at night."

"That will be all right," and she gave Sam her address.

Rosemary lived at the edge of the city beyond the Semmes University campus. The house had only four rooms, and the first impression Sam had of it was that it was overflowing with people and books. Rosemary was the eldest of the children, all of whom were in school. Since the house seemed to be the gathering place of all the children in the neighborhood, it was weeks before Sam learned which were Rosemary's brothers and sisters. School books, public library books, and the books the elder Jones had been able to acquire were aligned on shelves, piled on tables, and even stacked in a corner of the "front" room that was a joint sitting room and bedroom.

Rosemary's father was a short, squatty man with a pair of the most bowed legs Sam had ever seen. He saw instantly that the daughter did not inherit her looks from her father. He was reading when Rosemary introduced Sam to him, and while he chatted with Sam for the sake of politeness, it was obvious that he wanted to return to his book. As long as he knew him, there were few times Sam ever saw him when he was not reading.

Sam fell in love with Rosemary's mother. Here was where the girl got her looks. Trying to figure out how to feed and clothe eight people and pay for a home from a teacher's salary evidently was not discouraging to her, for Sam never saw her when she wasn't ready to laugh and play with the children. There was plenty of fun going on at the Jones' house. Everybody took part in the playing except the head of the family and, with a book in his hands, he was lost to his surroundings. Sam liked the Jones family. He began to spend his Sunday afternoons there. Later, when the family came to know him better, he was nearly always invited to stay and have the snack Sunday supper with them.

The entire family went to church on Sunday evenings, and about the only time he was ever alone with Rosemary was when they walked slowly home from church. It wasn't often that he got to see her during the week because of his work at the barbershop and his school lessons.

Sam and Rosemary had been to a party on the South Side. They were standing on a corner in the glare of a street light when a speeding automobile came down the street. As the car neared them, it started stopping with a screech of the tires on the asphalt, but traveled several cars lengths past them before it stopped. Immediately, it went into reverse and backed up to them. Sam grabbed Rosemary's hand and started to withdraw from the edge of the sidewalk when he saw Sergeant Odom of the police department behind the steering wheel. The officer was a regular patron of the barbershop. Another policeman was in the front seat with him.

"Nigger, what are you doing in this part of town and at this time of the night?" Odom asked him. "You belong on the other side of town."

"We have been to a party," exclaimed Sam, "and, believe it or not, we are really waiting for a bus."

"Grab your gal and get in. We'll take you to town," ordered the officer, nodding towards the rear seat.

Sam and Rosemary lost no time in accepting the invitation.

The car had hardly started when the officer glanced over his shoulder and said to Sam, "Shine, what are you doing with such a skinny brown gal? I thought you liked 'em dark and with plenty of meat on their bones."

Sam had been flattered that the police officer had stopped to give them a ride, but with the officer's words, he experienced a feeling of revulsion. His first impulse was to ask the officer to stop the car and let them out, but as quickly, his better judgment told him not to do this. The policeman undoubtedly would take his actions as an affront and might lead to an unpleasantness that would be embarrassing to Rosemary. He decided to make the best of the situation. To do this, he must act like a Negro.

"Mr. Odom, you don't know what kind of a girl I like," he replied in a manner which he hoped sounded like a Negro who was pleased at being joked with by a white man.

"That won't do, Shine," admonished the officer. "You can't crawfish out of it now just because you've got this brown gal with you. I've heard you say at the barbershop that you wanted them as black as they can be so you would know their mammy was a virtuous woman."

"No, sir, Mr. Odom. You've never heard me say anything about what kind of girl I like." Sam had difficulty in keeping his voice from breaking.

"Maybe you are not so particular about color as speed. After all, you don't care much about a horse's color if it's speedy and that gal back there looks like she was built for speed," and the officer laughed at this own joke.

Sam did not reply to this sally.

It turned out that the officers were going within two blocks of Rosemary's house.

"Why does the white man think he has always got to take advantage of his superiority over the Negro," Sam exclaimed vehemently, as the car drove away. "Don't they think we have any feelings? Now there is a white

146

man who ordinarily is just as nice as he can be. He stopped and gave us a lift just because he recognized me as the shoeshine boy at the barbershop where he gets shaved every day and I don't doubt but there are many white people he knows for whom he wouldn't have done that much. Yet, he had to spoil it all in trying to be funny by making suggestive remarks about you. Would he have made such remarks if we had been white?"

"Maybe you attach too much importance to those things," replied Rosemary, giving his arm a sympathetic squeeze. "It doesn't do a Negro any good to pay much attention to those things. It only leads to trouble. Don't mind on my account. I didn't pay any attention to what he said and I certainly appreciated the ride. My feet were killing me."

"I know, but how can they expect the black race to ever to amount to anything unless they encourage the individuals to maintain their self-respect? Are we forever to remain the butt of the white man's crude jokes?"

"Maybe the best thing for us to do is to make up our minds that we are 'niggers' and get all the happiness out of life we can."

"I'll never do that. I will admit I am a Negro and everything that it implies, but I am not a 'nigger' and never will be and I resent being treated as such. I want to be taken and accepted as a Negro by both blacks and whites alike. That surely isn't asking for much."

Chapter 23

Midway in the block between Sixth and Seventh Streets on Highland, there stands a two story brick store building, the only business structure on the block. This building, like everything else in the neighborhood, was old and weather-beaten, but unlike the houses that were built of wood and had sagged into all manner of postures never dreamed by their builders, it stood firm and erect like some drunken bum who had braced himself to pass an approaching policeman. If one looked close enough, there could be seen painted on one side of the building the dim outlines of an enormous glass of foaming beer. Under it was the price "5 cents" and above it in block letters two feet high was the name "Lafayette Wilkerson."

When the sign was newly painted, the lower floor of the building was occupied by Wilkerson's Family Saloon and the upper floor, reached by outside stairs, was a lodge hall occupied in turns nightly each week by the Woodmen, Knights of Pythias, the Masons, and the Eastern Star, thus making the place something of a social center of the neighborhood. At that time, the surrounding houses were occupied by solid and dependable skilled white people.

Gradually, the skilled workers, as economic conditions improved, moved away and their places were taken by the unskilled workers until an event took place that drove the white people out almost overnight. The city council passed an ordinance segregating the prostitutes and set Sixth Street as the western boundary of their area. Since there was no conflict of interest between the Negroes and the prostitutes, the Negroes promptly moved into the houses vacated by the white people.

In an effort to keep his cash register active, Wilkerson accepted the change and put a partition across the room. He continued serving his dwindling white trade in the front and served his growing Negro trade in the rear. Since it was beneath his dignity to wait on Negroes, he hired a Negro bartender.

He was doing all right under the changed conditions when another event took place that again altered the entire complexion of his business. Both national and state prohibition laws were enacted. He put his liquors out of sight, bought a stove, refrigerator, pots, pans, and dishes, and across the front window, he had painted "Lunches." No effort was ever made to prepare food that would induce a customer to return, but one could nearly always get a fairly good ham or cheese sandwich there. Wilkerson tried selling home brew, but it was a no go. In the first place, it was too much trouble to make and in the second, most of his customers soon learned that they could make it just as good and a whole lot cheaper. White corn whiskey proved to be his main and most profitable item of sale.

Prohibition was a boon to the poor ridge farmers in the country north of Rock City for many of them turned to making whiskey. Wilkerson financed many of them in getting them stared in the business. In return for taking their entire output, thus relieving them of the danger of peddling their product, Wilkerson insisted on the distillers maintaining certain standards in equipment and a uniformity of the product. It did not take word long to spread throughout the city that Wilkerson's corn could generally be counted upon as being the best and safest to drink, and he soon counted some of the leading citizens of the city among his customers.

When Wilkerson started selling illegal liquor, he took off his apron and left from behind the bar for good. He took his place at the front door where he could personally pass upon every person undertaking to enter the place. He got a comfortable arm chair that he placed just inside the door in winter and on the sidewalk in the summer. He was always in a position where the bartender could keep an eye on him. The regular customers entered and left without ever a word from Wilkerson, for he did not encourage friendliness with his customers and many of them did not want it. If a person he did not know undertook to enter the place, Wilkerson would stop him with an inquiry as to his business. If the answers were not satisfactory and it seemed that the person was intent on entering the place anyway, Wilkerson would flash the bartender a signal and the bartender would dump the entire stock of corn whiskey on hand down the drain and rinse out the container with a strong disinfectant. The bottles were behind a hidden panel beneath the bar.

Even after he had become the political boss of the ward and a power in local politics and no longer had any fear of the local officers and very little fear of the federal officers, Wilkerson probably more out of force of habit, kept his station at the door. He had always been a large man, and in the course of time, with his sedentary life, he became ever larger to the point that he had to have a special chair built for himself. He invariably slouched in the chair with his legs, crossed at the ankles, extended in front of him and his hands clasped about his enormous stomach as if to hold it in place. He wore soft shirts that were never buttoned at the neck and a black bow tie that was never tied.

Wilkerson was a man of few words. His conversations were carried on mostly in monosyllables and of short duration. He rarely looked directly at the person to whom he was talking, yet no detail of any person was ever overlooked. Most of the Negroes spoke to him as a matter of training on their part, but about the only response most of them ever got was a slight move of the right thumb, and this was considered an honor by the recipient. The only time any of his white customers ever spoke to him was to introduce a new customer. He apparently did not have any close friends and did not want any.

In Wilkerson's business, it paid to stand in with the authorities, and the surest way of doing this was by the delivery of votes. Wilkerson carried the votes of his ward in his vest pocket. So firmly did he control his ward in every election, the opposition conceded it to the administration, and never made any effort to capture it. They could expect only from two to six votes, depending upon how strong a campaign Wilkerson thought they were making and these were given just for protection. In an election contest, affidavits might be produced from several people that they had voted against Wilkerson's candidate.

He always controlled the machinery in his ward but that was not his chief source of control. He took care of his people. The Negroes knew that he would not allow them to be persecuted nor to become the victims of the fee grabbing officers. The women in the segregated district knew that so long as they kept orderly houses, they would not be subjected to periodic raids by the police. If any of them became ill, they received prompt admission to the city hospital and those in dire need would be cared for by public charities. If any of them were arrested on serious charges, they would not have to stay in jail until tried for Wilkerson would make bond for them. A person was never known to have been prosecuted for having liquor on him that had been purchased from his place.

The city as a whole benefitted by Wilkerson's rigid control of his ward. He had a vigorous hatred for thieves and robbers. As a rule, those criminals, after making successful forays, would naturally gravitate to the segregated section to spend their ill gotten gains. When any of the girls received any indication that one of their customers were of this element, she passed her suspicions on to her landlady. The landlady, in turn, communicated the information to Wilkerson, who passed it on to the police, and they were usually able to make successful use of it. If any girl undertook to shield one of these criminals, she was run out of town, and if a landlady was found who did not cooperate, she was forced out of business through constant raids by the police. Therefore, the police could partially justify, at least to themselves, any accusations of lenience towards Wilkerson. As for the crimes of violence that took place in the ward, the remainder of the city was unconcerned.

Most of his sales were delivered to his customers. For this purpose, he kept a Cadillac automobile and a Negro to drive it. When not being used, the car was parked in front of the place and was the admiration of all the Negro boys. Hardly less admired and greatly envied by them was the Negro who drove the car. This was a dapper yellow Negro in his early twenties who was generally known as "Hot Shot." He lived upstairs in one of the old ante rooms of the now deserted lodge hall, for one of his duties was to receive the liquor from the moonshiners, who, for obvious reasons, made their deliveries at night.

The other employee of the place was known only by his nickname of 'Thunder.' He probably acquired this name on account of his deep, rolling bass voice, and he hardly spoke any oftener than it thundered. He seemed to try to outdo his employer in taciturnity. He was a man of middle years, was almost as large as Wilkerson, and was as black as midnight. He presided over the bar, made all the sales inside the house, and kept order in the back room where the Negroes drank.

Chapter 24

One day, John Henry was passing the place when Wilkerson stopped him.

"Boy, do you work anywhere?" he was asked.

"Yassah, I works at the country club, caddying'."

"Make anything at it?"

"Yassah, sometimes I does right good. Other days I don't make so much."

"I need a boy to help clean up around here. I will give you five dollars a week. Do you want the job?"

Even if he did not want the job, John Henry was so in awe of Wilkerson, he was afraid to refuse the offer.

"Yassah."

"Come around here in the morning about eight. Thunder will tell you what to do," ordered Wilkerson with a jerk of his head. The white man lapsed into silence, and John Henry knew he was dismissed.

John Henry was elated at his good luck. He was glad to get a regular job, even though it paid only five dollars a week. He was proud to be working for a man as powerful as Mr. Wilkerson, for, like every Negro, he knew it was a distinct asset to have the friendship of some white man who would look out for him. He was flattered that he had even been spoken to by the great man. It had never occurred to him that Mr. Wilkerson would ever notice him, much less, offer him a job. His only fear was that he might not please Mr. Wilkerson, but if he didn't, it wouldn't be because he hadn't tried.

He did not say anything at home about his good fortune until after supper, holding the piece of news, just as if one would hold a sweet in the mouth, rolling it around with the tongue, trying to make it last as long as possible and getting the most good out of it.

"I've got a regular job. Go to work at eight in the morning," he announced, trying to be casual.

"Well, I'se glad you got a regular job," replied Maria. "I never did like you workin' at de golf club. Most of dem caddies ain't no good no how and all of 'em is goin' to wind up in trouble. But I don't know how you's ever goin' to get to any job any time in de mornin' much less eight, as hard as you is to git up. You better go to bed earlier'n you been goin'."

"Oh, I'll get up all right. The job don't pay much; just five dollars a week but I'm working for a mighty big man," rejoined John Henry, withholding the name of his employer until he had aroused more curiosity and he could announce it with the desired telling effect.

"Who you gwine to be workin' for?" asked his father.

"I'll be workin' for Mr. Lafe Wilkerson," proudly announced John Henry.

"Humph. Mind about how you workin' around a place like dat; you'll find yourself on de inside of de jail first thing you know."

"Aw naw, nothin' like dat. Mr. Wilkerson, he's too smart to get caught or let one of his niggers get caught. 'Sides, ain't no police goin' to catch him and none of his niggers. He tells the police what to do and who to arrest. They know better'n to bother Mr. Wilkerson."

"I'd druther you be caddyin' at de golf club dan workin' for dat man in dat kind of business," remarked his mother.

"Boy, you'se gettin' in a mighty dangerous kind of business. It's dangerous in more ways dan one. You jes' watch yourself, dat's all I asks 'cause if you don't watch out, you can get into more kinds of trouble in a minute than it would take a year to git out of," cautioned his father.

When John Henry reported to work, he was given a broom, mop, bucket, soap, and cloths and was put to work cleaning. The place was so dirty that John Henry wondered if the place had been given a real good cleaning in years. The rear windows were so covered with dust that when he had cleaned them, the contrast was startling. He had been hard at work for several hours when Thunder walked over to him, watched him a few minutes, and remarked, "Boy, don't work so hard. This job may last for years," and he returned to his place behind the bar.

During the afternoon, two policemen in uniform came up, and after speaking to Wilkerson who was sitting in his chair on the sidewalk, came into the place and went to the bar. John Henry made up his mind that if any trouble started, he was going to make a break out the back door. His fears were relieved when Thunder set two glasses, a bottle of Coca-Cola and a half-pint bottle of white corn whiskey on the bar. Each officer took a drink and then with a casual nod to Thunder, walked out. They paused in front to exchange a few pleasantries with Wilkerson who had not moved out of his seat.

Thunder saw John Henry staring goggle-eyed at the officers and the first time he could catch his eye, he called the boy to him with a slight jerk of his head.

"You know this business is against the law? You don't have to worry about the police. All we got to look our for is the federal men. If they ever come in here or pick you up, you don't know nothing, see? So long as you don't talk, you will be taken care of, but if you do talk, you will have to get out of it the best way you can. Understand?" John Henry nodded. This was the first of the three long speeches John Henry ever heard him make.

After cleaning up the place in the mornings, John Henry's duties were practically non-existent except for a few deliveries of whiskey which he might make on foot in the neighborhood. At the end of the week, Thunder paid him six dollars instead of the five dollars that he had expected. The job was thoroughly satisfactory in every way except one. That was Hot Shot.

Hot Shot lorded over John Henry every opportunity he had, and these were many. In spite of this, he was proud of his job for he knew he was the envy of every young Negro in that end of town. Wilkerson paid him well for what he did, so he was able to wear good clothes and spend freely.

While Hot Shot dutifully obeyed the orders of Wilkerson and Thunder, he keenly felt the lack of someone he could properly impress with his position. His hours of work were so long, he did not have much opportunity to "strut" among the Negroes. The coming of John Henry gave him this outlet.

The second day John Henry was at work, he had just washed a cuspidor and placed it near one of the tables in the back room when Hot Shot came in and almost immediately called for John Henry.

"Here, Boy, this spittoon belongs over next to the other table. Move it over there."

"Yassah," said John Henry, moving the cuspidor as he was directed and wondering what difference it made where it should be set.

"Be careful about these things in the future. We want things done just one way around here, and that's the right way." admonished Hot Shot importantly.

"Yassah," returned John Henry meekly.

When they came out of the room, John Henry noticed Thunder's eyes following Hot Shot as he crossed the room, but thought nothing of it at the time.

Hot Shot developed a genius at finding things for John Henry to do, particularly if there were any customers in the place. He delighted, while talking to some customers, in turning to John Henry as if some thought had suddenly struck him, give an order, and return to the customer with an air of "Please excuse me, but you know these things must be looked after."

John Henry executed all the orders Hot Shot gave him with good grace for it never occurred to him to do otherwise. No one had told him who was and who wasn't to give him orders and he naturally assumed that all three of them would. He soon noticed, however, that Thunder rarely ever told him to do anything and that even Wilkerson scarcely spoke a half-dozen words a week to him. He guessed he was working directly under Hot Shot.

One day, Hot Shot parked the automobile in its customary place after making a delivery, and coming into the saloon, he said to John Henry, "Boy, get yourself some clean soft cloths and go out there and wipe off the car."

John Henry started cleaning the car when Wilkerson called him. "Who told you to wipe off that car?"

"Mr. Hot Shot, Sir."

Without turning his head, Wilkerson roared, "Hot Shot."

Hot Shot came running.

"Yassah, Mr. Wilkerson, what can I do for you?" he asked.

"What the hell do you mean having that boy wipe off that car?"

"Boss, it needed it, and I knowd you wanted it done."

"Yes, and by God, you knew I wanted you to do it. That is your job. If you're getting too damn good to do it, let me know, and I will get somebody else to do it."

"Yassah, Mr. Wilkerson, that's all right; I'll do it. Here, Boy," he said turning to John Henry, "go back there and straighten up them soft drink cases. They look like they's about to fall down."

"And leave them rags there for this Coontown sport to use," added Wilkerson.

This incident, coupled with several glances exchanged between Wilkerson and Thunder, soon led John Henry to believe that Hot Shot was not in as good grace around the establishment as he assumed, and he began to take Hot Shot's conduct as a pattern of what not to do.

This rebuff was not recognized by Hot Shot as a warning of impending disaster. Previously, he was the porter, lackey, errand boy, and chauffeur. He was the one to whom all orders were given, but now there was somebody who was his inferior. He had an audience before whom he could display his importance and his ego had to be fed.

Where previously he had obeyed without question, he began to enter discussions with Thunder about what he was told to do. At times, he even offered suggestions to Wilkerson about the business. Neither paid any attention to anything he said, but he flattered himself that they did.

He began to adopt a proprietary air towards the customers, and when a white man would come into the place, he was effusive in his reception, kept up a running line of chatter while the purchase was being made, and show the customer to the door with cordial invitations to return. One day, two plain clothes officers came into the place. Even though they had spoken to Wilkerson as they came in the door, Hot Shot met them with an invitation to step right up to the bar and told them that the barkeeper would take care of them.

As customary, Thunder set a bottle of whiskey, glasses, and bottles of soft drinks on the bar; and the officers poured themselves drinks. When they turned to leave, Hot Shot approached them.

"Gentlemen, I hope everything was all right," he said.

"Boy, what has gotten into you?" one of them said. "You think you are running a nightclub?"

"Nawssah, nawssah. I jes' wanted to see that you gennemun are taken care of. You know Mr. Lafe wants his friends to have the best."

"We won't worry about that."

"You won't have to worry about that as long as Hot Shot is here," he said walking up behind them as they started to the door and placing a hand on the shoulder of each of them.

"Glad you came in, Gennemun. Hurry back," he called after them.

The officers stopped on the sidewalk and spoke a few words to Wilkerson before leaving.

In a few minutes, Wilkerson came into the store.

"Boy," he approached Hot Shot. "Go over to the filling station and have the two new tires I bought yesterday put on the back wheels."

"Boss, them tires on the back wheels is still good. We don't need no new ones on them."

"Damn you, don't you argue with me; do as I say and be damned quick about it."

"Yassah, yassah, Boss, goin' right now," with a light laugh as if humoring the eccentricities of a curmudgeon.

After Hot Shot had left, Wilkerson stared at the floor a minute, then raised his eyes to Thunder, who was watching him intently.

"I am going to have to get rid of that son-of-a-bitch."

Thunder slowly nodded his head in assent.

Wilkerson went to the telephone booth, and dropping a coin in the slot, called a number and barked a few short sentences into the mouthpiece.

In a few minutes, two uniformed policemen drove up in a car. Wilkerson had returned to his chair on the sidewalk, and there he held a brief conversation with them. The two officers nodded their heads in understanding and left.

Shortly afterwards, Hot Shot returned. When he started across the sidewalk to enter the building, Wilkerson stopped him.

"Boy, get two pints of whiskey and take them to 927 North Seventh Street. Deliver them to the last room on the right at the end of the hall on the first floor. Don't collect anything, it's already paid for."

Hot Shot went to the bar and slipped the bottles into his hip pockets, came back out, and started to get into the car.

"Don't take the car," yelled Wilkerson. "Damn it, walk. It's not but four blocks. It'll do you good to walk that far. You are getting so lazy that you ain't worth a damn. I am going to cure you of that and some other things."

Without replying, Hot Shot turned and started up the street. He didn't like the look of things, but he was not able to figure out just what was wrong.

John Henry had seen and heard all that had taken place and he, too, sensed that something was wrong, yet he had not noticed anything out of the ordinary. Mr. Wilkerson had spoken rather sharply to Hot Shot, but any Negro working for a white man could expect more or less of that.

In about twenty minutes, the telephone rang, and Wilkerson answered it.

John Henry heard him yell into the telephone, "Hell, yes, I know it. No, and I don't want his bond made. The bastard should have had sense enough not to get caught."

John Henry glanced at Thunder, but the latter had no more expression on his face than a wall.

Wilkerson came out of the booth and turned to John Henry.

"Boy, can you drive a car?" he asked.

"Yassah."

"Good. Hot Shot is not coming back. You can have his job. I'll start you on ten dollars a week. If you keep your mouth closed, tend to your business, and watch your step; you'll get more. If you don't, you will follow Hot Shot. Do you want the job?"

"If there ain't no danger of me gettin' into trouble."

"The only man you can get into trouble with is me. So long as you do what I want done, you will be protected, and when I get to the point I can't take care of you, I'll let you know."

"That's all right, Boss. I'll take the job. What about this portering work?"

"Hell, we don't need a porter," replied Wilkerson and went back to his chair on the sidewalk.

John Henry was completely mystified at what had taken place and at the same time, overjoyed at his good luck. It took a few minutes for it to dawn on him. He was to take Hot Shot's place. He was to drive that big Cadillac car. And he was to get ten dollars a week, maybe more. He just

159

had to talk to someone. He walked over to Thunder who was still leaning imperturbably on the bar.

"What happened to Hot Shot?" he asked in an awed voice.

"You have seen and heard as much as I have," replied Thunder.

"I don't know a thing except something funny happened," returned John Henry.

"I don't know, either; but if I had to guess, I would say that Hot Shot was arrested by them two policemen that drove up here a little while ago and that he is in jail. If he is, he is going to get about six months on the county road; but I don't know; I don't know nothin', Boy, and if yo' wants to stay on this job, the leastest yo' knows, is the bestest."

"I would like to know this. How come Mr. Wilkerson give me this job?"

"I don't know that either, but I'd say it was because he has been seein' you around for some time, that you are nice looking, got good manners, and some good sense if you would just use it. I'd guess you wasn't hired here as no porter; you was hired to take Hot Shot's place. I seen it coming for some time. That's all I know," and with that, Thunder lapsed into silence. This was the second long speech John Henry had ever heard him make.

Chapter 25

John Henry had a good job, and he intended keeping it. He knew the best way to keep it was to please his employer. His mother had always told him that when he was working for white people, to do what he was told and to keep his mouth shut. If he didn't like the job, he could quit it. He had no intention of quitting this job. The pay was good and promised to be better and how much better depended upon how useful he could be to Mr. Wilkerson. So far as he was concerned, Mr. Wilkerson would never have any cause to complain. He never gave a second thought to the fact that the business he was in was unlawful. He knew that a man who could put a person on the county road as easily as Hot Shot had been put there, could also keep a person off it. He carried out the orders Wilkerson gave him without question.

He knew he was lucky and he was going to make the best of it. He had the privilege of driving the Cadillac. He would have almost worked for nothing for this privilege, but he knew at the same time that if he started speeding around town in it, he would share the fate of Hot Shot. From time to time, Wilkerson raised his wages, and in a few months, he was making more money than most men earned.

He did not throw his money away, nor did he give any evidence of his affluence. He bought himself some good clothes of modest cut and color. He correctly guessed that Mr. Wilkerson would not like it if he started showing evidence of making good money. He never told anyone, not even his mother, how much he was making. He soon learned that he didn't have to try to make an impression on the Negroes who usually hung out on Felts Street. The fact that he was Lafe Wilkerson's boy gave him all the prestige he needed.

He didn't drink. Thunder had warned him against this, but the warning was needless. He had on several different occasions taken drinks and had decided that whiskey was not for him. He didn't gamble and his contacts with women were few and fleeting. He saw in the work he was doing an opportunity to get himself on Easy Street if he was careful and stayed close to the man who could put him there.

He really didn't have much opportunity to spend his money for his employer commanded most of his time. Wilkerson lived at a downtown hotel where John Henry picked him up every morning at ten o'clock in the Cadillac and left him there every night, usually around midnight.

He had to sleep on the place to receive the whiskey when it was delivered by the moonshiners. Wilkerson had furnished one of the ante rooms of the lodges as a bedroom, and in another, he had installed a bath. For the first time in his life, John Henry took a bath in a bathtub with hot running water.

The whiskey was stored in the basement of the building and John Henry's first duty each morning was to fill as many bottles as he thought would be sold that day and bring a supply of them upstairs and place them in the "crack" that had been made for them. Sometimes, if he was rushed with early morning deliveries, Thunder helped with the bottling, but this didn't occur often since most deliveries were made from about dark until close to midnight.

John Henry had been with him about four years when Wilkerson decided to expand his operations. He had started bootlegging to supply the Negroes in his neighborhood, but gradually over the years as the reputation of his whiskey spread, the biggest part of his business was in delivering. He counted some of the leading citizens of the city among his customers. He had all the protection he needed in an area larger than he could serve and he never objected to the Negroes bootlegging in the Twelfth and Felts area so long as they didn't get too big, but now he wanted that business for himself. He had long realized the risks he would have to run if he expanded his business. He could not afford to keep any kind of books because the federal agents might swoop down on him almost any time and seize them and use them as evidence against him. He didn't feel that he was in a position to handle any more details himself. Safety required that all transactions be in cash and all records be either in his head or in the head of someone he could trust.

In John Henry, he had found the person he needed to widen his operations. The boy had an uncanny memory for details and was scrupulously honest. As an experiment, Wilkerson bought a lunch room on Felts Street near Twelfth and turned it over to a Negro to operate. The operator was to sell Wilkerson's whiskey and turn over the entire receipts to him. For his compensation, the operator was to have all the profit he made out of the legitimate end of the business. This arrangement worked so well that Wilkerson had John Henry looking for other locations and people to operate them. In a few months, Wilkerson's whiskey was being sold through three lunch rooms, a drug store, and a filling station.

John Henry carried the inventory of each place in his head and no written record was ever made of how or what any of the places were doing. On one occasion, he found one of the operators was buying and selling whiskey on his own. After he reported this to Wilkerson, the place was raided by the police and the operator drew a stiff county road sentence. None of the other operators ever sold any but Wilkerson whiskey after that.

With his increased business, Wilkerson had to have a larger source of supply of whiskey. He had John Henry drive him into the hills and there contacted other moonshiners. After the contact was made and the price agreed upon, Wilkerson left other details to John Henry to carry out. In some instances, it was necessary for Wilkerson to finance the stills.

With the increased duties, Wilkerson was generous with his increases of salary for John Henry until he was making as much money in two months as his father made in a year. He was spending only a small part of his salary now and regularly banking the remainder. His extended authority and increased income did not change him in any way except to make him keep his mouth closed tighter. He was always polite and obedient to Wilkerson, differential to Thunder, properly humble in the presence of white men, especially if they were police or county officers, and to the Negroes who handled his master's whiskey. He was always an exacting but just steward.

Chapter 26

John Henry's rise to affluence had very little effect on the living standards of the remaining members of the Martin family. While Maria never understood just what John Henry was doing, it was sufficient for her to know that it had something to do with whiskey. Besides being deeply religious and fundamentally opposed to whiskey, she had also seen the trouble and woe it had brought to the people of her race. She knew no good could come from John Henry's work and so far as she was concerned, the money he made was worthless. The only compromise she made was that she allowed John Henry to pay her board but she would not take as much as John Henry wanted to pay her. What he did pay her was mostly profit since he made no pretense of eating any meal at home except the evening one, and most of the time, he did not show up for that. Of course, he did not sleep at home.

She objected violently when John Henry bought her a new stove and an electric refrigerator and only used them because she had no other alternative after he had had the old ones taken away. John Henry insisted that they move into a better house, but this she steadfastly refused to do. For a long time, she refused to buy herself some new clothes but did so finally when John Henry threatened to buy some for her himself. The sensation she created when she went to church in her new finery removed some of her scruples against using the money.

There was always in the back of Maria's mind that such good fortune was not meant for ordinary folks like them and that sooner or later, the "gravy train" as she expressed it, would be wrecked. She did not spend all the money John Henry gave her and for the first time in her life, she had money for which she did not have a pressing need. Several times when she thought of the money she had on hand, she wondered just what bill it was that she had forgotten to pay. It took her a long time to get used to the fact that she had money in the house. As her hoards grew, she began to be afraid that someone would break into the house and rob them and maybe kill them. After thinking the matter over for several weeks, she decided she would put the money in a bank. Not that she had any confidence in the banks, but even if the bank lost the money they would not be so likely to lose their lives in the losing.

She had never been in a bank in her life and she had no idea what she would have to do to put money in one. She knew there must be something about it that could not be done by an old Negro woman like her and she would be embarrassed before the bank men. Then the thought occurred to her that she did not have the right to put the money in a bank. After all, John Henry had given her the money to spend on her family, and if she hadn't used it, she should return it to him. When she offered to give it back to him, John Henry laughed at her.

"I gave it to you to spend. If you don't want to spend it, all right, but I don't want it back. Do what you want to with it," he said.

She finally mustered up enough courage to go to the bank. She put on her best clothes and slipped her money in the top of her stockings. That wouldn't do, she thought. She couldn't go into a bank where all those white folks were and pull up her dress to get out her money. She put the money in her pocketbook which she clutched tightly all the way to the bank lest a purse snatcher grab it from her.

Looking back over it, she found the ordeal at the bank to have been rather pleasant. She had walked past the bank several times before she entered it. Once on the inside, she didn't know what to do. There were so many people going in and out and the men sitting at desks and in cages were so busy that she was afraid to interrupt them. She was about to leave when the uniformed guard walked up to her.

"Something I can do to help you, Auntie?" he asked.

"No, Sir," she stammered. "I means, yes, Sir. I wants to start a bank account."

"Certainly, come with me, please," and he escorted her to a man who sat at one of the desks.

"Mr. Hopkins," the guard said. "We have a new customer who wants to open an account."

"That's fine. How do you do?" this to Maria. "Do you wish to start a checking or a savings account?"

"I don't know 'xactly," answered Maria. "I wants to put some money in the bank where it will be safe."

"I imagine you wants to start a savings account. Just sign this card, please."

Maria laboriously scrawled her name at the place indicated. The man took the money and came back in a few minutes with a book that he handed to her.

"Here you are. All fixed up. Now, anytime you want to put any more money in the bank or take any of it out, you just go to any of those windows over there and they will take care of you."

Maria took the book, and thanking him, started out. Before she got to the door, she opened the book and looked at it. There was her name at the top of the page and there was the amount of money she had given the man. It looked mighty little for the money she had given him. Just a little book with some scribbling in it. The money she had given him would buy a lot of food and clothes. She had an impulse to go back in and ask for her money. Then she looked around the bank. The massive columns and high vaulted ceilings gave her an impression of strength. Maybe her money was safe in there. After all, the man said she could draw it out any time she wanted it. She would leave it there for a time, anyway. Besides, the white folks who ran the bank were awfully nice to her.

If Maria was slow to accept the benefits of John Henry's unlawful activities, William had no such scruples. He was a fatalist so far as whiskey was concerned. He figured that if John Henry was going to drink, he would drink, whether he was selling it or had to buy it for his own use. He was not worried about John Henry getting into trouble. He had heard enough about Mr. Wilkerson's influence to know that John Henry was not going to get into any trouble so long as he did what Mr. Wilkerson told him to do and he constantly cautioned him along this line.

He had worked hard all his life and now he was getting along in years. His work had aged him before his time. Many a morning he had to crawl out of bed and go to work when he was barely able to be on his feet. The boon of staying in bed would have been the greatest gift that could have been given him, but he knew he had to make the effort for a day missed would mean that all of them would have to feel the pangs of some hunger. Now, if he didn't feel so good, he could turn over and go back to sleep, or indulge in the luxury of lying stretched out in complete relaxation with no guilt of conscience since there would still be food on the table.

William knew that Maria had put some money in the bank, but just how much, he did not know nor did he care. The fact that she had some no matter how little was a source of great satisfaction to him. She was the first Negro he ever knew who had money in the bank. He couldn't imagine that she had much in the bank for he had never been conditioned to think of money in terms of more than a few dollars.

As far as Samuel was concerned, his brother had become a "big shot," and that was a source of some pride to him. The food on the table had become better and more plentiful. He had better clothes to wear to school and church. Some had even been purchased new.

Chapter 27

Sam's contacts with Max Moskovitz had aroused his ambition to make something of himself and his friendship with Rosemary had spurred that ambition. Before he had finished high school, he had made up his mind that he was going to be a doctor-not a specialist like Max planned to become, for he felt that the field was not broad enough for a Negro to be a specialist, but just a general practitioner and surgeon. He knew that doctors were more generally respected by Negroes than any other class or group and most of them he knew seemed to be making money. At least, all of them maintained offices, drove nice automobiles, lived in fairly good homes, and from what little he had been able to observe along that line, they were usually well thought of by the white people. Just being a doctor seemed to set them apart from other people.

Sam's aim in becoming a doctor was purely for that of financial gain and prestige. It took Rosemary to give him some ideals for his ambition. Rosemary had been brought up with the idea that she would go to college. When their first child was born, Hannah and Cicero Jones had agreed that this child and all others they might have would receive a college education and the advent of each, until there were six in all, had not weakened this purpose. Out of each pay check, a small amount was put aside for the children's college education, and even though the fund had never grown to be a very large one, certainly not nearly enough to carry out their plan; yet, they knew that somehow some way, each child would get the education he desired. Each of the children accepted as a matter of fact that schooling would not stop until a college degree had been earned.

When she was eight years old, Rosemary had been helped through a serious illness by the care of a nurse employed by a life insurance company. From that time on, her course in life was clear; she was going to be a nurse when she grew up. As she became older and learned more about the profession, her aim became more concrete. She was going to be a public health nurse. To her, they were the most glamorous beings in existence. Rosemary pointed out to Sam that being a doctor was not just the means to make money and live good, but was an opportunity to be of service. More particularly, it was a chance to be of service to a particular group of people who badly needed her--their own race. The parallel of their ambitions strengthened the friendship between Sam and Rosemary.

They planned their careers down to the last details. Sam would take both his academic and medical degrees at Semmes University and she would take her training at the hospital that was operated by the medical school of the university. Since she would finish her course long before Sam would receive his medical degree, she would go to work, and if necessary, help him finish school. This provision Sam usually objected to, claiming that he would be able to make his own way; but she would lightly brush aside his objections. Then when Sam finished his internship and opened his office, she would go to work for him. With her training, she should be in a position where she could be a lot of help to him. He would not have to pay her any salary, and the money he would save there could be used towards buying a home and furnishing it. Then, in say two or three years, after Sam had built up a profitable practice, she would train a girl to take her place so they could be married and start a family.

While it was a beautiful picture and one that could be brought to reality by a few years of hard work, it failed to satisfy something deep down in Sam's heart, and in the months before he was to enter the university, he gave considerable thought to the matter of his career. There was nothing in Rosemary's dream that negated the fact that he was a Negro. Rather, it made him more of a Negro than ever. The customs of the country being what they were, he could only have Negro patients, and thus would be living in a practically exclusive Negro world. To be known as the successful Dr. Samuel Martin, a Negro, was not enough. He wanted to be something that would raise him above his race, that would break down the distinction between himself and the white man; maybe even do away with the barriers between his race and the white race. Just what this could be, he did not know, but the thought persisted that such a goal could be obtained.

He considered other professions as the way to achieve this aim. While teaching had a certain appeal, there he could reach a great number of plastic young minds and bring them up to his way of thinking, yet what he could accomplish would be slow and uncertain. His financial returns would be small, especially if he taught in any of the state supported schools systems in the South for there he could only teach in the Negro schools and the pay of southern Negro school teachers was notoriously small. He probably would have to have some political connections to get in a public school system in the North.

He might study law and move to some northern city which had a large Negro population and enter politics. From a personal standpoint, he might rise to great heights. He might become a judge or go to Congress or hold some other high political office. In the end, this did not satisfy him, for he knew what he got along this line would not be so much by his own ability but by trading his influence with his own race. There was no appeal in the private practice of law. He could hardly expect to represent anyone other than Negroes and since their per capita wealth was small, he could not expect to earn many large fees or have any prominent clients. Even those Negroes who would have the wealth to employ a highly skilled lawyer would be inclined to employ a white one.

The commercial world was given some thought, but there he could not see much promise. The best he could expect would be to own a grocery or a drug store serving Negroes and the poorer class of white people. He could not expect to enter the employment of some large corporation and rise to the top as any young white man could. He might get a job as a porter and spend the rest of his life at just about the same wages. Even if he did show exceptional talent, his color would prevent his being given an executive position. In this field, his chances of success were limited except in a concern that depended upon Negro customers.

The ministry received only a passing consideration. This profession was decidedly out. He was not at all religiously inclined, and he was intelligent enough to know what a great part superstition played in the religion of the average Negro. He could not see himself fostering those superstitions in order to eke out a meager existence for the ordinarily poor Negro congregation.

In the final analysis, his career would have to be either dentistry or medicine. For a while, he considered the former since he had heard of a Negro dentist who had white patients exclusively, but the thought of spending the remainder of his life staring into mouths caused him to decide in favor of medicine.

He knew it would take a lot of money and he would probably have to keep working during the afternoons, weekends, and vacations; but somehow, he knew he would get through. Others had done it and so could he.

One Sunday morning during the late summer while the family was at breakfast, John Henry asked Sam what he was going to study. When Sam replied, he asked, "Is that a four year course?"

"No, it takes eight years in school and at least one year as an intern in a hospital," answered Sam.

"Good God," burst John Henry. "Do you mean to say you have got to be paying out tuition and the other expenses of going to school all that time?"

"All but the year I am an intern. Then, I will get my room, board, and laundry. Most hospitals will pay a small salary, at least enough to stay supplied with cigarettes."

"How are you figuring on going to school that long?"

"I've got a little money saved up and I expect to keep my job at the barber shop."

"Won't you have to do a lot more studying than you did in high school?"

"I expect that I will have to do considerably more."

"I'll tell you what let's do. I've just started me a roadhouse. It's all mine and I've got Mr. Wilkerson's protection. It looks like it's going to be a real money maker. You quit your job at the barbershop and I'll lend you the money to go to school. You can pay me back when you start making money yourself. By that time, I may need your help. I'm clever now, but you can't ever tell what will happen in my business. Maybe someday I'll be glad to have the job as your chauffeur."

Chapter 28

Sam approached the administration building of Semmes University with a feeling that tended towards trepidation. He felt himself as a alien entering a hostile land. He had a feeling that he had no business here; that he could never become a part of this great institution. Those massive buildings lining the quadrangle of the campus had no place for him. This institution was dedicated to higher education. It was inconceivable that those in charge would allow him to enter and receive what was offered there.

Somewhere, he had read that every person was a part of all the people he had known and the surroundings in which he lived. If that were true, then what was entering Semmes University was hard work, poverty, hunger, and nakedness; the odor of boiling cabbage, freshly dumped wash water, open privies, and sweaty bodies--sometimes, so intense that it was acrid. He was Malvoy Tanksley, Max Moskovitz, Deacons Burke and Chadwell, Brother Hutton, Mattie Carr, and an assortment of public school teachers; Twelfth and Felts Streets on Saturday nights with its corn whiskey, its gambling, loose women, and quick and fatal fights. He was the son of a simple ignorant woman and a hard working laborer. He was the brother of a bootlegger's assistant. He was Mills Alley and now Mills Alley had presumed to accompany him to Semmes University.

His uncertain footsteps carried him up the wide stone steps and into a large room that was a ferment of activity. Around three sides of the room were tables behind which sat members of the faculty engaged in registering the students for the coming term. Placards over the tables indicated the departments of study. Prospective students were milling about, arranging schedules, and stopping to greet fellow students of the previous year. He did not know a single person here. He was the only member of his high school class to come here. Those few who were going to college had already left for the State College for Negroes.

Gradually, he began to catch the spirit of the place. He made his way to a table over which hung a placard on which was written "Adviser." There were two other students in line ahead of him. He could not help but overhear what was said between the students and the adviser. When it came his term, he told the adviser that he wanted to register for a premedical course and handed her his high school certificate and grades.

She looked them over, listed on a card the subjects he should take, and told him to have each subject approved by a member of that particular department.

In making the rounds to have his subjects approved, Sam was amazed at the number of white people connected with the University. Of course, he had known in a general way that the president and a number of teachers were white, but he had no idea what the actual relationship would be like. He saw white people talking and laughing with the Negro teachers and returning students on a friendly basis in which the difference in race apparently played no part. He covertly watched them while pretending to make out his class schedule. He looked for some evidence of condescension on the part of the whites, but in this he failed. Their every word and gesture was easy and natural. He wondered why the relations between the races could not always be as pleasant as this all the time and concluded that the answer was that of education. If that were true, he was all for education.

The table at which he presented himself to have his English course approved was presided over by a scholarly looking young white man who took the card, glanced at it, initialed it in the proper place, and handed it back to Sam with the remark, "There you are Mister Martin. From the number of freshmen who are signing up for the pre-medical course, there shouldn't be any lack of doctors in the coming years."

Sam could hardly believe his ears. He turned away in a state of confusion. He had been called "Mister" by a white man. He glanced back at the instructor to see if it hadn't been a gag, but the instructor was busy with another student. Apparently, he had intended on calling him "Mister." Semmes University was a confusing place and seemed to be long on formality.

Like all boys in growing up, he had wondered what it would be like to be addressed by that title. He figured as he grew older, he would first be addressed in that form by very young children, and it wouldn't be until he was in his twenties that other adults might use that title when speaking to him and then only by those who did not know him very well. He never expected to be called "Mister" by a white man. The white people who knew him well would always call him by his given name. When he started practicing his profession, a few of them would call him "Doctor," but most of them would settle for "Doc." He knew that white people deliberately refrained from addressing a Negro as "Mister" or "Mistress," and even under circumstances when common decency and respect for old age compelled a younger white person to address a Negro in some way other than by the given name, a compromise was effected by the use of "Aunt" or "Uncle." He had concluded that the extremes to which white people went to keep from formally addressing Negroes was based on nothing more than a deliberate attempt to humiliate them. He had made up his mind that after he had started his professional career, he would be amused rather than irritated by the efforts of the whites to avoid addressing him formally. He had never expected to be addressed as "Mister" by a white man, at least south of the Mason and Dixon Line; yet the very first time he was so addressed, it was by a white man. Truly, Semmes University was going to be a wonderful place.

Chapter 29

As a matter of policy, Dr. Luke Pearson, the head of the department, taught one freshman chemistry class, and it was an accident that Sam chose this one. When he entered the classroom for the first time, his first thought was that the janitor had been slow in finishing his work and had let the time for the meeting of class slip up on him. When the man he had mistaken for the janitor started addressing the students, he just as quickly decided that chemistry must not be very important if a man who could be mistaken for the janitor was teaching it. The man who was talking was low and heavy set with a massive head on which tightly curled snow-white hair fitted like a skullcap. The contrast between the hair and the blackness of the skin was arresting. He was wearing a bibbed blue denim apron that Sam was to learn later that he wore almost as much as he did his trousers. He donned the apron the first thing on arriving at his office and the only reason that he did not wear it home was that his secretary or some student would remind him to take it off.

Dr. Pearson habitually talked with his eyes downcast, as if peering through a microscope and he rarely raised them, even when lecturing. It was a standing joke on the campus that Dr. Pearson in his forty years of teaching, had never seen a student. But as the man talked about chemistry, he caught Sam's attention so that the hour passed as if it had only been a few minutes. Sam decided he was going to like chemistry, and particularly, he was going to like Dr. Pearson.

Sam soon learned that Dr. Pearson was the most famous man on the campus. His reputation was international and he was frequently consulted by leaders in the business and chemical world. As a result of some of the honors that had been heaped upon their teacher, the University had prepared a pamphlet that gave a short biography of the man that included a listing of his more important research attainments.

Dr. Pearson's mother had died giving him birth on a plantation in Alabama shortly after the start of the Civil War. His father had followed his master to war as his body servant, and both had been killed at Cold Harbor. The pickaninny had been cared for by the Negro women on the plantation. When the place was overrun and the buildings burned by the invading army, he was carried by the fleeing Negroes to the pine lands nearby where, apparently tiring of their burden, he was abandoned by them. His frightened cries attracted the attention of a poor white farmer who took him home and reared him. It was this man's name he bore.

He was given what meager education the poverty stricken neighborhood afforded but he learned with amazing ease. At the request of his benefactor, he was allowed to attend the white school that had longer terms and provided a few more years of instruction. He was given a desk at the rear of the room and was never allowed to recite his lessons with the white children. He was treated more as a curiosity than a student. He read everything he could get his hands on that had any printing on it, and he early developed that insatiable curiosity that was to bring him fame as a chemist. He was never satisfied to accept things as they were but was always asking the whys and wherefores.

When he was sixteen years of age, the white man who reared him realized how eager Luke was for an education. He gave him twenty dollars, all the cash he had, and told the boy to go North. There he would have better opportunities for an education. With all his personal goods in a haversack slung over his shoulder and the twenty dollars in his pocket, the boy started out with no idea where he was going except that it was in a northerly direction. Without ever being certain how he did it, he wound up at Semmes University. There, after some persuasion on his part, he was allowed to enroll. Four years later, he had earned his degree and a scholarship to Harvard University. With Harvard behind him, he returned to Semmes as its first chemistry teacher and there he had remained. He was the oldest member of the faculty both in age and in years of service.

He had seen the school grow from a makeshift building with a faculty of ten to a dozen modern buildings on a beautiful campus of many acres and a faculty of more that two hundred.

Dr. Pearson was one of the pioneers of agricultural chemistry. He had never forgotten the soul killing toil of the farm workers during his youth that barely kept the workers alive. He was one of the first to see that cotton, instead of being king, was a despot that was not only killing the men, women, and children who were its subjects but was also destroying the land that produced it. He realized that if the South were to develop economically, it would have to get away from the one crop system. He knew that the Emancipation Proclamation was mere idle words because his people were slaves to a master that was even more harsh than the cruelest of the white masters had ever been. In all of his experiments for the greater utilization of farm products, Dr. Pearson had never tried to find a different use for cotton. He left the wider use of that fiber to other scientist.

The results of his research had bordered on the miraculous. Many new industries had been built on the utilization of peanuts, sweet potatoes, and soybeans. Farm incomes had been greatly increased by his studies in the use of fertilizers, cover crops, and livestock. His experiments in nutrition had lowered the death rate and had developed healthier babies, particularly among those of his own race. He had had the satisfaction of seeing the number of independent Negro farm owners increase each year.

Sam learned that Dr. Pearson had been offered enormous salaries time and time again by various industries, but he had turned them all down to remain at Semmes University at a salary less than what his assistants would have made had he accepted any of the offers. As Sam came to know the man better, he learned that the teacher had no concept of money, but since his wants were simple, there had never been any complication in his life due to its lack.

The laboratory became an interesting place for Sam, and he spent as much time there as he could. He was greatly flattered when Dr. Pearson allowed him to help in some tests. On the other hand, Sam did not make much of an impression on the teacher. Dr. Pearson had seen too many students in the years he had been teaching who had become enthusiastic over chemistry when they first studied it, but after a while when so much of the work had become drudgery, they would lose interest and go on to something else. His policy had been to encourage the student a little but if more than a little encouragement was necessary, the student would never be anything but a routine chemist. But as Sam's interest in the study continued unabated, Dr. Pearson began to take more interest in him and occasionally discussed with him some of the work that led up to some of his discoveries. It was a great day for Sam when the teacher took him into the private laboratory the university had equipped for him. To Sam, this room seemed the veriest Holy of Holies. Here the famous scientist had worked out some of his most important experiments.

Dr. Pearson led him to the cabinet that contained samples of some of the many products he had developed out of ordinary plants, most of which were widely cultivated in the South, and pointed out how they had helped in changing farming economics of the region. At the present time, he was working on the soybean and he showed Sam the results of his work thus far.

"You see, unless chemistry can add to the wealth and happiness of mankind," explained Dr. Pearson, "it hasn't much justification for being. While the 'chemist' is the successor to the alchemist of old, the chemist of today is not looking for a way for his own personal enrichment but for all mankind. Our own section of the country has been cursed with poverty; this applies to the whites as well as the blacks. We have followed a one crop system so long that most of our farmers don't know how to grow anything but cotton. When cotton prices are high, everything is fine. Everybody makes money, and we have a year of prosperity. When prices are low, everybody suffers and the poor tenant farmer and sharecropper suffer worst of all. It isn't the fault of any particular group of people. It is just the viciousness of a one crop system. No class or group has the power to change it so we go on year after year, losing everything including our self-respect, in growing an unprofitable crop. Before we can undertake to help the poor people in the South, and I mean the poor of both races, we must provide them with greater incomes from their farms. This I have tried to do by developing those things that grow unusually well in the South. You will notice that I do not have any products made from cotton. I made some paper from the stalks once and I believe that it could be successfully manufactured commercially, but since it would just be another reason to grow cotton, I abandoned it. You can see many products that have been produced from peanuts or sweet potatoes. There is scarcely a farmer in the South but who knows how to grow these two crops. In fact, they are just as easy, if not easier, to grow than cotton. If I can succeed in making these regular money crops, more and more acres will be planted in them and less in cotton. This in turn should make cotton more profitable to grow.

"Recently, I have become interested in the soybean. The South offers almost ideal conditions for its cultivation and it looks as if the field for its use is almost unlimited. You are familiar with some of the more ordinary uses for the soybean such as its oil in paints and varnishes, its meal in bread as a conditioner and absorber, and its use in plastics. The possibilities of the soybean is almost unlimited. The only regret I have in undertaking its study is that I am an old man and will be dead before I can see a fractional part of its development.

"What has been done so far is merely the barest start. Take, for instance, grass. Grasses of some sort grow practically the year around in the South and vast areas that have been lost to economic gain when planted in cotton could be put in grasses. The cattle that feed on the grasses would produce enough meat and milk to feed the entire country.

"To give you an illustration of how wasteful cotton has been of both land and manpower, trees in the South grow rapidly. If the average acre that has been planted in cotton had been planted in trees instead, more actual fiber could have been produced by several times over. This fiber could have been more economically used by industry with a much higher economic return and in most instances, with a better product."

"That is incredible," exclaimed Sam.

"Nevertheless, it is true," continued the scientist. "Forestry should in years to come be one of the leading industries in the South, and great factories will be built to make its products into a myriad of commercial uses. And to those who grow the trees, there will come a more abundant and richer life than was ever dreamed of in the cotton fields. I despise cotton. It has held our race in bondage and it has held down the white race with whom we have had to live. The sharp economic struggle for existence brought about by the growing of cotton has engendered bitterness and hatred between the races where there should have been love and happiness. Industrial development through chemistry can do what no amount of prating of rights can ever do; bring peace and mutual respect between all men, regardless of color."

Chapter 30

By the time the Christmas holidays arrived, Sam had become so engrossed in his work and studies at Semmes University that he regretted the days wasted away from campus. He told himself that he wished he knew that he had nothing else to do the remainder of his life but to go to school. He debated with himself the idea of giving up his plan to become a doctor and become a teacher instead. He would certainly make the change if he knew he could attain a teaching position at Semmes University.

Sam dropped by the room of classmates Jim Page and Hank Ford to compare the results of an experiment in chemistry and found both boys deep in their books. Hank invited him to be seated and shoved a sheet of paper toward him. Sam compared the results with his own. The two boys continued their studies.

"Why in the heck are you guys studying so hard? Don't you know that is a habit that is likely to grow on you?" asked Eugene Rutherford as he entered the room.

"It's this damned French that's got me. Why in the good gosh they require so much foreign language is a mystery to me," replied Page.

"It's the mental training and cultural advantage, my boy. Some day you will appreciate its value," returned Sam in mock seriousness.

"Just what I was thinking," rejoined Rutherford. "But a hell of a lot of good it's going to do any of us. After we go through this grind and get our degrees, then will come the glorious opportunity to use all of this. While you are sitting in your office waiting for patients to come in and have their teeth fixed, which never get out of order because of a diet of cornbread and other rough stuff, and if they did need a dentist they wouldn't have enough money to pay you, you can just let yourself lean back in your chair, providing you can keep up the installment payments on it, and entertain yourself conjugating French verbs. And, Sam, while you are groping down dark alleys, wading through puddles of wash water to deliver babies at a price that won't average five dollars and wondering where your next month's office rent is coming from, you can keep your mind off your troubles by repeating a few Elizabethan sonnets. Now take me, I will get all the breaks. I will be sitting in a one room schoolhouse prettily nestled in the middle of a bare clay clearing by the side of a mud choked road in Alabama trying to teach a bunch of kinkie headed pickaninnies to read and write. Oh, I might sometimes think I would be better plying my time teaching them how to chop cotton but that will be incidental. I won't have to trot out any of this mental training and cultural advantage stuff to ease my mind of financial worries because when it comes to that, I can just sit there and gloat over that forty dollars I will get on the first of every month. And what's more, I will get it six times a year, maybe eight, you can't tell. It may be true that I won't get the cash, but I will get a county warrant. Then some big-hearted philanthropic white man, one who loves his country so much that from the feeling of highest patriotism, will cash my warrant for sometimes as little as a ten percent discount although he would really feel that he should have twenty. No, you boys will need all this. I won't. But I will go along with you on it because unless I get that damned degree, I won't be able to get to that school."

Sam laughed. "You don't paint a very cheerful prospect for the future."

"Seriously speaking," replied Rutherford, "I sometimes ask myself if it is really worth the trouble. Maybe this thing of higher education for the Negro is just a snare and a delusion. If I had not been bitten by the bug to obtain a better education, I would probably have become a satisfied and happy field hand, seducing the wenches until one day I would seduce one that I liked so much that I would marry her, providing of course, that I had enough money for the license. If I didn't I would probably just live with her. As it is, I will probably go through life a disillusioned, dissatisfied country schoolteacher, having a fine vision but completely warped through the lack of opportunity to take a step towards its realization. Sometimes, when I consider that I am a young, able-bodied man, not producing a thing, not even earning my keep and my poor old mammy and pappy way down in Alabama working their daylights out to help keep me here, I get discouraged. When I eat a meal, I wonder just how many shirts that old woman had to wash to pay for it. When I buy a book, I mentally figure up how many pounds of cotton that old nigger down there had to grow to pay for it. When I think of the sacrifices they are making and when I consider the limited opportunities I will have to justify those sacrifices, I feel like giving it up entirely."

"You are not very encouraging, to say the least," said Page.

"It is the truth and you know it. I could probably make more money and be better off by starting me a honky-tonk, or a numbers racket, or even a pig ear joint somewhere than I will ever get through anything I will get here."

"I will admit that the opportunities for a Negro are not so broad as that of a white man, but you will have to admit that they are greater than they were a generation ago, and there is no reason why they should not grow greater as time goes on," argued Sam.

"I knew it. I knew you would have to bring up the comparison between the black and the white," said Page. "That is the one thing that distorts our entire viewpoint. We look at everything we do or try to do through the eyes of the white man. We are dead wrong when we do that. We are Negroes and we can't change it. So realizing that, let's forget it."

"You can't forget it. It's all about you. Your entire life, from the cradle to the grave, is molded and influenced by the white man. He makes the laws, he establishes the customs, he designates the social strata, and he places the values upon things. It is his world and you have to take it as he ordains it and like it. If you protest about it, you will only get misery and unhappiness and maybe the loss of your life," added Sam.

"It's true that this country was founded on the proposition 'that all men are created equal,' and that this was a great step in the freedom of mankind," he continued, "but the very men who wrote the Constitution so recognized slavery that the Negro was considered only three-fifths of a man. The Negro never asked to be brought to this country. There was never any migration of them. But the white men raided the jungles of Africa and brought them over here against their wills, not to be free men, but slaves. They said to them in substance, 'This is our country. We have made it, but we don't want to do the hard work. Therefore, you are to do all the work. You are to do our bidding, live as we tell you to live, and where. You are a little above our mule, just a little lower than our race horse.' Then after the white men finished fighting over the Negro, they said to him. 'All right, you are free, but we dare you to do anything with your freedom. You are a citizen, but you can't vote. You can work, but you can't make much money. You have a certain place, and you must stay in that place. We are the Lords of Creation, and you must still look up to us'."

"Granting all that is true, but the picture is still not as bad as you have painted it. Even if the lot of the Negro is not ideal, whatever he has of value has been granted to him by the white man, his language, his manners and his customs, his mode of living, his ideals, and even his slowly enlarging opportunities for personal improvement," said Page.

"I am not going to agree with that last statement. The white man may be clothed with the generosity of acquiescing but it is the Negro who is forcing the opportunities for his betterment. No matter how much the white man might encourage, it wouldn't mean anything unless the Negro had the desire to do something with himself," replied Rutherford.

"You are probably right about that and I won't argue the point. But you will have to agree that most of the hatred for the Negro has come from the lowest class of white people. They are people born with advantages we will not likely attain for generations, if ever, but he does not make use of them. Rather, he goes into the open labor market and competes with the Negro and because the Negro will do better work for less money, he develops an intense hatred for him. It must be based on jealousy and envy for I have noticed that it is not confined to the Negro alone. He hates the Jew and Catholic as well and this is because most of the immigrants in the past several decades have been people of those religions. They also compete with him in the same market and usually even more successfully than the Negro. He won't admit this feeling is caused by these reasons so with the Negro, he blames it on the color of his skin. He can't use that same excuse on the Jew and Catholic because their skin happens to be the same color as his own but since the religions are different, he blames his hatred on religious differences."

As Sam uttered these words, his mind went back to an occasion a few years ago when two boys, one a Jew and the other a Negro, sat on the rear steps of a combined store and dwelling and discussed something along these same lines. That undoubtedly was the beginning of the faith in his ability to arise above the different racial coloring. He had not seen Max in months. Max was in his third year at college and didn't have much time for anything except school and work."

"All of that is true," Rutherford put in. "And you will have to agree that the opposition to the advancement of the Negro race is very real and definite. You must admit that the law doesn't apply to the Negro the same as it does to the white man. The opportunities in business are extremely limited. And no matter how valuable an employee a Negro might become, he must always have a white man as a boss. Whatever opportunity a Negro has to rise, it must be among his own race. To the white man, he is still a Negro."

"It all gets back to the same question of economics," stated Page. "You must remember that in the first place, the Negro has never shown much justification for a changed attitude of the white man. Yet, when the Negro has done an outstanding thing, the white man has been the first to honor. I have heard of Negro dentists who have a large number of white patients and there are any number of Negroes in business for themselves who work only for white people such as contractors and mechanics. There is no reason to believe that as time goes on that Negroes will not be more readily accepted by the white people."

"Yes, but not because he is a Negro, but in spite of being one," put in Ford.

"That is as it should be. Do you know of any white man who has been successful just because he was white?" returned Page. "None of us want social equality, whatever that means, in spite of what the white man might cry, in criticism of the Negro. We Negroes do not accept that belief. I feel that I am better than many Negroes. The white man feels that same way about white people. If there were such a thing as social equality, such as the white man has in his mind when he refers to Negroes, I don't know that I would have any different associates than I have now. Certainly, there are vast hordes of white people with whom I would hate to be forced to associate with, and I don't doubt that if such a condition should be brought about, the Negro would be the loser for the simple fact that there are more white people than Negroes. Just like the old saw about the white chickens laying more eggs than the black ones."

"You take a very broad-minded view point of the matter," observed Sam.

"Not broad-minded. Just sensible. There is no other course open to me if I want to live a happy, well ordered and successful life. The rules were made before I came into this world and all I ask is to be allowed to play according to them. If I can succeed in having some of the rules changed for my benefit, my race will be benefitted thereby, but they will have changed because I will have deserved it and not just because I have simply desired it."

"Listen, Smarty. How come you had to be born a nigger any way?" asked Rutherford mockingly.

"'Cause the stork dropped me down the chimney of the cabin instead of carrying me on up the hill to the white folks' house," returned Page in feigned sweetness.

"Seriously though. Did any of you fellows ever ask yourselves that question? Especially, after you have been subjected to some small injustice by a white man? Some little bit of unfairness that didn't amount to anything in itself, but wouldn't have happened to you if you had been white instead of black?" queried Rutherford.

"Who hasn't?" asked Page.

"I think that is silly," answered Sam. "What would be more sensible, if not more logical, if that is clear to you."

"I don't know what that means and I doubt if you do, but go on," interrupted Rutherford.

"Would it be," continued Sam, ignoring the interruption, "why were you born in the United States instead of Africa? All of the disadvantages of your birth are geographical, not ethnic. Had you been born in the heart of Africa, would there ever be any occasion for asking that question? Whatever limitation there is for you is the result of economics. Basically, you might say the whole fault lies in two things. One was that civilization did not advance above the upper falls of the Nile River and the other was that your ancestors were able to stand hard labor in hot climates where the Indian could not. Had civilization spread to Africa as it did throughout Europe, the Negroes would have been able to resist the slave traders, and they would not have been brought to America where there was a great demand for cheap labor. Why, for all you know, if history had been different, you might have been a chief in Africa today with fifteen or twenty wives with lips as big as soup plates."

"Not me," protested Rutherford. "My ancestors were Ashanti. We have always been noted for our beauty, both men and women. You are talking about those weak Gold Coast niggers. The reason the women have developed such large lips was to make them so ugly the slave traders would not have them."

"Yeah, but the fact remains that most of the slaves came from the west coast and they were taken mostly from the Congo River tribes. From the first, they were only considered as beasts of burden. Their only value lay in the man hours of work they could produce. They were given whatever good treatment they received, not for humanity's sake, but because it was good business to care for a valuable asset. He was housed, fed, and clothed to keep him in good health, for a sick slave was a liability and a dead one was a total loss. He was encouraged to make love, not through a desire to make him happier, but because it inevitably resulted in the birth of more valuable chattels," continued Sam

"The Negro was set free, not through the kindness of the white man but because of economic forces. The people in the North felt that the slave labor in the South was enriching that region and was nullifying the struggles of the masses in the North. The cry of the abolitionists was merely the overtone. The Negro was not freed from any humanitarian point. It was purely economic. And the ridiculous thing about the 'Southern Rebellion' was that the slave labor was fast becoming unprofitable in the South. If the southern people had consulted their pocketbooks instead of their hearts, there never would have been a Civil War. Soon, they would have freed the slaves themselves.

"A free Negro could be hired just when he was needed and paid only for the work done. The rest of the time, he had to shift for himself and considering the few days out of the year that the labor was needed in the cotton fields, it would have been cheaper to hire him than to own him.

"It was when the Negro began to compete in the free labor markets with the white man that his troubles began. He started off ignorant and without ever having to shoulder responsibilities. All he knew was hard work and naturally he worked harder and for less money than the white man. All the trouble the Negro has had in the South, and elsewhere for that matter, has been caused by what the Negro calls 'pore white trash'.

"When the South realizes that it can only be as prosperous as its lowest class and begins to fully cooperate with the Negro in raising his standard of living, then the standard of the low white people will rise and the whole section will prosper."

"All that sounds good but it is not helping me a bit on this French. How about you philosophers taking it somewhere else."

"Come on, Sam, I can see we are not wanted around here," commanded Rutherford. "Besides, they are apparently that rare type of a student who go to college and waste their time studying. If we stick around any longer, they might infect us."

"I believe you have something there. So long, Suckers," Sam called to the grinds.

Chapter 31

"What shall we do now?" asked Rutherford as they paused on the steps of the dormitory in indecision.

"Come on down to the drug store and I'll buy you a Coke," invited Sam. "There should be somebody down there we could chew the rag with for a while."

"Thanks, but I have just thought of something. What's the use in spending good money for something to drink. Let's go down to Susie Ray's house. She is giving a party for her Bible class," and Rutherford looked at his watch. "She should just about be ready to serve the refreshments by the time we get there."

"We don't have any business barging in there," objected Sam.

"Don't be a fuddy-duddy. You know Susie well enough to know she will be tickled to death to see us and she always has plenty of refreshments. We won't have to stay long."

If Sam had any doubts about their welcome, they were dispelled by the hearty welcome they received. Rutherford's prediction about the time for serving the refreshments was almost perfect as Susie's little granddaughter was passing out the paper napkins. Sam and Eugene were given generous portions of cookies and a fruit juice concoction that Susie called "frappe". The refreshments were being rapidly consumed with much good natured joking and laughing when rapid, heavy footsteps were heard on the porch, the door was flung open, and a white man rushed into the room crying, "What's going on here? You are all under arrest," and threw back his coat to flash a badge.

Another white man who had evidently entered the house by the rear door to forestall possible escape attempts, herded Susie and a woman who had been helping, from the kitchen.

"What have you found?" he asked the first man.

"Nothing yet, but I haven't had time to look around. From what I have seen of this gang, we are going to have a good night."

"What is the meaning of this?" cried Susie. "Coming in here and breaking up a party like this."

"We're deputies, and you are all under arrest."

"For what?" asked Sam.

"Disorderly conduct."

"When did that get to be a state law and give you men the right to arrest for its violation. That is a city ordinance, and you are not city police."

"Wise guy, eh?" and he turned to the other man. "Keep an eye on this s.o.b. and bust him the first chance you get. Look around and see what you can find."

The men looked into drawers of the furniture, in closets, in cupboards, and under beds until they had completely searched the house.

"Who is in charge here?" the first man asked.

"I am," replied Susie.

"Where is your liquor?"

"There is no liquor here."

"The hell you say. This many niggers having a party and no liquor. Don't make me laugh. Search 'em." This last to his partner and they quickly ran their hands over the pockets of the men.

"Nothing here. What are we going to charge 'em with?" asked the second man.

"I don't know yet, but we'll find something," answered the first man, and he started looking in the closet again.

"Here, I got something," he called out, picking up a deck of playing cards. "Whose are these?"

"They are mine," replied Susie.

"That's it then; we'll charge them with loitering around a gambling house. Call in the squire."

The second man left, and in a moment he returned with a potbellied, watery eyed individual who had been waiting outside in a car.

"Here they are. Charge them all with loitering around a gambling house," the first man instructed him.

The magistrate sat down at a table and, pulling a pad of legal looking blanks and a fountain pen from his pocket, started filling in the names of those present as the officers called them off to him.

With the blanks filled in, the magistrate, assuming what he thought was a judicial manner, addressed the group.

"Court is now open. All you niggers are charged with loitering around a gambling house. The fine's two dollars and the cost is three. Who's ready to pay up?"

"But this is not a gambling house," protested Susie. "And how could we be guilty of loitering around a gambling house?"

"Here you are, here is the evidence," and the first deputy threw the deck of cards on the table.

The magistrate picked them up, removed the cards from the box and spread a handful of them in a practiced manner, but looked at them as if he had never seen anything like them before.

"M-m-m, that's right," he said. "Regular poker and black jack cards," he said. "Who do these belong to?"

"Me," replied Susie.

"And you run this house?"

"Yes."

"Looks to me as if you were running a gambling house," interjected one of the officers.

"These are playing cards, ain't they?" asked the magistrate.

"Yes," replied Susie.

"You can gamble with them, can't you?"

"You could if you wanted to, I suppose."

"Well, that fixes it," triumphantly replied the magistrate. "That makes this a gambling house. That makes all of you guilty of loitering about a gambling house. I am ready to take your money for your fines."

"But I am not guilty of running a gambling house," again Susie protested.

A look of annoyance flashed across the magistrate's face. Then with what he hoped would be construed as judicial patience, he held out the cards to Susie.

"You admit these cards are yours, don't you?"

"Yes."

"Then that makes you guilty of owning cards, doesn't it?"

"Yes, if you want to put it that way."

"Then you plead guilty?"

"I don't plead guilty to gambling or to running a gambling house."

"What the hell difference does it make what you plead guilty to, just as long as you plead guilty and pay your fine and get turned loose. Hell, I'm not going to sit around here all night chewing the rag. Either all of you plead guilty and pay off, or I will bind you over to the grand jury and you can lay in jail until they try you in criminal court. That may take months and your costs alone in that court will be over forty dollars. You had better plead guilty now and pay off when you can get out for five."

"Squire, I ain't got that much money," one man said.

"How much have you got?"

"Lemme see. I got two dollars and a quarter."

"Let me have it. Where do you work?"

"Supreme Chemical Works."

"Come around to my office Saturday and pay the other three dollars. Here's my card, and if you don't come Saturday, I will send for you and put you in jail. Now who is next?"

Several paid the five dollars.

The party was obviously over, and as those who paid were released, they left the premises.

"Are you going to pay off?" whispered Eugene to Sam.

Sam shook his head.

"I got about fourteen dollars. I'll lend you the money to pay your fine if you haven't got it.

"No, I am not going to pay these fee grabbers one cent. I am going to let them take me to jail," returned Sam.

"You will have to stay in there for some time unless you make bond, and it will cost you a lot more in criminal court."

"That's what they tell you. Do you think that any decent court, presided over by a half honest man, would fine us for anything that we did here tonight?"

"No."

"I'll have my brother called as soon as I get to the jail and he will come down and sign my bond. Yours, too, if you want him to, and that will be the last of it. These fellers can't afford to take this sort of case to court. They are just out for what they can get. They will split that three dollars cost and probably keep the five, too."

By this time, the crowd had thinned out to only three or four.

The next man called before the magistrate entered a plea of not guilty.

"So, you want to go to jail, do you?" barked the magistrate.

"I don't know. That's what my boss man told me to do. He said when I got arrested to always plead not guilty and send for him. Then, he would tell me what to do."

"So, who is your boss man?"

"Mr. Dick Ambrose."

"The feed man?"

"Yes, Sir."

"All right. Stand to one side. Next," and he pointed to Sam.

"Not guilty."

"Not guilty, damn. This is getting to be a habit. Who do you work for?"

"I don't work anymore; I go to Semmes University."

"Oh, yeah, an educated bastard. All right, what about you?" and he pointed to Eugene.

"He pleads not guilty, too," said Sam.

"Oh, a pal of yours, eh? I suppose you told him what to do. Damn you, let him do his own pleading."

"You want me to bust him one, Squire?" asked the first officer, making a suggestive movement to his hip pocket.

"Hell, no. When in the devil are you guys going to learn that you can't spend a damn thing but money? You are going to hit one of these niggers some day and get into a hell of a lot of trouble. 'Get their money and let the bastards go' is my motto."

Finally, everybody had either paid off or made arrangements to pay, except Sam, Eugene, and the Negro whose "boss" had told him to plead not guilty. The officers carried them out, put them into an automobile, and started to jail. They had gone but two blocks when the magistrate ordered the driver to stop the car. Turning to the three Negroes, he ordered them to get out and keep going.

The three were left standing on the corner.

"What did I tell you?" asked Sam. "All those bastards are out for is whatever they can get. If there is any difference between what they have just done and highway robbery, I would like to know what it is? They expect the Negro to obey the law, yet permit the law to prey upon them like it did tonight. There is nothing fair about it."

Chapter 32

Towards the end of his second year in college, Sam was disturbed by a vague unrest. It worried him because he could not determine the cause of it. Up until now, he had thoroughly enjoyed his college life. So far as he could see, nothing was going wrong. Everything was all right at home; no one was sick; John Henry was still making good money and gave liberally to their mother so that his father did not have to work unless he felt like it; he and Rosemary got along fine together; and his grades in school were satisfactory. He had once toyed with the idea of giving up his ambition of becoming a doctor and prepare himself for teaching, but he had decided that so long as John Henry was willing to finance his education, he would stick to medical training.

Soon after the beginning of that year, he had been alone in the laboratory late one afternoon winding up some experiments, when Dr. Pearson came in and asked if he would like to help with some work. He was flattered at the offer and promptly accepted it. It would be something of a distinction to work in Dr. Pearson's private laboratory. They had worked late that evening. Thereafter, it became a regular routine for Sam to help Dr. Pearson two or three afternoons a week.

Dr. Pearson would set Sam to running tests, and most of the time, Sam would not know the objective. He did not like the idea of working late, but he had learned that time had no meaning for the teacher when his younger and more demanding appetite would remind him it was time for the evening meal. He would call that fact to Dr. Pearson. Immediately, the doctor would give a startled look that concurred that fact, and they would quit for the day. Sam would remind the doctor not to wear the apron home. Maria had learned not to expect Sam at the mealtime, and she would keep his supper warm for him when he was late.

One evening, they had spent several hours in the laboratory when Sam paused a few minutes for an experiment to develop. He glanced at Dr. Pearson who was studying some slides under the microscope. Dr. Pearson would study a slide for a few minutes, make some notes on a pad, and put another slide under the microscope. He was totally oblivious of his surroundings. Sam grinned at the older man's preoccupation. Then with a start, he realized he had been just as intent on what he had been doing. He glanced at the clock. The hours had passed like minutes. A sense of peace and satisfaction stole over him. This is true happiness, he thought, doing this thing that he wanted to do. What would be better than spending the remainder of his life doing this sort of thing, he asked himself. A laboratory would be an ideal place in which to pass an existence where the only laws were the immutable ones of Nature and one could, by harmonizing those laws, achieve what men call success, but what the individual would call happiness; in a laboratory where there was no place for racial problems, the injustices of mankind, and the hatred of one group for another.

Why not give up the study of medicine, stay here, and take a degree in chemistry? He could probably teach the subject, if not here, then in some other college. Then, as quickly as the thought came, he put it out of his mind. It would not be fair to Rosemary. She was counting so much on him being a doctor, and she was certainly doing her part to realize their ambitions by the zeal with which she was doing her work at the hospital. No, he could not let her down. He would go on and get his degree in medicine.

It was not so easy to put the thought out of his mind, and when it recurred to him time and again, he knew the idea of giving up chemistry and Dr. Pearson permanently was the cause of his unrest. Several times, it was on the tip of his tongue to say something to Rosemary about it, but he could not bring himself to open up the subject. He finally decided he would put off a final decision until late in the summer. Dr. Pearson was to spend the summer with the United States Department of Agriculture, and Sam figured that several weeks away from the man and the laboratory would lessen the charm, and he would be more willing to enter the medical school when the fall term commenced.

The summer vacation had the opposite effect. With the approach of school opening, Sam became more eager than ever to go back to the laboratory. In his own mind, there was no longer a question; the unrest had been quieted. He would not enter medical school. He would go back to Dr. Pearson and take his degree in chemistry. He knew now, though nothing had ever been spoken to that effect, that Dr. Pearson believed he had possibilities as a chemist.

The only hard thing about his decision was having to tell Rosemary, but sooner or later, she would have to know.

One Sunday evening, they were in the midst of a conversational lull while idly swinging to and fro in the porch swing.

"Rosemary, would you be very much disappointed if I should not become a doctor?" Sam asked her.

"What do you mean?" she quickly asked.

"Just that. I don't want to study medicine. I want to study chemistry."

Rosemary waited a long time before answering him.

"I am not surprised," she finally replied. "I have been expecting you to say something like that for some time now. In fact, I am relieved that it was no worse. I knew there was something on your mind."

"How could you tell?"

"I don't know. A woman's intuition, I guess. Have you given the matter much thought?"

"Plenty of it in the past few months. I like the subject. I like the man who teaches it, and I don't believe I can ever do anything else that I will enjoy so much. What do you think about it?"

"You do whatever you want to do. It is for you to decide; not me."

"I was afraid that you would take it that way. That's why it has been so hard for me to mention it."

"You misunderstand me, Sam. I don't mean it that way at all, and I don't want you to think it. I mean that you've got to live your own life the way you want it and not try to live it for me. If we are to be together in the future, there must be happiness in it for both of us and I know you can't be happy or successful doing one thing when your heart is in another. As the woman, it's my place to adapt myself to your life. While I had been planning on being a physician's wife, I can just as easily plan on being the wife of a chemist."

"Do you really mean what you are saying or are you just trying to keep me from feeling like a heel?"

Rosemary turned squarely around, and in the dim light, looked directly into Sam's face. "I mean every word of it, Sam," she said sincerely. "You are a strange boy but I love you for that very strangeness. There is something about you that won't let you get used to being a Negro. Unless you do that thing that will completely absorb your thoughts, I am afraid it will cause you and all those who love you, many heartaches. You have never been as interested in medicine as I would have liked. You have never considered it an end but merely the means to an end. You have become wrapped up in chemistry, and it has made you happy; all but this uncertainty. You take chemistry. Get your degree in it."

Sam studied her for a few minutes as if seeing her for the first time. He then slowly took her in his arms.

"You are a darling to look at it that way," he said. "But I am warning you, chemist don't earn much money."

"That doesn't worry me. People don't have to have money to be happy. I know. My mother and father have been happy and they've never had much money. And I know something else you don't," and Rosemary partially withdrew herself from his arms and took his chin in her hand and gave it a shake. "Negroes aren't supposed to make money and gain fame. They are supposed to find their happiness in other things."

When Sam announced his decision at home, the only comment was from John Henry who grinned and said, "That's fine. If you can't find anything else to do after you graduate, I'll see if I can't get you a connection with some good moonshiners. Some of them could certainly use a good chemist."

Doctor or chemist, it was all the same to William and Maria.

To the announcement of his decision, Dr Pearson replied, "My boy, you have picked a hard row of stumps to hoe but unless I am badly mistaken, you will enjoy every bit of it. I had hoped you would continue your studies with me, but I would never have advised you to do so. That is one of those things a man must decide for himself. I believe you will be very satisfied with your decision."

Chapter 33

John Henry got the idea for his nightclub about the same time Sam entered Semmes University. He had mulled over it for several days, and when he caught Wilkerson in a placid frame of mind, he broached the subject.

"Boss, I see in the papers that the white folks in New York have gone crazy about them nightclubs in Harlem."

"All right. So what?"

"How 'bout us startin' one here. It oughta use a lot of whiskey and make good money on the food."

"Don't niggers and white folks both go to them in New York?"

"That's what they say."

"You can't mix blacks and whites in the South like that without causing trouble."

"I don't mean to run jes' that way. Let it be a club run by colored folks with colored entertainers and all, but jes' let white folks go to it. It oughta be a big hit."

Wilkerson eyed him speculatively. At last, he asked, "How come you think you could get by with it in Rock City? Don't you know it would cause so much talk, the church people would close it down before it got started good?"

"Don't have it in town. Put it 'way out in the country somewhere in an outa the way place. I knows jes' the spot for it. Out on Scott's Lane in that pore rock section near the river."

Wilkerson remained silent for so long that John Henry was beginning to think he had dismissed the subject from his mind. When the white man finally spoke, he asked John Henry, "Have you got enough money to pull it off?"

"Yas-suh," replied John Henry, wondering what was back of the question.

"I don't want to take on any more projects but I would like to make money faster right through this gap. If you think it's a good thing, you start it, but there are two things I want clearly understood."

"What's them, Boss?"

"It is not to interfere with your work here and you have to buy all of your liquor from me."

John Henry bought a worn-out farm on Scott's Lane. He remodeled the four room house on the place and added a combination dining room and dance floor. He employed a good chef, and through a booking agency, he lined up some good Negro acts. He named the place Rosy Dawn.

Rosy Dawn was a success almost from the beginning. A visit to the place became a "must" for those out to enjoy the night life of the city. John Henry consistently maintained the high standard he had set for the food, the liquor, and the entertainment he provided.

The chief factor contributing to the success of the place was the order he maintained. The most staid and respectable people of the city, but not so staid and respectable that they were above drinking illicit liquor on occasions, learned that they were running no risks to their reputations by the possible outbreak of brawling or rowdyism at the Rosy Dawn. John Henry knew that if anything ever occurred in which a white patron was killed or seriously injured, it would be the end of the business.

In maintaining order, John Henry had to develop tact and diplomacy to the highest degree of perfection. Because he was a Negro, he could not lay his hands forcibly on any white man, and he could not, under any circumstances, ever touch a woman. To do so would invite immediate trouble in which he would always be in the wrong. When a customer showed an inclination to cause trouble, he could not ask him to leave for no Negro could ever order a white man out of any place. If soft talking persuasion would not calm the person, John Henry would usually entice him into one of the rooms, usually under the pretense of sampling some particularly outstanding liquor, and John Henry would ply him with booze until he passed out. In spite of all his precautions, some trouble did occur, but none of it ever developed into anything serious.

Contrary to what he had expected, John Henry learned that women caused more trouble than liquor. A drunken man could usually be handled in one or more of several different ways, but a jealous man or woman was incapable of being controlled, particularly if the jealousy had been inflamed by alcohol. He developed an uncanny ability to detect this sort of trouble while it was still a long way from exploding and was usually successful in forestalling any unpleasantness. In spite of the money he was making, it was always with a sigh of relief when he saw the last customer leave every morning.

John Henry began wearing a dinner jacket, and it seemed to do something for him. He began to watch his speech and even had Sam give him lessons in diction and grammar. His manners became so smooth and he developed so many ways of dispensing subtle flattery, it became something of a distinction to receive the personal attention of the owner of the Rosy Dawn.

One day Wilkerson called John Henry and Thunder into the back room, and seating himself at one of the tables, ordered them to be seated.

"I've been examined by a doctor," began Wilkerson, "and he tells me I've got a bad heart. There is no way of telling just how long I might live, but it is not going to be more than just a few months at best. I've been to the bank and got all my affairs straightened up so when I kick off, there won't be much trouble in passing on what I've got to my two children.

"You didn't know I had any children, did you?" he continued, noting the look of surprise on John Henry's face. "They live in New York. Their mother and I separated twenty years ago and she took them. So far as I know, they don't know the kind of business I've been in and I don't want them to know. Thunder, I put two thousand dollars in the bank today in your name to be turned over to you when I die. I put the three businesses on Felts Street in your name, John Henry. My advice to you is to sell them off. You might get a few hundred dollars out of them but if you want to run them, don't try to sell any whiskey. You won't be able to get the protection in the city I've got. You might continue to run your nightclub if you make the right connections to get your whiskey. I wouldn't try to handle it myself if I were you. That Henderson crowd from the South Side will probably take over my liquor business and if they do, don't try to oppose them. That's all."

"Boss, I am mighty sorry. Maybe the doctor is wrong," consoled John Henry.

"No, he is right. I've known something was wrong for some time. Don't say anything else about it. I don't want any sympathy or pity. Hell, we've all got to die sometime, and one time is as good as another. Let's just go on the way we have been."

Two months later, John Henry walked in the door and found Wilkerson slumped down in his chair. He raised the man's head but a quick glance at the face told him that his boss was dead. In spite of the shock of the sudden death, the thought occurred to John Henry that this was the first time he had ever touched the person of a white man.

"Well, what are we going to do now?" John Henry asked Thunder as they were walking back to the bar after the ambulance had left with Wilkerson's body.

"Do just what he said," replied Thunder, taking off his apron. "In just about five minutes, I am going to be gone from here, and I ain't never coming back; not even to this part of town. You can get the money out of the cash register and give it to whoever takes charge. I suppose the rest of this stuff is yours. I've had to work for that bastard for fifteen years because I was afraid not to, not knowing at what time I might get sent to the county road or to the pen. Hot Shot wasn't the first man he ever got rid of. I hope he left me that two thousand dollars like he said he would but if he didn't, I ain't going to worry. I've got a little farm out on Green Hill Road and it's paid for. I've got a little money in the bank. That's one thing I'll say for him, he did pay good. I'm going out to that farm, where, if you didn't know it, I got me a wife and four children, and I ain't never coming back here. Any time you are ever out that way, drop by and see me."

John Henry was surprised at the feeling expressed by Thunder's words, but when he realized Wilkerson had kept the Negro in subjection for all these years, he had to grin. As for himself, he sincerely regretted the white man's passing. Wilkerson had always been fair in all their dealings and had allowed him to go into a business in which he was making good money. Even by the white man's standard, he could be considered well fixed.

He followed Wilkerson's advice and sold the Felts Street businesses. He received considerably more for them than Wilkerson had estimated they would bring.

One night John Henry noticed a young woman in a particularly happy party. She seemed to be having as good a time as the people with her, but every time he glanced at her table, he caught her looking at him. He didn't like the looks of things but he couldn't tell why. All of the people in the party were strangers to him except one man and this man had been in the Rosy Dawn once before. Once, when he glanced at the table, this man caught his eye and motioned for him to come to the table.

"Yes, Sir, what can I do for you, Mr. Richardson?" asked John Henry.

"Not a damned thing, John Henry. I just wanted to tell you that you have one damn good club here and I wanted you to know these folks so that if any of them want to come back, you will know that they are all right."

"That's mighty nice of you," smiled John Henry. "I hope all of you will come back. Is everything satisfactory?"

"Fine, fine," boomed Mr. Richardson. "It couldn't be better. The food's good; so's the liquor and that's a damn good orchestra."

John Henry realized that the man had had a little too much to drink and was getting into that expansive and demanding mood that could lead to trouble. He hoped he would not have to take him to the private room before the night was over.

"Thank you, Mr. Richardson. I am glad you like the place." He felt it a good idea to be as impersonal as possible.

"You are damned right, I like it and I say you are a damn good nigger."

The woman spoke up. "Big Boy, did anybody ever tell you that you are a fine looking man?" she asked.

"Lady, it is mighty nice of you to say so." John Henry replied with a slight bow and in a tone of voice that he hoped expressed the proper amount of humility. "But I reckon folks don't pay much attention to a man's looks, 'specially if he's colored," he added.

"Don't kid yourself about that. Women notice a man, regardless of his color."

One of the waiters tapped him on the shoulder and told him that he was needed at another table. Excusing himself, John Henry left the group.

In a short while, to his relief, the party left.

The next night, he noticed the woman sitting at a table by herself.

He went to the doorman and asked him why he had let the woman in alone.

"Boss, she came out in a taxi by herself and when she started in, I told her about the rules that women without escorts can't come in. Then, she said that her boyfriend had to go somewhere else but for her to come on out and he would be out later. Boss, she acted like a woman what usually has her own way and I didn't think it best to cross her."

John Henry shook his head. He didn't like it. Unescorted women could cause trouble.

The woman sat quietly sipping her drinks until after the floor show, when, catching John Henry's eye, she beckoned him to her.

"Big Boy, why haven't you been over to see me tonight? Is this the way you do your customers? Just let them sit by themselves without a word of welcome?"

"I've been sort of busy tonight. Besides, I've been watching for the rest of your party to arrive."

"There won't be any rest. I'm here by myself."

"I'm sorry."

"Why?"

"We just don't like for a woman to come in alone. Some man might try to get fresh with her."

"Don't you worry about that. I can take care of myself. Sit down."

"I'm sorry, ma'm but I can't do that."

"You could if you wanted to. You own the place and I, as one of your guests, demand it."

John Henry smiled.

"I am sorry, Miss, but I can't. You must remember you are white, and I am black. All of my customers are white and they wouldn't like it if I sat down at table with a white woman."

"To hell with that. I want you to sit down."

"I am sorry, Miss, but I can't. Please don't ask me."

"If you can't sit down, then don't hang over my table." she yelled in sudden heat.

John Henry bowed and turned away.

Later that night, John Henry was in his office when the door opened, and the woman came into the room. John Henry rose to his feet.

"Listen, Big Boy," she exclaimed. "I like you and I don't mean maybe. The next time I make a play for you, don't run or there will be trouble," and before John Henry could reply, she left the room.

A few minutes later, he strolled into the dining room and did not see the woman. He went to the main entrance where the doorman told him that she had left in a taxi that she had previously called for.

"Boss, do you know who that woman is?" the doorman asked.

"No; do you?"

"Her name is Hattie Carver and she is Captain Browington's woman. He's crazy as hell about her." Browington was a police officer who had gained his position through political influence rather than ability. He was reported to have become wealthy by selling police protection to law violators.

John Henry grunted and went back into the club.

One night a week or so later, after seeing that everything was in order and locking the club for the night, John Henry came out to get his car and found Hattie Carver in it.

"Howdy, Big Boy," she greeted him.

"What are you doing in my car?" demanded John Henry.

"Everybody went off and left me, and I know you don't mind taking me to town."

"Where have you been all night? You haven't been in the club."

"I didn't feel like going inside. I waited outside, and my people went off without me."

John Henry didn't believe a word she said, but it was up to him to make the best of the situation.

They drove several miles without speaking.

"You are not very sociable outside your club, are you?"

"I get paid for giving white people a good time there. A nigger ain't got no business having a white woman in his car this time of night when he ain't her chauffeur."

"You must be afraid, Big Boy," she taunted.

"I ain't what you call afraid, but I ain't looking for trouble and I don't want to find it. I know I'll find it if you keep monkeying around me. How come you have to pick on me?"

"Because I like you and if you would let me, we could have some good times together."

"We couldn't have no good times together, woman, and you talk foolish. Your skin's white, and mine is black, and that ends it. You ain't got nothin' to lose that you ain't already lost, but I got everything to lose."

"What do you mean by that crack?" she flared.

"Figure it out for yourself. I ain't smart."

"Listen, I set out to make you because I like you, and I am going to do it. Black or white, it doesn't make any difference to me. You are a man, and that is all that counts. But if you go acting up with me, I will make trouble for you. Do you play or not?"

"I wish I had never laid eyes on you, that's what I wish."

The car was passing through a deserted street in the industrial section of the city. The woman leaned against him and gently slipped her arm around his shoulders. With the other hand, she turned off the ignition switch and pulled out the key.

John Henry grabbed for the key, but she slipped it in the top of her stocking with a laugh.

"Do you want to get it from there?" she taunted.

John Henry steered the car to drift over to the curb and stopped it. His intention was to get out of the car and away from it as fast as he could knowing that she would leave the car on the street somewhere, and he could get it later.

Her arm around his shoulder restrained him. "Don't be foolish," she pleaded.

By the dim glow of the dash light, he could see the warm soft white skin of her neck and shoulders, and her lips were provokingly near.

"You don't want to leave me here do you," she coaxed and laid her head upon his shoulder.

John Henry slipped his arm around her and gave her a slight squeeze. She nestled closer in the pit of his shoulder with her face upturned. He bent his head down, and their lips met. He seized her in both arms and held her body close to his. She passionately returned his kisses. He lost all sense of caution and restraint. He forgot the color differences. He didn't care what the consequences might be.

The woman pulled away from him.

"We can't stay here," she said. "Someone might come by and see us."

They went to his old room above Wilkerson's saloon, for which he still had a key, and spent the night.

The next day, John Henry rented rooms on the second floor of a building near Wilkerson's place, the lower floor of which was occupied by retail stores. The Negro woman who had charge of the rental of the rooms was under obligation to him, and he knew she would keep her mouth closed. The room was near the rear stairs, so it was possible by driving his car into the alley, for him and Hattie to slip into the room unseen.

John Henry knew what he was doing was wrong; that he was treading on dangerous ground and that there was nothing he could promise himself in the relationship except the pleasure of the present. Sooner or later, the white woman would tire of him and there would be nothing he could do about it. He would not have the privilege of trying to win her back as a white man could. On the other hand, if he should ever tire of her, he could not quit her. If the relationship became generally known, she would be forced to give him up. There might be even more serious consequences. When these thoughts entered his mind, he quickly brushed them aside. He was willing to risk anything the future might hold for the nights he spent with this woman's soft white body in his arms. He forgot the cost he might have to bear.

One night, they were together when there came a knock on the door.

"Who's there?" called John Henry.

"It's me, open up," cried a voice on the other side of the door.

"My God, it's Harry," cried Hattie.

John Henry had to swallow before answering.

"What do you want?" he asked.

"Damn you, open the door and find out."

"I ain't done nothing for you to arrest me."

"Listen, you black bastard, I am not going to stand here and argue with you. You either open that door or I'll bust it in and if I do, it won't be good for you."

John Henry nodded to the next room that had a door opening into the rear hallway. Hattie hastily donned her clothes and fled. John Henry opened the door. Captain Browington stalked into the room and looked about. He wore his uniform, something he rarely did.

"So she's gone, eh?"

"Who's gone, Mr. Browington?"

"Damn you, Boy, you know who I'm talking about." looking at the open door to the next room, "and there ain't no use in me looking either. Damn it, I don't want to find her now; I just might have to kill her."

John Henry did not reply.

"Now listen, Nigger. I'm gonna tell you something." The man's voice was cold. "I ain't going to kill you like I ought to and like I would if you were a white man. Damn you, Boy, I ain't going to honor you that much. I know who was here and I know about her being with you. I am going to make you pay for it and pay plenty. I'm not going to kill you now. I am going to get you, you black bastard. I am going to make you die a thousand times and die cursing me, but not now. I'm going to get you later."

And with that, he stalked from the room, slamming the door behind him.

Chapter 34

About two miles beyond John Henry's place by the road, but not quite half that distance across the fields, there was a worn-out rocky farm. At this time, it was rented by a man by the name of Spence Perry. His family consisted of only himself and his wife. At the cluster of stores and filling stations down on the highway where he soon established friendly relations, he said he had rented it only because of his wife's health. She had to get out in the sunshine and fresh air.

John Henry kept a caretaker at the roadhouse all the time, except on Saturday and Sunday so he always spent Saturday night there. As a rule, the customers stayed later on Saturday night, or rather, Sunday morning, than any other time and since his help did not report for work until late Sunday afternoon, John Henry liked to sleep all day Sunday.

One Sunday morning, he had just lain down to sleep when he heard someone calling from the road. Thinking it was one of his customers, who, not being satisfied with the night's celebration, had returned for more, as sometimes happened, he got up, slipped on his shoes and pants, and unlocked the front door.

"What is it?" he called.

"My car broke down," the voice in the darkness called. "Do you have a telephone? I want to call a garage."

The owner of the voice came within the light from the front door. John Henry saw he was a white man. He wore overalls and a faded blue shirt. His beard was of several days' growth and a shapeless felt hat surmounted a mass of unruly hair. Although the man's appearance was unprepossessing, he was a type with whom John Henry was not altogether unfamiliar since he bought a lot of liquor from men like him.

John Henry stepped back out of the door to allow the man to enter. As he did so, the man suddenly drew a pistol and covered him with it.

"Throw up your hands, you black bastard," he commanded.

John Henry inwardly cursed himself for a fool, but believed his only danger was the likelihood of losing his night's receipts. He complied with the demand.

"Now turn around and march out that door. At the first funny move you make, I'll plug you," the man ordered.

Wondering what this was all about, John Henry obeyed. When he reached the edge of the porch, he stopped.

"Keep moving, damn you," ordered his captor. "When I want you to stop, I'll tell you."

With his mystification increasing, John Henry obeyed.

Although there was no moon, the sky was clear, and there was enough starlight to enable a person to see large objects at quite a distance. John Henry decided that there was nothing to be gained by suddenly ducking and trying to run away. By leaving the house, John Henry concluded that robbery was not the motive and he was at a complete loss to account for the intruder's actions. The thought flashed through his mind that this man might be a representative of some of the white people who lived in the district and had decided to run him and his business out of their neighborhood, but he dismissed it since this man did not look as if he had any concern about the morals of others.

He was forced to cross his grounds, then over a fence onto the adjoining property. This was a pasture that was overgrown with weeds knee high, and John Henry was conscious of the cold dew striking his bare ankles.

"Boss, what are you goin' to do with me?" he was impelled to inquire.

"None of your damn business. Keep goin'."

The two made a wide semi-circle through the pasture and came within a dozen yards of the road. Here John Henry was halted and forced to turn his back to the road.

"Now, Nigger, you stand here and if you make a move until I tell you to, you'll wish you hadn't. Do you get me?"

"Yassuh, Boss."

In a minute or two, John Henry heard an automobile start, and out of the corner of his eyes, he could see the headlights passing on the road.

"Hey, Boss," he called. Getting no reply, he called several more times and finally turned around. Seeing no signs of his recent captor, he cautiously made his way over to the road. There was no one there.

Deciding the man had gone back to the house and was now rifling it, John Henry made another long swing through the pasture and came up to the rear of the house. Crouching close to the ground, he cautiously raised himself up and peered in a window. The light was still burning in the dance hall and it lit up most of the interior. He slipped from room to room, peering into the windows, but since he still did not see anyone, he finally approached the front; and taking all precautions against a surprise attack, he slipped in the door. He still could see no one or any sign that anyone had been inside the house since he and his captor had left it a short time before.

He bolted the door and went through the house, turning on all the lights and searching it thoroughly. He finally satisfied himself that he was the only human being there. A cautious glance into the hiding place of his money proved it had not been bothered. He was at a complete loss to explain what had happened.

Finally, deciding that he had been the victim of an insane man or a practical joker, he again went to bed.

He was not destined to spend the remainder of the night in undisturbed slumber. Dawn was just breaking when he was awakened by a heavy pounding on the door. Fearful, lest his visitor of earlier in the night had returned, he slipped on his trousers and shoes and quietly made his way to one side of the door in case the man should start shooting.

He could hear more than one voice, but he could not make out what was being said. The pounding was repeated.

"Who's there?" he called out.

"Open this door, Nigger. We are police officers."

213

"What do you want?"

"We want to talk to you."

"What do you want to talk to me about?"

"Damn you, open that door."

"Have you got a search warrant?"

"We don't need a search warrant for what we want. Open that door or we will bust it down."

Realizing from the tone of the officer that nothing was to be gained by delay, John Henry switched on the lights and opened the door.

When he unbolted the lock, the door was flung back against him. Before he could recover himself, three men rushed into the room and covered him with drawn pistols. One of them was Captain Browington.

"Go to the back door and tell the others to come in," Browington commanded one of the men. "We've got him."

One of the men pocketed his pistol and went to the back of the house. He returned in a few moments with two other men. One of them had on the uniform of a city policeman, but the other one was in plain clothes. Browington was also in his uniform.

"We've got your man, Sergeant," Browington said to the other man in uniform.

"Has he made a statement?"

"He doesn't have to make a statement. I know what I'm talking about."

"Boss, what is this all about?" John Henry asked.

"Damn you, Boy, you know what you've done. Sit down. We want to ask you some questions, Where have you been tonight?"

"I haven't been anywhere. I've been here all night. Why? What has happened?"

"Listen, Bastard, we'll ask the questions. When did you close up tonight?"

"About three o'clock. Why?"

One of the men in plain clothes drew a blackjack and hit John Henry over the head with it, laying open his scalp and blood spurted from the wound.

"Damn you, didn't he tell you not to ask questions?"

John Henry sank into a chair. "You didn't have any reason to hit me like that. I just asked you what happened," he exclaimed.

He was met with two more blows from the blackjack knocking him onto the floor.

Two of the officers seized him and shoved him back into the chair.

"Where did you go after you closed this joint?" demanded the officer with the blackjack while holding the instrument in a menacing manner.

"Hell, don't hit that nigger again," spoke up the sergeant. "What are you trying to do? Let him beat the rap on a forced confession?"

"Answer my question," demanded the officer, lowering his weapon.

"I didn't go anywhere. I went to bed," replied John Henry, wiping the blood out of his eyes.

"You are a damn liar. What are your shoes and pants legs doing wet?"

"A man came by here tonight and got me out of bed, and with a pistol, he made me walk down through the fields on the other side of the place. That's why I was slow about opening the door. I thought he had come back."

"Nigger, you ought to be a better liar than that. I thought you were smart."

"That's the honest truth, so help me God."

"What did he carry you down in the fields for?"

"I don't know. He just made me go down there and left me."

"Nigger, you will have to think up a better one than that to beat the hot seat."

"What do you mean, Boss?"

"You know damn well what I mean. How come you thought you could rape Mrs. Perry and get by with it?"

"Rape Mrs. Perry? Why, Mr. Browington, I don't know what you are talking about. Who is Mrs. Perry?"

"Don't pretend you don't know who she is. She is that woman you raped down the road tonight. If her husband hadn't come back when he did, I expect you would have killed her."

"So help me God, Mr. Browington, I don't know what you are talking about. I haven't been off the place tonight except like I told you. What time did this happen?"

"Come on, let's take him down and let Mrs. Perry identify him," suggested the sergeant.

"On your feet, you," commanded Browington, grabbing John Henry by the belt and jerking him to his feet.

"Let me wash my head and put some more clothes on."

"Hell, no. You are going just as you are."

"Now wait a minute. Don't be in such a hurry, Harry. Let him wash that blood off his head. Hasn't that woman had enough of a shock tonight without having to look at a bloody headed nigger? Besides, we want those pants and shoes for evidence," said Sergeant Bullard.

After he had washed off his head and stanched the flow of blood and changed clothes, John Henry was taken by the officers and led to an automobile. Two of them held him by his belt and waistband and the others walked with drawn revolvers.

They carried John Henry farther out the road and turned off into the yard of the house where Spence Perry and his wife lived. One of the officers got out of the car and went into the house to see if they were ready to have John Henry brought in for identification.

They returned in a few minutes, and John Henry was taken out of the car and started towards the house.

Said Sergeant Bullard, "Jenkins, you walk in just ahead of us and stay right behind Perry. If this is the nigger, we don't want any shooting." Jenkins hurried ahead to carry out the orders.

The front door opened directly into the bedroom.

John Henry was led into a cheaply furnished room, faintly illuminated by a kerosene lamp on a small table at the head of the bed. On the bed, there was a woman with closed eyes. Her head slowly rolled from side to side and with every breath, she gave a low moan. Her hands tightly clutched the covering. On the far side of the bed stood a roughly dressed man whom John Henry took to be Spence Perry. Jenkins stood at his side. He took a good look at the woman.

She was no longer young. She had hard lines on her face and her faded hair was disarrayed. She had narrow thin lips and a sharply pointed chin. John Henry thought to himself that he would have to be forced to have anything to do with her, much less attempt a rape.

"Mrs. Perry, can you open your eyes a minute and take a look at this man? We want you to identify him if you can," asked Browington solicitously, leaning over the bed.

"No, no, I can't," moaned the woman rolling her head faster.

217

"I know it will be hard but it must be done," urged Browington.

The woman stopped rolling her head and slowly opened her eyes. When they fell on John Henry, she screamed and cried out, "Oh, my God, yes. That's him."

John Henry involuntarily took a step forward.

"Please, Lady," he pleaded. "You don't know what you are saying. Tell them that you have never seen me before."

"It's him. It's him. I would know that voice anywhere," cried Mrs. Perry. Her husband started around the bed. Jenkins grabbed him.

"Here now, none of that," cautioned the officer. "The law's got him and the law will take its course."

"By God, let me at the black bastard. He will never look at another white woman again. Just let me kill the son-of-a-bitch."

"Take him out," ordered Bullard, motioning to John Henry. "Take him to jail and lock him up. This woman has gone through enough for one night."

John Henry was hustled out to the car. The drive to the jail was made in silence. Browington did not accompany the other officers to town.

Chapter 35

When word of John Henry's arrest got to the Martin home that morning, Sam immediately went to the jail to see him.

"What in the name of goodness has happened?" Sam asked as his brother came up to the barred window.

"I don't know. I can't figure it out. I'm charged with rape."

"Rape?" echoed Sam.

"Yeah. A white woman. A white woman who lives about two miles beyond the club. It's only about a mile across the fields."

"My God. How did that happen?"

"I don't know. Several screwy things happened last night," and John Henry told Sam about his visitor who marched him around in the fields, about his arrest, and the identification as the rapist. "Somehow, I think there is some connection between the two, but I can't make heads or tails of it?"

"Did you know this woman?"

"I never laid eyes on her in my life."

"She was probably not herself when she identified you. As soon as she calms down, she will change her statement," consoled Sam.

"I'm afraid she won't. In the first place, she is not likely to see me until the day of the trial, and it will be too late for her to back up. She will have to go through with it then to save her face."

"Do you suppose anybody could be so heartless?"

"I don't know, but it looks serious now."

"Can you make bond?"

"No. I've been told that bond will not be allowed."

"What are you going to do?"

"I want you to do it for me. I want you to employ a good lawyer. Get the best you can. Mr. John Clayton, if he will take the case. Try to get him for a thousand dollars, but don't go over twenty-five hundred."

"That much money? Great God! Can you afford to pay that?"

"Yes. That part will be all right. I will probably have other expenses."

"It is a good thing school has just started. I will quit and save you that much."

"No. Whatever you do, you stay on in school. This is your last year, isn't it, since you have decided to become a chemist instead of a doctor? I've got enough for that. After you get out of school, you might have to look out for the old folks. There ain't no telling how long I will be in this jam, if I ever get out."

"It is not all that serious, is it?" asked Sam.

"Hell. Look at it this way. I am a nigger charged with raping a white woman. You ought to know I've got two strikes and no balls on me now. Of course, the whole thing may blow over. It may be a frame-up to get some money out of me. They might think I've been making a lot of money out there. If that is what it is, I will probably get out. It may cost me a couple of thousand, but what the hell? It would be worth it. If that ain't what's behind it, I don't know. You get a lawyer and get him to work. Let me tell you something else. I want you to know it in case anything ever develops. I've been sleeping with a white woman."

"The hell you have. How did you ever come to do a dumb thing like that?"

"There's no reason why I shouldn't tell you now. Her name is Carver. She used to be Captain Browington's woman, and he was one of the policemen who arrested me this morning."

"That doesn't look so good."

"No, but he never said anything out of the way this morning. I've been thinking it over, and I don't see any connection."

Sam employed Clayton to defend John Henry. The lawyer went to the jail with Sam and talked to his client. John Henry gave him the full account of the night's happenings and told of his relationship with the Carver woman. The lawyer whistled at this. "That looks bad," he commented. "If that ever gets out, you won't have a Chinaman's chance. It's going to be a tough case as it is."

The lawyer talked to the attorney general and talked to all of the state's witnesses except the Perry woman. He sent for Sam to come to his office.

"I've gone over this case thoroughly," the lawyer said, "and frankly, it looks bad. You know how these cases are when a Negro is charged with raping a white woman. He is convicted to start off with. John Henry was in the neighborhood, or at least just a mile away when the crime happened. His shoes and pants legs were muddy and wet with dew, as if he had been crossing the fields between the two places and the woman identifies him. He has no witnesses to establish an alibi since the club had been closed for some time when the crime took place. He was by himself. We simply can't let him tell the tale about the man marching him around with a pistol. While he may be telling the truth, and I've got no reason in the world to doubt his word, we can't let him tell that to a jury. Nobody could be expected to believe that."

"Yes, but he said it happened, and I believe he is telling the truth."

"Grant that he is telling the truth. Could you make twelve white men believe it? Or could you get one man out of twelve to believe it enough to hang a jury? It just doesn't make sense."

"How about a frame-up and that being a part of it?"

"We can't do that. The only reason we can give for a frame-up is his affair with the Carver woman and if we bring that out, the jury will convict him on general principles. You know how southern men are about Negroes where white women are concerned. I don't care how common the white woman is, that never excuses the Negro.

"Since talking further to your brother, I am convinced that the whole thing is a frame-up, but I don't see how we can prove it. I have talked to Dr. C. R. Burton, who is a reputable physician. He says he was called in to see the Perry woman that night and that she was in a highly nervous state, evidently suffering from some violent shock, that she had several bruises on her body, but he could not tell from what evidence he found whether or not there had been penetration. It is testimony that while in itself is not damaging, yet will not be helpful to the defense.

"I have investigated the Perry's and from what I have been able to learn, they have not been in this county for more than a couple of years," continued the lawyer. "They came here from one of the upper river counties. I have written up there for a full investigation into their past but I don't expect much from it. Probably, just what you would find in the average sharecropper's biography."

"What can be done for him?" asked Sam, his stomach weak with dread.

"It doesn't look as if there is much we can do. He has a good reputation, except for the bootlegging, and that won't be held against him in a case like this. Maybe we can get him off without the death sentence and in a few years, get a pardon for him. Or we might get a reversible error in the record and by the time the case goes to the Supreme Court and back, something might happen that it would not be tried again. This woman might leave town or simply refuse to go through with another trial."

"How long can this trial be put off?"

"It can't be put off. The attorney general dropped by my office this morning. He made as if it was a social visit but I knew he had something on his mind. He mentioned it casually, but I knew that was the true purpose of his visit. He said that if we didn't bring it up, he would not introduce anything about the Carver woman. Then he told me that the case had to be tried next week. It had been especially set, and the judge would not grant a continuance. He is afraid if the case is put off, a mob would be formed to storm the jail."

"God forbid," breathed Sam. "But why did he have to say anything about not bringing up the Carver woman into the case? If it would have the effect you say it would, it seems as if he would want it? What do you make of that?"

"I've been trying to figure out that one myself, but I can't. Knowing the attorney general like I do, he won't overlook any bets to get a conviction. Maybe the Carver woman has connections who have gotten to him or maybe Browington was afraid that his name would be brought out and he talked the attorney general out of it. You know no white man would like to have it a matter of record that a Negro man took his woman away from him."

"Yes, maybe that's it," agreed Sam. "You do all you can for him," he continued. "He's been a good brother to me. All we can do is hope and pray. At least I hope, and my mother and father will pray," and tears came into his eyes.

On the afternoon of the day John Henry was arrested, William and Maria went with Sam to visit him in the jail. John Henry undertook to assure his parents that nothing would come of the charge, that he had done nothing, and that he had nothing to fear.

"I know, Son, but still when a colored man is charged with having something to do with a white woman like that, it's a mighty serious thing," observed William.

When they returned home, Maria went to bed, but she refused to allow Sam to call a doctor. William would wander the house and then go out into the yard and back in again. Frequently, he would sit down, but he remained sitting only a few minutes before he would get up and start wandering again.

A feeling of nameless dread hung over the house.

Sam took John Henry's advice and remained in school. He realized that nothing was to be gained by quitting, but it was difficult for him to keep his mind on his studies. There seemed to be an air of futility about everything he was doing. He felt as if he was going through motions over which he had no control; that he was a helpless automation in an action in which all facets were rushing headlong to doom.

His fellow students were sympathetic and made offers of assistance. This had an effect on Sam that was contrary to the intentions.

It reminded him of similar offers made to those who had just lost a loved one by death, but of course, there was nothing they could do. One of the students said to Sam, "Somehow or another, it seems to me that you are facing a problem that isn't one that just affects your family, but is one that affects the entire colored race."

"I appreciate your feelings and somehow or another, I, too, feel that way; but at the same time, it is a most personal one for me."

One afternoon, when he was working in the laboratory, Sam had stopped what he was doing, and was staring out a window with unseeing eyes when Dr. Pearson came up behind him, placed a hand on one of his shoulders, gave it a slight squeeze, and without saying a word, passed on. Sam was more grateful for this expression of sympathy than he would have been for any words the teacher could have spoken.

Chapter 36

Two days before the trial, Sam went to Clayton's office to discuss the case with him. When Sam seated himself, the lawyer asked him, "Do you know a Negro woman by the name of Tanksley, Malvoy Tanksley?"

"Yes," replied Sam. "Why?"

"What do you know about her?"

"She lived across from us when we first came to live in Mills Alley. She was a tough character, but after her father and stepmother died, she took charge of her three younger half-brother and sisters and has been taking care of them ever since. She moved away some time ago, but just where she lives now, I don't know. My mother always took an interest in her and the children. Why do you ask?"

"This morning, she came to my office and began asking some questions about the details of the case against John Henry. I answered her in a general way without giving any pertinent facts. Since I did not know what she was up to, I did not want to say too much, but I did want to know what she was up to. Finally, she asked me if it would help John Henry any if it could be shown that he was somewhere else at the time the crime was supposed to have been committed. I told her that such proof would just about clear him. Then she stated that John Henry had been with her, at her house, in her bed, for about an hour, early on the morning the crime took place."

"What do you know about that?" declared Sam. "Wonder why John Henry hadn't said anything about that?"

"Wait a minute. I'm coming to that. I asked her if she knew any reason why John Henry shouldn't have told me about being with her. She replied that she knew why he hadn't said anything that would involve her. It seems that some years ago, the juvenile court gave her custody of those children only during her good behavior. The reason John Henry hadn't said anything was that he was afraid that if the fact became known that he was in bed with Malvoy, the court would take those children away from her. In other words, he was trying to protect the Tanksley woman. However, she declared that she was not going to allow John Henry to do that for her. She would take a chance on losing the children."

"Have you talked to John Henry about this?" asked Sam.

"No, I have been busy since she came in and couldn't get away. I can go down there now. Do you want to go with me?"

John Henry listened with interest to what the lawyer had to say but when Clayton had finished, he smiled and shook his head.

"There is not a word of truth in what Malvoy told you," he said. "Why, I haven't seen her in almost two years and then nothing more than to exchange greetings."

Sam had been elated since the lawyer had told him about Malvoy. He had visions of John Henry being quickly cleared of the charges against him, but at his brother's words, his spirits sank.

"Why do you think she would tell a story like that?" asked Sam.

"I don't know but I can guess," replied John Henry. "My mother was always good to Malvoy. She believed in her as a girl when no one else did, and it was on a statement of hers that the judge granted Malvoy custody of the children. I expect she is just trying to return those favors."

The lawyer grunted. "It is a little bit surprising to see such a beau geste in one who is so unprepossessing," he observed.

"If you mean by that, you are surprised at her doing it; I can say the same thing. However, I think it damned swell of her to make the offer," replied John Henry.

"Why can't we use her testimony anyway?" asked Sam, who had been in a deep study.

"What do you mean by that?" asked John Henry.

"Let her go on the stand and give her testimony to that effect."

"Only over my dead body," answered the lawyer, shaking his head. "Even if professional ethics permitted me to use her testimony, as a practical matter, I would say 'no' a thousand times. Anything could happen to break down her story. A casual passerby, the officer on the beat, one of her children, most anything, and rest assured that the state would move heaven and earth to disprove her statement in addition to going back and digging everything up on her which you guys say is pretty bad. The failure to sustain an alibi is the next thing to pleading guilty. In fact, it could be even worse. Mercy might be granted on a guilty plea, but the proof of a fictitious alibi would probably arouse prejudice on the part of the court and jury. It could even result in the Tanksley woman being sent to prison for perjury. No, let's forget that angle as a defense."

When Sam got home, he told his mother what Malvoy had tried to do.

"What did I tell you?" she remarked. "I always did say Malvoy Tanksley was all right. I knowd dey was good in dat gal."

The more he thought of it, the more Sam was puzzled by the offer of Malvoy to make the sacrifice for John Henry. He couldn't reconcile the offer with the girl he had known. He always figured his mother had been prejudiced in favor of Malvoy because she did not have a mother. The only creditable thing she had ever done, so far as he knew, was in caring for the children and he thought that she had done this to satisfy her natural maternal instinct.

He had obtained her address from the lawyer and that evening, he went to see her. She was living in a small Negro settlement in the southern suburbs of the city. At first, she insisted that John Henry had been with her that night, but when Sam told her that the lawyer would not use her testimony, she admitted that she had not seen John Henry in months.

"Yo' mammy had always been so good to me," she sobbed, "dat when I heard about your brother being in trouble, I made up my mind to help him in any way I could 'cause I knowd Aunt Maria must be worried near crazy. I'se sorry dat I can't help him enny."

"That's mighty fine of you, Malvoy, but didn't you know that when you came out with that story, the juvenile court would likely take the youngest children away from you?"

"Yes, I knowd dat, and I thought about hit some but dey done got so big dey couldn't keep dem from Malvoy for long."

Sam left her clinging to a post of the porch with tears in her eyes.

"Tell Aunt Maria not to worry more'n she can help," was Malvoy's parting words to him. "She's been so good to de orphaned dat de good Lord ain't goin' to let her suffer much."

Tears came to Sam's eyes as he stumbled through the sagging front gate.

Chapter 37

The trial didn't consume much time.

Mrs. Perry testified that she was at home alone and had been asleep for some time when she was awakened by someone knocking at her door. When she opened the door, that man (and she pointed to John Henry) came in and seized her, and despite her struggles, threw her across the bed and there accomplished his purpose. Her husband came home about that time, and the Negro, seeing the lights of the approaching car, jumped up and ran out the back door. On cross examination, she admitted she had never seen John Henry before that night but she was positive in her identification.

Her husband testified that as his car came up the drive, the headlights swept around a curve, and he noticed a man run towards the west between the chicken house and the barn. It was proved that this was the direction towards John Henry's place. When he went into the house, he found his wife in a hysterical condition and after a long time, she was finally able to tell him what had happened. He then aroused a neighbor and sent her to stay with his wife while he went to an all-night service station to call the sheriff.

The night dispatcher sent Jenkins and two other men on the call. Captain Browington happened to be at the jail at the time so he went with them. On the way to the Perry home, they had passed Sergeant Bullard and had picked him up to go with them.

Jenkins, Browington, and the other officers told about the arrest and identification.

Dr. Burton told of his findings.

When John Henry took the stand in his own defense, he related his movements of the night he was arrested, leaving out the episode in which he was forced to walk through the fields at the point of a pistol. To explain his wet shoes and trouser legs, he stated that after he had gone to bed but before he was asleep, he heard a noise in the direction of his chicken house and went to investigate it. He admitted that he had been a bootlegger for years.

229

He denied in full the charges brought against him and said he had never laid eyes on Mrs. Perry, to his knowledge, until he was taken to her house by the officers that night.

He had no other witness to offer on the charge but he did have a number of character witnesses, most all of whom said that while they knew he was a Negro who bootlegged and ran a roadhouse, that he was of good character otherwise and could be believed on his oath.

Sam had been in constant attendance throughout the trial as had William. Maria wanted to attend but after one day of it, Sam and John Henry advised her to stay at home. They saw the strain on her was too much, and they were afraid she would not be able to bear up under it. Sam sat at one side of the lawyer and John Henry on the other side at the defense table while William sat directly behind them.

Throughout the trial, Sam minutely watched every development of the case, and he could see as it progressed that it looked worse and worse for his brother. Every bit of the state's evidence seemed relentlessly to pile up against the defendant, but when John Henry took the stand in his own behalf and underwent a grueling cross-examination without breaking down or becoming involved in any contradictions, Sam could not see how the jury could fail to turn him loose after he was so convincing in all of his statements. During the lulls in the lawsuit, he studied the faces of the jurors in the hope of finding some indication of what their feelings might be, but all twelve were as inscrutable as so many stone faces. For the most part, the only sign of life they betrayed was the batting of eye lids, and the slow and unceasing chewing of tobacco and the occasional leaning over to expectorate streams of amber.

When the judge had charged the jury and it had retired to consider its verdict, the air of tension in the courtroom let up. Clayton walked over to the attorney general and exchanged some pleasantry with him. Just a little while before, during the heat of the trial, Sam thought they were going to fight. One of the court officers joined the two lawyers and told a joke at which all three laughed heartily. The judge came down and joined them, In a few minutes, Clayton came back to Sam and John Henry.

"The judge said he was going to keep the jury out until six o'clock. It is now two," said the lawyer looking at his watch. "In case they have not reached a verdict by then, he is going to send them back for the night and have them report back at nine in the morning."

"How does it look to you now?" asked Sam, knowing John Henry was anxious to hear the answer, but was afraid to ask the question.

"I can't tell. I certainly don't expect an acquittal. We can just hope for the best."

Sam thought he would get up and take a walk, but immediately changed his mind. The jury might report while he was out. Besides, John Henry couldn't leave and he should stay there with him. In a little while, they would know John Henry's fate. The jury would see the truth of the matter and would come in and so report. Then he and John Henry could leave the courthouse together. There would be a lot of happiness in those rooms in the back of the little restaurant out near Semmes campus tonight. No, that couldn't be. The lawyer said he did not expect an acquittal and he should know. That was his business and he had been in it for years. Then that meant John Henry would be found guilty. Found guilty of rape. Of raping a white woman. John Henry was a Negro and he would be guilty of raping a white woman. Oh, God! No! No! That couldn't be. That meant electrocution for John Henry. John Henry was his brother. The brother who had been so good to him. He mustn't think about those things. In a few minutes, he would be in a panic. He must remain calm for John Henry's sake. He glanced at his brother. John Henry was staring at the floor. At least, he was calm. He was taking it like a man, not like some hysterical fool. He leaned over and gave John Henry's arm a slight squeeze. John Henry glanced at him with a shy grin and returned to studying the floor. Sam looked at the jury room. What was going on behind those doors? What were they fixing to do with his brother? Even if they should find him guilty, would there be someone among them who would hold out against the death sentence? My God, how long did it take twelve men to make up their minds? Should there be that much doubt one way or the other? The judge said he would keep them out all night. Why not give John Henry a break? If they couldn't agree in four hours, why think they would ever agree? Why not dismiss them, even if that did mean John Henry would have to remain in jail until the next term of the court? That was better than being in the penitentiary, and no telling what might happen at the next trial. Aren't those men ever going to knock on that door? He must stand it. After all, he was a grown man. He must

231

show the stuff of which he was made. He must not think himself into a near panic again.

John Henry asked Sam to get his father out of the courtroom before the jury reported, explaining that he didn't believe he could stand it if a jury returned a verdict against him with his father present. Sam explained John Henry's feelings to his father, and the old man readily agreed with him. He said he would rather not be present and was staying only because he did not want John Henry think that he was deserting him. Sam gave his father taxicab fare home in spite of the old man's insistence that he had money for that.

In about an hour, there was a knock on the jury room door. One of the court officers went to the door, opened it, and stuck his head inside. He turned around and called to another officer near the door, "Call the judge. The jury is ready to report."

The judge came in and took his place on the bench, Clayton took his seat between the brothers, and the attorney general stood at his table.

"Tell the jury we are ready," ordered the judge.

The officer opened the door and the jury filed out in solemn procession. Sam looked at each face as it came into view in the hope of reading a verdict. They were still blank. He felt his pulse pounding at the base of his neck. The palms of his hands were wet with sweat. All arose to their feet.

"Gentlemen, have you arrived at a verdict?" asked the judge.

"We have." answered the foreman.

"What is it?"

"We find the defendant guilty as charged in the indictment," was the response.

"So say you all?" asked the judge and all twelve heads nodded in assent.

That's not true thought Sam. That couldn't be happening. The jury was still out. They had made some mistake in their verdict. They had found John Henry guilty. There was nothing else said. Nothing about a sentence. The judge said they would have to fix the sentence if he were to be sent to the penitentiary. That meant------Oh, my God! They had condemned John Henry to death.

Sam slipped behind the lawyer and put his arm around John Henry who was standing immobile. Not a muscle moved.

"I am sorry, John Henry," said the lawyer.

John Henry came to life. "You did the best you could."

"I suppose there will be a motion for a new trial?" asked the judge.

"Oh, yes, Your Honor. I will file it as soon as the stenographer prepares the transcript," replied Clayton.

"That's all right," returned the judge. "If you need any extra time, prepare an order, and I will enter it for you."

"Maybe, that was supposed to be a favor," thought Sam. "It was easy enough to grant favors after they had condemned his brother to die. He shouldn't say that about the judge. He had been fair. The judge didn't make the law. It was only his job to interpret it."

The officers took John Henry in custody and started to lead him out of the courtroom. Only then did Sam see any signs that the verdict had affected him. John Henry's eyes were filled with tears.

When John Henry got to the door, he turned and called to Sam, "Tell the old folks not to worry. Everything will turn out all right," and with a quick wave of his hand, he passed through the door to the jail.

Sam didn't see how he could go home and tell his parents. He tried to think of some excuse for not going. That wouldn't be right, he thought. They are probably dying of suspense now. He had better call a cab and hurry with the news. It had to be done. He would try to use some of John Henry's courage. He had taken it like a man. John Henry, who had never been anything but a common, bootlegging Negro, could stand up under a thing like this better than he could. Even though Sam was in his fourth year at college with the benefits of those years of mental training, he felt that John Henry was a better man than he was. Yes, in every respect. At least John Henry could stand up and take what "Life" had to give. He had never felt closer to his brother than he did now.

The trial court overruled the motion for a new trial. His lawyer made the formal motion for an arrest of judgment, which was also overruled. An appeal was taken to the Supreme Court. The case was duly placed on that court's docket, but it was February before it was argued. The court held the case for two months before giving its decision. The opinion was brief. The court had not found any errors in the trial below and overruled all the defendant's assignments of error and set the execution date for May 15. Sam was in the Supreme Court when the decision was given. From the opening statement of the justice who delivered the opinion, Sam knew all hope for help from the courts was gone. The only power left to save John Henry was the governor of the state.

On the day the Supreme Court affirmed the conviction, and while he was making ready to be removed to the state prison, John Henry was called to the visitor's gallery. When he walked up to the window, he was facing Browington.

"Nigger, I told you I was going to get you and I have," declared the white man. "This is what happens to niggers who sleep with white women. I framed you right, you black bastard. Even if it did cost me plenty, it was worth it. Hell, they ought to have me in Hollywood. The plot was perfect."

John Henry grinned.

"What the hell are you laughing about? Have you gone crazy?" demanded Browington.

"The thought has just hit me that I am the winner and you are the loser," replied John Henry.

"How in the bloody hell can you say that?"

"In a little while, I'm going to be dead, and some day you will die but I hope it will be a long time off because as long as you live, you will live with the thought that a nigger took your woman away from you. Until your dying day, you will know that I was a better man than you and you will rage and curse and scream in your anger, but there is nothing you can do about it. I will be beyond your power to hurt. The only thing you can do is to come to my grave and piss on it, and I hope you do because if they catch you, you'll be put in the nut house."

Browington leaped to the heavy wire mesh screen and pounded on it with his fists.

"You black bastard. If I could get to you, I would kill you with my bare hands," he screamed in his frenzy.

"The state will do the job for you and do a much neater job."

The guard, who had strolled to a discrete distance, rushed to John Henry at Browington's outburst, and grabbing him by the arm, escorted him back to his cell block.

Chapter 38

A week before the date set for the execution, John Henry was removed from the main building to the death house, a narrow, two-story red brick building in the far corner of the prison yard. A guard was placed in the corridor outside the cell, day and night, with instructions to keep his eyes constantly on John Henry. The lights were so arranged at night that John Henry could sleep with his head in a shadow but the light would fall across his body. These precautions were to prevent him from taking his own life. The state insisted on that privilege.

All restrictions regarding visitors were removed for the final week. He was allowed as many visitors as he cared to see, and there was no time limit on their visits. William and Maria came to visit him every day and remained all day.

John Henry tried to get them not to stay with him so much. It was a strain on him, and he knew it must be an even greater strain on the old people. On the fifth day as Maria started to leave, she kissed him and embraced him through the bars. She became hysterical and would have fallen had not John Henry held her up. William and the guard took her from John Henry's arms. She had to be taken home in an ambulance. She never returned to the prison.

On the afternoon preceding the execution, John Henry was taken out of the death house for the last time. He was carried to the barbershop of the prison where his head was shaved. It was a clear day, and the sun shone in all of its splendor. In spite of the heat, it felt good to him for it had been almost a year since he had been outdoors with the sun shining full on him. When he re-entered the door of the death house, he gazed for a moment into the blue depth of the sky above him. "This is the last time I will ever see it," he thought.

In accordance with a long established custom, the wife of the warden visited him and asked him to select his menu for dinner. John Henry thanked her for her thoughtfulness but replied that it didn't make any difference what he had because he felt as though he could not eat anything. He was prepared a meal of fried chicken, cream gravy, hot biscuits, corn on the cob, ice cream and watermelon topped off with viands which were supposed to be a favorite with all Negroes. He scarcely touched his food.

Early in the night, the death watch of Negro preachers began to arrive. Each would solemnly shake hands with John Henry. Then, each in turn would take a seat in a semi-circle of chairs in front of the cell which widened with the admission of each newcomer. They talked in undertones and for the most part in monosyllables as if they were already in the presence of death. Due to the number of people in the death house, the warden increased the number of guards.

His visitors thought of Death; John Henry's thoughts were on Life. As the slow minutes of the night dragged, John Henry became more and more nervous under the strain. To relieve the tension, he began to talk. He talked of the people he had known in the past, of the things he had done as a boy, the escapades he had been in at school, and his experiences as a caddy at the country club. He talked himself into a state of hysteria. He began to rail against the witnesses who had testified against him at the trial, the judge of the trial court, and the judges of the Supreme Court, the officers who had arrested him, and the governor of the state who refused to interfere in his behalf. He shouted curses against them and cried for the vengeance of Heaven to be directed against them. His friends gathered at the bars of the cell and tried to quiet him. Then, suddenly, his mood changed. He clung to the bars and begged the guards to execute him immediately that to wait would be only prolonging his agony.

One of the guards, seriously and patiently explained to him that such a course would be impossible, that the execution could not be carried out until the time provided by law. John Henry sank back on his bunk and buried his face in his hands and cried repeatedly, "I'm sorry." At other times, he paced up and down in his cell, clasping and unclasping his arms.

By the time William and Sam arrived, he was calmer so that when his father clasped him through the bars of the cell, he was able to calm the sobs of the older man. He did give way to weeping when his father explained that his mother was physically unable to come to see him, but that she had sent her love, and to tell him that she would soon meet him again in Heaven.

At midnight, one of the ministers suggested holding a song and prayer service. So, the crowd gathered about William who was sitting at the bars holding John Henry's hands. They raised their voices in the old hymns that had been such a comfort and consolation to their race since its implantation on the American shores.

The soft voices filled the small brick building with a fervent melody. The still dark hours of the morning bore their singing to the main prison where few prisoners were asleep. It seemed as if the entire race was giving expression to a soul filled with the longing and sorrow of a people only a few years from the bondage of slavery but had yet to make its way in a world which apparently had no place for it. They sang the old revival hymns and the spirituals which the Negro had given to the world with all the fervor of true artists.

During the prayers, the two brothers and their father stood with their arms about each other's shoulders with the cold impersonal bars in the middle of the group, mute reminders of the separation which was soon to come and would last throughout this world for all of those concerned.

John Henry seemed to feel better after this and chatted with his father and brother. When they seemed at a loss of what to say, he would pick up a thread in the conversation and carry it forward.

No longer was he hysterical, nor did he express any animosity or ill-feeling towards anyone for his plight. He had finally accepted the inevitable.

The first gray fingers of dawn had just begun to tinge the eastern sky when two men in overalls entered the death house and passed through the swinging doors into the mysterious depths of the room beyond. Everyone knew who they were and what they were doing, but everyone studiously avoided looking directly at them, and no mention was made of them. If they had been wraiths from another world, unseen by mortal eyes, their passage would have attracted no more attention. All eyes avoided the pencil of light beneath the door and no attention was paid to the occasional noises from the other room as if ignoring these things could, in some mysterious way, halt the preparations for the act which was soon to be performed.

The line of darkness was being driven higher into the sky and the tinge of gray was widening and whitening at the base when the warden and prison physician arrived. The warden nodded to the assemblage and shook hands with several of the Negroes whom he knew.

The white coat of the doctor looked oddly out of place. Instead of being worn, as customary, to save life; here it was being worn to play its part in the taking of a life. Instead of its wearer trying to prolong life, here it was his job to announce when that life had been extinguished.

"I am sorry, but all of you will now have to leave," the warden announced to the crowd. "The law does not permit the presence of anyone here at this time except the necessary officials."

"Just a word of prayer before we go," begged one of the preachers.

"All right. But just a minute, please."

"I know. I won't be long. Let us all kneel."

John Henry slipped to his knees as if glad of that moment of respite now that the final moments had come. Sam and his father each held one of John Henry's hands as they knelt.

"Almighty Father in Heaven," began the preacher. The warden looked about him, as if at a loss what to do, and then making a concession to the religious atmosphere, he also kneeled. The doctor compromised by bowing his head. The guards maintained their positions, fearful lest something happen to their prisoner. "Into Thy hands for keeping we commend this, one of Thy children. Oh, God, in Thy infinite mercy, judge him not as he has been judged by the sons of men, but judge him by that loving kindness which caused You to give Your Son that we might be saved through Everlasting Life. This we ask in the name of That Son, who died at the hands of men, that all of us may live through Eternity with Thee. Amen."

One by one, each passed by the cell and shook hands with John Henry and tried to utter a word of consolation to him. Instead of strengthening him, their kindness helped to unnerve him. With tears streaming down his face, he sobbed so convulsively that his father had to hold him up against the bars.

"You really must go," said the warden as one of the guards unlocked the cell door.

Sam grasped John Henry and pressed his cheek against his brother's. "Take care of our mother," John Henry whispered. Sam nodded, as he choked back a lump in his throat and turned away. At the head of the stairs, both William and Sam turned and looked to get a last glimpse of son and brother. A guard was kneeling at John Henry's feet slitting his trouser legs with an enormous pair of shears. Sam went slowly down the steps. When he got to the bottom, he saw the preacher standing in a group outside talking in whispers just as people do at funerals. He realized his father had not followed him. William had started down the stairs, but had collapsed against the wall, sobbing.

Sam started to him when he was arrested by the sound of footsteps on the floor above him. He strained his ears, listening for further sounds from above. Suddenly, the electric light above his head which had been dimmed by the growing dawn, grew dimmer still. There came a crackling sound from the room above and the light grew bright again. Before he could move, the light grew dim again and again there was a crackling sound from above.

The meaning of these things was not lost on William. "Oh, God. My son, my son," cried William and blindly started up forgetting that he was still on the stairs. Sam sprang to him and caught him to keep him from falling down the steps. Sam led him out into the yard where others took charge of him and began to utter futile words of consolation.

"Let's get him away from here before they bring the body down," whispered one of the preachers.

When Sam and William returned home, Maria was sitting in a straight chair, her hands folded in her lap, her body slowly rocking to and fro. She glanced into her husband's face, and there read the message he could not steel himself to tell. Her wail of sorrow rent the morning air. William stumbled to the floor at her feet and buried his face in her lap. Her hands stroked his kinky white hair while heavy sobs shook his body.

"My boy's gone to Jesus," moaned Maria. "Oh, God, why did You let my boy go? Oh, dear Jesus, he will be so lonesome there without me. Why didn't you let me go before him? I wanted to welcome him over there, standing by Your side. Oh, my baby, my pore, sweet baby's gone," she cried over and over.

Rosemary came in from the adjoining room with a glass of water in her hand. Sam shook his head at her, took her by the arm, and led her into the kitchen where some of the neighbors had gathered.

"Let them alone with their grief," he told her. "There is nothing we can do for them," and he walked to the door and stood with unseeing eyes looking at Maria's flowers in the yard which William had so zealously attended that summer.

Chapter 39

Sam did not grieve over John Henry's death. He was in the grip of a stronger emotion--hatred. During the time the body was in the house, he wondered aimlessly from room to room evading, as much as possible, the condolences of sympathetic friends and neighbors. The lamentations of his grief-stricken parents during the funeral service served only to increase his hatred and his resolve.

His attitude was the cause of much comment among the visitors to the home. They could not understand a person who did not show visible signs of grief over the death of a member of the family. It was whispered that since he had been going to Semmes University, he had become so high and mighty that he was ashamed of his brother, ashamed of the way John Henry had made his money, and ashamed of the manner of his death.

Sam wished he could break down in grief. It would be a blessed relief from the way he felt now. On the return from the cemetery, he felt if he had to stay and watch the sorrowing of his parents, he would lose his mind and start killing people. It wouldn't matter whom. He asked Rosemary to stay there until he got back and then left the house.

He had no particular place to go. He wanted to get off by himself. He wandered aimlessly until he found himself on the embankment of a railroad spur track and sat down on the end of a crosstie.

He tried to analyze his feelings. He did grieve over John Henry's death as was natural. He would miss his brother, miss him terribly; but after all, sooner or later one of them had to die. That was a part of the scheme of things over which no one had any control. John Henry's death in itself was not so important. It was the way in which it came about that counted.

A little while ago, John Henry had been alive, and he had loved life. He hadn't allowed the fact that he was a Negro bother him. He took life as he had found it, and he had made the best of it. He had been financially successful and had been generous with his success. Now, he was dead. He hadn't died of an illness or in an accident over which no one had any control; but he had been taken as a strong healthy man from one room to another and in the space of a few short minutes, he was carried from that room as a mass of inert matter. That result had been brought about by reason of one fact and one fact only; he was a Negro.

It hadn't taken John Henry's protestations of innocence for him to believe his brother was not guilty of the charges against him. He knew his brother well enough to know he wouldn't have committed such a crime. John Henry was not convicted for committing the crime of rape. John Henry was convicted of being a Negro.

John Henry's only guilt was in violating one of the white man's taboos; the one against the Negro having sexual relations with a white woman, no matter how much the white woman might be willing nor how low or debased she may be. And in John Henry's case, he could not be held morally guilty for he had been faced with a temptation that few men could have resisted. Had that same charge been brought against a white man and under the exact conditions, the authorities would have investigated the matter and turned him loose.

Sam's hatred was not against Browington and the Carver woman. They were only the instrumentalities through which this horrible thing was brought about. His hatred was directed at the entire southern white people and it was they that he wanted to make suffer for the crime they had committed.

He tried to think of ways in which he could get his revenge. The thing he would like most to see would be the dilution of every southern family with Negro blood. That would be retributive justice with a vengeance. Then the whites could no longer look down upon the Negroes and keep them in their abased state, but would have to embrace them as brothers. Obviously, such a thing would be impossible.

Maybe he could be the leader in developing such an intense racial spirit among the Negroes that on a certain day, which would not be too far off, at a given signal, they would rise up and destroy all the white people in the southern states. The Negroes would seize control of all state and local governments before the remainder of the nation could realize what was happening. They would then be in a position to force the recognition of their control by the rest of the country and of their right to keep what they had seized. No, this too was impractical for the white people not only in the remainder of North America, but also in Europe, realizing their duty to carry "the white man's burden," and seeing in such a course, the removal of their very profitable assets and land would destroy every Negro in the country.

A general strike of all Negroes seemed to present more practical possibilities. So dependent was the South on the Negro labor, all industry would be at a standstill, and the Negroes could obtain far reaching concessions before calling off the strike. The person who brought it about would become a national figure. Such a course would take years of organizing, and it would have to be done quietly and undercover. If the white people ever had an inkling of what was coming, they would take drastic steps to forestall it. An immense amount of money would be necessary to lay the groundwork, but if the proper contacts could be made, the communists would probably furnish much of the money.

The final means of exacting his revenge which presented itself to his mind would be the economic liberation of the black race. While its results would not be so dramatic and would take a long time and an infinite amount of education and training in cooperation, its results would be just as effective. It could be done by inducing the Negro to live on even less than he was now doing, if such a thing were possible, and put his savings into the purchase of the effective means of production such as factories and processing mills. In the course of time, they would be able to control the whole area through their economic power, and thus put the two races on a parity. The only flaw he could see in this plan was as the Negro became more economically independent, he would tend to become more conservative and be reluctant to cause any upset in the system in which he had his investments.

Each of his possibilities depended primarily upon one thing and that was the united action by an overwhelming majority of the Negroes. The thought occurred to him that in spite of being a Negro and having lived with them all of his life, he really did not know much about the susceptibility of the masses to any new thoughts or movements. He must make a study of these points.

It was not strange that nearly every idea Sam developed for punishing the white race carried with it the betterment of the condition of the black race, for in his thought processes, the two were indissolubly linked together. He blamed the white race for all the ills of the blacks.

The chill of a rising dew brought him back to the consciousness of his whereabouts. He struck a match and looked at this watch. He had been sitting there for several hours. When he started to rise, his limbs were so cramped he could hardly move. He stood up and stretched. All the thinking he had done helped him or so he told himself. The great burden of dread and worry he had borne for months had been lifted. Gone was the uncertainty of the future. He had outlined for himself a definite course of action.

He realized he was hungry; hungry for food and human companionship. He would not go home. Rosemary would be there, and she would be sympathetic. He did not want that. The time for sympathy was past. Nor did he want to tell her yet of the decision he had made, of his plans to avenge John Henry's death and free the Negroes of white domination. He wanted lights and noise and laughter. He walked the tracks to an overhead crossing over the street and scrambled down the embankment to the sidewalk. When he came to a street light, he counted his money. He had twenty-eight dollars. That could go a long way on Felts Street.

He went into a "good time" house and ordered some whiskey. It was vile tasting, but its effect was something like what he was seeking. He took another drink and went into the back room. A dice game was in progress. He stood at the table until the dice came around to him. He shot a dollar and won. This was more like it. He rolled dice for more than an hour and won almost a hundred dollars. A girl came over to the table and started a conversation with him. He went upstairs with her.

When the girl entered the room, she pulled her dress off and kicked off her shoes. She had nothing else on but her stockings. She laid down on the bed and held her hands invitingly. Sam choked back an impulse to vomit. He walked over to the bed, threw a five dollar bill down to her, and stalked out of the room.

The girl quickly followed him downstairs.

"Big Boy, I thought you wuz goin' to spend the night wid me," she complained.

"Well, you thought wrong. I'm sorry I went upstairs with you."

"Whut's the matter wid me?"

245

"Nothing."

"Den how come you is sorry?"

"You wouldn't understand. Come on over to the bar. I'll buy you a half pint if you'll leave me alone."

"Dat's a deal. Somehow, I don' like you much ennyway, even if yo' is got money. Dere's somep'n strange about you."

Sam bought the liquor and gave it to the girl. When she went into the back room, Sam ordered a drink for himself.

"How do you like being a Negro?" Sam asked the bartender as the latter laid his change on the counter.

The bartender gave Sam a hard look and went to the other end of the bar where he began mopping it with a damp cloth. He rubbed in circles until he went back to where Sam was standing.

"Did you ask how I like being a nigger?" the bartender asked, stopping the wiping motion but leaving his hand on the cloth.

"I said Negro instead of nigger, but I suppose to some people they are the same thing."

"That's what I thought you said. Let me ask you something. Have you ever been anything else but a Negro?" and the bartender accented the last word.

Sam shook his head.

"I don't know what you are talking about," said the bartender, "but from the way you look and talk, you don't seem right to me. You ain't looking for any trouble, are you?"

"Oh, no," replied Sam.

"Well, even if you ain't, you are in a good way of finding it. It don't do a nigger any good to be talking the way you is."

"I suppose you are right," replied Sam, turning away. "Well, good night. Any time you get tired being a nigger, let me know."

Sam tried to slip in the house, but Maria was up and waiting for him.

"Oh, Sammy, Sammy, I know it's been hard for you," she cried, taking him into her arms.

"I know I did wrong, running away today like I did," and he began to cry. It was a relief.

"Yo' did the right thing, honey," she consoled. "Yo' couldn't do no good stayin' about de house. Hit wuz better dat yo' git hit over yore own way. Let me fix yo' something' to eat. Yo' mus' be hungry."

"No, I'm not hungry. I just want to go to bed."

Maria did not say anything about the liquor she smelled on his breath.

Rosemary had heeded Sam's injunction to remain at the house until his return and had spent the night there. The next morning at breakfast, Sam and Rosemary lingered over their coffee. Sam told her of his thoughts of the night before and his plans. Rosemary listened to him until he had talked himself out on the subject.

To her, the whole idea was fatalistic. No one in his right mind would give a second thought to such an impossible task. Any efforts along such lines were doomed to failure and could lead to serious trouble, particularly for some innocent people. She knew it wouldn't be any trouble to start any sort of organization among Negroes. They were natural "joiners", especially, if the organization had promises for some pleasures but would lose interest if it had some serious purpose. But Sam was not in his right mind. He was suffering from the shock of John Henry's tragic fate. In a few days, he would have recovered his normal good sense. She wisely decided it would not do to oppose him directly.

"What do you propose to do about going back to school this fall?" she asked.

"I am not going back. All that is behind me. I will devote all my time to building up my organization?"

"You may be right. I don't know, but it looks to me as if it would take years to build up to what you propose to do. Meanwhile, you are going to have to have money to live on. It seems to me that the logical thing for you to do is to get your degree and then get a job that will pay a decent salary so you can do this other work on the side."

"I won't be drawn away from my plan," declared Sam, doggedly. "Most any kind of job will do me until I get started. The members will pay small monthly dues and in time, I will be able to draw a small salary from that source."

"If what you plan to do is going to take years to accomplish, I can't see that one year, more or less, in getting it started is going to make much difference. On the other hand, this final year in school may mean a great deal to you in about five years. If you do not return now, you may never go back to school again."

"I don't intend to, not now or in five years time. I am through being a Negro imitating a white man with the economic cards stacked against me. From now on out, I am going to be strictly, exclusively, and solely a Negro with but one thought; to do everything I can to destroy the smugness of white people."

"There are a great many of them and very few Negroes," said Rosemary with a wry smile.

"You are wrong there. Only about one-fourth of the people in the world are white. While the remainder are not all Negroes, they are colored so far as the white people are concerned. I have the majority with me to start off with. The colored peoples of the world only need leadership. I propose to help furnish that leadership and I know of no better place to start than in this country."

"I hope you know what you are doing," replied Rosemary lamely, realizing that further discussion was useless.

Chapter 40

For several days, Sam indulged himself in an orgy of idleness and never left the house except to get some cigarettes. Maria became convinced that he was ill, in spite of his protestations that he was all right, and she prepared some of his favorite dishes for him. When she set a bowl of milk toast in front of him, a dish which to Maria's way of thinking, was the only food a sick person should eat, Sam decided to relieve her anxiety about him by remaining away from the house most of the day. The Negro branch of the public library and the Negro YMCA, which had comfortable chairs in the lobby, became his favorite haunts.

One day Sam was sitting in the YMCA when a brisk walking middle aged man with a handlebar mustache started through the lobby, saw Sam, immediately changed his course, and came to a halt in front of Sam's chair.

"Isn't your name Sam Martin?" he asked

Sam acknowledged that it was.

"Wasn't your brother, er-ah, executed a little while back?"

"Yes. What of it?"

"My name is Lloyd. Grover Lloyd," replied the man. He grabbed a chair, whirled it around so that it faced Sam, and sat down in it. "I am the southern field agent for the Negro Development League."

Sam had heard of the League, but had only a vague idea of what it was.

"The League has never been very active in this section because the leaders at Semmes University have always preferred to work with our larger and probably better known rival. We have decided to become more active in this area and have a new secretary here, a young man from Chicago, and we want to make this one of our best chapters. We are in need of some local field workers. How would you like to have a job with us?"

"I don't know," replied Sam. "First of all, tell me just what is the purpose of the Negro Development League?"

"Just as the name implies," answered Lloyd. "To develop the Negro. It is our job to investigate all acts of injustice committed towards our race, to get the truth out of each lynching and publish it, to see that Negroes are given proper recognition in all civic enterprises and movements, to help all Negroes who have political aspirations, and to organize the Negro as far as possible into voting blocs. In other words, to do anything that will help or develop the Negro race."

"I see," returned Sam. "My brother was framed and railroaded to his death. Why didn't you investigate that?"

"Oh, we did," blandly replied Lloyd, "but our investigations showed there was a political connection there we couldn't go up against. Besides, we couldn't prove anything definite. Sometimes, there are things we are absolutely forced to overlook. I hope you can understand."

"I think I do. What do you want me to do?"

"General field work. You will be under the direction of the secretary. It will be your job to go around to churches, lodges, schools, and other Negro groups and make talks on behalf of the League and its work. Of course, one of our main jobs is to get new members and raise money to carry on our work. That will be your principal job at first. Then you will be expected to serve on the various committees that will be appointed."

"Primarily, all of your work is directed against the white race then?" inquired Sam.

Lloyd looked uncomfortable. "I wouldn't say that. Our purpose is to develop the potentialities and capabilities of the Negro," he replied. "Since the white race predominates, of course, some of our work must, of necessity, conflict with some of the white interests and ideas."

"That suits me all right," returned Sam. "When do I start to work?"

"Fine, I like that spirit. Our office is upstairs. Come on up, and I will introduce you to our secretary."

The secretary, Thomas Hockett, proved to be a thin nosed and tight lipped light yellow man of bustling energy. His acknowledgment of the introduction was done with so much hand-shaking and expressions of gratification, the simple act became something of a ceremony. Lloyd briefly explained to him who Sam was, and Hockett displayed enthusiasm at every statement and beamed on him like a doting father. Sam was beginning to think he had not been giving himself due credit for who he was.

"Don't we have a meeting with the mayor this morning to see about getting some more Negro firemen?" asked Lloyd.

"Yes, and it is about time we were leaving," replied Hockett, glancing at his watch. "We are to meet the remainder of the committee over at the Negro Chamber of Commerce."

"You come on and go with us," invited Hockett.

"I am not on the committee, and I really don't think I should go," demurred Sam.

"Oh, yes, by all means," urged Lloyd. "We will make you a member of the committee. The more we have, the better it will be."

At the Chamber of Commerce, Sam was introduced to the president of that body, a doctor, a real estate man, and the presidents of two women's clubs. All of them went to the city hall to see the mayor.

They did not have to wait long to see the officials. They were ushered into the office, and after some scurrying around, chairs were provided for all of them.

"Mr. Mayor, we understand the city is planning to put on several more firemen, and we have called upon you to ask you to make those appointments from members of the colored race," explained Hockett.

"We already have two colored fire halls," explained the mayor, "and at the present time, there are no vacancies in either of them. These appointments will be made to take care of vacancies in the white fire halls."

"We understand that, and that is why we are here. What we would like for you to do is to transfer all the members of one of the present white fire halls to take care of those vacancies and appoint Negroes to man the vacated fire hall," and Hockett went on to explain the disparity between the number of Negroes in the city and the number who were firemen, citing statistics showing the area of the city occupied by Negroes as compared with that occupied by white people and gave several other reasons along the same line.

At the conclusion of his statement, the mayor expressed his appreciation for calling those matters to his attention, thanked all of the committee for their interest in the welfare of the city, congratulated them on their interest in the members of their race, assured them of his own undying interest in the welfare of the colored citizens of the city, and politely ushered them out of his office. The net results of the visit, so far as Sam could see, were exactly nothing, and he was somewhat surprised at the enthusiasm of Hockett of the probable results.

The next day, Sam went with Lloyd, Hockett, and another similar group of Negroes to call on the governor to urge him to adopt as part of his administration's program, the creation of an Interracial Commission composed of both whites and blacks. Since the legislature did not meet for eighteen months, and it was obvious that such a commission would have to be created by that body, the governor seemed a bit surprised at the visit, but explained that he thought the matter was a worthy project, would take it under advisement, and would be glad to meet with them again at a later date.

That afternoon, Sam was helping Hockett check some mailing lists of Negro churches when he asked the other man just what was the purpose of the visit to the governor.

"It had two reasons," explained Hockett. "One was to impress Lloyd that I was on the job. The other was to bring me and this organization to the attention of the governor."

"What good would that do?" asked Sam.

"If I keep on calling on these public officials, they'll get to know me pretty well. I'll make them think I've got a lot of influence with my people, and I'll get a good job out of one of them," replied Hockett, leaning back in his chair and stretching his arms over his head.

"You mean you are using this place to get a political job?"

"Yea, and preferably under the Civil Service. I'll do it sooner or later. You just watch me."

One Saturday morning, Hockett explained to Sam that on Sunday night, he was to go to the Southside Baptist Church and make a talk on what the League was doing. A collection was to be taken, and Sam was to bring it to the office Monday morning.

Sam carried some of the League's pamphlets home with him to study for his talk. There was a good attendance at the church, and he thought he made a fairly good impression. After the meeting, he was given sixteen dollars and fifty cents. That was half of the collection; the church kept the other half.

As soon as he entered the office the next morning, Hockett eagerly asked him how much money the collection had amounted to.

Sam told him and dumped the money on the desk. Hockett separated it into two piles and gave one of them to Sam.

"What is this for?" Sam asked.

"That is your salary for the week."

"My salary!" echoed Sam.

"Yes, didn't Lloyd explain that to you? You get one-half of all the money you solicit for the League."

"You mean that's the way this organization is run?"

"Hell, yes; how else did you think it got money or you were to get your pay."

"To be honest with you, I had never given that any thought. Why, this thing is just a racket," declared Sam.

"Sure, what of it?" asked Hockett with a shrug of his shoulders. "It is really not quite that bad. The worst you can say about it is that we are just professional Negroes; that is, we make a business being Negroes. You take that visit to the mayor last week. Do you think he is going to appoint any Negro fireman? He is not. I've got sense enough to know that. All we accomplished was to give the members of the committee the satisfaction of making their wants known to the mayor, of sitting down in his office with him and receiving his assurance that their wants will be given due consideration. They know the mayor is not going to appoint any more Negro firemen and would probably be the most surprised people in town if he did. In a way, they are professional Negroes, too; but they are not doing it for pay. They are doing it for the satisfaction of an egotistic desire. We've got the best end of the deal. We get the money."

"I don't think I'm going to like this job," replied Sam, placing the money back on the desk.

"Don't look at it that way. It's a living and not a bad one. With your looks, your education, and the fact that you have a brother who was executed for raping a white woman; you could give this angle a good play. You can make a good thing out of this job."

"No. If I should do anything like this, I will do it in such a way that I can keep all the money."

"You won't find it so easy without the prestige of the League back of you," warned Hockett.

"It might be worth a try," countered Sam.

Chapter 41

Sam went to the library, and getting a magazine, he moved a chair behind the stacks and sat down to read. He could not concentrate on the printed page, and his gaze kept wandering to the open window. His thoughts recalled to his memory the story he had once heard about the Negro, who, when asked why there were so few suicides among the Negroes, he replied, "Boss, hit's like dis. When a white man's got trubbles, he sits down to think 'em over and de more he thinks about dem, de more upset he becomes until he gits up and kills hisself. But when a nigger's got trubbles, he sits down to think 'em over and pretty soon he gits sleepy, and he goes to sleep. When he wakes up, mos' of de time, his trubbles is gone."

He decided he had just about reached that point. At least, he was at the thinking stage. But if he went to sleep, he was going to wake up with the same thoughts on his mind. His experience with the Negro Development League had convinced him that there was a strong possibility that he could build up such an organization as he had planned. He would have to start from the ground up. The first thing he would have to do was to meet some of the people from whom he expected to draw the majority of his followers--the laborers. Tomorrow, he would get a job and go to work with them; become one of them.

The next morning, Sam put on a pair of his father's overalls and went to the wharf to wait for a job. The wharf was the city's unofficial, unmanaged, and un-housed employment agency for common labor. A laborer, seeking work, went to the wharf; and an employer, seeking labor, went to the wharf. A Negro, without regular work, was nearly always certain of picking up a little money loading or unloading the steamboats. If he remained there long enough to become known by some of the boat's crew and had shown a willingness to work, he might be hired on as a regular deck hand on one of the boats.

There was once a time when the broad cobblestone paved bank of the river was bustling with activity. At times, as many as a dozen boats were tied up loading or unloading their cargos. The goods were piled high and long lines of wagons awaited their turns to load or unload. The chant of the laborers rose from the riverfront from early in the morning until late in the afternoon when the last of the boats would slip their moorings.

With loud blasts from their whistles, the boats would back out and turn up or down the river, and the last of the incoming cargos were moved from the wharf. Silence would again reign until later in the night when the incoming boats would dock, land their passengers, and wait for the morning for the work of trans-loading their cargos.

Now the wharf was reduced to a smaller size, not much larger than an ordinary city lot and most of its area was covered by the enormous city owned river terminal where the loading and unloading of goods from the capacious barges that had replaced the steamships, was done by cranes, pipes, and automatic conveyors. The signs of activity were few, in spite of the fact that the river now carried a far greater volume of freight than it ever had in the days of the steamboats. The only steamboats which now docked at the wharf were an occasional excursion boat from St. Louis or Cincinnati during the summer months.

The passing of the steamboats did not end the custom of Negro laborers coming to the wharf for work and for another purpose. Not all Negroes who came to the wharf wanted work. Some came purely for the companionship to be found there. It was something in the nature of a men's club. One individual might be temporarily aloof from work, having just finished a job that lasted for a week or more, and with cash in his pocket, there was no reason for work. Another might have a wife with a good job so he had no necessity for work, and another might be living on the proceeds of unlawful activities carried out during the hours of darkness.

The loafer and the bum enjoyed a few hours of immunity from arrest for the police never arrested anyone on the wharf for vagrancy or loitering between sunrise and noon. They went along with the idea that all those on the wharf during the mornings were seeking work, but those who had not been employed by noon, presumably would not be employed and would have to leave.

If the weather were cold, fires would be made from the abundance of driftwood furnished by the river; and the Negroes would stand around them, alternately turning their front and back sides to the heat. If the weather were hot, they would sit like a row of blackbirds on the retaining wall at the upper end of the wharf where a few willows sprouting from flood borne seeds in the rich alluvial soil caught behind the wall furnished some measure of shade. Few friendships were ever formed among the Negroes on the wharf, and conversations among them were, at best, desultory.

Sam arrived at the wharf just before six o'clock. There were some fifteen men already there. Most of them had a lunch wrapped in newspapers and rammed into a pocket. Sam looked the men over. Including himself, less than a handful of young men were present. Most of the men were in their late middle years and two of them were aged. He stopped for a few moments and except for a few glances in his direction, no one paid any attention to him. He walked over to the wall, threw up his hand, and said "Hi." There were a couple of grunts in response. Backing himself up against the wall, Sam drew himself up onto it.

"Has there been much work lately?" he asked the middle aged man next to him.

"Enough for them as wants hit, but the pay ain't much."

"What's the pay?"

"Twenty-five, thirty, thirty-five cents an hour, dependin' on de kind of work."

A truck stopped at the top of the wharf and a white man got out. He walked down to the wall and announced, "I need ten men for grading."

The result of this announcement was anything but electrifying. Several of the men made twisting motions with their bodies, but the motions never engendered enough force to propel the body off the wall and on its feet. Several of the men looked at those sitting nearest them with expressions that seemed to say, "Did you ever hear of such foolishness in all your life?"

"All right, what about it? Do any of you men want work?" shouted the white man.

Several of the Negroes slid off the wall as if they thought some action was expected of them, but they were uncertain as to what it should be.

"How much you payin', Boss?" one of the Negroes finally asked.

"Thirty-five cents an hour."

257

Several shook their heads and some turned and looked out over the river as if something on the other side had attracted their attention.

"I wouldn't do that kind of work for less'en forty cents an hour," one man declared.

"I can't pay over thirty-five, and I can't stand here all day. Do any of you want the work?"

Two of the men started towards the white man, and others fell in behind them until eight had tacitly signified their intentions of taking the offered jobs. Sam slid off the wall and joined this group.

"I'll take you and you and you," said the white man, pointing to individuals. "How old are you?" he asked one man.

"I'se forty-two, Boss."

"Hell, you'll never see sixty again. Can you work?"

"I kin keep up wid de rest."

"That probably won't be so fast. All right, I'll take you. You all get in the truck. I'll take you two," he said, pointing to two more men.

He had reached Sam and looked him up and down.

"Let me see your hands."

Sam held out his hands, palms upward.

"Humph. They don't look like you've been doing much hard work. What about it?"

"I can do what you want done."

"All right. I'll soon find out. Get in the truck."

The white man selected two more men and after they were on the bed of the truck, he slid into the cab with the driver.

The contractor for whom Sam had been hired to work was engaged in grading the ground for an airport. He was given a long handled shovel and put to work with six other Negroes leveling the dirt after it had been dumped by a truck. Sam started spreading the dirt with a zest. In a few minutes, one of the Negroes said to him, "Boy, this is goin' to be an awful long day before hit's over."

"What are you driving at?" asked Sam.

"You ain't goin' to last long at de rate yo' is workin'. Take hit easy."

Sam saw the logic in the advice and set his pace to match the others. At first, he found their pace frightfully slow, but as the morning dragged on, he realized they were spreading a lot of dirt. In a little while, he raised blisters on his hands and when they burst, his hands were painfully raw. However, he persisted in spite of the searing pain every time he lifted the shovel.

"Don't do all yore liftin' wid yore arms and hands," one of the men suggested to him.

"What do you mean?" asked Sam.

"Git de shovel acrost yore knee and let hit hep you do de liftin', lak dis," and he showed Sam what he meant.

Sam tried it that way and found that lifting the shovel of dirt was easier besides easing some of the pain in his hands.

During the noon hour, he went to a nearby grocery for his lunch, and while there, bought a pair of cheap cotton gloves that gave his hands some protection. Once, the man who had hired him came by, and asked about his hands.

"Oh, they are all right," replied Sam.

"Let me see them."

Sam slipped off his gloves and showed his hands.

"Mmm. Look pretty bad. Maybe I shouldn't have hired you. Be careful with them and don't get them infected."

"I'll be careful," promised Sam. "Thanks for the interest."

"Hell, I'm not interested in you. If you get laid up with those hands, you'll get compensation, and it will go against our record with the insurance company."

"Oh," responded Sam, at a loss of anything better to say. "I suppose that was the reason the slave owners looked after their slaves so well," he mused. "Sickness or injuries to the slaves was costly."

The afternoon seemed to stretch out interminably, and several times Sam thought he would not be able to finish the work. Every movement of his hands was torture, and every muscle in his body cried for relaxation. He glanced at the other men several times to see if any had noticed his sufferings, but none had since each was always engaged in his own shoveling in an even and methodical rhythm. When the quitting time finally came, in an excess of relief, Sam told himself he believed he could have worked an hour or so longer if it had been necessary.

On the way back to town in the truck, the men laughed and joked with each other in the reaction to their labor. Sam came in for some kidding about his blistered hands. This pleased him, for in so doing, he felt the men considered him as one of themselves. In spite of his pains and aches, the day had been worth what it had cost for he had made contacts in the group in which he planned to start his campaign.

He was so tired that he could hardly stay awake long enough to eat his supper. A dreamless sleep left his muscles sore, but his body refreshed. His hands were so sore and stiff, he could hardly close them over his knife and fork at breakfast. Maria urged him to quit the job and get an easier one, but when he refused to do so, she grunted in disdain and remarked, "A lot o' good all dat college goin' did you. You ain't doin' no dif'runt frum what yo' pappy done all his life."

When he showed up at the place where they were to meet the truck, one of the Negroes called out, "There he is. Who said he wouldn't be back?"

"I sho' didn't think we'd ever see him enny more," commented another.

"We didn't think you'd be back after what you went tro' wid yist'day," one of the men explained to him.

"Boy, you sho' must need de work to be back on dis job."

"Maybe he done got a gal in a fix and he's got to git de money so's he can mar'y her," offered another with a cackle.

"Ain't no gal gonna let me hang around her long enough for 'at," returned Sam to this sally.

The good-natured bantering of Sam was ended by the arrival of the truck.

Sam again followed the pace set by the other men and in a short while, he had worked all the soreness out of his muscles, but he was still bothered by his blistered hands. To his surprise, the work seemed easier today. While they were working and during the intermittent conversations which sprung up, Sam studied the men whom he thought he could more easily interest in his program. He picked as his most likely prospect a big Negro in his late thirties whom everybody called Jumbo, but whose real name Sam learned later was Henry Newsom.

He remembered that the night before, Jumbo had gotten off the truck a couple of blocks before he had. So, when Jumbo got off the truck that evening, Sam got off with him.

"I gotta git me a drink," called Jumbo as they started up the street together.

"I wouldn't mind having one myself," remarked Sam.

"We can get a drink over there at Sis Cornwell's but my ole lady jes' gives me enough ever' day to git one drink."

"That's all right. I got a little money," replied Sam.

Sis Cornwell's place looked like any of the other weather-beaten frame houses on the street, except for a crudely painted sign tacked over the door which read "Fried Catfish." She had made what she hoped would be considered a restaurant by the police by putting two oilcloth covered tables and eight chairs in the front room of her house. Sam and Jumbo had hardly seated themselves at one of the tables when a skinny black woman, who reminded Sam of Malvoy Tanksley, came in. Her face lighted up when she saw Jumbo.

"Does yo' want yore regular?" she asked.

"Yeah, but make hit two, Sis," replied Jumbo.

Sis retired to the depths of the house and in a few minutes, she returned with two soft drink glasses that were nearly filled with a clear liquid and placed them on the table.

Jumbo picked his up and drank half of it in one gulp.

Sam gingerly took a taste of his. It was terrible. Jumbo drank the remainder of his, and setting his glass down, said to Sam, "What's de matter? Can't yo' drink hit?"

"It's all right," replied Sam, "but since you drank that one so quickly and I've still got mine, have another."

"I ain't go no money for no more."

"Take it anyway. These are on me."

"Alright, if yo' is got dat kind of money. I don't kere. Sis, bring me anudder. How come yo' workin' on 'at job?"

"What do you mean?" asked Sam.

"Yo' ain't been doin' 'at kind of work."

"Oh, I jus' got to the place where I had to do it," casually replied Sam. "How long you been doing that kind of work?"

"Who? Me? I been doin' 'at kind of work all my life. 'At's de only kind of work I'se ever did. Jes' common labor on de public works."

"Don't you get awfully tired of it?" asked Sam.

"Sometimes, I gits tired but den I gits rested up ag'in."

"I mean don't you get tired of doing that kind of work all the time?"

"What other kind of work kin I do?"

"Suppose the man who has that job had one of those graders to level off the ground. You could get the job of running it."

"Not me. I don't know how to run 'em. I jes' wouldn't have a job."

"You would if the white man couldn't get anybody else. He would teach you how to run it. You know how much common labor gets up North? They gets sixty cents an hour."

"How come dey gets so much?"

"Because they are organized up there and make the bosses pay it."

"You mean dey got unions?"

"Yes."

"Hit won' do for colored folks. De white folks won't let colored folks in de unions and colored folks can't do no good wid unions by deyselves. When de white man says to de nigger 'go to work' de nigger goes to work. If he don' work, de police gits him for vagrancy."

"Then you don't think Negroes can do any good by organizing into unions or clubs?"

"All dey'll git is trubble. I don' want no part of hit."

263

"I thought maybe the clubs should have some good purpose and that would be it. We can do something else."

"I wouldn't mind join' some sort o' social club but dat's de only kind, lessen maybe hit's got some sort of insho'ance benefits lak de Knights o' de Golden Cross. But dey don' have much social life."

Chapter 42

In the next few days, Sam gave a lot of thought to what Jumbo had said and realized the truth of the statements. He had heard that a few of the unions had admitted Negroes, but usually that was in cases where the Negroes were skilled in their work and were in such numbers that their presence in the community was a threat to a successful strike by the white workers. The Negroes were admitted to membership as a matter of self-defense. It would have to be done slowly and would probably take years. All right, at least, he would make a start.

One afternoon, when the sun was beating down on his back, a flash of inspiration came to him. He was so appalled by the simplicity of the idea that he left the shovel of dirt poised across his knee while he was lost in thought.

"Hey, Boy, you on WPA?" yelled the foreman.

He came back to reality with a start.

"I just had a catch in my back," he explained.

"If you aren't able to work, check out and you'd better see the company doctor."

"I'm all right now."

"Then take the lead out."

For several days, Sam mulled over his idea. He spent several evenings doing extensive reading at the public library.

One day when he and Jumbo were eating their lunches together, he said, "You remember a week or two ago you said something about how you would like to join a lodge which had some social activities?"

"Yeah," and Jumbo's face lit up with a smile. "You know some kinda lodge lak dat what don' cost so much?"

"I've been thinking about organizing a lodge with social activities."

Jumbo's face fell.

"Dem lodges wid social activities costs too much. I know. I done tried 'em. Dey tries to get too high falutin' to suit me."

"This lodge I am thinking about will have very small dues. It won't take much to operate it."

"Dat sounds purty good to me. Now de ole lady, she don' mind lodges iffen dey don' cost too much."

"Let's get some people together and talk it over," proposed Sam.

It was agreed that they would hold the meeting at Jumbo's house.

Twenty people were invited to the meeting and eight showed up.

"I have an idea for a new lodge and it is one that I believe will be popular," explained Sam. "It is based upon the history of the American Negro. There will be three degrees in it and each degree will portray an epoch in the history. The first degree will show the life of the Negro in Africa and will end with the initiating of the candidate into the rank of Warrior. Naturally, this will be known as the Warrior Degree. The second will show the Negro as a slave on a plantation; of how he must work and serve his owner; of how he is denied all but the barest of necessities of life, and how he aspires to better things. This will be known as the Slave Degree. The third will show the Negro after he has been freed and how, instead of being helped by the white man, he is exploited and kept in a condition that in many instances is worse than that he experienced as a slave and finally, through his own efforts, he is able to raise himself to a decent level of living, with hopes of greater and better things in the future. This will be known as the Citizens Degree; for when he passes through this one, he has finally attained full citizenship not only in the lodge, but in the community."

There was a chorus of approval.

"How are you going to do all of this?" someone asked.

"I have been working on the script and in a week or so, I should have it finished," said Sam. "We will have to have certain props, particularly for the Warrior Degree. We should have several shields and spears and some feathers for headdresses, anklets, drums, or tom-toms. I will arrange to get all those things. For the Slave Degree, we won't need much; just an arrangement for a camp fire. Most of the action in this degree takes place in the woods where the slaves have secretly met to plan their possible escapes. The things we will need for the Citizens Degree, we can easily get.

"In each degree, it is absolutely necessary to have three people to confer it, but as many more as may be present may take part. It is my thought that we can be the first members, and we can take turns in putting on the degree work until each one of us has been initiated into all three degrees. Of course, after that, no one can confer a degree who has not already taken all three degrees."

"What is it going to cost?"

"We will have to work out the initiation fees and dues after we get started and find out what it is going to cost to operate. I think if we try to keep the costs down, it should never amount to very much. Our largest item of expense should be the lodge hall rent. Of course, whatever we want to spend on social affairs will be left up to the membership as they arrange them. I thought we might make a charge of two dollars for each degree and two dollars yearly dues, payable quarterly.

"What's quarterly?" someone asked.

"Every three months and a member will be dropped if he is more than one full quarter behind in his dues."

"Dat seems fair enuff."

"At every lodge meeting, there will be a fifteen minute orientation period."

"What's dat?"

"At this period, one or more talks will be made by some member of the lodge on some subject dealing with the history, art, social, or economic conditions of the black people with suggestions on how the Negro can improve himself or his race. This period must always be observed. It is hoped that the talks for the most part will be original by some member of the lodge, but in case that is not always possible, we will send out material from time to time from headquarters for this purpose.

"The purpose of the lodge will be three fold. First, to inculcate a feeling of brotherly love towards all Negroes. Second, to teach the Negro something of the history of his people and encourage him to take pride in those Negroes who have made outstanding records in any field of activity. Third, to teach the Negro to take full advantage of all economic, political, and social opportunities that may be presented to him."

"How 'bout de social activities?"

"We will always keep in mind that people work together better if they play together, so we will stress social activities. There will be dances, games, picnics, suppers of various kinds, even card playing; but we must not allow gambling or drinking to be indulged in under any circumstances."

"Dat's a good idear. I'se seen lots o' clubs busted up because dey got to drinkin' an' gamblin'."

"We want to keep the organization on a high plane," continued Sam, "because if we do, it will continue to live and grow and will be of great benefit to all Negroes but especially to those who are members.

"And that brings up something else. While we will want to take in as many members as we can get, at the same time, we should screen the applicants. We don't want to take in chronic trouble makers, drunks, gamblers, or people who have served time for crimes. All of this will be set out in a manual that I will prepare."

"I'm in favor; let's get hit started."

This response met with general approval.

"Then the first thing we should do is to elect officers. There will be a president, a vice-president, and a secretary-treasurer. I will act as chairman and we will go into the election of officers."

"Since you got hit up, you ought to be de president," one woman suggested.

"No, I would rather be the secretary-treasurer for he is the one who will have to do most of the work. Suppose you elect someone else to be the president." replied Sam

Jumbo was elected president, and Sam learned his name was Henry Newsom. Mattie Green was elected vice-president and Sam was elected secretary-treasurer.

"I would suggest that at our first few meetings that we take turns in conferring degrees on each other. After we have all been initiated, no one can confer a degree unless he himself has obtained that degree."

Since Sam still had some work to do in preparing the material for the three degrees, it was agreed that they would hold the first meeting in two weeks. Someone was appointed to arrange a meeting place.

"What's gonna be de name of dis lodge?" another asked.

"I had thought of calling it 'Citizens of the Sun' because the native home of the Negroes is Africa where the sun shines intensely. When he is taken into slavery, there comes a time of darkness, but with the help of this organization he will again come into the Light and stand in the full Sun of Civilization."

"I like dat," said Jumbo, and the others agreed with the thought.

The first meeting of the Citizens of the Sun was held in a Sunday schoolroom of the church of one of the group and several hours were spent in rehearsing and conferring the Warrior Degree. A week later, the charter members were divided into two groups and each took turns into conferring the degree. In the course of six weeks, all three degrees were practiced and conferred on all the members; and plans were made to bring in new members.

During these weeks, Jumbo was so enthusiastic about the Citizens of the Sun, that he talked to Sam about it every chance he could get while they were at work. Others who overheard him, expressed their desires to join the lodge so that the first new members came from Sam's and Jumbo's fellow laborers.

There was a worker on the job who did not seem to have any clearly defined duties. It was his job to check out the tools each morning and to check them back in at night. Occasionally, he would drive one of the dump trucks if the regular driver was absent. At other times, he would run errands and bring out supplies or light equipment in a small pick-up truck. He seemed to make himself handy wherever he was needed. The other men said he was a "flunkey" and seemed to resent him because his job was relatively easy. His name was Charles Patterson, and naturally, he was called Pat by everyone. Occasionally, he would eat his lunch with the laborers and was friendly enough, but Sam detected a slight restraint among the others when he was present.

One day, after a lunch that Pat had eaten with them, Sam asked one of the men why he didn't like Patterson.

"I likes him all right," replied the man, "but I jes' naturally don't feel easy around a preacher."

"He's a preacher?"

"Yeah. Leastwise, he's a studin' to be one and hit's almost de same."

"What is he doing here?"

"He jes' works durin' de summers. De rest of de time he's in school. He's been wid dem for years. His ole man worked for 'em until he got killed on a job. De bosses thinks a lot of 'em."

A few days later, Pat was eating lunch with them again. They were sitting in the shade of the tool shed.

"They tell me you are studying for the ministry," observed Sam.

"That is correct."

"Where do you go to school?"

"Riverside Seminary."

"What denomination is that?"

"Methodist."

"I suppose the ministry is a pretty good racket. You are not likely to make much money, but from what I have seen, it is a rather easy life."

"I am not particularly concerned with the money angle and I don't expect to find it easy. It is not an easy life for a conscientious minister, and that is what I hope to be."

"You mean that you have the 'call'?"

"I suppose you can say that."

"Well everybody to their own notion, as the old lady said when she kissed the cow," stated Sam, "but from what I have seen of it, religion is nothing but a snare and a delusion, if I may be permitted another bromide."

"Religion can be the salvation of everyone's life."

"Oh, for God's sake. Don't start asking me about my soul and where will it spend Eternity and all that sort of religious pocus."

"I am not thinking so much of life in the Hereafter as I am of life on this earth. Religion can make it finer, richer, and more worthwhile."

"Baloney. That is old stuff. Religion is one of the few doubtful privileges the slave owner allowed the Negro. It was a good means of keeping him under control. The religion they gave him taught him that if this life was one of sorrow, toil, and suffering; he would get his reward in the Great Beyond. All he had to do was to do as his master or the overseer told him, work hard and do his work well, be faithful to his owner; and when he died, he would go to a place where there would be no more work. There, he would be supplied with all of his needs, and he could spend all Eternity strumming on a harp, singing hymns, and having a good time in general. Religion probably held down many a slave revolt. It was a good gimmick for the white man to help him control the Negro.

"Religion has always been a good racket. Its victims have been the ignorant, preying upon their fears of the unknown, taking from them their hard earned means and giving them only a promise of a pie in the sky in the by and by. It is the most one-sided deal ever contrived by the mind of man. There is no way to enforce the promises."

271

"You don't have much faith, do you?" responded Pat.

"If you mean in religion, none at all. The only faith I have is that which I have in myself. I believe I can do certain things and I will do them. The fact that I am a Negro will not stop me. I will do them because I am inspired and driven by the most moving of all human emotions; hate. Hate will drive a man long after religion has lost all of its force."

"Your contrast is not exact. The opposite of hate is love."

"A mere sentimental expression that quickly fades away when hate enters the picture. Our aims are the best criterion of what we are trying to do. You are trying to hold the Negro down to a low level of existence. My whole thought is to raise him to a higher one," stated Sam.

"You are wrong about my intentions. I know that some of the criticisms you have just made of religion are partially justified. Religion has been perverted at times by self seeking individuals or groups; but on the whole, it has made the life of Man better. Thoughts change in religion just as it does in other fields. No longer does the understanding minister preach of the agonies of hell and try to frighten the sinner into joining the church, but through his religion, he preaches a more practical way of life on this earth based on the teachings and the life and death of Jesus."

Sam could no longer contain himself as he responded, "A myth. That is one of the oldest and most persistent myths that has befogged the mind of man and it is one of the most difficult to eliminate. The myth of a resplendent half-god, half-man; born of the union between God and mortal and partaking the qualities of each, who dies and comes to life again like Attis, Osiris, Dionysus, and many others. Your Jesus was a piker when it came to the resurrection business. Some of them such as Demeter, died and were resurrected annually."

"There is one great difference between Jesus and all those others that you are talking about."

"Such as?'

"Love."

"Bosh. An emotion for weaklings. Give me hatred. That is a man's emotion."

"I believe you could use a little religion," concluded the would be minister.

"It is not for me."

The lunch hour was over.

Chapter 43

The Citizens of the Sun was a success from the start. Sam's insistence that every participant in the degree work should know his part perfectly was largely responsible for this. He was attempting to stage a drama and he knew that if the story was to be effective, it would have to be adequately presented. Fortunately for his purposes, the actors caught the spirit of the theme.

There was no lack of applicants, and Sam quickly realized that if they were required to wait awhile before admission, membership would be even more desirable. So, he instituted a procedure by which each application was referred to a committee on admissions. This committee was required to investigate the character and reputation of each applicant and make a formal report. Then a vote was taken on the application if the report was favorable.

In a few weeks, the membership outgrew the Sunday school classroom and Sam began to look for larger quarters. He found the ideal meeting place. It was upstairs over a grocery store and had originally been used as a Masonic lodge hall. In the course of years, as the white people left that section of the city, the lodge had moved farther out. The rent was ten dollars a month but the owner refused to do anything about the condition of the place except keep the roof and the stairs repaired. He had to keep the roof in good shape anyway to protect his property and the merchandise of the tenant on the lower floor. The stairs he kept in good condition lest he be sued if someone were injured.

The place was cluttered with an accumulation of debris and dust and several of the window panes were missing. The plumbing, while old, with a few minor repairs, was usable. A work party was organized and one Saturday afternoon, some fifteen of the more zealous members met at the place armed with mops, brooms, buckets, cloths, and soap powder. Before the afternoon was gone, the place was brought to a satisfactory state of cleanliness. The following Saturday afternoon, the treasury was drawn for paint, brushes, and glass. When the work party had finished, the lodge hall was ready for regular meetings.

One day, Sam was eating his lunch in the shade of a grader, when Pat came over and sat down beside him.

"What is this new lodge you have organized that Jumbo has been telling me about?"

"I don't think you would be interested," replied Sam.

"From what Jumbo has been telling me about it, I believe I would."

"What has Jumbo been telling you?"

"He says it's based on the history of the Negro race and has for its purpose, the uplifting of the Negro."

"Seems as though Jumbo has pretty well caught the spirit of the thing."

"If that is true, I would like to become a member. As a future minister, that is in line with some of the things I hope to do in the ministry."

"There is nothing religious about it."

"Religion can take many forms and can be presented in many ways. Whatever is aimed to better the lot of man, whether spiritual or economical can be a practical application of religious principles."

"Well, if you think you would like to join, I will bring you an application tomorrow."

By the time Patterson's application was passed on, he had left the job and returned to school so Sam saw very little of him. In the course of a few weeks, Patterson took his initiations. After he had received his degree of Citizen and became a full fledged member of the Citizens of the Sun, he came over to Sam and taking him by the right hand, he said, "Brother Martin, I think you have something fine here. It has a great power for good."

"Thank you," replied Sam.

"But at the same time, I see a dangerous potential in it. It is a thing that can easily get out of hand and cause a lot of harm. I hope you will always keep a close eye on it to prevent anything detrimental from ever happening."

"What do you mean by that?" asked Sam.

"You have some things in the rituals that with just a little more development, could arouse some powerful emotions and cause great harm in the field of interracial relations."

"Maybe that is what I have in mind," suggested Sam.

"If you have, it will only lead to trouble and it could be very serious trouble. The Negro cannot win by force. Force leads to violence and in violence, the Negro will always eventually lose simply because he is so vastly outnumbered."

"Not if that force were properly applied and if properly applied, it does not have to lead to violence. What would happen if all the Negroes in the South were to go on a strike?"

"In the first place, the idea is fanciful. There is no such leadership that could bring about such a thing. And the strike would end in two or three days, just as soon as the Negro got hungry."

"Then he could take the food."

"And get shot in the process."

"Of course, I am not thinking of such a thing as a general strike. I realize that such a thing is virtually impossible. But there is such a thing as economic force."

"With that I won't disagree--if properly used. It is fairly obvious that the more important the Negro becomes in the economic life of a community, the more consideration he will receive. That is why I think you have a powerful force for good in this organization. If you can teach the Negro to improve himself so that the white man will pay him more for his talents, the money he receives will buy him more material possessions and more privileges. When a dollar goes into a cash register, it counts just as much whether it was spent by a white person or a Negro."

"That road is too long."

"But its destination is more certain."

Sam decided he had made a mistake in allowing Patterson to join the lodge, but as the weeks passed and Patterson regularly attended the meetings but never took part in the discussions at the orientation period, he concluded that perhaps he had been hasty in his opinion.

The membership of the lodge grew so fast that Sam decided that he had better organize another lodge to meet at a different night. To prevent members attending one night from attending a meeting at another night and thus defeating the purpose of the second lodge, a by-law was passed prohibiting the number of visitors from exceeding ten percent of the members present.

By January, a third lodge was organized and Sam quit his job to devote all of his time to the work of the Citizens of the Sun. He fitted out an office in the lodge hall and began to make plans to organize lodges in other parts of the city.

Chapter 44

One day, Sam was at his desk checking the lodge accounts when a well-dressed Negro man in his late twenties came into the office and introduced himself as B. J. Spalding. Sam acknowledged the introduction and asked him to be seated.

"I had better tell you something about myself," said Spalding.

"Go ahead," replied Sam thinking that this was certainly a novel approach for a sales talk.

"I was born and brought up in Brooklyn, New York, and I have a degree from Columbia University where I majored in sociology. I am now working on my masters' degree with my thesis on the life of the average Negro in a southern city. I have picked this city as the scene of my study."

"That's fine," said Sam for lack of anything else to say.

"I have only been here for a week. but I have heard about the Citizens of the Sun. I have always heard that the southern Negroes like to join lodges and particularly one where they can dress in costumes. I have decided that I would like to be a member of your lodge; that is, if you will have me. It would provide me with fruitful material for my studies."

"I don't know about that."

"What do you mean?"

"Well, I don't think I'd like the idea of my members being studied for some sort of report on them."

"Please understand that my entire approach would be sympathetic. After all, I am a Negro, too. I certainly don't intend to make fun of my own race or hold them up to ridicule."

"I suppose there is no harm in your joining then with that attitude. I will be glad to take your application."

In the course of a few weeks, Spalding was approved for membership and quickly received all three degrees. One day, he came to Sam and said, "Look here, I am here on a grant so I don't have to worry about making a living. I would like to have the opportunity of working closer with the southern Negro. Why not give me a job, without pay, of course, of helping you organize new lodges. I would like to see what I could do along that line."

Sam thought over the proposition for a few minutes before replying. "I don't see why you can't do it. In fact, I will appreciate the help. I am kept rather busy as it is."

They outlined a plan of expansion and Spalding went to work. Scarcely a week passed without him organizing a new lodge. Sam checked behind him and found that he was organizing the lodges along exactly the same lines Sam had done. In a short while, there were twelve lodges with a total membership of close to a thousand and the number was growing weekly.

"What do you get out of this?" Spalding asked Sam one day.

"What do you mean?"

"What pay do you get?"

"I don't get any."

"Then why are you doing it?"

"I have an idea."

"That is fine and noble, but you have to eat."

"I hadn't given much thought to that so far."

"I have an idea. Why not form a central council with a representative from each lodge. That council would take care of the overall operation of the lodges. Each lodge would be required to pay into the central council so much money for each member. Sooner or later, that will have to be done for the organization cannot continue to expand unless there is someone to do the job, and that someone should be paid. Also, there are expenses that need to be paid by the members. You should draw a salary."

"That would come in handy."

"Suppose you leave it up to me to dun the lodges. I will see that it is worked in a fair and acceptable way."

Through the efforts of Spalding, the central office was formed and Sam was voted a salary of fifty dollars a month with the suggestion that this salary would increase as the membership grew.

In the course of a few weeks, Spalding became a distinct asset to Sam and the Citizens of the Sun. Not only did he organize new lodges but he paid close attention to them, seeing that the newly elected officers knew their parts and properly conferred the degrees. He paid particular emphasis on the orientation period by insisting that each one be fully carried out at each lodge session.

To insure that the printed material for this period would not become monotonous to the members, he prepared many new programs, some of which were based on particular days of the year; such as, Labor Day, Christmas, Easter, and from the standpoint of the organization, Emancipation Day.

It was Spalding's suggestion that all the material be printed instead of mimeographed, and that the lodges be required to pay for it. When Sam objected to the added cost, Spalding said he would bear the initial expenses and the central council could pay him back after the lodges had purchased it. The central council made a small profit on the literature.

"How can you afford to do this?" Sam asked.

"The scholarship grant by which I am making my studies was based on the living costs in the North. My living here is considerably less that I thought it would be. I am actually saving money on the grant. Since I am learning more about the southern Negro through the Citizens of the Sun than any other possible way, I don't mind helping you out. If you never pay it back, I won't be out anything personally, but I am sure there will be enough sales to insure the return of my investment."

Occasionally, Sam and Spalding discussed the subject of Spalding's studies.

"I have been surprised at the complacency of the southern Negro," Spalding remarked one day.

"And how in particular?" responded Sam.

"From what I had heard all my life, I thought the average southern Negro was always just at the boiling point because of the injustices done by the whites. On the contrary, I have found them to be more or less indifferent about the whole matter."

"Maybe, it is because they don't realize they are being imposed on."

"It could be, but at the same time, they are not entirely ignorant. In fact, I have found some who have plenty of good common sense and are fairly well read, but they don't seem to be aware that they are victims of a vicious system."

"Maybe, that is because they find the system not altogether bad. The white man hires him, pays him for his work, and allows the Negro to spend his earnings more or less as he pleases. It seems that so long as most Negroes have a roof over their head, something to eat, the minimum amount of clothes, and enough money left over to have a good time over the weekend, they are more or less satisfied. The indifference of the average Negro toward his lot is provoking to me."

"I haven't seen any evidence of communist leanings in the Negro South. I wonder why?"

"I suppose it is because no one has made the effort to educate him in the program."

"But surely some of them must have heard of the Communist Party and made an effort to find out something about it."

"Most Negroes don't seem to be interested in ideologies. Their main thought is to make a living and get a few simple pleasures."

"Yet their livings are so precarious that it would only seem logical that they would have turned to something that would promise them more than they are getting."

"The Negro has never been taught to work in unison. That is one of the things I hope to accomplish by the Citizens of the Sun. Not that communism is the answer to his problem. From what little I know about communism, he would probably be exploited just about as much under it as is being done under the capitalistic system."

"In it, there might be a hope for better conditions."

"There may be, but I doubt it. His best chance is to use the present established system for his own good. When he has been brought to the point that the present system will depend absolutely upon his labor, and he knows it, he can get his rewards by making the white man come to his terms. What do you know about communism?"

"Oh, nothing. That is, practically nothing. I was just curious, that's all."

At another time, Spalding asked Sam, "What made you use the noun 'citizens' in the name of this organization?"

"Oh, no reason specifically. It was probably because I wanted to help the Negroes realize that they are citizens, not only in this organization, but in the community as a whole. Why do you ask?"

"Did you know that the French Revolutionist called themselves citizens? I just wondered if there was any connection."

"I didn't have that in mind, but maybe it is an omen. Maybe my organization can be as revolutionary."

"Do you want it to be?"

"I have a score to settle with the white race."

"It looks to me as if you are on the way to doing it. At least, you will have the means, and maybe I can help you."

"How?"

"All in good time," Spalding terminated the conversation by leaving the office.

For a long time, Sam did not tell Rosemary about the Citizens of the Sun, but his work in training the members in their parts and in organizing new lodges kept him so busy at night that he finally had to tell her to explain his absences.

Her reaction was the practical one.

"What do you expect to get out of it?"

"What do you mean?"

282

"Is it the financial returns?" asked Rosemary.

"I hadn't given it that much thought."

"Don't you think you should? You are organizing these lodges for just one of two reasons. One is that you are still angry at the white world for what happened to John Henry, and in some way you see in what you are doing a possible chance to get even. If that is so, your ambition is unrealistic and doomed to failure. You can't revenge yourself on one hundred fifty million people. You can't even do it on the few hundreds of thousands who live in this area. Any attempt to so will destroy you and will injure thousands of innocent people of your own race. The other reason is to make money, and it doesn't seem as if you are going about it with this idea in mind."

"I am not thinking of the money angle."

"Then you should abandon the whole idea."

In spite of her views, Sam asked her to become a Citizen of the Sun, and Rosemary agreed. In the course of three weeks, she was awarded the three degrees.

She expressed to Sam her admiration for the ritual he had prepared, but she did not attend any of the lodge meetings except on special occasions.

Chapter 45

There was an election for mayor of the city approaching. Outside of noting, by glancing at the headlines in the papers, that Mayor Spears, who had held the office for several terms, was being given a spirited contest by his opponent, Sam had not given the race any particular thought. He had no interest in politics. That was something for the white people and in which the Negroes took little part. He knew that in a general way, the Negroes voted in the city elections, but had no choice in the county and state elections since the nominees were always selected in a party primary from which Negroes were barred, and those nominations were tantamount to election. No matter how much the candidates might fight each other in the primary, once the nominee was selected, the followers of the defeated candidates would fall in behind him and support him in the general election.

Sam heard someone coming up the steps and when he looked up, he saw Police Inspector Odom come in.

"Hi, Shine," he greeted Sam.

"You have a good memory," replied Sam.

"That's part of being a cop. A good memory and keeping up with people. I've been keeping up with you."

"Why?"

"For no good reason, except that the knowledge might come in handy some day like I think it is going to do now."

"And just what does that imply?"

"I understand you have organized some sort of a lodge and are doing pretty well with it."

"I have organized a lodge all right; in fact several; but there is nothing illegal about it."

"Don't get me wrong. I am not here to cause trouble. I am here to get some help and to give you some help."

"In what way?"

"How many members do you have?"

"About eleven hundred."

"My God; I'll say you are doing well with it. I need their votes for the mayor."

"What's that got to do with me?" asked Sam.

"I want you to deliver them."

"You mean you want me to get each of them to vote for Mayor Spears?"

"Yes."

"I don't know how I could get them to do it even I were inclined to do so."

"Here is something to make you 'inclined' to do it," and Inspector Odom pulled out a billfold, extracted some bills from it, and laid them on the desk. "These are for you," he said. "That's your part to stick in your pocket and do with as you please. Now here's how you get the votes. In the first place, you just let it be known to as many of your lodge members as you can that you are for Mayor Spears. Then in about two weeks before the election, I suggest that you pitch a barbecue for all of your members. Have plenty to eat and to drink, non-alcoholic of course, with plenty of entertainment and as a special treat, invite the mayor to make a talk."

"That will cost a lot of money."

"We'll take care of that. We'll go as high as four thousand on it."

"My gosh; you'll do what?"

"Give you four thousand dollars. With that much money, you should be able to provide enough food and entertainment to get every one of your members to attend. After they are there and having a good time and are full of good food and drinks, you can let it be known that it was all provided by the friends of Mayor Spears and that the mayor will speak to them. We can time it so that he will arrive just about the time you make the announcement. That is all we are asking you to do, and this money is yours for your trouble. What about it?"

"Let me think it over for a couple of days," and Sam picked up the money and handed it back to the officer.

"No, you keep that. That is for your trouble. If you decide for any good reason that you can't go through with it, then you can give me back the money," and with that, the officer left.

Sam picked up the money and saw that he was holding a stack of one hundred dollar bills. He counted them. There were ten of them.

"One thousand dollars," he shouted. That was more money than he had ever seen at one time in his life. And it was his just for having a barbecue for the Citizens of the Sun. It didn't take much thinking to arrive at a decision. The Citizens of the Sun would have their barbecue.

Sam undertook to earn the money. At the next regular meeting of each of the lodges, he let it be known that he thought it was in the best interests of the Citizens of the Sun to vote for Mayor Spears in the coming election. At the same meeting, he announced that a "get together" for all the members of all the lodges and their families in the form of a barbecue picnic would be given. He hoped that he had not left an impression that there was any connection between his political preference and the event.

He had found it surprisingly easy to get permission to hold the event at one of the city's parks for Negroes.

When he had gone to the secretary of the Park Board to get permission to use one of the buildings in the park for preparation of the food, the secretary hesitated about granting the request. But when Sam casually mentioned that the mayor would appear and make a talk to the group, the secretary's hesitancy quickly vanished.

Sam appointed committees from each lodge to handle the affair. He arranged with one of the bakeries to prepare the meat and furnish the bread, a dairy to furnish milk and ice cream, and one of the bottling companies to supply soft drinks and ice. He had each lodge select ten women to prepare a bowl of either potato salad or coleslaw. For each bowl furnished, a dollar was given to the lodge charity fund.

The picnic was a huge success. It was held early in the evening so that few would have to lose any time from work to attend. There were plenty of food and drinks. Mayor Spears appeared as scheduled. Inspector Odom was in the car with him.

Sam wondered if the mayor would remember that he had been a member of a committee that had called on him almost a year ago to ask for the appointment of Negroes to the fire department. He concluded that the mayor had probably received scores of committees on so many matters that there was no reason why he should have remembered him. He decided that he would not say anything about that meeting. It might embarrass the mayor since no Negroes had been appointed firemen, at least so far as Sam had heard, and he was not proud of the visit.

"Mr. Mayor, I want you to meet Sam Martin, the man who got up this meeting. I have known him since he was a shoeshine boy at the courthouse barbershop."

"I am certainly glad to know you," boomed the mayor, extending his right hand.

"Say, don't I know you?" he asked, peering into Sam's face. "Wait a minute. Don't say anything," and he held up his left hand in a halting gesture while his right hand still held Sam's hand. "I know. I have it now. You were on a committee from the Negro Board of Trade who called on me about appointing colored men as firemen. You made an impression on me at the time and I thought then that I would not forget you. I haven't forgotten about the matter of your visit, either. I am going to appoint some Negro firemen as soon as I can arrange for them to take over a fire hall completely. I can't do it now because my opponents will say I did it just to get votes for the election but, believe me, I will do it just as soon after the election as possible. And I will be returned to office. Have no doubt of that--with your help and all the good people like you."

Sam knew that the mayor's promises were so much "hog wash" but at the same time, he was flattered that the man had remembered him. He had heard that one of the requisites of a successful politician was the ability to remember names and faces, but this was the first time he had ever seen it in practice.

What Sam did not know was that someone on the mayor's staff had remembered about Sam being a member of the committee, and the mayor had been briefed on him just before the party got to the park.

At Odom's suggestion, Sam got up on a table and summoned the crowd about him and introduced the mayor. The applause which greeted the mayor was started by members of the mayor's party. The mayor was assisted to the table and throwing wide his arms in a gesture of friendship, he assured his listeners that he was not there to make a political speech and keep them from their fun and social activities. He thanked them for their loyal support in the past and hoped that he could count on their loyalty in the future. He recounted some of the things that he had done for the colored people; the schools he had built (the old ones were in a state of collapse before they were replaced), the parks he had built (which were woefully inadequate), and promised them that if re-elected, that he would give them even more and better recognition of the many fine outstanding leaders of their race by the appointment of one of them to the Board of Education and the appointment of Negroes as firemen and policemen. His remarks were lustily cheered. When he jumped down from the table, he was hustled back to the car by Inspector Odom, but he shook hands with a number of the Citizens on the way.

Sam was disgusted at the enthusiasm evoked by the glib words and false promises of the incumbent. Most of the crowd undoubtedly believed the man was sincere in what he said. What the hell he thought, if it wasn't one politician they believed, it would be another and all the politician wanted was their votes. What did he care? It made no difference to him who was mayor, and besides, he had made a thousand dollars out of the deal. When he got enough of them organized and properly trained, he would use them for his own purposes. The event had taught him that the Negro vote was another weapon he could use even if it was limited to the local elections.

Chapter 46

The lodge meeting was over. Quite a few of the members remained for a while talking among themselves, but finally they had drifted away until only Charles Patterson remained in the lodge hall. Sam had gone back to his desk to post the payment of some dues.

"How long before you will be through?" asked Patterson.

"In just a few minutes. Why?"

"I thought we might stop at the drugstore and get a Coke."

Sam finished his work, locked his desk, and turned out the lights. The two men went down the dark stairs together and Sam pulled the front door closed behind him and tested it to see if the lock had engaged.

When they entered the drugstore, Pat suggested that they sit in a booth. After they had ordered the drinks, Sam asked Patterson, "What's on your mind?"

"What makes you think there is something on my mind?"

"You never remain long after the lodge meetings and asking me to come in here and have a drink gave me the idea."

"As a matter of fact, there is. What do you know about Spalding?"

"Not too much. He says he is a student at Columbia University and is here on some sort of a grant to make a study of the life of the average Negro in the South. I figured one of those 'do-gooder' organizations is furnishing the money. Why do you ask?"

"Has he ever said anything to you about the Communist Party?"

"No, why?"

"I have an idea that he is a communist organizer and is planning to organize a cell here."

"He could do that all right. He is a good organizer. He has been most helpful to me in organizing new lodges for the Citizens of the Sun. In fact, he is working on a new one tonight."

"And he has never said anything to you that would suggest he was a member of the Communist Party?"

"Not directly. Once he said something about being surprised that Negroes had taken no interest in communism."

"What is his position with the Citizens of the Sun?"

"Officially, he has none. Unofficially, he has helped in organization work. He says it gives him a good opportunity to go into the homes of Negroes and see how they really live. I had an idea that his grant was just enough to support him for one year. That is all most of them amount to. I figured that he would be leaving soon and take the remainder of his year to write his report or thesis or whatever it is he has to write. That is, if he is supposed to write anything."

"Is he not in a position to take over the Citizens of the Sun and make a communist organization out of it or use it for the Communist Party?"

"I certainly wouldn't allow him to take over what I have built up. On the other hand, I might go along with him on some of the things he wants if it should coincide with some of the things I want."

"I have not had any fear so far as you are concerned. I have an idea you will overcome your bitterness in time and more or less forget your grudge against the white people."

"I'll never do that."

"You can't hold a grudge against hundreds of millions of people, especially since they control the economic and social conditions of the world."

"The white people are in the minority in the world. The colored races outnumber them several times over. It is only through their grasping qualities and control of most of the natural resources of the world that they have done what they have."

"They didn't have control of the resources originally. They figured out a way to use them and did it. It is the fault of the colored races that they didn't use them first."

"Conditions are changing. All over the world the colored races are awakening to what has been done to them and are going to do something about it. They will no longer be exploited."

"And you said Spalding has never talked communism to you?"

"That's right."

"What you are saying sounds like communist propaganda."

"That may be, but that is only because the things I have just said happened to be the truth, and they are the truth whether spoken by me or some communist leader."

"The main reason I wanted to speak to you about this matter is this. You are not going to get anywhere with communism with the southern Negro."

"How do you know so much about the southern Negro?"

"Mainly, because I am one. The second reason is that I am preparing myself to be the spiritual leader of a group of them, and I have been studying them. Maybe not with the intensiveness of Spalding, but in a very great degree. I don't believe the southern Negro will fall for the communist line. The southern Negro is inherently conservative and will not go for anything that is too new and different."

"He has never had a chance to do anything new and different."

"No, and he has not been educated to grasp new and different ideas. If that is what you are planning on, you are headed for trouble."

"I'll tell you now. This is the first time communism has ever been mentioned to me. I'll tell you this further. You have given me some food for thought. There may be something in communism after all and I may get a lot of help from the Communist Party."

"What may seemingly be help will only be an assist on the road to destruction. And I'll tell you this. If I ever see any indication of communism in the Citizens of the Sun, I'll take steps to stop it."

"Why don't you want the Negroes conditions to be bettered?"

"I want it bettered, but it can't be done through force. Force begets force, and force is always evil."

"Force is something that even the white man understands."

"I hope you are not naive enough to believe you could bring about a revolution so that the Negro would have the controlling voice."

"The white man could be forced to terms."

"The white man would meet the Negro's force with an even greater force, and since the Negro is overwhelmingly out-numbered in this country and there is no organization of the colored people outside of this country that would come to their aid, such a scheme could not and would not succeed."

"There is Russia."

"Don't depend on their help. You might find you are leaning on a frail reed. Forget force. There are two ways in which you can accomplish what you desire."

"What are they?"

"One is the law of the land. We are citizens and have equal rights and protection under the laws."

"Try and get it, especially in the South."

"It can and is being done. The white people cannot set aside their own laws insofar as the Negro is concerned without setting them aside for themselves. The Negro needs to contribute from his means to employ the best legal talent possible to enforce his rights within the law. He may lose time and time again, but eventually the right decision will prevail. There is an organization which has done much along this line."

"The white man will always interpret the laws to suit himself. Hasn't the Supreme Court ruled that schools can be separate as long as the Negroes have equal facilities and teachers, and can anyone claim that Negroes have equal facilities?"

"Yes, but that is not a good law, and sooner or later, that ruling must be set aside."

"You can't expect anything from the white people."

"Don't forget, it was the white people who set us free."

"Yes, and it was the white people who made us slaves in the first place and it wasn't through any love that they had for the Negro that made them set us free. There were a few religious fanatics who bellowed long and loud, but basically, it was because paid labor in the North could not compete against the free labor in the South."

"Suppose tomorrow that all segregation barriers were broken down and thrown away. Would your life be greatly different from what it is now? I am afraid it wouldn't be."

"You mean it wouldn't be different if I could go into any restaurant I wanted to and be served, take any seat I wanted to in a public transportation system I had paid for, go to any school I might choose, go to any public park, or any other public place?"

"On the surface, it would be. For a while you might enjoy a new found freedom, but in a little while, you would run up against something that would cause you more anguish than you could now experience, and that is discrimination."

"Discrimination?"

"Yes. And there would be nothing you could do about it. All the laws in the world couldn't stop it. You might walk into that restaurant and take your seat. The white waiter might even pull out your chair for you and shove it under you as you sat down. He would hand you a menu and walk off presumably to attend to duties elsewhere and those duties would take a very long time. Eventually, he would return and take your order. After another long wait, your food would be brought to you. The meat would be tough and stringy, the vegetables watery, and all of it cold.

293

If you protested about the service or food, you would be met with bland apologies and excuses. And what would be the result? The next time you wanted to eat at a restaurant, you would go to a restaurant where Negroes were welcomed. And what sort of restaurant would that be? Either an all Negro restaurant which no white person patronized where you probably would get good food and good service but you would be in a Negro world; or a restaurant where both races were served but where there would be a class of white people that would look down upon you."

"Why should I?"

"Because they would not be the same class of white people you would find in the better restaurant. Or take, for instance, the matter of schools. Suppose your children should go to a school where the white children are in the majority?"

"Why not the Negroes in the majority?"

"Because the whites will not go to a school where they will be in the minority. They will leave it and go to a school where the whites are in the majority."

"Why couldn't laws be passed to require them to go to the nearest school?"

"How can you ask that the laws which now restrict Negroes in school attendance be set aside so far as the Negro is concerned and enforced as to the white child? You can't have your cake and eat it too."

"What would happen?"

"Your child would get the same instruction as the white child but suppose your child did not learn so easily as the white children? The answer would be obvious to the white children. It would be because he is a Negro. Or suppose a white child has a party and invites all the white classmates. Your child is not invited. He is hurt. He asks why he wasn't invited. What are you going to tell him? Are you going to tell him that he wasn't invited because he is a Negro? If you don't tell him then, sooner or later he will learn the reason. How is he going to feel when he has been discriminated against because he is a Negro. Discrimination can hurt worse that segregation ever can."

"Not if the Negro is big enough to take it."

"Very few people are big enough to take social discrimination. His only refuge is with his own kind, and then you have segregation again."

"But will there always be discrimination?"

"Yes. Except in a few isolated cases. If you don't think there will be discrimination, ask a Jew. He will tell you it exists."

"But if the courts can declare that segregation is illegal, why can't the courts declare discrimination is illegal?"

"Because discrimination does not involve a legal right; there is nothing tangible or definite about it. Take the case of the restaurant. How can you prove that the delays were deliberate, that there was no way to prevent the food from becoming cold or that the meat was not the same served to other customers? Discrimination is indefinite but effective, and that is what makes it so maddening. It cannot be fought. It's like shadow boxing. You can wear yourself out but you can never land a punch. Between discrimination and segregation, I will take segregation. Under segregation, the rules are clear and defined. Your area is set aside. Within that area, you are free to move about as you please. If you recognize the bounds and limitations, you can live as an individual. It is only when you pass the bounds of segregation that you are made to realize that you are a Negro. With discrimination, you have the bounds and limitations, but you can't see them so you can avoid them. It is as if you were in one of those houses of mirrors in amusement parks. You think you have an open passageway when suddenly you walk into a solid wall. Just when you think you are moving freely as an individual, you are brought up suddenly by the invisible wall of discrimination, and there is nothing you can do but turn away and try to find another way?"

"What is your other way?"

"It is so simple that I am afraid to tell you lest you laugh."

"Then give me a laugh."

"Love. The Man of Galilee gave us the answer almost two thousand years ago. 'Love those who despitefully use you. Love your enemies. Love your neighbor as yourself. Turn the other cheek. God is Love.' It is a workable formula if men would only try it."

"It is too pitiful to garner a laugh," replied Sam and he did not laugh. "Try to apply that rule and what will you get? More exploitation. More insults. More degradation. A continuation of the bars between the races."

"You are wrong. Just as wrong as you can be. Love can overcome all things. Love will break down the barriers of segregation and remove discrimination."

"But how long will it take? Centuries?"

"I don't know, maybe, but I doubt it. Perhaps only a generation or two; maybe longer. I don't know. But time is not an element. It is the final result that counts. Meanwhile, the Negro will be happy. Love brings happiness; hatred brings unhappiness."

"That sounds good. You should enlarge on that theme. It would make a good sermon. That would sound all right from a pulpit, but like so many things said in a pulpit, they won't apply in everyday life."

"They will apply. You can shatter your skull beating it against barriers you can't hammer down. If you take up the sword, you will die by the sword. You can go into the courts and break down all the barriers of segregation, but in the end, you will find that you have won a hollow victory. Meanwhile, you will live a miserable life. I will follow my course and I know I will be happy."

"I wonder."

"I think so. Let me give you an illustration. I know of no southern church which bars Negroes."

"Some of them broke away from the northern churches of the same denomination because of the slavery issue."

"That is true but they didn't bar Negroes from church membership. In fact, most of the churches had Negro members. That was particularly true in the rural and suburban churches. I'll admit that most of the time, the churches had balconies to which the Negroes were restricted, but they were members just the same. After the Civil War, what happened? The Negroes left the white churches and formed their own and in a comparatively few years since the war, they have had a remarkable growth in membership and assets. Some of the Negro churches maintain printing plants that are among the finest in the country. Why did they do it? Because they could never become leaders, could never assume places of responsibilities in the white churches; so they preferred their own churches, poor and miserable though they might be, with pastors who could scarcely read and write, and in doing it, they achieved a measure of happiness and a justifiable pride in their accomplishment."

"Yet, the Negro and his religion has been the source of much amusement among the white people."

"That is true to some extent, but it has not stopped the growth of Negro churches nor restricted the religious experiences of the individual Negro."

"Religion is so much bilge. To that extent, I will go along with the communist. It has been a narcotic which the ruling classes have dished out to the exploited masses to dull their sense of pain. In substance, they have said to the Negro, 'It is true you have it hard now. Yours is a life of hard work, with little or no rest and very little pleasure; but the time will come when all this will be changed. Then you will have a high backed canvas seat on the front row and all those who lord over you now will have to look up to you. You may be hungry now but in time to come there will be pie in the sky for you.' No, I can't go along with that."

"You haven't kept up with the changing concepts of religion. That 'pie in the sky' deal is almost a thing of the past. Religion of today is for the lives of today. It teaches people to live in the present as well as to hope for the future."

"When you begin to talk about the present, you begin to make sense," said Sam. "I want something done in the present but not in vain efforts to attain some high moral or ethical goal. The white man has never let ethics or morals stand in his way of attaining what he wanted. The first explorers of this continent came with armies led by the Cross of Christ, yet they killed and robbed many Indians and exploited the remainder. Later, they came in great waves and took the land away from the Indians and reduced them to a state worse than slavery. When they found that the

Indians would not work as slaves, they brought our ancestors over from Africa to do their hard work. Then, when they filled their pockets with gold they made selling our bodies, they began to pray over our souls. The white man got what he wanted by action and the Negro should get what he wants by the same course."

"But you are outnumbered and your way will lead to destruction, not only to you but to many innocent people both black and white."

"It will not be done boldly and publicly. It will be done through economic pressure, by the withholding of badly needed labor, by sabotage of the white man's most vital efforts."

"And you say that you haven't been talking to Spalding about communism?"

"That is correct."

"You have picked up a lot of it along the line somewhere."

"Maybe my ideas and communism are the common result of things along the same lines."

"Remember this. Though you are a Negro, you are an American first and in spite of some injustices directed towards you because of the color of your skin, nowhere in the world does a person of your race have as much freedom and as many opportunities to better himself and his family as you do."

"I can't see that."

"'There are none so blind as those who will not see.' Come on. It is getting late. I've got to get to bed. I have a hard day tomorrow."

Chapter 47

In spite of the thoughts he had expressed at the time, in the course of the next few days, Sam thought a lot about the conversation with Patterson. In spite of the phenomenal growth of the Citizens of the Sun, he realized he was getting nowhere with it because the matter of education was slow and tedious. It would take more than a lifetime to get what he wanted by this method and he did not have that much time to spare. He wanted results quicker. If Spalding was really a communist organizer, why hadn't he said something that would suggest that role? So far as he could remember, Spalding had never said anything that would suggest he was other than what he said he was. Spalding asked him about the use of the citizen in the name of the organization and coupled it with the French Revolution, but that could have been nothing more than academic interest. He must have a talk with Spalding and he would like to have a talk with Max Moskovitz.

He hadn't seen Max for several years. The Moskovitz's still ran the store and in spite of the fact that they lived on the same lot, they really lived in different worlds. While Sam had been busy at school, he had heard that Max had finished his academic work and was in medical school. With a start, he realized that even if little Negro and Jew boys played together, when they grew up, they didn't maintain their contacts with each other.

The next Sunday morning, after his father and mother had gone to church, Sam crossed the back yard and knocked on the rear door of the Moskovitz's house. The door was opened by Mrs. Moskovitz.

"It's Sammy Martin. My how you have grown up. You wanted something from the store, maybe?" she asked.

"No, I would like to see Max," he replied and the thought flashed into his mind that if he were true to his upbringing and the southern tradition, he would have asked for "Mister" Max since Max was now old enough to be referred to by that title.

"He just got up. He studies so hard. Wait a minute and I'll call him. Won't you come in?" she asked hesitantly.

"No, I'll wait here."

"Max, Sammy Martin from out in the back wants to see you," she called into the house.

In a minute or so, Max appeared.

"Hello, Sam, don't tell me you are being chased again."

"Not this time. I would like to talk to you for a few minutes. Can you spare the time?"

"Gladly. Shall we sit here on the steps?"

"If you don't mind."

"Something on you mind?"

"Yes. I have been doing a lot of thinking about race relationships during the past few months. Particularly, since what happened to my brother."

"Yes. I am sorry about that. I wish that there was something I could do."

"You did all you could. Your mother sent some food to our house at the time. I am sure Mama has thanked your mother."

"Think nothing of it."

"You know, the Negroes are giving serious thought to desegregation. Some think that it can be accomplished within the framework of the laws of the country. That may be possible. I don't know. But in a discussion the other night, the question arose about what would happen if desegregation was accomplished. If discrimination would not be worse that segregation. Someone mentioned that Jews are discriminated against and I thought I would presume upon our years of acquaintance to ask you about it. I don't mean to pry and I don't want to hurt anyone's feelings, but since you are the only Jew I know, I thought I would ask you. What about it?"

Max thought for a minute before he replied.

"My people have experienced both, you know?"

"I didn't know that."

"Yes. For centuries, we were segregated into areas known as ghettos in the cities of Europe. We were segregated even more that the Negroes in the United States. We could not own land, we could not enter any of the professions, we could not hold public office; there were certain public places to which we were forbidden; we had to wear a distinctive costume; we were subject to special taxes; and at all times, it was impressed upon us that we were different. We were cursed and hated and subjected to all sorts of indignities. At times, many of my people were destroyed by mob violence known in recent years as pogroms."

"All that is news to me."

"You evidently have not been a deep student of history."

"I'm afraid history has been one of my weaker subjects."

"Here in America, we have not had segregation. We have had the equal protection of the laws. Only occasionally have we been persecuted but not to any great degree. The Ku Klux Klan of a few years ago is an example. We did have the protection of the laws and except for some economic boycotts, it didn't amount to much. But discrimination--yes. We are different; chiefly, because of our religion. We are not Christians while most people in this country are. Many of the people are immigrants of the past few decades such as my mother and father. To others, we seem to have strange ways. We have dietary rules that many Jews observe. We work hard and we save our money; we try to better ourselves, and people do not like us for all these things. Since we are white, we can't be subjected to the segregation laws such as apply to your race, but we do face discrimination. Segregation is bad although I have not experienced it, but my mother and father have told me about it. But discrimination I know. I have experienced it all my life."

"In what way?"

"By being made conscious of my Jewishness. Haven't you heard the ditty: 'Jew baby, Jew baby, how you sell your sox'?", and Sam nodded his head. "I think I must have heard it the very first day I attended school. I didn't know what it meant. In fact, I don't know what it means now, if it has any meaning, but somehow I knew it wasn't nice."

"I attended the public schools for twelve years," continued Max. "There are Gentiles with whom I went all the way through school. Never once was I ever invited to the home of one of them. I have known some Gentile girls toward whom I was attracted, but I never dared ask one of them for a date. Had I done so, I probably would have been insulted for my presumption and I might have been waylaid and beaten by some of her friends. I have to walk the narrow path of restrained friendliness."

"I am now attending a great university. It is noted for its liberal attitude. Although it can't be proven and the university authorities deny it, it is said that they will take only a certain number of Jewish students. There are some colleges that openly limit the number of Jewish students and there are some private schools of higher learning that won't take Jews at all. If I should want to join a fraternity, which I can't afford, my choice is restricted. I cannot expect, nor would I receive, a bid from any except the two Jewish fraternities. I've never seen them, but they tell me that there are many hotels, principally at resorts, that display a sign that reads: 'Restricted Clientele' and that means 'No Jews'."

"Suppose a Jew should attempt to register at a hotel?"

"They would ask him if he had a reservation and when he replied that he did not, they would tell him that they were sorry but there were no vacancies."

"Suppose he had written and made a reservation?"

"If his name was distinctively Jewish, he would never get the reservation. If he had an Anglo-Saxon name, and many Jews have adopted them, and they could tell he was Jewish when he presented himself, they would tell him that they were sorry but there had been some mix-up and his reservation had been lost or misplaced and they had no vacancies. If he succeeded in getting in, he would by indifferent service and other subtle ways be made to feel unwelcome."

"I didn't realize those things were being done."

"They are. Now, you are interested from the standpoint of your race. There the discrimination will be easier. We Jews are white. The color of your skin is a dead giveaway. No matter how cultured or how refined you may become, there is always the skin which can't be disguised.

If you get rid of segregation, then you must face discrimination. And the sad fact of it is that you never know when it is going to face you."

"Isn't there any way of combating it?"

"Yes, and I think I have told you this before. 'Tell it not in Gath, publish it not in the streets of Askelon'."

"I believe that's from the Bible."

"It is and it is almost the first passage from the Bible I knew. Now matter how much it hurts, never let them know. And it's a good rule to follow, whether it's segregation or discrimination."

"Are you not studying medicine?"

"Yes."

"How do you expect to be successful if you are going to be discriminated against because you are a Jew? Are there enough Jews to give you and the other Jewish doctors all the business you can handle?"

"I am not only studying medicine, but I am going into a specialized field. I am going to be a surgeon. I expect to get a good portion of my patients from Gentiles. I expect to be such a good surgeon that people will demand my services. They will forget I am a Jew and will only remember that I am the man they will want to perform their operations."

"Suppose you don't become that good? Suppose you don't build up the practice you anticipate?"

"I will have a practice of some kind--but, it will never be known in Gath, nor will the people in Askelon read about it."

"Discrimination is so unfair. Why does it exist?"

"Our people have been asking that question for almost two thousand years. In our case, we have assumed that it stems from religious differences. That can't be true in your case for your people have adopted the religion of those who discriminate against you. Basically, it is probably ignorance or fear or a combination of both. In our case, it is a difference in religion; in your case, it is a difference in the color of the skin. There are other differences but these are the fundamental ones. There are several possible ways in which discrimination might be overcome. One is education. All people could attain such a high level of education that they would realize that there is no real reason for discrimination. The other is love. Men might develop such a feeling of love for others that the real or imagined differences would be overcome. This seems rather hopeless, for the very people in this country who practice discrimination profess to believe in the teachings of the Man who taught them that 'God is Love'."

"You sound like a friend of mine who is studying for the ministry. He says the only answer is Love. Love as exemplified by Jesus Christ. It's odd that you two would say practically the same thing."

"Maybe it is not so odd after all. You must remember that Jesus was a Jew, and from what I know of Him, he was a very devout Jew. He did not teach a thing that had not been taught in our homes and our synagogues for centuries. 'Thou shalt love the Lord thy God with all thy heart, with all thy soul, and with all thy might'. I understand it was on this premise that Jesus based all his teachings."

"It looks like Love is out then. If you and Christians have been teaching the same thing for centuries and there is still the intense feeling which maintains discrimination, it looks as if that answer is a lost cause."

"It may be. I don't know. I told you my answers were more or less theoretical because we do not have that degree of education and love we should have. The only definite answer I can give, and it is one you need to live with in the present, not in some Utopian future, and that is live with conditions as you find them, make the best of it, and if it hurts, don't let them know."

"Not a very happy prospect."

"It can be. You can live in a little world of your own. Most of us do anyway, whether we are white or black or Jew or Gentile. We have our families, we have our friends, we have our work, we have our church. First and last, we will know only a few hundred people in a lifetime and not more than a dozen or so intimately. Why get excited about what is happening to millions of other people when we can do little or nothing about it? The best help we can give them is to live our own lives so that they are worth most to us. If we face segregation, if we face discrimination, conform to it for the moment, withdraw into your own world as quickly as possible and don't let it spoil your life."

"That may be all right for you but I want to do something about it. I want to fight. I want to get some action."

"Go to it, but I am afraid you are asking for trouble and will accomplish little."

"At least, I will have fought the fight."

"The pages of history are full of martyrs and no doubt there are thousands of others whose names have been forgotten."

"What's the use of living a life of misery; of trying to conform when you can't conform?"

"All people live by rules. I doubt if there is anyone who is absolutely free. It is just a question of how many rules you are going to live by. Sometimes, people can be happy in living by rules."

"What do you mean?"

"My people are orthodox. That may not mean anything to you."

"It doesn't."

"It means they live according to the ancient laws and customs of the Jewish people. Meat and dairy products can't be served at the same meal. The dishes can't be used for two meals in succession. No meats can be eaten unless the animal has been killed after an inspection by an official of the synagogue and it must be killed in a certain way so that the blood is certain to drain from it. There are many rules about cleanliness, about prayers, and about religious observances. To a person not familiar with them, they seem to be rules that limit and restrain, yet my mother and father have been happy in observing them. I don't observe them, but I will never let them know that I don't. In not observing them, I am not certain I will be any happier than they have been."

"But they are rules of a religion."

"Not so much religion as a way of life."

"At least they are at liberty to quit them anytime they want to."

"They couldn't quit. They would die first. We live in this world as physical beings but our real living in this world is in our minds. We create the world in which we live by our concepts of it. You happen to be a Negro in the southern part of the United States of America. You don't like it. Suppose you had been born a Cockney in England? I don't know much about England, but I understand the social position of the Cockney is not very high. Would you want to revolutionize the social conditions of England or would you do as the Cockneys do, accept your social position as a matter of course?"

"I could leave England."

"You can leave America."

"But I don't want to leave. This is my home."

"Then why don't you enjoy it as it is, as you have found it. Don't try to make it over to suit your own ideas. You can't make it over and will only succeed in making yourself unhappy in your efforts. Whatever you do may have some effect, but it will be so small that you can't see it in your lifetime. Maybe, in a thousand years, maybe in five hundred years, maybe even sooner, there will be no blacks in this country. They will have become so completely amalgamated just as the Saxons and the Normans became one to make the English of today but you are not going to live long enough to see it. If I were you, I would do just as my people have done for centuries; enjoy the present as best you may. When things happen that hurt, 'Tell it not in Gath' and retreat into your own little happiness."

"It is something to think about but I am afraid I can't see it your way. Thanks for the talk."

"I am glad you came by. Good-bye now."

The matter of discrimination toward Jews did not appear important to Sam as his thoughts reverted to the conversation with Max, during the next few days. Basically, the attitude of the non-Jews towards the Jews was one of religion and was the dying aftermath of the intense religious fervor of the Dark Ages, Sam decided. At least, the religion of the Jews was their own. The Negro did not have even this consolation. Whatever religion the Negro had was given to him by the white man as a sort of 'hand me down'.

306

He had always known that Jews were considered different from other people because of their refusal to accept Christ as their Savior but that had never particularly impressed him because he had never paid much attention to religion. In fact, he had come to accept the fervor of the average Negro toward religion as one of the factors that hindered the development of the race.

That religious difference could extend to social discrimination was something of a surprise to him, and he wondered just how many points could be advanced and just how far they could extend as a basis of social discrimination. He wondered if the ideal of the communists of a classless society was really possible anywhere except among the most primitive people. He knew vaguely that there was a caste system in India with its great number of "untouchables" and that in most parts of the world that was considered backward. There was an upper ruling class, usually based on wealth or power with the vast majority of the people composing a lower class, who for the most part, existed on a subsistence level. He knew in a general way that in the countries of Europe there existed a lower class known as peasants who, from what he knew of them, more or less corresponded to the place of the Negro in the United States. Even in the democracies, there were class distinctions and in some of them, such as England, the distinctions were almost as hidebound as the caste system of India, so that it was difficult for a person of a lower class to rise to a higher class. Practically all of these distinctions were based on birth, wealth, or tradition and not on color. It was only when the whites and blacks came in conflict that the difference of skin color became the distinguishing factor.

There must be an answer, and since he had set himself the task of trying to find it, he would continue on the course he had set for himself. In the long run, his efforts must contribute something toward it. At least, in some way and in some measure, he would exact some of the revenge due him for what the white people had done to him and to his family.

Chapter 48

He kept in mind what Patterson had suggested to him about Spalding. In his conversations with Spalding, he tried to detect some indication of the northern Negro's political ideas but he never found anything that aroused his suspicions. Spalding seemed to be only what he represented himself to be, a student on a grant studying the home life and living conditions of the Negro in an average southern city.

As a rule, when Spalding organized a new lodge of the Citizens of the Sun, Sam was always notified of the first investiture service so he could be present and most of the time he conferred the first degree. He got into the habit of dropping into some of the lodges and paid particular attention to the orientation periods but he found nothing to indicate that Spalding had introduced anything communistic into them. He heard nothing more than what he had outlined in the guides.

He had just about made up his mind that Patterson was entirely wrong in his suspicions when one day Spalding came into the office.

"What are you getting out of this Citizens of the Sun business?" he asked.

"What do you mean? I thought we had discussed that once before?"

"Just what I said. What are you getting out of it? This thing has the potential for a money-making business. All you have to do is to put on a small tax per member, say fifty cents or a dollar a year, and with the sale of the rituals, literature, and other paraphernalia, you could really make some jack out of it."

"I am not interested in making money out of it. I have another purpose in mind."

"Yes, I know, but frankly, that is too vague, too indefinite, and too uncertain of realization. If you don't want to make the money out of the members, there is another way you can profit personally and at the same time, attain your objectives."

"What is that?"

"By affiliation with another group that is more powerful and has the money to operate with."

"What group?"

"The Communist Party."

"The Communist Party?"

"Yes. Your aims are not so far apart. The Communist Party aims to destroy the capitalist class; your plan is to destroy the ruling white class and the two are practically one and the same. The party and your organization could be mutually helpful. It could be handled so that there would never be any known connection between the two. Your organization could be used to spread the party propaganda and those receiving it would not realize it until they were indoctrinated with the principles."

"Are you a member of the Communist Party?"

"Need that question be answered now? I'll tell you this. Here is ten thousand dollars," and Spalding reached into his inside coat pocket, brought out an envelope, and handed it to Sam. "That will be your annual salary."

"What will I have to do to earn it."

"Nothing more than you are doing now. We will arrange things so that you and I can get small salaries out of the Citizens of the Sun so we can have an explanation for how we live. I will continue to organize new lodges, and we will gradually, from time to time, change the ritual and the material furnished for the orientation periods to conform to the party principles."

"Is that all that is required of me?"

"That is all."

"Let me think about it for a few days," and Sam handed the money back to Spalding.

"You keep it. You can give it back if you change your mind. Remember, you have everything to gain and nothing to lose." admonished Spalding as he got up to leave.

So Patterson was right, mused Sam after Spalding had left. I wonder how he knew? Did Patterson have connections he didn't know about? If Patterson knew, how many other people knew about Spalding? He could be letting himself in for some serious trouble. On the other hand, he could allow Spalding to go ahead with his ideas, then if anything did happen, he could always say that Spalding had wormed himself into the Citizens of the Sun and had directed it along communist lines without his knowledge. It could be a case of eating his cake and having it too. The communist had been waging war on the ruling classes for years and probably had definite programs worked out. What difference would it make to him if his aims were carried out through his own efforts or through the efforts of a larger and better organized group?"

At the same time, he could make good money for himself. Ten thousand dollars was a lot of money, even if he never got any more. There was the promise of that much a year, plus what he could make out of the Citizens of the Sun. It was an opportunity too good to pass up. He would line up with Spalding and the communist.

The next day, Spalding came into his office.

"Well, what is the verdict?" he asked.

"How do you propose to work it?" asked Sam.

"I think the first thing we will do is to re-write the material for the orientation periods. We must first inculcate the members with the ideology of the Communist Party. Then, we can carefully select the members we think have become susceptible and institute another degree. We can make it appear that only those who have met certain requirements can petition for this degree without you letting it be known just what the requirements are. That degree will be full membership in the Communist Party."

"Do you think it will work?"

"It is bound to work. Those who receive the Party Degree will be bound to absolute secrecy. The first three degrees will merely be the field from which our recruits will come. With the backing of the money from the party, in a few months, a year or so at the most, we can spread this organization throughout the South. We can make it a powerful force in the economic and political life of the region and when the time comes, we will have the nucleus for the revolution."

"Revolution?"

"Yes. That is the aim of the party. Revolution in all countries and the establishment of the dictatorship of the proletariat. Communism is the only answer to the ills of the world. Under communism, each shall be rewarded as he deserves and shall give according to his talents. In a classless society, all economic struggles are eliminated, and all share equally in the means of production."

"Yes, I have heard those things, but I never had much faith in them. I am not interested in any of those aspects, except that of the classless society."

"It has its appeals in many forms. Suit yourself. What is your answer?"

"I'll go along with you."

"Good. We'll get started immediately."

The changed scripts for the orientation periods apparently made no impression on the members of the Citizens of the Sun. Sam had figured Patterson would be the first to say something about them and had mentally debated with himself how he would handle the situation. He decided he would allow the tenor of Patterson's complaint to set the pattern for his reply. He attended several lodge meetings when Patterson was present and on several occasions during the orientation periods, he caught Patterson looking at him but not at any time during the meetings or the social periods afterwards did the theology student ever have anything to say more than the usual pleasantries.

Sam had about decided that the communist tinge would have to be heightened by a fresh infusion for it to be effective when the first objection came from a most unexpected quarter. Jumbo came early to the regular weekly meeting of the parent lodge and went into Sam's office.

"What about dem changes in de teaching part?" he asked Sam.

"What are you referring to?"

"Dat's what I asked. Hit don' sound jist rite to me."

"Have you said anything to anybody about them?"

"I ast Pat if he knew ennything about 'em, and he said he didn't."

"Did you say something to him or did he say something to you first?"

"I said sumpin' to him. He didn' have much to say. He seemed kinda puzzled like. He said he'd noticed 'em, but he didn' know nothin' about 'em, but iffen he found out he would let me know. I don' like 'em, but dat ain't important. I don' think de white folks is goin' like 'em."

"What have the white folks got to do with it?"

"Dis is de white folks country, en I have noticed dat whut dey don' like, dey usually don' put up wid. Now dat stuff about changing de guvenment, dat don' sound so good to me."

"Don't we change the government every four years when we elect a president?"

"Dat don' say anything' about enny elections. 'Sides, we don' change de guvenment. We jes' changes de mens whut runs hit. De guvenment goes on jist de same."

"Don't you think it's time that the government should be changed, and people be given better opportunities to improve themselves than they have now?"

"Not by no niggers. Now if de white folks wants to change it, dat's dey business. Ez fur as I'se concerned, ebberthing's all rat lak dey is. I'se got a job, I eats regular, and I has a good time. You start messing things up, dey ain't no telling what will happen."

"You don't have the proper ideas of what we hope for."

"All I know is dat de white folks ain't goin' to lak hit, and when niggers start doin' sumpin dat de white folks don' lak, de niggers get de wurst of hit."

"I wish you wouldn't say nigger. Say Negro. You are not a nigger; you are a Negro."

"To Negroes, I may be a Negro, but to white folks, I'se jes' a nigger, and I'se found out I gits along best wid de white folks so long as I'se a nigger."

"That is not the right attitude. So long as you think of yourself as a nigger, you will always be a nigger."

"I'se been a nigger all my life and as fur as I'se concerned, I'll die a nigger. I don' know too much but frum what I do know, I'd druther be a nigger in the United States dan a Negro ennywhars else in de world."

"What did Pat say when you spoke to him about the changes?"

"He jist said he didn' like 'em but not to say ennything to ennybody; dat things would work deyself out all rat."

"That is pretty good advice. Have you said anything to anyone else?"

"Nope. I made up my mind that I'd speak to you. I don' lak de way things are going. If I don' lak hit, I'll jes' drap out o' de lodge, dat's all."

"Maybe you would be happier if you did drop out."

"I jist don' wat to git in no trouble, dat's all."

The fact that Patterson had noticed the changes and had said nothing to him about them caused Sam some worry. He said something about it to Spalding.

"I wouldn't worry about it," advised Spalding. "You see, we are beginning to separate the sheep from the goats. Let Jumbo drop out. I don't think Patterson is particularly concerned one way or the other. He will soon finish school and probably will go off somewhere to preach.

We can expect things like this occasionally. We will just have to use our heads and not try to make an issue out of everything that comes up."

A few days later, Sam met Patterson on the street.

"What did you tell Jumbo about the changes we have made in some of the lodge material?" he asked Patterson.

"I am glad you said we," replied Patterson. "That saves me asking you a question."

"I didn't mean it exactly as you have taken it. That is something of an editorial 'we.' But that is not answering my question."

"I don't know that you are entitled to an answer but I will give it to you just the same. He asked me about the changes. I told him not to say anything about them. I had already noticed them and was waiting to see if anyone else had. Since Jumbo had noticed them and I doubt if there is anyone in any of the lodges who knows less about government and economics than he, I have summed that others had although no one else has mentioned it to me."

"Why haven't you asked around? You seemed to be interested."

"That wouldn't be fair."

"What wouldn't be fair?"

"My calling attention to the situation. If I don't say anything, and no one else says anything, the whole matter might blow over. I see no point in stirring up trouble."

"But it is not going to blow over. I am going to see to that."

"Then you have definitely lined up with Spalding and the Communist Party?"

"I don't like it being stated that way but it is more or less the truth. I can get more help from them to aid me with my aims than I could hope to accomplish by myself in years."

"I think that you are riding for a fall. Omitting for the moment what the authorities might do, I have made up my mind not to say or do anything about the matter, at least until I think I have to do something, because I have faith in the Negro."

"What do you mean by 'faith in the Negro'?"

"I think the average Negro is a patriotic American citizen. I don't think he can be led astray by communist propaganda."

"What has he got to be patriotic about? The moment he is born and for all of his life, he is a second rate citizen. Communism make no distinction between classes or races. Under communism, he will be a first class citizen or rather on an equality with all other citizens."

"That is a delusion and I don't believe the Negro will fall for it. At least, I am going to wait and see, and I think I am right." and with that, Patterson turned and walked away.

After several more weeks, and no one else had said anything about the changes in the orientation programs, Sam was just about to decide that their efforts had been wasted. He mentioned their apparent lack of success to Spalding.

"That's all right. We don't have to move too fast. We must build up our ideas gradually. The changes will come almost imperceptibly."

315

Chapter 49

On September 1st, 1939, German troops invaded Poland and two days later, Great Britain and France declared war on Germany. American factories, in spite of the Neutrality Act, began making war materials for the Allies. On November 4th, the President of the United States signed a bill removing the arms embargo. Immediately, American factories began to accelerate the production of armaments for the war effort.

Spalding came to Sam one day.

"I have here a list of the factories in this city which are producing war material for the Allies," he said. "There are seven of them."

"All right. So what?" asked Sam.

"What do you mean--so what?"

"What is that to us?" asked Sam.

"Don't you see that this is just a capitalistic war? Why should we help England and France who have held millions of the colored peoples of the world in subjection for centuries. Are we going to allow them to continue that system?"

"I don't see that the Germans are any better. They got into the colony business late and lost what they had in the last war. England and France promised Hitler some colonies in an effort to avert war. Aren't the Germans boasting of their Aryan blood, and Hitler has said that the people of that blood are destined to be rulers of the world. I don't see any sense in jumping out of the frying pan into the fire."

"But you don't understand. Stalin and Hitler have an understanding. Russia and Germany will be the only two great nations left in the world and in time, Russia and the communist ideal will conquer Germany."

"How does all that have anything to do with us?"

"We can do our part by sabotaging the production of war supplies for the Allies."

"In what way?"

"There are scores of ways. A handful of sand in important bearings; fire; the alteration of instruments to throw them out of alignment; electric power outages; accidents that will tie up conveyor lines. There are plenty of ways. The first things we will have to do is to find out how many of our people are working in these factories. Then we will have to work on them to do the sabotaging."

"Did it ever occur to you that not many of our people would have jobs working with machinery?"

"The chances are, our people are holding the best jobs to do the work."

"In what way?"

"As porters. Nobody pays any attention to a porter, and they usually have access to the entire place. And nobody would ever suspect one of them."

"We have no record of the jobs held by our members."

"Suppose I have some cards printed. We will send them out with the announcement that we want to get information on the members so we will know just what their qualifications are in the event we will need to call on them for special lodge work and on committees. In addition to their home addresses, we can ask their church membership, schooling, place of employment and their duties there, hobbies, and so on. Nobody will ever suspect what we are doing."

"It won't hurt to have that information, in any event."

The cards were printed and distributed with instructions to all lodges to have each member fill out the card and turn it in as quickly as possible. Within a week, many of the cards had been returned. The first batch of cards showed that seventeen members of the lodges worked at five of the factories that Spalding had listed. Four worked as porters, three in maintenance, four as laborers on construction to additions to the plants, one as a garage worker, and the remainder worked on trucks either as drivers or helpers.

Spalding was enthusiastic over the information. He decided his best prospects were with the four porters and the three maintenance workers. He told Sam that he would immediately start learning all that there was to know about the seven men and armed with this knowledge, he would be in a good position to know whom to approach and just how that approach could best be made.

Sam recognized the inherent danger in what they were doing. He knew that if any of the men could be induced to commit sabotage and were caught, he would immediately tell who it was who had put him up to it. He didn't know just how far the law could go in connecting him with the crime, for a crime he was certain it would be. The destruction of property to change the course of a war in Europe was something he had not had in mind when he started the Citizens of the Sun. His objective was closer to home and was aimed at the people who continually heaped injustices and shame on the people of his race.

Up until now, the war in Europe had been more or less academic as far as he was concerned. Spalding's proposal had made it more real for him. He began to read all that there was in the city's two daily newspapers about the war. He went to the library and pored through back copies of the papers. He went through the files of several magazines. What he read, he didn't like.

The people they were undertaking to help had proclaimed through their leader that they, as a particular group of the white race, were superior to all other people and races; that they would impose their will upon all the other peoples of the world since they were so inferior that they were incapable of leadership. And when he read how Hitler had refused to make the awards to Jesse Owens after winning gold medals in his events at the Berlin Olympics in 1936, he decided that Spalding was leading them down a blind alley. He decided that he would not take any part in Spalding's plans and he would not allow Spalding to use the Citizens of the Sun for his purposes.

How to stop Spalding was the problem. Of course, he could report to the FBI what Spalding was planning, but at the same time he might be getting himself in trouble because he had cooperated with Spalding. Such a course might mean the breaking up of the Citizens of the Sun, and he didn't want that to happen. There was but one thing to do; he would have to handle Spalding himself and run the risk that Spalding hadn't so far entrenched himself in the organization that he could take it away from him.

After he had made his decision, several days passed before he saw Spalding. As each day passed, he sensed a small feeling of relief for he dreaded the showdown.

One night, about half an hour before the meeting of Number One Lodge, Spalding came into his office. He was in a happy frame of mind.

"I've got all the information I need," he exulted. "Out of all the men I've investigated, I think I have five I can depend on to a certainty. The next thing is to go to work on them."

"I don't think you had better do that." replied Sam.

"What do you mean?" demanded Spalding.

"I have done a lot of reading and studying. I don't like anything about your plans. It looks to me as if we are helping the Nazis."

"Certainly, we are. I hope you didn't have any doubt about that."

"Why should we help them? They have proclaimed themselves the master race. The colored people of the world have no place in their plans except as slaves."

"That is just a lot of talk. We are lined up with the greatest force in the world and at the proper time, the communist will take over. What Germany is doing today is just a weakening process for all of Europe that will make it easier for Russia when the time comes."

"Germany will become stronger instead of weaker. It will have all the people it is conquering to use as slaves to further build up the German power."

"What are you driving at anyway?"

"It is simply this. You are to stop what you are doing and give up your connections with the Citizens of the Sun."

C. Vernon Hines

"Oh, no. You have gone too far to turn back now. You are in this just as much as I am, and I am going to finish what I have started."

"No, you are not. You are going to quit and I suggest that you go back to New York immediately!"

Members had begun to arrive for the lodge meeting. When Sam and Spalding had unconsciously raised their voices, several men came to the door of the office. In the number were Patterson and Jumbo.

"Let me tell you something," said Spalding with deadly earnestness. "I haven't been working this thing alone. Where do you think the money came from that I gave you? I have been making constant reports on what I have been doing. I can't go back. I have to go through with what I started. The Communist Party does not tolerate failures. My life is at stake, and I don't intend to lose it for you or anyone else."

Patterson and Jumbo stepped into the room.

"I have heard part of what has been said, and Sam, I want to tell you that you are on the right track," Patterson said. "You can't get by with what you are planning," he said to Spalding.

"I can, and I will," declared Spalding.

"Let me tell you something, Mister," spoke up Jumbo. "I have had nothin' to do wid my folks bein' brought over hyar as slaves but if they hadn' a been, I'd be livin' in Africa today, an' I'm tellin' you, I'd rather live in America 'en enny place on earth. I may be a nigger, but I'm an American nigger. I'm free, and I'm proud of hit."

"You are just an ignorant laboring lout, interested only in a job that will give you a bare living. You don't know what you are talking about," declared Spalding, waving a hand with an air of dismissal.

"I know what I am talking about," said Patterson. "I am not just an ignorant nigger, and I know this; what Jumbo said is true. The Negro is a loyal American regardless of the conditions under which he lives, and if America should get into this war, which I hope it won't, the Negro will fight for it just the same as the white man."

"You are a damn fool. A sanctimonious damn fool, who is planning on living a life of ease while cramming the fables of religion down the gullets of other damn fools. I am telling all of you that I am going through with what I have started. I am taking over the Citizens of the Sun and I'm telling all of you to clear out," and with that, Spalding pulled a pistol from his pocket and backed up against the wall. "I'll give all of you one minute to clear out, and then I am going into that lodge room and take over."

"You are not going to take over because those people in there will not follow you," asserted Patterson. "They don't like biggetty Yankee Negroes telling them what they can or cannot do."

"We will see about that," and Spalding waved his gun suggestively.

Meanwhile, Jumbo who was nearest to Spalding and on his right, began to ease towards him.

Spalding noticed the movement and pointed his weapon towards Jumbo.

"No, you don't," he shouted. "Come one step closer and I'll shoot."

Spalding had turned partially away from Sam, and Sam started moving toward him. Spalding noticed that movement and turned and pointed the pistol towards Sam.

"No, you don't," he declared. "Besides, I'd like to shoot you anyway."

As he turned, Jumbo dived for Spalding's feet. The blow unbalanced Spalding who threw up his hands to catch himself. As he did so, Patterson grabbed the arm which held the gun and all three went down in a heap. There was a struggling mass for a minute or so, and then there was the report of a pistol, followed in a second or so by another. Patterson rolled to one side and Spalding the other while Jumbo came up off the floor with the pistol in his hand and handed it to Sam, who stood transfixed in his tracks.

The commotion had attracted all the lodge members to the door of the office but as the shots rang out, all of them, some sixty or more, broke for the stairs. It had been a chilly night, and Sam had made a roaring fire in the stove. In the rush for the door, several of the members were shoved against the stove and their screams of pain added to the pandemonium. Most of them thought shots were being fired into the crowd. The stove was eventually knocked over and the glowing coals were scattered across the floor. Some of the coals were knocked into the open door of a closest where there were mops and cleaning rags stored as well as a can of kerosene that was used to start fires in the stove. Immediately, the rags were ignited. In a few minutes, the closet was engulfed in flames.

Sam stood for a few seconds staring unseeingly at the pistol in his hand. Then he laid it down on the desk and dropped to one knee at the side of Patterson and felt for his pulse.

"I think he is still alive. Let's call an ambulance and get him to a hospital," and he stood up and reached for the telephone on the desk

"Forget callin' de ambulance," shouted Jumbo. "Dis place is on fire, an' we'll all burn effen we don' git outa hyar. How 'bout de udder one?"

Sam turned to Spalding. He felt for his pulse and then turned back one of his eyelids.

"If I am any judge, he's already dead. We have played the devil tonight, haven't we?"

"I'm tellin' you dis place is on fire. Effen we don' git out in a minnit or so we ain't goin' to git out at all. You git his feets, and I'll git his head and let's git goin'."

Sam became conscious of the fire. It was between them and the door and spreading rapidly. He picked up Patterson's feet as Jumbo grabbed him under his shoulders and they started out. The fire had become so intense, they had to skirt the walls to reach the head of the stairs, and they were almost stifled by the smoke. Just as they got to the stairs, the can of kerosene exploded and in a second or so, the entire lodge hall was seething in flames. Sam and Jumbo made their way down the stairs with their burden. Sam could hear the sirens; and as he and Jumbo stumbled to the foot of the stairs, they were met by the firemen.

"Is anyone else upstairs?" one of the firemen demanded.

"One more, but I think he is dead."

"Is there a back way?"

"No. No back way."

"Fleming, get your mask on and see if you can go up these stairs but don't take any chances. They say there is another one still up there. He might be still alive. Lay that fellow down. Johns, get the pulmotor and go to work on him. He looks like he is in bad shape."

As Sam and Jumbo laid Patterson on the sidewalk, another fireman dropped on one knee and started loosening Patterson's collar. He drew back his hand and looked at it.

"Hey. Captain," he yelled to the fireman who had been giving the orders. "A pulmotor is not going to do this man any good. He's been shot or stabbed. Look here," and he held up his blood-stained hand.

"I'll be damned. That's a matter for the police. They'll be here in a minute."

By this time, the firemen had driven the spectators back, most of whom were lodge members, and had several fire hoses playing on the flames. A police squad car drove up and two policemen jumped out.

The lead fireman motioned for them to come to him.

"That man has been shot or stabbed and they tell me there is another one upstairs. I suppose he was shot or stabbed. What was it?" he demanded of Sam.

"Shot," replied Sam.

"Go to the car and call an ambulance," one of the policemen told the other. "I'll take charge here. Who shot him?" he demanded.

"I don't know," replied Sam. "They were scuffling over a gun, and it went off twice. Each one must have been hit by a bullet."

"That is evident," replied the policeman, "unless one bullet went through both of them."

"De one upstairs had de pistol, and he pulled it on us," explained Jumbo. "Me and this one jumped him," pointing towards Patterson. "He grabbed his gun hand and all of us went to de flo'. De gun went off jist as I got my hand on hit and as I twisted hit to take hit away, it went off again. Both of dem drapped back and I come up wid de gun."

"Where is the pistol?" demanded the officer.

"I handed it him," and Jumbo pointed to Sam.

"I laid it on the desk when I started helping Jumbo bring him downstairs. It is still up there."

"You'll never get it now," declared the officer, glancing up the stairs.

By this time, the ambulance arrived. Patterson was placed on a stretcher and put in the ambulance which left with a low moan of its siren.

"All right, you two," said one of the policemen to Sam and Jumbo. "Get in the car, and let's go to the station."

At the police station, Sam and Jumbo were asked to tell what happened. Sam was as brief as possible about the Citizens of the Sun, explained that Spalding had planned to take the organization over and make it an adjunct of the Communist Party; that he had told Spalding that he would oppose Spalding's plan. Spalding then became excited, said that his life was at stake, and that he was going through with his plans. At that, he drew a pistol and held it first on one and then another and was holding it on Sam, threatening to kill him, when Patterson and Jumbo jumped him. In the struggle, the gun went off twice. In the rush to get out, the stove was knocked over and the place was set on fire. When he saw that Spalding was dead but Patterson was still alive, he and Jumbo carried Pat down the stairs.

"What have you got to say about it?" Jumbo was asked.

"He tole it jist about lak it happened," responded Jumbo.

324

"Who had the gun when it was fired?"

"Dat Spalding feller. Hit wuz lak dis. When he had dat gun pointed at Sam hyar and was about to shoot him, I see Pat make a dive fer de hand what held de gun. Ez he did so I dived for the feets. We all went down in a heap. I retched up to try to git my hand on de gun. Hit went off jist as I grabbed hit and as I did, hit went off again. I reckon I must uv twisted Spalding's hand when he pulled de trigger de second time. I never did git my hand on hit rat good. When de gun went off dem two times, boff uv dem sorta fell back. So, I picked up de gun and handed it to Sam. Dat's about de way hit happened."

A clerk made notes as both Sam and Jumbo talked. When Jumbo finished, one of the officers told him to write out the statements so Sam and Jumbo could sign them. As the clerk left, Inspector Odom came in.

"The hospital just called and the other one is dead," he announced. "What does it look like?"

"Nothing we can pin on these two," one of the officers said. "It seems that the one that burned up in the fire was a communist and was trying to take over the lodge. This one," pointing to Sam, "seems to be the organizer and chief mogul and was opposing him. This other fellow, whose name was Spalding, pulled a pistol and threatened to shoot Martin. As he did so, this one," pointing to Jumbo, "and the other one jumped him. All of them went to the floor, and in the struggle, the gun went off twice. The first shot must have hit Patterson and the second one got Spalding. Jumbo said he never did get his hand on the pistol real good until after the shooting. There ain't nothing you can pin a murder rap on him, 'specially when it looks like he was trying to prevent a killing even though it ended up with two killings."

"As soon as they sign their statements, let them go. I want to see you two at one o'clock tomorrow afternoon," the inspector said to Sam.

In a short while, the statements were brought in. While Sam read his, Jumbo's was read to him. After both of them signed the statements, they left the station.

"Hit was sum night," Jumbo remarked as soon as they were on the street.

"You can say that again. I want to thank you for what you did. It took a lot of nerve," said Sam.

"I wouldn't have done hit except I see Pat make de move. I knowd dat no one man could handle him, but I figured de two of us could take keer of uv him. I didn't think about gittin' shot or I wouldn't have done hit."

"Thanks just the same. Somehow or another, I am not sorry about Spalding, but I sure feel badly about Pat. I didn't realize until now just how much of a friend he was to me."

"What he did took nerve. He didn't have much uv a chance," observed Jumbo.

The next afternoon when Sam went to Inspector Odom's office, Odom said, "Come in. Close the door," and when Sam had closed the door, the officer invited him to be seated.

"That was a nasty mess last night," began the officer.

"It sure was," admitted Sam.

"It might interest you to know that a New York undertaker contacted us this morning and what is left of Spalding's body will be sent there."

"Was there anything left?"

"Not that you would recognize as a human being. Now about this organization of yours. What's back of it?"

"Just what do you mean?"

"Just what I said. What's back of it?"

"I organized it as a lodge for Negroes. Its ritual is based on the history, the hopes, and the aspirations of the Negro in America."

"It sounds good. I thought that was what it was when I first heard about it. I appreciate what you did for us in the last mayor's race, but after that meeting, we began to get some bad reports on it. We took it up with the FBI. They told us to lay off; that they knew all about it."

"The devil they did."

"Yes. It seems that they had not paid any attention to it until Spalding came to town. He was a known communist, and every movement of his was known. You've been on the suspected list but they had nothing definite on you. After what happened last night, they are satisfied with you. That is on one condition, and I think you would be wise to accept it."

"What is that?" asked Sam.

"That you either disband the Citizens of the Sun or let it die of a natural death. They seem to think it won't last if you are not there to keep it alive."

"And I have been on the list of suspected communists?"

"You have. It was through your association with Spalding."

"I'll tell you one thing and you can pass it on to the FBI. Southern Negroes will not fall for communism. They may be ignorant, but they are not dumb."

"The FBI had reached the same conclusion a long time ago, although yours and Spalding's activities gave them some room for doubt. I think that doubt has been removed. I say this--forget your lodge. Forget Spalding. Get into something else, and I don't think you will be in any trouble. That's all. Thanks again for the help in the election. If I can ever do you a favor, let me know."

Chapter 50

Sam went to the undertaker where Patterson's body had been taken. He knew the assistant who met him at the door with a decorous greeting.

"I thought I would come by and see Charles' body before the funeral," he explained.

"I understand. Come on back to the chapel. We have him lying in state. His mother and father just left but they will back at eight o'clock."

"I don't know them."

"No, but they would like to meet the man their son gave his life to save. However, his sister is here."

The undertaker's assistant escorted Sam through the anteroom, across a hall, and into the chapel. The chapel was dimly lighted, and at the far end in front of a bank of flowers, there was a casket. Half of the top was thrown back displaying all of the corpse except the legs and feet. A soft light was shining on the body. Sam noticed that there were several people sitting around the walls of the room. As they approached the casket, a young woman arose and approached them.

"This is Samuel Martin, Miss Patterson," the undertaker's assistant said.

"How do you do?" replied Patterson's sister as she carefully examined Sam from head to feet as if trying to identify some unusual feature.

"I hardly know what to say under the circumstances," replied Sam. "Except to say that I am extremely sorry. I realize Pat gave his life to save mine. I am certain that Spalding had every intention of killing me."

"I know it is not your fault. At least directly. Of course there is no use in saying that if you had not organized the Citizens of the Sun and Charles had not been interested in seeing that it was not used for an evil purpose, all this would not have happened. The causes are too remote. I am just wondering how much the world is the loser by exchanging his life for yours."

Sam hesitated a moment before replying. He could detect no tone of rancor in her voice.

"To give you an honest answer," he replied, "I am afraid it was a bad swap. He was a far better man than me."

"I appreciate your saying that. For not only was he a good man, but he was a wonderful brother. He delayed his own education to help me finish school. I am to start teaching this fall. Come on and see him," and taking Sam by the arm, she led him to the casket.

Sam gazed down at the figure. While the features were familiar, it seemed to him as if he were looking at a complete stranger. He realized of course, that the absence of life made the difference. The sight of that lifeless form made him realize fully for the first time, that if it had not been for what Pat had done, it would be him there in repose. He wondered what it was that had prompted Pat to grab Spalding and lose his life. Certainly, Pat was under no obligation to him. It would have been the sensible thing for Patterson to have turned away and leave him to get out of the mess which had been his own doing. Pat had sense enough to realize the risk he was taking. What Jumbo had done was not so hard to understand. Jumbo was trying to help Patterson.

"He looks so peaceful, doesn't he?" asked Miss Patterson with a slight sob.

Sam nodded his head in assent. He could think of nothing to say. Abruptly, he turned and left.

Funeral services for Charles Patterson were held the next day in one of the largest Negro churches in the city. The sanctuary was filled and the overflow filled the vestibule and front steps. The services were conducted by Dr. Josh Fleming, Dean of the School of Religion where Patterson had been a student.

There were some dozen or more white people present. Sam recognized several of them as officials and employees of the construction company where Patterson had worked. He wondered if they were there, not so much out of respect for Patterson, but to impress on the other employees who were present that they took an interest in them, even after death, and thus gain a greater measure of loyalty and more work out of them.

He had steeled himself for the funeral ordeal. Since he had entered college, he had avoided funerals as much as possible and had only attended them when there was no alternative. He knew the pattern. There would be one or two mournful hymns sung by the congregation, a long prayer by the preacher during which he would remind the Lord, and incidentally, his listeners, how brief and uncertain Life was, and the Awful Fate awaiting those who had not died Saved in Grace and an imprecation that the hearts of all those present who had not been Saved would be so moved that they would Save their Souls before it was too late; then another hymn. Then the preacher would read several passages from the Bible and launch into a exposition of the virtues of the deceased, many of which he had never possessed, would gradually work around to reminding those who loved him most how much he would be missed, bringing the family to tears and sometimes into hysterics, with many others joining in the weeping through sympathy or mass contagion. The services would close with another mournful hymn.

After the casket was brought into the church and placed before the alter, the services opened true to form, but instead of the congregation doing the singing, the choir sang "Abide With Me." The Reverend Fleming opened his Bible and started reading from it. Sam made up his mind that he would not listen; that he would close his mind or direct his thoughts into some other channel. He would not allow himself to be harassed by what the preacher would say. He paid no attention to the reading of the Scriptures. He did not know when the preacher stopped reading and started talking. All he knew was that the voice droned on, but in spite of everything he could do, his mind would pick up some word or phrase of the preacher. He had to admit the preacher had a good voice and did not indulge in any dramatics which made it easier for him to direct his thoughts elsewhere. In spite of everything he did, his mind kept wandering back to the words of the minister, but would not stay long enough to grasp any connecting thought.

Sam was wondering how he would go about carrying on his fight against the white race, since he could no longer operate the Citizens of the Sun. Probably the best thing for him to do would be to identify himself with some of the more solid organizations, such as the National Association for the Advancement of Colored People. His objection to that organization was twofold. In the first place, it was always headed by a white person or a lackey of the whites so that no matter what it might accomplish for the Negro people, in a measure, the whites could claim credit for it. The other was that they insisted that everything be done within the framework of the law. He didn't believe the Negro would ever get his rights by law. Practically all the laws upon which they depended had been on the books for decades, and it had availed the Negro nothing. If the Negro ever got anything, it would have to be by force.

The words the minister was saying impinged upon his thoughts. "Greater Love hath no man than this, that he lay down his life for his fellow man." He was talking about me, said Sam to himself and started listening. "We may well ask ourselves why this young man deliberately placed himself in a place of extreme danger to save the life of another. We may ask ourselves if it would not have been better that the two lives could have been weighed and the choice made as to which one was to be saved and which one was to be lost. That was not for us to decide, and only God in His infinite wisdom is in a position to answer that question. We can evaluate lives in terms of our own existence but only God can evaluate them in terms of the Eternal. The world might have been better off if the one had lived and the other had died or if the other had lived and the one died. That question can never be answered for us for we do not have the privilege of seeing each life lived out to its fullest and then be allowed to make our choice. Those things are only idle speculation. The one question I think we can safely answer is given in the Scripture I have just quoted.

"I had the privilege of having this young man as a student in my school. I think I knew his character well and it was a beautiful character. At an early age, he dedicated his life to God, and in his conception of the duty imposed upon him in so doing, it meant that he had dedicated his life to his fellow man. The rule of his life was Love. He had a deep love for his fellow man, based upon an abiding faith in the inherent goodness of all men. When the test came to him, he did not hesitate to face it. It was not a moment for speculation, for weighing the pros and cons of the situation, and after mature deliberation making the wise and judicious decision. The rule of Love guided him. He saw a brother in imminent danger of losing his life. That was enough for him to act. Taking no thought of his own life, of what it might mean to him in terms of happiness or success or the material things which would come to him in the future, he acted upon that rule which he had accepted as his guide and willingly and gladly laid down his own life for his fellow man. Greater Love has no man than this. We can only thank God for the privilege of knowing lives of such as this one that has just ended. May the blessings of God attend you now, through life, and through all Eternity. Amen."

Sam sat stunned. What would his life be compared to what Patterson's might have been had he lived? Of course, there was no answer to such a question. But was there an answer? Could there be an answer? There could be an answer, but only he could provide that answer. God, what a burden had been placed on him! He had been given a duty he could not shirk. He owed that much to Patterson.

The choir sang the final hymn during which the undertaker closed the casket and placed the pall of flowers on it. The minister led the pallbearers in a slow march up the aisle followed by the casket which was pushed and guided by the undertaker and his assistant. The congregation arose out of respect for the passing of the body. That is, all but Sam. He kept his seat. He was too dazed by the force of his thoughts to take any action. When the people started out of the church and some of them had to crowd by him, Sam came back to reality.

He had not planned to go to the cemetery. Now he would go. He would see the final act in the drama. He was too greatly concerned by it not to see the last final curtain. He found an acquaintance who had room for him in his car for the ride to the cemetery.

Little was said on the ride. One or two efforts were made to start a conversation with Sam, but he did not notice them. The others thought it was because of his grief for his friend who had given his life for him.

The services at the cemetery were brief. The minister read a short passage from the Bible and said a prayer. The casket was lowered into the grave, a concrete vault was placed over it and locked into place, and the grave was filled. The pall was placed over the mound, and the flowers arranged around the grave site. When the setting was completed, the minister gave a benediction, and Charles Patterson was buried.

Sam took his place in the line of people who filed by and solemnly shook hands with the mother, father, and sister of Charles Patterson. His friend who had given him a lift to the cemetery was waiting for him.

"Go ahead. I am not ready to leave yet, and I don't mind the walk. After the past few days, I think the walk will do me good. It's only a couple of miles."

Sam wandered aimlessly about the cemetery reading inscriptions on the gravestones. Occasionally, he came across the name of a person he had known. The shadows of the trees and shrubbery began to lengthen. Soon, he must leave for he had heard that the gates were closed and locked at sundown. He glanced about him. On the far side of the cemetery, two workmen were busy shoveling something into a wheelbarrow. He was reluctant to leave. A calm and soothing peace had come over him.

He sat down on a stone bench. It was on a lot on which there was a large stone bearing just the name "Murdoch." There were several graves on the lot and space on it for several more. He idly wondered how many more Murdochs there were to be buried here, and if there were any of them still left who came here and sat on this bench and communed with their dead.

He let his gaze wander over what he had heard preachers call the City of the Dead. The first time he had heard this expression at a funeral service he had thought it "corny." Now it seemed expressive. There were thousands of people buried here, enough to form a small city. All of them had been loved and except for the extremely young, had loved. Each stone, from the simplest ones at the foot of the graves, through the larger tombstones, many of which bore more details of the lives of the persons lying beneath them, some bearing quotations, most of which were from the Bible, to the more elaborate monuments, had been placed as a loving memorial to one who had been loved.

Beneath each mound of earth there were people who had made countless small sacrifices for those they had loved. Depending upon the length of life they had attained, many had made greater sacrifices. Some had made the supreme one, as was evident by the two graves he had noticed, one of a woman and by her side, that of a child whose death occurred only five days after that of the woman.

What had all these people lying dreamlessly about him gotten out of life? Considering that they were Negroes and judged by the standards of white people, they hadn't gotten much. Simple luxuries had been only to a few. For most of them, their lives had been ones of struggle and toil, wresting a living barely above the subsistence level. Their greatest financial achievements had been the payment of the small weekly premiums on the insurance policies that had paid for their funerals and the stones above their graves. If any had had ambitions, they were lucky if the ambitions had been simple ones for they had had no opportunity of realizing great ones. At the best, their lives could only have been called drab and dreary. Yet, there was one thing that sustained them but they never realized it, with the possible exception of a few, just what it was, and it was something for which they had a God given infinite capacity. That thing was Love. If they had only realized what this virtue was and had developed it to the fullest, their lives would have been richer and fuller. Unfortunately, they, like almost everyone else, failed to realize that Love was something more than an incident to life. Love was life itself.

It was such a simple thing to understand that Sam was amazed that he had not realized it before, but he had had to learn it the hard way. It had taken the tragic death of a good man to teach it to him. That was too big a price to pay for a lesson. It wasn't reasonable to think that half the people should die to teach the lesson to the other half. One life had been sacrificed and that should have been enough. The Man of Galilee had said "Love ye one another," and had ascended the cross and died a horrible death because of the Love He bore for mankind. When men died as Patterson had done, it only proved the truth of Christ's words.

For the first time in his life, Sam was really happy, and for the first time in his life, he had a worthwhile goal in view. He wanted to spend his life telling others of this truth he had just learned and particularly he wanted to tell the people of his own race. He wanted to tell them how they could transform their lives, how they could forget the evils the white people had imposed upon them. No, they were not evil; it was just something the white people had done because of their ignorance. He wanted to tell them to make their lives something so fine and clean that the white people would be glad to learn from them. He had an understanding of God's greatest gift to man--Love, and he wanted to pass it on to others.

The power of love was amazing. Only a few short hours before, he had hated white people; he had hated them so intensely that he was devoting his life in organizing Negroes to further that hatred. Now he did not hate them. He was sorry for those who had exploited and humiliated the Negro, for in so doing, they were not only denying themselves the wonderful ecstasy of love but they were degrading, not just the white race, but all mankind.

Now, he knew he did not hate white people. Not as a whole and not as individuals. And strangest of all, he cared nothing about being like a white man. There were no privileges or rights denied to him as a Negro, that he would get up off this bench to accept. Those things did not matter anymore. The white people, in drawing a line of distinction, were only debasing a God given soul and the Negroes in chaffing under the distinctions, were denying themselves the opportunity to arise above the white people. Life was too short to spend even the shortest moment of it in hatred. There was not enough time for a person to give all the love of which he was capable, without wasting any of it on hatred.

Why hadn't he learned this before? The lesson had been there all the time for him, but he had been too blind to see it. He had expected perfection and in failing to find it, he had held everything else of no account. He hadn't realized the importance of even the smallest amount of love in every individual. He had felt sorry for his mother and father. To him, they had been living miserable, dreary lives as untrained, uneducated Negroes, but now he could see that he had been wrong. They loved each other, they loved their sons, they had loved their church, their neighbors, and their friends. They had been happiest when giving of their meager means and their time to others.

He had considered Malvoy Tanksley as degraded as a person could become. Her only interest had seemed to be whiskey and men, yet that spark of Divine Love in her had caused her to take on the responsibility of caring for and rearing her half sisters and half brother. She had even offered to risk the love she had found in an effort to help John Henry in his trouble, for had she testified that John Henry had been with her when the crime he was charged with committing had taken place, the juvenile court would have taken the children from her.

Jumbo was nothing but a common laborer; certainly not very high in life's social and intellectual scale. He seemed to live only for his daily drink of whiskey. He was very much in love with his wife and she was in love with him. He knew nothing of politics and political trends, yet he had the good sense to realize that communism offered nothing to the Negro. When the test came to him, he risked his life to save another. John Henry's money had made it easy for him to go to college, and his brother had seemed to take a pride in his academic accomplishments. Yet, it would have been so easy for John Henry to resent his brother's apparently easy life and refuse to furnish the money for him to continue his education.

Come to think of it, he knew no one who did not at times, display qualities of completely unselfish love. And all of them were the happier for the action. Why couldn't people realize that the only way to happiness was through love? But who was he to ask such a question? Had it not taken a tragedy to make him see it? Through Love, one was enabled to see the Divine in each individual.

After all, wasn't that all that Christ had taught? He had said many things but all had revolved around this one central theme. Didn't He say "God is Love"? How many times had he heard this in Sunday school and church? But up until now, it had never had any meaning for him. To him, it had been a meaningless phrase. He doubted that no more than a few whom he had heard say it, had come anywhere close to understanding its real meaning. Hadn't Christ also said, "Thou shalt love thy God with all thy heart, with all thy soul, and with all thy being, and thy neighbor as thyself?" Such a simple but meaningful statement. That must be what being like God is. Love. The more a person loved, the more he became God-like.

Why were there all the divisions into denominations by people who professed to believe in the Man who had spoken those words? How could there be room for division? On what points could people differ who sincerely believed that God is love and that every person should love God with all his heart, soul, and being. They just say they do and make a few conventional gestures as proof of that statement. Why, if every person was imbued with the Love of which Christ spoke, the whole world would be transformed within a few hours. There would be no problems such as the one that had concerned him so much recently. Just from the standpoint of the Negro alone, he could have no resentment toward the white man no matter what the white man might do to him. Would he not feel as He who died for the things in which He believed, who with His dying breath prayed, "Father, forgive them for they know not what they do."

The example of Love by the Negro would transform the white man. Had he not suddenly realized a simple truth? Hate breeds hate and love breeds love. By hate, men die, and by love, men live. He could no longer sit here. He must be up and about his new business of telling people of what he had learned. Suddenly, he felt humbled and awed. He slipped to his knees, and his lips formed silent words. "I thank you, God, that I have learned before it was too late."

He walked home. He did not hurry. For the first time, he was going somewhere but not at a break-neck speed. He looked at the people he met. He saw them as personalities and not vague figures to be ignored, if possible. Several returned his looks, and they seemed so friendly that he began to nod to them. Soon, he was speaking to all whose eyes met his. Most of them seemed surprised, but many returned his greetings.

He met a white man who had on greasy overalls and was carrying a lunch box. Sam spoke to him. The man responded with a "Howdy," and smiled. It seemed to Sam that the man's weary shoulders went back a bit.

"It must be contagious," said Sam to himself. A few days ago, he would not have dared to speak to a white man he did not know. He had spoken to one and had met a friendly response. "All of which proves the truth I have just discovered," he mused. "Hate breeds hatred, and love breeds love."

His mother was putting the supper on the table when he arrived home.

"Wuz hit a pretty big funeral?" she asked him.

"Yes, it was, but after all Pat had lots of friends."

"I'll always remember him in my prayers. Iffen hit hadn't a been fer him, you would be daid."

"I don't doubt that."

When they had partially sated their hunger, Sam said, "I made a mighty important decision this afternoon. I have decided to become a minister."

"De Lord be praised," shouted Maria.

"How come you make up your mine to do dat?" asked William.

"I don't know that I can answer that question. I could say that it was something the preacher said during the funeral service, but I am not sure that would be correct. It has probably been building up in me for a long time and it took the death of Pat and the preacher's words to turn the tide. I know that I had built up such a store of hate within me that something had to happen, either for the worse or for the better. Fortunately, I believe it was for the better."

"You ain't been right, Son, since John Henry went away," said Maria.

"I know. Many little things had happened before, but I suppose it was John Henry's death that set me off on a course of hatred. I see now that I was wrong. I think the best thing I can do to make amends, to salvage something from the loss of Pat and help overcome the causes of my hate, is to devote my life to my fellow man."

"Dat sounds might fine, Son," stated William.

"Now, the first thing we want to do is to move out of this alley. I think living here had a lot to do with the way I felt," but he had no sooner uttered the words than he regretted having said them. Here he was trying to impose his will upon others, even though he thought what he had just proposed was for the best interests of his mother and father. "That is, if you all will consider moving."

"I don't know, Son; I been living hyar so long dat won't no other place seem like home," said Maria.

"I sorta feel de same way," said William. "I ain't never lived in but two houses. De one in Brierville. I wuz born dar. And dis one hyar. 'Sides, de rent is not so much."

"I have enough money to pay rent on a better place. I can do that and still have enough money to see me through the seminary."

"We'll see about hit. Dere ain't no use in bein' in enny hurry."

"I am going over to see Rosemary after supper. That is if she will see me."

"I'se glad to hear you say dat, son. Rosemary is a good girl. You ain't been doin' her right lately and you couldn't blame her iffen she got her another fellow," said Maria.

"That is a chance I'll have to take. I don't know whether she will like my becoming a preacher. She always wanted me to be a doctor."

"I wuz hoping you'd be one, too," said his mother, "but 'twixt being a preacher and a doctor, I'd druther you'd be a preacher. Most folks'll get well ennyways when dey body gits sick, but when dey soul gits sick, hit takes a powerful good preacher to cure 'em, and savin' dey soul is de most important thing a person can do."

"I don't know whether I will be able to save their souls for the world to come, but I hope I can be able to save their lives for the world in which they are living."

Rosemary answered his knock on the door.

"Why, Sam, this is indeed a surprise. Come in."

"Am I forgiven?" he asked.

"Forgiven for what?" Rosemary asked, and before he could answer, she went on. "I have been making out some reports. Excuse me a minute until I get them out of the way," and she began to gather up papers scattered over the table.

"No. Go right on with your work."

"No. I can do that any time. I really should have done it at the office. What am I to forgive you for?"

"For not coming to see you any oftener than I have been doing."

"I gathered you were busy. I am sorry about what happened. I was uncertain whether to come to you or not but I decided that since you hadn't been hurt, I really had no excuse."

"I have been busy. Probably, you wouldn't have been able to locate me."

"Did you lose all your records of the Citizens of the Sun?"

"Yes, but it makes no difference. I would have burned them all anyway."

"What has happened?"

"I was ordered by the police to break up the organization. But that is not important. I know it sounds corny and a few days ago I wouldn't have believed such a thing could have happened. I have been made to see things in their true perspective. I have been trying to correct some of the faults of the world through hate when the real good in the world has been done by men; men like Patterson because they loved. I have come to the complete realization that the only thing worthwhile in this world is Love."

"I know it is everything that makes life worthwhile."

"I know you do, whether you realize it or not. You have done something I have not been able to do. You made up your mind while you were still a child that you were going to be a nurse. You have worked straight through and attained your goal. I know the monetary reward is not your primary concern. You would almost do the work for nothing. I am sure you would if your living problems were taken care of. And you have been happy in what you have been doing. You have been happy and I have been miserable. From now on out, I am going to be happy, too; and I am going to do it by forgetting myself."

"What are you going to do?"

"A potentially great minister died when Patterson gave up his life for me. I am going to try to take his place. I am going into the ministry. I am going to try to teach my people how to live full and rich lives. I am going to try to teach them that being black is not an evil thing. I am going to try to teach them how not to be hurt but to grow and to become loved and respected. I don't how long it is going to take. I must spend at least three years in seminary. Will you wait for me? I know it is selfish for me to ask, but believe me, I need you."

"I will wait for you," replied Rosemary, softly.

"There is just one thing I must do first."

"What is that?"

"I have ten thousand dollars to which I have no right. I am going to give it away, but I don't know to whom I shall give it."

"The county health service has been trying for years to get the county court to appropriate money for a greatly needed Negro baby clinic. You could consider that."

Sam's money provided the seed capital to establish the baby health clinic.

Chapter 51

On June 6th, 1954, the Reverend Samuel Martin delivered the baccalaureate sermon to the graduating class of Semmes University at the Highland Street A. M. E. Church. In this sermon he said:

"In spite of examinations and all the other activities connected with the completion of your university careers, I have no doubt, that everyone of you has heard of a recent decision of the United States Supreme Court which declared that segregation of the races in public schools is unlawful. All over this nation, prominent Negroes have hailed it as a great victory for the colored people. Some have likened it to the Emancipation Proclamation. To hear them talk, it has ushered in a new era for the Negro. It is the beginning of the end of the distinction between the races.

"My friends, I am afraid it is a hollow victory. The only immediate good I can see come out of it is possibly some slightly better educational advantages for a few Negroes, but I am fearful that these advantages will be dearly bought. Judicial decisions and legislative enactments cannot change prejudices and customs, nor do they replace ignorance with learning.

"There seems to be something in the make-up of the average person to make him look down upon certain classes or groups of people. Probably, it is a self-pampering of the ego. To the average white person, all Negroes are the same, with only slight variations as to honesty, industry, or intelligence. We know that Negroes have class distinctions. We may deny that fact as a matter of principle, but in our hearts, we know it exists, and it is nothing new. During slavery, the house servants looked down upon the field hands. The field hands, conscious of their market value as workers, looked down upon the white sharecropper, who, not owning slaves, had to work in the fields to earn his meager living. He, in turn, looked down upon the slave because he was not a free man. The large landowners looked down upon the hill farmer and the sharecropper. The business and professional people looked down upon the workman and the laborer.

"That condition prevails throughout the country today, leaving the Negro out of consideration. On the Pacific coast, the white people look down upon the Japanese and Chinese. In some sections of the

North, you will find, for instance, that Italians are not permitted in certain communities. Jews are not permitted in that community and other distinctions are drawn along racial, religious, or national origin lines. It hasn't been so many years since there was a great social gulf between the 'lace curtain' Irish and the 'shanty' Irish. This contempt of one group for another has given us such words as nigger, kike, Jap, Yid, Chink, wop, bohunk, hunkle, Rusky, greaser, cross-back, wetback, mick, hillbilly, redneck, cracker, yokel, kraut, frog, limey, and possibly others that I do not remember at the moment, but each one of them carries with it the idea of the superiority of one individual of a group over an individual of another group,. You will notice that very few of these names refer to Negroes. Practically every one of these words carry with it the idea of insult and an implication of the superiority of one person over another.

"In the recent war, it seems that certain phases of it were referred to as operations. There was Operation This and Operation That. While I don't like to refer to myself as a Negro, I try to think of myself as just simply a human being. I wish to say that we Negroes are completing Operation Segregation and are entering into Operation Discrimination, which I am afraid we will come to think of as Operation Heartbreak. The tragic thing about it is that there will be nothing we can do about it because there will be nothing tangible we can fight. There will be no courts into which we can go to enforce our social rights. There will be no laws which we can charge have been violated.

"What are you going to say to your children when they come home in tears from a desegregated school and tells you that a white classmate had called them 'niggers'? If you complain to the teacher or the principal, you will probably be told that it was only childish thoughtlessness and nothing can be done except to caution the offending child not to do it again. What are you going to tell your little daughter when she tells you that the little white girl who has been so friendly with her, who sits next to her in class, who eats at the same table with her in the cafeteria, and who always chooses her first when they select teams on the school grounds, is going to have a birthday party and has not invited her? What are your boys and girls going to think when they reach their teens and find their white classmates are drawing farther and farther away from them until they are no longer included in the white social groups?

"Let's leave the children out of it and take a look at the grownups. How are your women going to feel when the white women with whom you work on committees at the PTA never invite you to their homes and always have an excuse when you find that the white men will treat you as an equal at the school group but will never invite you to join their luncheon clubs, their lodges, their civic clubs, or other similar organizations? It will be something of a shock to find that the white people will meet you as an equal on certain occasions and ignore you on others. Formerly, you could have said that the whites were hiding behind the segregation laws which they had made. Now, you are denied that feeble consolation.

"I am afraid what is going to happen is this; the schools in the predominantly white neighborhoods will soon revert to wholly white schools, and the schools in the predominantly colored neighborhoods will be wholly colored, and you will learn to swallow your social snubs.

"There is not one of us but who will admit that the Negro has been mistreated by the whites and particularly in the South. Now, I am going to let you in on a little secret. It may shock you at first, but if you will give it a little thought, I believe you will see that I am right. The white people have mistreated the Negro because he is afraid of him. I don't mean the white people are afraid because of any physical violence which the Negro might do. The laws and the enforcement agencies are sufficient to take care of that situation. The white man is afraid of the Negro because he is fearful that the Negro will rise to the status where the white man will have to look up to him. Now, I don't mean all whites feel that way. The better educated white people know they have nothing to fear from the Negro, and what amelioration has come about for the Negro has been because of this small group. The fear is in the group, which for lack of a better term, we shall call the low class white and they are numerous and vocal. This is the group that have often been referred to as 'pore white trash'. The Negro is the only group left for them to look down upon and if the Negro, by education, by industry, and by culture raises himself, there will be nothing left for that group to look down upon. They are fighting for their position in the world. And since they are so loud in their cries of protest, the politicians must of necessity, listen to them.

"Don't allow what I have said to discourage you. There is a clear-cut answer to the whole problem. It is being gradually answered by people of good will of both races and it is those people who will finally work out the solution. Most of the work will rest upon the shoulders of our people. We must keep in mind the simple words of the Galilean, 'Love ye one another.' The speed by which the problem will be answered is in proportion to the capacity of the Negro to love.

"You are graduating from a great university and in a few days, you will be entering your chosen fields for your life's work. Don't go as Negroes. Forget you are Negroes. Go as individuals. Go as one in which a Divine Part of the Eternal God lives.

"Since we were brought here from Africa, we have allowed the white man to set the standard by which we live and we have trailed along behind that standard. We have aspired to be as the whites. There is absolutely no hope for any race which sets as its ideals the ideals of another race. The difference in color is an everlasting barrier as long as one or the other uses it as a matter of distinction. Since this barrier is practically impossible to break down, at least for the present, there is but one course for the Negro to follow. That is to set his own standards and set them so high that the white race will be forced to try to attain those same standards. And there is but one standard. It is the one given by the Man of Galilee. He best expressed it when He said 'God is Love.' That is the answer for all these problems for the Negro. And when he adopts the standard of love, he will find that the problems will have faded into insignificance. It is a standard that will raise him high above all present levels of human existence.

"I have dedicated myself to that principle and I no longer think of myself as a Negro. I am a child of God with an infinite capacity for Love if I will only develop that capacity. My friends, only in love will you find happiness. In love, you will no longer be a Negro. In love, all men will look to you; and in your love, you will reward them by teaching them to love in return. That is the answer, not only to the problems raised by the differences in race, but it is the answer to all the problems which beset mankind."

THE END

About the Author

C. Vernon Hines was an attorney in Nashville during the 1930s, '40s, and '50s. He was very active in civic affairs as an Elk, as a scoutmaster and district chairman in the BSA, and as the teacher of a Methodist men's Bible class for 29 years. He probably represented more blacks in legal matters that any other attorney in the mid-South at that time and usually with little or no compensation. Until his death in 1958, he was continually attempting to bring down the legal and social barriers that prevented blacks in the South from attaining their full potential. Although the characters depicted in the book are fictitious, the events are typical of instances in which the author was called upon to provide legal representation against the injustices imposed. The book is presented as it was written almost a half century ago.

Printed in the United States
34442LVS00003B/169-180